THE EASTERN
GREATEST v

Yuuki
Kagurazaka

Damrada

Emperor
Ludora

Velgrynd

N EMPIRE'S
VAR POWERS

VELZARD

The
Four
Knights

Tatsuya
Kondo

FUSE

Illustration by
Mitz Vah

That Time I Got
Reincarnated
as a SLIME
14

That Time I Got Reincarnated as a SLIME

14

FUSE

Illustration by **Mitz Vah**

YEN ON

New York

That Time I Got Reincarnated as a SLIME ⑭

FUSE

Translation by Kevin Gifford

Cover art by Mitz Vah

TENSEI SHITARA SLIME DATTA KEN volume 14
© Fuse / Mitz Vah
All rights reserved.
First published in Japan in 2019 by MICRO MAGAZINE, INC.
English translation rights arranged with MICRO MAGAZINE, INC.
through Tuttle-Mori Agency, Inc., Tokyo.

English translation © 2022 by Yen Press, LLC

Yen On
150 West 30th Street, 19th floor
New York, NY 10001

Visit us at yenpress.com
facebook.com/yenpress
twitter.com/yenpress
yenpress.tumblr.com
instagram.com/yenpress

First Yen On Edition: July 2022
Edited by Yen On Editorial: Rachel Mimms
Designed by Yen Press Design: Wendy Chan

Yen On is an imprint of Yen Press, LLC.
The Yen On name and logo are trademarks of Yen Press, LLC.

Library of Congress Cataloging-in-Publication Data
Names: Fuse, author. | Mitz Vah, illustrator. | Gifford, Kevin, translator.
Title: That time I got reincarnated as a slime / Fuse ; illustration by Mitz Vah ; translation by Kevin Gifford.
Other titles: Tensei Shitara Slime datta ken. English
Description: First Yen On edition. | New York : Yen ON, 2017–
Identifiers: LCCN 2017043646 | ISBN 9780316414203 (v. 1 : pbk.) | ISBN 9781975301118 (v. 2 : pbk.) |
    ISBN 9781975301132 (v. 3 : pbk.) | ISBN 9781975301149 (v. 4 : pbk.) | ISBN 9781975301163 (v. 5 : pbk.) |
    ISBN 9781975301187 (v. 6 : pbk.) | ISBN 9781975301200 (v. 7 : pbk.) | ISBN 9781975312992 (v. 8 : pbk.) |
    ISBN 9781975314378 (v. 9 : pbk.) | ISBN 9781975314392 (v. 10 : pbk.) | ISBN 9781975314415 (v. 11 : pbk.) |
    ISBN 9781975314439 (v. 12 : pbk.) | ISBN 9781975314453 (v. 13 : pbk.) | ISBN 9781975314477 (v. 14 pbk)
Subjects: GSAFD: Fantasy fiction.
Classification: LCC PL870.S4 T4613 2017 | DDC 895.63/6—dc23
LC record available at https://lccn.loc.gov/2017043646

ISBNs: 978-1-9753-1447-7 (paperback)
       978-1-9753-1448-4 (ebook)

10 9 8 7 6 5 4 3 2 1

LSC-C

Printed in the United States of America

That Time I Got Reincarnated as a SLIME

14

CONTENTS | DRAGON AND DEMON COLLIDE

THE CLOWNS' DECISION

That Time I Got Reincarnated as a Slime

Word had yet to reach the Empire… But as far as the loyal subjects of that Empire were concerned, perhaps ignorance was bliss. The imperial generals who were supposed to be invading the Western Nations after storming their way through the Forest of Jura—in other words, their beloved fathers, brothers, their very family—were all killed without having any say in their fates.

Nearly a million troops had gone on the attack. Defeat was simply unthinkable. There was no doubt in anyone's mind that the Empire's long-cherished dream of conquering the West would be accomplished in all its glory, the entire land united as a single nation under the lofty name of Emperor Ludora. The Forest of Jura was a formidable obstacle, no doubt—but now that the evil dragon Veldora had been weakened, there was nothing for anyone to fear.

That was how things were supposed to turn out.

And so in the reign of this greatest of emperors, the imperial army—considered the strongest that history had ever known—had finally begun its invasion.

That, in essence, was how the imperial citizens felt. None of them expected a hard fight, let alone a stinging defeat. None had imagined that the Empire would never even reach the Western Nations before their dreams of world conquest were crushed within the Forest of Jura. But that was exactly what happened—the imperial army was wholly eradicated without accomplishing any of their goals.

Thanks to an ambush at the hands of the Jura-Tempest Federation— a strike that wasn't even on the Empire's radar—these citizens would be reminded of just how vast and unpredictable the world could be. But now, for just a few more days, the Empire's subjects would remain blissfully unaware.

●

In the headquarters of the Composite Division in the imperial capital was a large, ornate room where certain people were now gathering in secret. The meeting was chaired by Yuuki, with Kagali, Laplace, Teare, and Footman—the Moderate Jesters—accompanying him. Misha, one of the three leaders of Cerberus, was also present; her coleader Vega was not, as he was on a mission with the Magical Beast Division.

Laplace and Misha were currently delivering their reports, and their tales couldn't help but make Yuuki chuckle a bit. He had pictured several potential scenarios in his mind, but *these* results were singularly unexpected. It was all too overwhelming—and all too soon. The demon lord Rimuru and his band had pulled off such a mind-boggling performance that they would need to rethink their entire strategy urgently.

The most astonishing thing of all, of course, was how the demon lord had actually expanded his army's power since their last meeting.

"Impossible… Just wiping out an army that size without breaking a sweat, you know? I figured he would win in the end, but suffering zero casualties? That's just too much."

"It's simply unbelievable. With the Empire's force, they could have taken on three demon lord factions at the same time and *still* maintained equal footing…"

"Well, compared to the Ten Great Demon Lords, the so-called Octagram is on another level in terms of fighting ability. Guy still reigns over them all, granted, but Luminus and Daggrull have been fighting for influence with each other for ages now, haven't they? We're all aware of Leon's power... And Milim, notorious for not even bothering to have anyone serve her, now has both Carillon and Frey—each former demon lords themselves. That leaves Ramiris and Deeno as the last solo acts, doesn't it?"

Kagali wanted to fire back against Yuuki. But as his analysis continued, she began looking increasingly convinced. Certainly, things were different from back when Kagali lived among the demon lord ranks. No need to mention Guy again, but Milim now ruled over a vast territory south of the Forest of Jura. Luminus and Daggrull both governed large forces—armies that hadn't thinned out even after several clashes against angelic troops. There were wild cards like Leon, yes, but this crop of demon lords was nothing at all like when they were the new guys, back in Kagali's heyday.

Even if you had a decent-size legion serving you, after all, survival as a demon lord often came down to dumb luck—and that was just as true for Kagali, back when she was Kazalim the Curse Lord. That was why she tried to keep her wits about her back then and build cooperative relationships with the other demon lords, taking every measure possible to ensure she stuck around.

Even Roy Valentine, the Bloody Lord, was nothing but a stand-in. The One God Luminus was the true demon lord, and even Luminus couldn't fully put down Daggrull's force. I used to be so jealous of people like that—people who could rip me to shreds. Carillon and Frey played it smart by comparison. Would that I were that intelligent—then I wouldn't have saddened so many others, and I wouldn't have lost Clayman...

Looking back, all the effort Kagali expended forcing so many magic-born under her command seemed pointless now. Playing the numbers game didn't really matter against someone who had more than a certain level of strength; Clayman's failure made that pretty obvious. What Kagali's side really needed was more friends she could've had frank, honest discussions with.

...Ah, but I can only say that now, can't I? As many times as we've all been betrayed, it's all but impossible for the likes of us to trust in others.

It was true. If she had never met Yuuki, she'd probably still be holding a deep-seated grudge against the whole world. But, she thought, it was too late—so she bottled up the regret in her heart.

But the conversation continued, regardless of how she felt about it deep down.

"You've had a hard time, haven't you, Laplace?"

"Boy, you said it. And it sure didn't get none better this time, either." Laplace nodded, looking fatigued.

"Ha-ha-ha! You had to fight for ten days straight, I heard?"

"Yep. That Treyni lady—lemme tell ya, she's gotten crazy strong. If I went easy—or hell, if I let up at all—she woulda killed me, no doubt. And I was fighting her in the middle of the forest, too! I think I put in a real good effort, if you ask me."

Laplace continued to whine for a while longer. It was a likely story, coming from him—he couldn't help how fishy he looked and acted—but for once, maybe he was actually right.

Yuuki raised a hand to assuage him. "But she believed you in the end, didn't she?"

"Yeah, right. They had me bound up so tight that I couldn't move an inch! The demon lord Rimuru's own officers were watchin' over me! You call that believin' me?"

Yet despite that, Laplace had negotiated his way out of there and brought back some truly valuable information. Talk about living up to your reputation.

"I'm amazed they let you go unscathed, actually."

"Well, supposedly, the demon lord Guy pulled a few strings for me. Not really trusting *you*, Boss, so much as takin' advantage of the situation."

If they were still clearly enemies, there was no way the captured Laplace ever would've been released. More to the point, Laplace wouldn't have gotten that involved in the first place.

After Laplace finally stopped complaining, Yuuki breathed a sigh of relief. But it was too soon to be relieved.

"And *I* had a hard time myself," Misha added. "This has been *so* exhausting. My job was to incite Commander Caligulio into prolonging the war, and I knew what I was getting into and all, but I swear to you, I seriously requested a withdrawal right in the middle of all that. When he turned me down, I was just about to really kill him and desert, even..."

The bitterness was evident in Misha's voice. Of course, by the time she made that suggestion, it was already too late. Misha had only been spared because Yuuki had built a war alliance with Rimuru. If not, Diablo would have personally seen to her grisly death by now.

"Well, we're all lucky, aren't we? Lucky that Rimuru's the type to keep his word."

"That slime is just the most extraordinary thing. Because I remember some people in the Armored Division being demon lord caliber in their fighting skills, but..."

"Yeah."

"You're right. Of course, Rimuru's forces dispatched them before he even had to lift a finger..."

As a still-shocked Misha explained, the demon lord had not just one, but several Demon Peers under his command. Not even she seemed convinced of the truth she was speaking, but there it was. The very height of the demon hierarchy, right here on the ground— fully unleashed—and still wholly devoted to serving a single demon lord.

"But the real surprise was seeing two Single Digits defeated before my eyes like cows at a slaughterhouse. Honestly, it's silly to even think of challenging monsters like those."

Everyone listened on in disbelief as she laid out the whole story. Yuuki felt it proper to change the subject.

"Bernie's and Jiwu's identities were another big surprise, weren't they? Knowing that I've been dancing in the palm of Damrada's hand is *so* frustrating."

Yuuki fully meant that. Now he was sure that Damrada was a traitor, and that revelation was a great shock to everyone in the chamber. He had been Yuuki's close confidant for many years, earning his sincere trust over that time, and he served as a top-level leader at the core of Yuuki's camp. He had even entrusted him with the Cerberus secret society, their main foothold inside the Empire. His turning traitor required them to redraw their entire game plan.

Two of the Empire's most powerful fighters had been attached to Masayuki, someone they dismissed as a peon to be ignored. That, too, showed just how much foresight Damrada had. He was influencing Yuuki and his cohorts, likely seeing matters from a much broader perspective than anyone else—and realizing that cut Yuuki's pride to tatters.

"It certainly is," Kagali added, lost in thought. "Thinking about it, I suspect Damrada was involved in Clayman falling out of control as well."

Yuuki nodded. "I don't think I can deny that, no. It's really kind of strange, looking back, how all our plans have failed. But I don't think Damrada benefits from that. It's only with his help that we've become so powerful, after all. If he wanted to take it away from me, he shouldn't have given it to us in the first place."

"That's what I'm wondering. I believe Damrada was quite fascinated by you, Sir Yuuki. That much wasn't an act, I don't think—the loyalty he showed you was the real thing. And think of all the projects we *have* completed, thanks to his assistance."

"As a former colleague of his, I can tell you that Damrada really was working hard for our organization. He had some impressive accomplishments, and I imagine his loyalty to you really was sincere, Boss. But that man did have his more ruthless, coldhearted side. His obsessing over money is evidence of his more pragmatic side as well. So perhaps it's possible that he could...betray you, for some reason."

Misha seemed convinced. But Yuuki shook his head at her.

"He betrayed me, no doubt about it, but... You know, I'm not sure if that's what he really wanted. Or maybe he did?" he asked, grinning.

"I agree with you, Boss. If all of it was just an act, then why would Damrada have done everything he did?" Kagali seemed to reach the same conclusion as Yuuki. "Allow me to explain. It was Lord Gadora's report that made us aware of Damrada's betrayal. Gadora was killed within Emperor Ludora's palace, and the man he saw standing before him was Lieutenant Kondo—the man hidden behind the Empire's shadow."

"The palace...? I see. So Damrada had enough status to be allowed in there?"

Yuuki nodded at Misha, adding more information of his own. "That's right. And based on the intel you brought back, I have an idea of who Damrada *really* is, too. There's only a few people out there besides the emperor who can give orders to the Single Digits."

Everyone looked taken aback.

"Yeah... Yeah, I'll bet. It just takes a little thought, and it's so obvious, huh?"

"Right. I don't think it was Damrada betraying us...so much as following the emperor's orders."

"Maybe he didn't intend to do any of it... But it doesn't matter much at this point."

Perhaps he was an enemy of Yuuki's from the start. Perhaps not. Right now, all that mattered was Damrada's traitorous behavior, and Laplace and his cohorts were out for blood.

"Yeah, you're probably right, Boss. But y'know, if he was tryin' to trick that idiot Clayman, too, then don'tcha think we oughtta make him pay for that?"

"Right! Right! Let's go and kill him right now!"

"Hoh-hoh-hoh! For fixers like us, trust is our most valuable asset. No mercy must be given to traitors!"

Laplace was ready to stage the purge today, Teare and Footman eagerly agreeing to the idea. But Yuuki stopped them.

"Hold your horses. We know Damrada is actually a high-ranking member of the Imperial Guardians. Rest assured he's a lot more dangerous than your run-of-the-mill demon lord. I'm not sure even *you* guys could beat him."

"...True. I hate to admit it, but even in my own demon lord prime, I don't know if I could have beaten Lord Gadora. And if Damrada's good enough to stage a sneak attack on Gadora, I think it's safe to assume he has the talent to back his reputation."

"Okay, maybe, but..."

"And also—I think there might be a message hidden in everything Damrada did."

The words came from Yuuki after a few moments of deliberation.

He began outlining his thoughts, cautioning that it was all hypothetical for now.

"Damrada is a cautious man. He knows us well, and he also knows about the demon lord Rimuru in close detail. Someone like him would certainly have known about the Resurrection Bracelets."

"What do you mean?"

"I mean that I think he was aware of the possibility that Gadora could've resurrected himself all along."

"But then... Wait. Do you mean...?!"

Now it dawned on Misha as well. What if Damrada wasn't trying to kill Gadora at all? What if, instead, he was offering him a way to flee the Empire?

"The last man to speak to him was Lieutenant Kondo, right? The 'stalker of the halls of information,' as they say. If Gadora had been left alive in there, he would've fallen right into the lieutenant's hands. Then he would've been able to extract every bit of information Gadora had—by any means possible."

"And then all our objectives would've come to light, you think?"

"Probably, yeah. But there's still a few things I don't understand. Keeping Gadora's mouth shut ensured that the Empire remained oblivious about Rimuru. The Empire paid gravely for that, as we all know. But I don't think Damrada dealt all that damage to them just because he wanted to do us a favor, you know?"

Yuuki grinned. "That, sad to say, I don't have much explanation for."

"I think that Damrada is more faithful to Emperor Ludora than you, Sir Yuuki," Kagali replied. "There's no doubt about that. But at the same time, he also saw all of us as friends...or not. What if he thought he could use us or have us play some kind of role for him?"

"Mm-hmm. Go on."

"There's a chance, perhaps, that the defeat of the imperial force was in accordance with Emperor Ludora's wishes."

"That's absurd!"

"No way, man. That's crazy talk."

Misha and Laplace immediately denied it, but Yuuki was piqued by this hypothesis.

"What purpose do you think Damrada would have in this scenario?"

"It's quite simple. A large number of deaths is essential for the performance of any large-scale ritual. The awakening of a demon lord requires many souls. Could it be that Damrada and Ludora were using the imperial army itself as a sacrifice?"

"It's feasible, yes."

"And if that's the case, it'd make sense that they'd want to meddle with Lieutenant Kondo, given how he was expecting to win this war. And that also gives me a vague impression of why he wanted us to survive…"

Gadora was visiting the emperor in order to give him a warning. Damrada kept him from doing so. But what if Gadora's information had been passed on to Kondo? The imperial army wouldn't have been nearly as devastated, for one—and even before that, they would've taken on a far different battle strategy against Rimuru and his band. It was easy to believe that a man of Damrada's intelligence would have noticed this, and thus it was safe to assume his actions were intentional.

But what was his purpose?

"Maybe he was testing the waters?"

"Perhaps, yes." Kagali gave Yuuki's suggestion a satisfied smile. "You have to tolerate a lot of sacrifices in order to create someone truly strong. Perhaps he was trying to use us as pawns for the creation of this force as well?"

"Or maybe he was trying to take us in."

"…?"

"You know how Kagali and I were pretty much the only people Clayman accepted orders from, right?"

"Yeah."

"Uh-huh."

"No doubt about that."

"So if he managed to set Clayman loose like that, maybe he had some kind of secret trick to accomplish that?"

"True. Brainwashing, for example?"

Yuuki nodded at Kagali. "I think he might have cast a Thought

Guidance spell on him, even if it wasn't all that powerful. Maybe that spell was driven by a magic item like what we had—or for all we know, he had some kind of mind-domination ability like Maribel's."

The reasoning hardened the faces of everyone in the room.

"Sounds like trouble," Misha said to a nodding audience.

Looking at them, Yuuki smiled. "I wouldn't worry, though. That kinda power doesn't work on me. So what I'm gonna do right now is touch each of you in turn. Is that all right with everyone?"

They all agreed to it. Refusing would be akin to confessing that you were someone else's puppet. Yuuki was giving everyone a chance to prove their innocence, and none of them were about to turn it down.

"Well, it looks like nobody here's brainwashed anyway. I mean, I would've noticed if you suddenly started talking differently. I knew you'd all be fine, as long as none of you were out there alone."

"So I was in even more danger than I thought, huh?" Laplace said, standing up and looking around. But Yuuki and Kagali both spoke up to deny it.

"Nah, nah, you're fine."

"Right. You're the last person who needs to worry about that."

That brought the grouchy Laplace back to his seat. "What the heck? You could at least pretend to worry a little more about me..."

It was more than enough to quell the chamber's gloomy atmosphere. Everyone shared a laugh, their thoughts shifting away from darker topics. Yuuki, appreciative of that, spoke up to guide the conversation back his way.

"So regardless of what Damrada's motivations are, the question is: What should we do now?"

"Yes... I'd like to ask him about how much our plans have been compromised."

"Whoa, whoa, ya sure we have the time for stuff like that? He knows exactly what we're up to already, don't he?"

"Yeah, I told Damrada everything we were planning to do. We didn't exactly keep it a secret."

"Okay, so shouldn't we be gettin' outta here?"

"Well, that's not too possible, either."

Yuuki's faction was now soundly based in the Empire. He still had a few people undercover in the Western Nations, but that was only a tiny handful. There was no way he could lie low over there, and preparing a new hideout wasn't a very easy thing even in the best of times. Most of all, they had neither the time nor the right preparation to allow all the members of his faction to escape safely.

"One thing I can tell you for sure is that I can't run Cerberus by myself," said Misha. "I relied heavily on Damrada's work skills for that, and I don't even know everyone he had working for him."

Vega, the third leader of that group, was good for little more than wanton violence. It was very unlikely that he could serve in any kind of managerial capacity. Misha's point seemed valid there.

"Oh, I know that. This is one Cerberus that's gonna have to make do with less than three heads. We can get rid of all of Damrada's employees, maybe, but the biggest headache is the Composite Division. It'd be a real shame to let go of that force—or rather, to lose all its associated bases."

They could cut their losses and run, maybe, but the losses were just too great to contemplate. There was no place in this world that could accept a force of one hundred thousand out of nowhere. That meant Yuuki would have to leave them all in the lurch— and that, in turn, meant those who didn't escape somehow would doubtlessly be purged. Besides, given what they could guess about Damrada's intentions, it didn't seem like he was telling people about Yuuki's secrets.

"Okay, so there are a few reasons why Damrada wanted to keep Gadora quiet, but I think one of them was to keep Kondo from learning our information. The Imperial Guardians probably aren't a monolith, you know. And the coup we're planning in the capital—I think Damrada wants that to succeed, right?"

"We don't know what his intentions are, but if he wanted to keep us hidden, that would be the only reason why, yes."

Yuuki and Kagali seemed to be anticipating each other's thoughts. The rest of the group looked on in confusion. Then, as if unable to bear it any longer, Laplace interrupted.

"Whoa, whoa, whoa, wait a sec, Boss. The whole idea that he let Gadora go on purpose is just a guess on your part, huh? Ain't it more likely that Damrada and Kondo are all buddy-buddy, and we're gettin' them all wrong?"

That sounded like common sense to most of them. But not to Yuuki.

"I doubt it. Look, the whole reason we planned this coup was because of the deal we made with the demon lord Guy. Damrada knows that, too. So instead of trying to meddle in our plans, wouldn't he think it better to sow chaos in the capital and pull one over on Guy?"

"Mmm... Is that even possible?"

"I sure don't know."

"Hoh-hoh-hoh!"

Teare and Footman looked pretty lost, instead focusing on some juggling balls they had on hand.

"But would someone so close to the emperor want to see the capital in chaos?" Misha asked after organizing her thoughts. But she still failed to understand Yuuki and Kagali's point of view.

In a way, that was a totally normal reaction. After all, Yuuki's train of thought was feasible only from an absolutely rational perspective, where any sacrifice is fair game if it achieves your goals. It allowed Yuuki and his band to leverage their abilities in any way they wanted, and from Misha's outsider view, it was as contradictory as it was insane. Asking her to understand it was ridiculous.

"Don't think too hard about it, Misha. The important thing is to understand who Damrada had his eyes on as a potential hostile element. Damrada, you know... He never saw Sir Yuuki or Rimuru as his enemy from start to finish. For him, that was Guy Crimson—and nobody else. And once you realize that, it makes sense that he'd look the other way while we ran wild all over the capital."

"Yeah. And Kondo's different. To him, the enemy's not just Guy, but anybody else who's against the Empire. He serves Emperor Ludora with a completely different perspective from Damrada's."

That, Yuuki concluded, probably meant they were in conflict over assorted matters. It made sense to Kagali.

"Well, all right. If you and Lady Kagali say so, Boss, I'll believe ya."

Laplace was unhesitant in his agreement, Teare and Footman nodding along. Then Misha looped back to the core question.

"So, Sir Yuuki, what are your plans for the future? If Damrada turns out to be an enemy, then obviously we can't trust him, regardless of his true intentions. So should we call off the coup and force our way out of here, consequences or not? Fortunately for us, we've got sixty percent of the Composite Division blockading the Dwarven Kingdom's eastern city. Add the remaining forces in the capital to that, plus as much support as we ourselves can provide, and it'd be easy to seize a regional city or two. Use those as a base, and…"

"…And the conquered nations with a beef against the Empire will rise up and form a grand anti-imperialist coalition?"

"Y-yes. Wouldn't that be the best way to secure an army and give us the highest chance of victory?"

"Not a bad idea, no. You don't need to look for long to find regions oppressed by the imperial nobility. Maybe we could style ourselves as a liberation force instead of a rebellion in those areas."

"So…?"

"But sadly, the answer is no."

Misha was about to ask why. Yuuki continued before she could open her mouth.

"The only way for us to survive is to stage the coup as planned. Isn't that right, Damrada?"

Before Misha could comprehend what he meant, the clowns immediately readied themselves for combat. Then the heavy chamber door opened, and in walked a man.

"Well said. I'd expect nothing less from you, Boss."

It was Damrada, dressed in his usual merchant garb. But his demeanor was pure military, and he had no interest in hiding that. The air in the room grew tense. Laplace attempted to make a move, but Damrada stopped him with a quiet command.

"Don't try it. My men have already surrounded the building."

Yuuki, observing the situation, relaxed his body and sank into the sofa.

"Do you have time to talk a bit? If so, why don't you sit down, too?"

"Boss, we can't just sit here all day—"

"It's fine, it's fine. You just take a seat, okay?"

Yuuki enjoined the dubious Laplace to return to his seat, then eyed Damrada with a bold smile.

"So what do you want?"

"I'm afraid you've misread my behavior, Boss, so I've come to explain that I have my own problems to consider as well."

Damrada took a seat as instructed. Seeing his perfectly calm, collected demeanor made Laplace's crew nervously chuckle. Then, leaving everyone else in the room behind, Yuuki and Damrada began conversing.

"Problems, huh?"

"Yes. My thoughts, you see, are that I truly do wish you success in this coup, Boss."

"Okay. Then why did you let Gadora go?"

"Heh-heh-heh… He's safe, then? I took a gamble on that one, but he always was a very cautious man. I assumed he'd find a way to survive."

"And you did it to keep Kondo from getting his information?"

"That's right, yes."

"Didn't you swear an oath of loyalty to the emperor?"

"I did, yes."

"You *did*? Then what about now?"

"I've said this many times before, and perhaps you may choose not to believe it, but my loyalties are to you, Boss."

"Like I can trust you in that."

"I suppose not."

Both of them smiled as they let their tongues do the fighting.

"I can tell you that burying Gadora's information has effectively destroyed the Armored Division. In addition, the Magical Beast Division is now outside the capital city. Even if word of the Armored Division's status has reached them, it will take some time for them to turn back. The forces currently guarding the capital are greatly reduced in number. The time is now, don't you think?"

"I do. It's so convenient for us that it almost feels like it's been set up."

"Yes. I've been spending years setting this up for you."

"Damrada, are you...?"

"Look, Boss, I have lived my whole life in order to defeat Emperor Ludora. That is the only path left for saving him. The best way to achieve that was by having you take over the Empire. My thoughts on that have not changed, and now everything has been put in place. The rest is up to you to decide."

"Pfft..."

Yuuki snorted, not enjoying this topic at all. Everything was going the way Damrada wanted it, and he was deeply uncomfortable with that. But was rejecting him out of hand the right way, either? Just as Damrada said, the situation couldn't possibly be better right now. The only question was whether to trust him on that.

"Let me ask you something."

"Go ahead."

"Why did you use Clayman like a pawn without consulting me?"

Yuuki and the Moderate Jesters had sworn to each other that no one would betray the other. To the members of this band, there were few others in the world they could even think about trusting. Clayman was one of them, a vital friend to Yuuki, and the question brought Kagali, Laplace, Teare, and Footman all to attention. Their gazes were focused on Damrada, as if they'd never allow him to deceive them. But despite the near-murderous atmosphere, Damrada remained calm.

"I had nothing to do with what happened to Clayman. I have an idea of who did it, but I hardly expected him to go to such lengths..."

There was a moment of silence. Then Yuuki broke it.

"Is that Tatsuya Kondo?"

"..."

"You seem to know a lot about Kondo. There's a lot of secrets around, you know? So don't you think us trusting in you is a little too convenient?"

Damrada listened to Yuuki's theory silently, a pained expression on his face. Then, after Yuuki was done, he spoke up softly.

"...I cannot tell you everything, because it would be against the law for me. All I can divulge for the moment is that not even I am aware of all of Kondo's capabilities. But even so, I still want you to believe me. His Majesty's salvation is at stake, you know."

The clowns' cold gazes pierced Damrada. The looks on everyone's faces proved it—he was well below their trust. Yuuki was among them.

However, there was no denying that the current situation wasn't exactly rosy for them. Damrada's forces were waiting outside the building; they all felt a presence from outside the room that couldn't be ignored. He must have brought along some of the most talented Imperial Knights with him. Neither Yuuki nor his friends would have an easy time breaking through this siege.

If it were only me, I think I could manage it... But I don't think I can bring everyone else to safety. That leaves accepting his proposal as our only choice, huh...?

Yuuki calculated his options. Then, suddenly, he noticed Damrada's gaze pointed straight at him, unwavering. Those eyes hadn't changed at all from the day they first met.

Yuuki closed his eyes, thinking back to the past. Ever since that moment, Damrada had been nothing but fearless and brazen, willing to accept any request—for the right price. But he was also a man of contradictions, willing to invest hordes of money for the sake of his friends. *"I'm willing to make any sacrifice for the sake of those I believe in,"* he once said. But who was Damrada picturing in his eyes when he said that?

It wasn't me, I'm sure. But I really did like those eyes of his...

He called Yuuki his boss, swearing his loyalty to him. But there was always something about Damrada that made him seem somehow untrustworthy. Looking back, Yuuki realized, it made him feel unconsciously sad for his comrade.

So he opened his eyes, looking toward him.

"I sense lies in your words. Your allegiance is to me, but at the same time, it's always been to Emperor Ludora. That much hasn't changed, am I right?"

"Heh-heh... There's no pulling the wool over your eyes, Boss."

That murmured affirmation was, in its own way, motivation enough for Yuuki to trust Damrada.

"All right. Instead of fighting you guys here, why don't we go out there and make this coup a success?"

Nobody expressed any dissatisfaction with this.

"Well, our hands are tied. If Sir Yuuki's made that decision, it's up to us to obey him."

"Yeah. But if you two-time us, Damrada, I'll see that you pay for it."

"You have our support, Damrada!"

"Hoh-hoh-hoh! Don't forget about me."

So the clowns made their decision. They opted to trust Yuuki, their boss—a sign of their bonds of friendship, as true as ever. And Damrada was just as much a part of those bonds.

CHAPTER 1

REWARDS AND EVOLUTIONS

That Time I Got Reincarnated as a Slime

The day after I revived approximately seven hundred thousand imperial soldiers and officers, we had our troops who played an active role in the defense of Tempest lined up in rows across the coliseum. The rank-and-file soldiers had filled every available seat in the house.

Today, we were holding a victory celebration. We were still at war with the Empire, technically, but we planned this as a necessary tool for boosting morale. Bacchus, dispatched from the Crusaders, and the overcomers serving Luminus were also in attendance. Jiwu had killed them, but fortunately, everything took place inside the labyrinth. They had all been properly revived, and they were kind enough to accept our apologies. "It's our lack of experience," they told me, but—you know—this crime was committed on our land, after all. We could at least treat them well.

Anyway, I'm just happy the damage was kept to a minimum. We had a deluxe feast planned for the second half of the celebration, so hopefully they'd indulge to their hearts' content.

We also had a few guests from abroad in the VIP seating. That included Alvis, who joined the defense, as well as Phobio and the Twin Wings who arrived after, elite troops in tow.

"Lady Milim is restless and worried, so Lady Frey sent us to assist you."

"Yes, but I'm not sure she had anything to worry about. We were convinced you'd win all along, Sir Rimuru."

Lucia, the blond Twin Wing, and Claire, the silver-haired one, gave me their reassurance in the most sonorous of voices. I guess I made Milim worry for me, but the news of our victory ought to set her straight again. Our city was safe, thanks to Veldora and Ramiris, and I was sure things would be pretty peaceful soon.

"I was sent over as a contact," Phobio told me. "The magical calls weren't coming through anymore, so I was dispatched just in case. And also... No, pardon me."

The way he put it, he would go back at once and bring reinforcements if things were looking bleak for us. As the fastest member of their group, Phobio was selected for the job, based on the possibility that magic wouldn't be an option due to magicule disruption. He was about to say something after that but stopped midsentence. The way he was looking at Alvis bothered me, but I decided to ignore it. I figured it was already finished business.

I thanked the three of them and showed them to their box seats.

After that, there was another group—guests from Dwargon. I saw Jaine there, arch-wizard of the Dwargon royal court. Dolph, captain of the Pegasus Knights, was serving as her bodyguard.

Jaine, for the most part, used me as her personal complaint board. "No forbidden spell casting in the Forest of Jura," she told me—but she was even angrier about me having Primal Demons under my wing. To be honest, I *did* have my regrets about that, but what could I do now? They just kinda showed up when I wasn't paying attention. They call that a force majeure in insurance contracts, don't they?

"No, it's *not* merely a force majeure! I've lived for quite a long time, I'll have you know, but I've never been so shocked and dismayed in my entire life!"

"I'm sorry."

I had no choice but to apologize. I appeased her as best I could, explained my side of the story, and after enough cajoling, she seemed to be a bit more satisfied.

It would've been nice if Jaine could've left like that, but we needed to have a meeting to discuss the future. In fact, that seemed to be the purpose of her visit. Sixty thousand troops were still deployed in front of Dwargon's eastern city, all under Yuuki's command. I told her that I had a tentative war alliance with Yuuki, and that was why war hadn't broken out over there. Tensions were still running high, though, so we couldn't leave things like this. Basically, I wanted to discuss matters with Yuuki and figure out a future course of action. We'd released the captured Laplace, entrusting him with a message from me, and now we were just waiting for Yuuki to contact us.

So I took Jaine and Dolph to the VIP seats as well, inviting them to celebrate our victory with us.

It was thus an international audience watching the proceedings that day in the coliseum. I was seated on a chair placed atop a raised podium, in slime form. Behind me were Rigurd and Rigur, the rest of our civil servants lined up behind them on both sides.

Among the columns below me were the Ten Dungeon Marvels, people who normally wouldn't be seen in public. They were the stars of the day, though, so their presence was perfectly natural. Showing off the labyrinth bosses to the world normally wouldn't be a great idea, but today, at least, it was fine—there were no civilians in the audience, after all, or adventurers from our Volunteer Army.

The first one to speak was Shuna, who was standing next to me. She gave a long, impassioned speech, explicitly stating beforehand that these were my words. It was a great performance, but I didn't write any of it—that was all Shuna. In a way, she's a much more effective secretary than either of my actual ones. I'm terrible with this speech stuff, and she's been a huge help on that front. Shion's not really suited for public speaking, and I'd be anxious leaving that job to Diablo—he'd just talk about how great I was from start to finish.

As I internally thanked Shuna for her presence, I thought over our next steps. During this event, I wanted to announce our achievements and, as I did, give out rewards to my people. In other words, I was going to try "awakening" (or whatever it turned out to be) my staff.

....
......

...

According to Raphael, granting someone a hundred thousand souls would "awaken" and evolve them, granting them strength equivalent to a "true" demon lord. Only those qualified would be eligible for this, but much to my surprise, twelve total candidates fit the bill: Ranga, Benimaru, Shion, Gabil, Geld, Diablo, Testarossa, Ultima, Carrera, Kumara, Zegion, and Adalmann. Only those connected enough with me on the soul level to obtain a demon lord "seed" were allowed; that was the condition.

The one who piqued my interest the most is undoubtedly Adalmann. He's the only one I didn't name myself. Why does he have the right to an evolution?

Understood. The subject Adalmann's faith in you has surpassed the level required to establish a firm connection with you.

Oh, right. I taught Adalmann the "secret skills of faith and favor" I learned from Luminus, didn't I? Thanks to that, we've built a connection that rivals the kind we'd have after a naming. That's just amazing. It's like he'd qualified for it all on his own, thanks to the unbelievable amount of faith he possessed. It's a little awkward how all that faith was aimed at me, but I have to admire him for it.

So that makes sense. But the next question was: How many of these people can be evolved? Based on a quick count, I had a little over a million souls stored inside me. That didn't quite match the number of people who died, but Raphael explained the reason why.

Proposal. The obtained souls were found to have a range of individual variances. Do you want to redistribute and reconstruct them to be uniform?
Yes
No

I thought *yes* without really understanding, and the next thing I knew, the total number ballooned to just over a million. The resurrected imperial soldiers would have a small amount of energy returned to them, so I'd figured the number would shrink a bit, but it actually grew instead. Some of them (like Caligulio) had been awakened themselves, and a lot of other really strong dudes stormed the labyrinth as well. People like that had much more energy than usual—and although I was technically borrowing it, I also took a ton of energy from Jiwu and Bernie, what with the ultimate skills they had and all. Each one of them had the energy of between several dozen and several tens of thousands of souls in their bodies.

So between this, that, and the other thing, I had enough souls to awaken ten people. But I had a few points of concern for this experiment.

The first was word of this leaking out. Was it really safe to do something so show-offy in front of guests like Alvis and Jaine? But I decided to trust them on this regardless—not because we were all part of an alliance, but because I knew they'd find out anyway. It was utterly impossible to fool Milim, and King Gazel had already put his trust in me with Diablo. Jaine was already pissed off enough at me, so it was kinda too late to keep her from learning about the labyrinth gang. I was sure the labyrinth-running community would start spreading rumors about how unnaturally strong the bosses had gotten before long anyway. No point, I thought, in concealing anything from anyone in this coliseum.

Next up was the uncertainty factor. This was the first time I had ever tried an awakening on someone else; there was always a chance something unexpected would occur. Thus, harnessing Ramiris's powers, I had the entire coliseum blocked off from the rest of the city. That should prevent any damage from spreading to the outside world, no matter what happens—and it'd also maintain confidentiality, so we'd really be killing two birds with one stone.

The last concern of mine was the Harvest Festival that'd likely occur to each target, much like the one triggered by my demon lord awakening. In my case, it put me in a catatonic state for three days straight. If something similar happened to them, it'd mean the majority of our main leadership would take a days-long nap in the middle of a war. They'd be totally off the grid for a few days, and if something went haywire, it'd certainly suck for us.

But despite stewing over it for a while, I decided this wouldn't be a big problem, either. There was zero imperial army left—nobody in the Armored Division, according to what Caligulio and his officers told us, that could mobilize at a moment's notice. We *did* just kill nine hundred and forty thousand of their soldiers and officers, after all, so I kinda doubted there'd be anyone left.

The Empire had nothing but their Magical Beast and Composite Divisions to wage war with. We had an alliance (more or less) with Yuuki's Composite Division, and right now the Magical Beast Division was being transported in a wholly different direction by the Flying Combat Corps, the pride and joy of the Armored Division.

My Eye of God skill was more than enough to keep track of those airships, and we calculated that even if they suddenly changed direction, it'd still take more than three days to reach our country. They had a normal cruising speed of around two hundred and fifty miles an hour; they could allegedly break the sound barrier at maximum combat speed—but only for a short period of time due to the comical amounts of magic force it consumed. We weren't even sure they could stay in the air for the long stretches of time it'd require without resupplying.

These airships ran incomparably faster than ships or trains, but being in the air brings its own threats. You may run into surprise turbulence or points where the magicules are too disturbed to access magic at all. Some areas were also home to monsters who patrolled the skies, so the safest route wasn't necessarily the straightest one every time. The fact that supersonic flight was possible in this world at all was a huge threat, but perhaps it wasn't as advantageous as you might think. I didn't see much need for alarm there.

That just left the possibility that the Imperial Guardians would go on the move. We whipped their asses this time, but only because we had the advantage of fighting on our home turf in the labyrinth. We could revive anyone who died in battle, which let us handle any situation with the utmost calmness.

If I was fighting the Guardians, I figured I could find a way to win. So would Benimaru, probably, at the end of the day. But what about Shion or Ranga? Wouldn't it be pretty iffy for Gabil or Geld?

If so, we'd need to address that as soon as possible. That way, even if they unexpectedly encountered a powerful enemy, they'd at least be able to buy the rest of us some time. We all had soul connections—in the form of soul corridors, to be exact—so they had a solid link with me still. No matter the situation, we'd always be able to Thought Communicate with each other. They could contact me as soon as they made an encounter, and then we could stage a pincer attack to kill off the threat.

Either way, I wanted to awaken everyone immediately, in preparation for what was to come. Every possibility, I thought, needed to be addressed. And this was the best time possible to do it.

....

......

...

So not to hurry things, but let's get started.

My first nominee, it goes without saying, was Benimaru. As our commander-in-chief, he had done an excellent job leading all our forces. He didn't look too happy about what Testarossa and the other demons got up to, but hey—every war comes with its unforeseen developments. It certainly wasn't his fault—and it *definitely* wasn't mine! It all worked out fine in the end, besides, and I think everyone involved did amazing.

After ending her speech, Shuna called Benimaru's name. He took a step forward and kneeled down in front of me.

"Very good! Now, Benimaru. I am ready to grant you a reward right now—"

"I don't even *want* to know what this is. You're scheming something again, aren't you?"

What the heck? I haven't even done anything yet, and he's on to me.

This whole awakening thing was actually meant to be a surprise. I knew I'd field objections if I brought it up with certain people, so I decided to carry this out without telling any of them. We continued talking as Shuna read out all of Benimaru's glorious war achievements.

"Well, y'know, I actually won a lot of souls in this war. I guess Testarossa and her gang have been offering them to me, and it looks like I can use them to awaken those closely connected to me enough."

"I heard nothing about this."

"Hey, I'm telling you now, right?"

We looked each other in the eye. He totally would've turned it down—I'm sure of it. Benimaru's a lot more serious-minded than you'd think, and he's got a serious drive to become stronger on his own, I guess. He even seemed to have some thoughts about my own evolution to demon lord. I'm sure Diablo and Shion couldn't wait to snap this reward up.

"So what is this awakening?"

That was a good question. In my case, it boosted my magicule count and magic power tenfold, as well as gave blessings to all the monsters in the lineage of my own soul. I couldn't say how much *he'd* grow from it, but I was sure it'd be a pretty big bump.

"Um, well, to put it simply, I evolved when I became a demon lord, right? Think of it as kinda the same thing. You'd have a demon lord–type evolution."

"What?! So it'll change not only me, but all who serve me?"

"I think so. Probably."

It was unclear to me just how much of an impact it'd have, but I'd bet it'd have its effects on Team Kurenai, at least.

"Oh, no, no, no, I can't accept something so important happening to me without any warning—"

"Hold on, hold on. Okay. If you put it like *that*, then maybe you're right, but now's not the time to argue about it. We can't be sure how strong our enemy's going to be right now, so we gotta do everything we can to strengthen our forces, right?"

"I'm sure you're right, but…"

Benimaru closed his eyes, troubled. Then he opened them again, looked at me, and heaved a long, heavy sigh. I guess he made up his mind—that or gave up, but same difference.

"But it's not just me being awakened, is it? I think a paring down of our forces right now is dangerous, but what are your thoughts on that?"

"There are twelve people who're qualified for this, but I'm only gonna do nine at this time. I'm gonna leave the demons to guard things, so I decided that a few days off-line won't be a big problem."

"I see. That—and we have the labyrinth. Perhaps they could buy enough time for us, at least."

That approach convinced Benimaru well enough. Next was the issue of things going out of hand on me.

"There *is* one thing bothering me still, however."

"What is that?"

"Right now, you're stronger now than I was when I evolved. I don't know exactly how strong you'll get through this process. You might even wind up stronger than me, you know."

If he did, I think it'd still feed back to me through the Food Chain feature of my ultimate skill Belzebuth... But regardless, the possibility is there. Plus, like, there's no *way* Diablo won't wind up stronger than me. I don't think Benimaru and his kin will betray me, but I can't deny the possibility that the sheer onrush of power could sweep them beyond control. I *think* they'll be fine, and I set up this isolation chamber around the coliseum just in case, but there is still that anxiety in my mind, yeah.

"So even with that concern, you still want to go ahead with our awakening?"

"Yeah, pretty much."

"Well, I certainly feel loved anyway. You're pulling out all the stops to ensure no enemy could ever defeat us, is that it? I'll do whatever it takes to live up to those expectations, then."

I don't know if it'll be true for everyone, but Benimaru, at least, understood my thoughts. He was all but assuring me that he'd never let himself go berserk with power. I'm glad I can count on him.

"I'll trust you on that."

"By all means."

Shuna chose that moment to end her rambling speech. It was time for the award ceremony.

✳

"Benimaru! Your command in this battle was truly outstanding! From this moment forward, you may style yourself as the Flare Lord!"

"Yes, my lord! Thank you for this glorious honor!"

The ritual was underway.

Benimaru is usually a pretty friendly guy, but in front of his soldiers, he's a high-ranking officer of the corps. He's perfect at separating public and private affairs like that.

I had just granted him the title of Flare Lord. I meant that as kind of a stand-in for "demon lord," just in case he actually did become a true demon lord like me. The "flare" part was meant to indicate intense fury. He may seem to keep his cool now (despite his more short-tempered past), but he's still got that flame burning deep down as his essence. It's just that he's able to control it—bring it down to a casual campfire, if needed. As a sort-of demon lord in my service, I couldn't think of a more appropriate title.

Question. Do you wish to use the prescribed amount of one hundred thousand souls to evolve the subject Benimaru?

Yes
No

That's a yes.

As soon as I gave the word, a soul corridor was created between Benimaru and me—not the thin, wirelike link from before, but a solid, hefty industrial cable of sorts. Through it, a hundred thousand souls coursed over to Benimaru—and with them, the evolution began...

...or didn't.

Nothing happened. Oh, great. Did I mess this up? I wondered for a moment before a thoughtful-looking Benimaru spoke to me.

"It would appear one more condition needs to be fulfilled."

"How so?"

"Oh, er, not you, Sir Rimuru. The problem seems to be on my end..."

He sounded oddly hesitant. Huh? Something's weird.

"What kinda problem?" I asked in a whisper. The answer came like a ton of bricks.

"Well, actually, I heard the 'voice of the world' just now, and it told me that I can evolve from an oni to a god-ogre—but if I do, I won't be able to father any children."

As Benimaru put it, becoming a god-ogre meant having a de facto infinite life span, so there was no need to have offspring at that point. Which...I guess is true? The oni race is pretty long-lived as it is, so if we're talking the next level after that, I suppose having no natural life span at all is logical. God-ogres must be a kind of spiritual life-form, then. It doesn't sound like demons have children, either, so I suppose that's what happens if your natural life suddenly stretches on forever. You can come back from the dead anytime you want, so it's not like you have to worry about preserving the species.

"Okay, so what's the problem with that?"

Sadly for me, I'm in the same boat—I can't have any children. Not that it's much of a problem or inconvenience for me, but...

"...Well, it seems I have some lingering desires from back when I was still a mere ogre. I had forgotten all about it, but apparently I need to finish up my duty as the chief of our tribe."

"And does that 'duty' mean you have to have kids, or else you can't evolve?"

"Y...es. I sort of have to make sure there's a generation after mine..."

Benimaru and I exchanged stares. We were right in the middle of this celebration, you know; couldn't this wait until later? To the audience, I must've looked like I was congratulating Benimaru; but if I didn't do something fast, everyone was gonna realize there was a problem.

I gave him another look, panicking a little. Then Benimaru awkwardly turned away. That was a rarity for him. He's usually so fearless. It was quite moving to see, in a sense.

"Well, Benimaru, you need to figure this out, okay?"

"No, but...?"

"Right," I said, raising my voice as I ignored Benimaru's attempt at an excuse. "So you want to get married as your reward? Who did you wanna get married to?"

"Whoa! Sir Rimuru?!"

At times like these, it was best to show off my more manly side— I was treating this as if it were someone else's problem. With all the arrangements I'd made for this day, Benimaru just needed to firm up his resolve and get over himself. It was a rough way of doing it, but it was a must for handling someone as reluctant as he was.

...Report. This behavior might lead to him strangling you.

Huh?

Raphael wasn't giving me many answers. I mean, c'mon, it's fine, isn't it?

As I told myself that, the coliseum erupted in cheers. I supposed the audience picked up on my voice enough to know what I was saying.

"So you've finally made up your mind, have you?" Shuna chuckled.

"Well?" Hakuro asked, hand on sword. "Who are you going to choose as your bride?"

Before Benimaru could begin to answer the question, Momiji stood up—along with Alvis in her VIP box.

"Sir Rimuru! Permission to speak, please!"

"And for me as well, I hope? I have the same request as Lady Momiji!"

The emotional force from them both was palpable. I was starting to think this was getting out of hand.

"Okay, okay, okay. Will you two come over here for me, please?"

We were in the middle of this event, but there was no helping that now. The soldiers in the seats were now witnesses to an entirely different kind of ceremony. Nobody was complaining—in fact, if I interrupted this right now, they'd probably all howl about it. So I let the two women say their piece.

"My lord, I would like to ask for permission to marry Sir Benimaru as a reward for his services."

Momiji was the first to speak, and she was certainly swinging for the fences. Hakuro wasn't far behind her.

"Sir Rimuru, a reward is something that must be given by someone else. It's not polite to simply ask for one. However, with that in mind, I hope you do my daughter a favor and grant her request."

He was willing, as he explained to me, to give up his own military decoration if it'd help Momiji realize her dreams.

This was an arrangement far too difficult for me to refuse by this point. Benimaru was frozen in place, unable to keep up with us. He's normally a man of very good judgment, but I got the feeling he was having trouble thinking straight.

Then someone else spoke up to make things even more confusing.

"Rimuru, my lord, please allow me to state my candidacy for the position of Sir Benimaru's second wife."

"What?!" Benimaru and I both exclaimed at Alvis's offer. She and Momiji were in a heated battle over Benimaru, that much was for certain. "Love on the battlefield," as it was famously referred to around Tempest—but since when had they come to *this* kinda truce over it?

"Okay, so...Momiji would be his 'first wife,' and Alvis, you'll be the second?"

"Yes, my lord!"

"That is correct."

Their faces couldn't have looked happier. Benimaru, meanwhile, was about ready to faint. I wasn't really sure what happened with these two women, but it seemed they'd established a clear pecking order.

"I would be a failure as a wife if I did anything to trouble Sir Benimaru. I will never ask him to choose between Alvis or me. Instead, we beg you—please marry us both simultaneously."

"Wait, um, I can't—"

"Don't worry. I've discussed this thoroughly with Lady Momiji, and we've come to the conclusion that someone of your ability, Sir Benimaru, would not have difficulty with this arrangement."

Uh, what kind of conclusion is *that*?

Benimaru looked my way, pleading for help.

Y'know, this is just as perplexing for me, too. I'm not sure if I can do much—

Understood. Under current Jura-Tempest Federation law, polygamy is permitted for the purpose of providing sufficient offspring for a species. However, the law as it stands restricts any additional marriage partners to widows seeking to bear children. In this particular case, a second wife would not be allowed.

Ohhh!

Right, yeah, I remember that. No clue why Raphael's such an eager participant in this nonsense, but now I figured I could lend Benimaru a hand.

"...Sadly, Alvis, in our nation, a woman can become someone's second wife only if they are widowed and seek to bear children. Now, there's a chance we'll change the rules once we make more progress on our legal infrastructure, but for now, we can't allow you to—"

I tried to sound as apologetic as possible as I dismissed Alvis's request. Benimaru nodded to me, visibly relieved, but any hopes that this would end the topic were quickly dashed.

"No need to worry about that, my lord. I've been doing some research of my own into the rules, and in fact, I just got married the other day..."

Huh? What do you mean you got married the other day? Like, with who? And doesn't that make it even more impossible to marry Benimaru?

That was what I thought, but Alvis then blew my mind once more.

"...but I regret to tell you that my betrothed has recently passed. Thus, I have fulfilled the conditions required to become Sir Benimaru's second wife."

Huh?

Wait, wait—this wasn't because of the war, was it? Because if so, we've got big problems... But Alvis's argument was so deviously clever, protesting at all began to seem silly to me.

"H-hang on a second, okay? C-can you tell me who you married, exactly?"

"That would be Phobio in the VIP box over there," Alvis said with a smile.

...

Um, Phobio's alive, isn't he?

Benimaru and I looked at each other, incredibly confused.

"What's up with all this?"

"I don't have any more answers than you!"

"True..."

We didn't even need Thought Communication. It took just a few glances to have that conversation.

Phobio carefully approached us, kneeling with a contrite look on his face.

"I'm really sorry about this. Alvis just started talking out of nowhere, and..."

"No, like, you *married* her? And now you're *dead*?"

"Well...about that."

And so came the big reveal. Between Momiji's, Alvis's, and Phobio's guidance, I finally understood the whole story behind the plan, although it took a few moments.

To put it simply, Momiji and Alvis had engaged in combat with each other so often that they had developed a kind of friendship. Thanks to that, instead of fighting each other, they decided to team up. They both had a common goal, after all—so how could they arrange it so they were *both* Benimaru's wife?

After racking their brains on the topic, they concluded the answer was to have Alvis marry Phobio. Then, after that, the wedded couple would go down to the labyrinth and battle to the death. Alvis emerged victorious, and now she was a widow—but since it was all down in the Dungeon, Phobio was instantly resurrected.

"She said we could marry for real if I beat her, but...I think I deserve to have a cry about this, don't you?"

That was the motive for Phobio to play along, huh? Seeing him slumped over like this was so sad to see that I couldn't help but sympathize with him. Like, what *does* happen after this, then?

"Rigurd, is this, uh, legal?"

"My lord, this is clearly the theory of power in action, the result of combining your wisdom and strength to gain what you want. As far as I'm concerned, it's completely on the up-and-up!"

It is. And Rugurd, Regurd, and Rogurd were all nodding along with him. Seriously? I guess that, for monsters, what Alvis did was perfectly acceptable.

"You see, my brother, just how much determination Lady Momiji and Lady Alvis have shown for you? Please, be a man and give them an answer!"

Shuna was all for it, too, then? And not just her.

"If you hate her, say it. If you don't want this attention, say so. That's all you need to do, isn't it? So why all the agonizing?"

Shion may have looked like she wasn't using her head, but this was actually a very good argument. She wasn't opposed to the arrangement at all; she was just urging him for an answer.

No opposition so far, then—nobody feels this is unethical or gross. And yeah, when it comes to monsters, survival of the fittest is the name of the game. The laws I've set in place are mainly there to ensure the strongest of us don't hog all our resources. As long as everyone's on the same page, and nobody's complaining, I don't see why I should object.

"Benimaru, how long are you going to stew over this? If you keep acting all indecisive, your father in the afterlife's gonna laugh at you."

"Soei... You say that, but my father loved none but my mother, and they brought Shuna and me into the world. What's so wrong about me wanting to do the same?!"

He was unusually agitated. Soei's observation must have hit home... But he wasn't giving an inch.

"I am not saying it's wrong. You seem to be lost over who you love, but that's exactly why you should have children, isn't it? A man and a woman can't have a child if they don't love each other. If you didn't have any love for either of them, then simply tell them no from the start. But if you *do* have any sort of feelings for them... then take them and show us the results!"

That's awfully straightforward of you, Soei. Surprisingly close to harassment, actually—but he looked so *cool* saying it, too. The guy drives me nuts.

But this argument also made sense to monsters. I had forgotten about this, but you couldn't really have a child if there was no love involved. I guessed Benimaru was at an impasse because he felt it'd be unfaithful to love two people at the same time—but choosing only one would make the other sad. That was why he had put off giving an answer all this time. I certainly don't mind that kind of thinking. But if he followed Soei's advice and "showed some results," wouldn't that solve his problems?

"Alvis! Let's see who can conceive Sir Benimaru's child first!"

"You won't beat me on that, Lady Momiji. My love is real—all I have to do is turn Sir Benimaru's heart toward me!"

I thought that'd be the hardest part… But either way, they didn't seem to be worried about much. It was just a matter of how Benimaru felt.

"Benimaru, we're in the middle of a national celebration right now. A place where we're meant to honor your military service, too. You're allowed to be as selfish as you want, all right? So please give me a sincere answer. Will you answer to the love of Momiji and Alvis or not? Which is it?"

If Benimaru says no, this conversation is over. But if not…

"Momiji… Alvis… As the samurai guarding Sir Rimuru, I may not be able to stay close to you for all time. If that becomes the case, will you still choose me?"

Benimaru was nothing if not sincere. He was even showing concern for their future. If he became a father and had no lingering regrets in life, he would evolve into a god-ogre—and once that happened and he gained de facto infinite life, would he be in any position to care for Momiji and Alvis? That was a good point. He was the only one doing the evolving, so his wives would be left behind…in assorted ways.

It'd be kinda mean to ask for an immediate answer in a situation like this, wouldn't it? It was a little hard for me to picture it, but I sure wouldn't want my loved ones passing on before I did. And I don't mean anyone in particular—that applies to all my friends. So I could understand Benimaru's concern, and I thought Momiji and Alvis might be upset by it—but my fears were unfounded.

"That's not a problem at all! Once I raise our child, I'll find my own way to evolve as well."

"I agree. And even if evolution is not possible for me, I know that my children will comfort you in your loss."

Wow. Strong women. Totally unfazed in their sheer determination. And when Benimaru heard this, he flashed a breezy smile.

"Sir Rimuru! Will you allow me to take two wives, then?"

There was no way I could say no here, nor was I about to. Maybe I was setting a precedent I'd live to regret, but if people saw it as me making special exceptions in exchange for exemplary military performance, maybe it'd give them some more drive and motivation to work harder. So fine, then. Benimaru may pretend to be all gruff and unflappable, but he's actually very pure of heart. If I hadn't stepped in, he probably would've been single for all eternity, so let's just see this as the right opportunity at the right time. If there's anything I'm worried about, it's the job he faces loving both Momiji and Alvis at the same time... But let's just have faith that Benimaru can juggle that.

Right. Time to give him some final words of encouragement. I hopped off my chair, transformed into a person, and raised my voice high.

"It is granted! By my name, I hereby authorize the soul union between Benimaru, Momiji, and Alvis!"

For monsters, "marriage" is treated as a union of souls. And that's more than just a metaphor—remember, you can't have a child without love. That's why I thought the new coinage here was appropriate.

Hearing my words, a smile erupted over Benimaru's face. It was tinged with joy, his cheeks bright red—but he still stood tall as he hugged Momiji and Alvis.

"I thank you. And I promise you that I will demonstrate my full sincerity in loving them both!"

The majestic words from Benimaru made tears of joy flow from Momiji's and Alvis's eyes. They were so overcome with emotion that they seemed to be at a loss for words. Honestly, I envy Benimaru. A beautiful young girl on one side, a more mature beauty on the other—like having a flower for each hand. But as much of a late bloomer as he is at this stuff, I'm sure he'll have a lot of adversity to overcome in his future. Of course, I'm not really one to comment. I'm asexual and genderless at this point, so it's no skin off my nose...

The coliseum burst into applause at Benimaru's promise. Shuna happily congratulated her brother, and Shion was clapping proudly for reasons only she knew. I could hear some jealousy and resentment among the cheering from the crowd, but it just showed how much everyone cared for him.

And so Momiji, Alvis, and Benimaru celebrated their new union in the midst of raucous cheering in the coliseum. I'd like to move right on to the party phase, but we're still in the middle of an event here, and I want to get the evolution rituals done with first. For now, we'll keep it to just that announcement. Once this evolution event masquerading as a victory celebration is over, we'll have more time to hold Benimaru's wedding in an unhurried fashion. There's another party scheduled for later today, but—hey—the more excitement, the merrier.

So allowing the happy trio to return to their posts, I ordered Shuna to make the necessary arrangements for them, raising a hand to quiet down the incessant cheering. It was a very unexpected turn of events. I could see Gobwa breaking down in tears out of the corner of my eye (and Phobio consoling her for some reason), but there was no time to think about that. Let's keep this thing going.

✳

Back in my slime form, I settled down on my chair. Once I was up there, Shuna's dignified voice echoed across the coliseum, the atmosphere still electric.

"Our three great commanders, please step forward!"

These referred to the commanders of our First, Second, and Third Army Corps—in other words, Gobta, Geld, and Gabil. All three were kneeling before me.

Let's kick things off with Gobta. He was looking right at me, face expectant.

"A-*hem!* Gobta, I will grant you *no reward!*"

"Huhhh? Aw, what the hey? That's so mean! Why'd ya call me up, then?"

"A fine question! I may not have a reward for you, but instead, I'm going to give you a new privilege."

"A privilege?"

All the souls in the world wouldn't evolve Gobta. He might have been a bundle of budding talent, but he didn't qualify for this prize, and I couldn't help that. I considered granting him some weapons or armor, but I didn't think he'd be capable of handling anything more than what I already gave him. Besides, he and Ranga could already transform into that combo beast, so I didn't think he needed any kind of half-assed armor anyway.

And forget about a cash reward—not like he'd use it for anything worthwhile. He already took in a fat paycheck as an army commander; I gave him a ton of points each month that he could trade in for money, so I was sure he was living comfortably. If this was a human kingdom, I'd probably be assigning him territory and making him an earl or something, but Tempest didn't really work on that system. It wasn't like he had any kind of governance skill regardless, so it was pointless to think about.

So I decided to grant Gobta a special privilege instead. The concept was hard for Gobta to wrap his head around; calling it just a "privilege" was probably too vague to understand. Let's give him the answer.

"I hereby grant you the privilege of continuing to address me as you do now, in your casual tone of voice!"

I grinned at the puzzled Gobta as I spoke. And before he could understand what I'd just told him, a cheer—or maybe more like angry shouting—rang out even louder than the one for Benimaru. It was sheer jealousy, and there was no way to hide it. Even Shion and Shuna were giving Gobta terrifying gazes. I couldn't even guess how envious they were.

"Um... You serious, sir?"

"Like, you don't even know *how* to talk all fancy, do you? You'd royally screw it up if you tried, so I'm taking this opportunity to make it your formal right instead."

I can sense that Gobta respects me, of course, but that's not at all prevalent in his tone of voice. I mean, I always tell people that they can be as casual as they'd like with me, but it seems to be difficult for a lot of people. Meanwhile, we'd frequently receive complaints from dignitaries about how flip Gobta's more natural speaking style was. People wanted me to do something about it, I was told, because otherwise it'd make everyone else look bad.

It was turning into a big hassle, so I decided to grant him the "right" to speak that way. We had foreign guests like Phobio and Jaine in the audience, so I figured taking this chance to spread the word would help solve the Gobta problem. I'm sure things like appearances and authority are big problems for some people, but as monsters, we never have anything as rigid as that. I just do what I wanna do. It's what's on the inside that counts, not the outside, and Gobta's a great example of that. He may sound like a little punk, but his loyalty is the real thing. I could see it in his eyes—eyes that're fully willing to die for me. That's why I gave him this "privilege."

"Thank youuuuuuuuuuuuuuuuuuu!"

With a huge smile, Gobta stood up and bowed until he was forming a right angle with his body. He was clearly overjoyed—maybe he had been working on correcting his tone, although if he was, he failed miserably. In a way, this was the best reward I could give Gobta, and that made me happy, too. He's *such* a hard person to shop for.

✳

That took care of Gobta. Next was Geld.

"Now, Geld—from this day forward, you may style yourself as Barrier Lord!"

"I gladly accept the title, my lord! And I, Geld, promise to do my best to live up to that name!"

Good. Strong response there. And as the crowd cheered, I lowered my voice to a whisper.

"And I'm gonna try the same evolution ritual I did with Benimaru on you."

"What on…?"

It was gonna be a pain in the ass to explain it every time, so I set up a Thought Communication with everybody I intended to grant souls to. Once they were all hooked up, I explained to everyone what evolution entailed for them, not forgetting to use Hasten Thought as well. That way, we could have this important conversation in less than a few seconds of real time.

Once I wrapped that up, Geld answered via Thought Communication.

(I am grateful for the offer, my lord, but I wonder if there are those more qualified than me for it. Carrera, serving as our observer, was far more successful in this war. If she, too, is qualified for this, then by all means, let it be her instead of me...)

Hmm. So he was declining the offer to be awakened? Well, I had no intention of evolving Carrera this time. She *did* contribute a lot, yeah, but if she was *this* much of a menace in her current state, I couldn't have her flying off the handle with even more power. We needed to see how this evolution stuff would unfold at first, and that was why I wanted to evolve more of the old guard for starters, since I trusted they'd be safe with it.

I relayed all that to Geld, but he still seemed a little torn.

(Yes, but me, I don't know...)

Ah. I guess Geld was also a little anxious about the potential to go berserk after this? Plus, maybe this was his way of expressing his atonement. The orcs' rampage a while back spread disaster all across the Forest of Jura, and as the leader responsible for that, Geld always placed himself under severe discipline. His eyes were shining with a strong determination, and right now, they were pointed straight at me. So I told him:

(Don't worry about that, Geld. The Geld they used to call the Orc Disaster might have gone out of control, but even that was for the sake of your friends, wasn't it?)

I didn't think he'd go berserk now. If he had that kind of determination, he ought to be able to control whatever power he had at hand. And nobody among us would ever shun Geld for the events of the past by now.

(I know you still feel responsible about it, but I trust in you. And I know you can use your newfound powers to help protect us all!)

Once Geld evolved, his followers would receive blessings as well. That, in turn, would strengthen the defenses of our entire nation. Explaining it this way to him, I noticed Geld's eyes sparkle even brighter than before.

(...If that is the case, then I will gratefully accept the offer!)

Great; he said yes. *That's* the Geld I know. A man who works not just for himself, but for all his compatriots.

By the way, only one other person besides Geld refused the offer at first. It felt like some of them had their qualms, but their expectations for the future outclassed their anxiety. It's my fault for not checking things with them beforehand, but momentum was important with this, as far as I was concerned. Seeing everyone agree to it greatly relieved me.

So I turned off the Thought Communication and got back into the party groove.

"You have done a great job for me. As a reward, I shall grant you this."

I signaled to Shuna. She nodded with a smile and handed Geld a set of equipment we prepared in advance. It was an armor-and-shield set, both Legend-class gear picked up from the battle, which I further customized after consulting with Garm. This gear reacted to Geld's own aura, meaning that only he had the right to handle it; it worked along the same lines as Holy Spirit Armor, something that not even Garm could reproduce.

The difference between Legend- and God-class gear lies in the maturity of the gear itself—in other words, the gear's skill capacity. The armor evolves over the years, in a variety of ways, and the number of years required depends on the materials used. Add a talented owner to the equation, and that dramatically increases evolution speed as well. Geld's talents are geared toward defense, so even though this gear is Legend class, I predict that it'd immediately up his defense to the point where it'd rival God class. Plus, as Raphael sees it, there's a high possibility that the armor will receive additional blessings from Geld's evolution. If that happens, a God-class ranking would be a shoo-in, and Geld would have some incredible defense boosts.

So Geld reverently accepted his reward, bowing to me.

Question. Do you wish to use the prescribed amount of one hundred thousand souls to evolve the subject Geld?
    Yes
    No

As I thought *yes*, I called out to Geld again.

"I have been giving you a great deal of hard work all this time. Now is a good opportunity for you to rest and relax, while envisioning what you want for the future."

I planned for Geld to continue playing a big role not only in battle, but in the construction of our city. He's been working incredibly hard this whole time, and he almost never even takes a full day off. He may very well be the hardest worker I know, and I really hope he takes this opportunity to chill out a bit.

"Yes, my lord! I truly appreciate this offer!"

Geld smiled warmly at me. Then he nonchalantly returned to his column, as if fighting off the evolutionary slumber the Harvest Festival would bring to him.

✳

How could he beat away that sleepiness? I have no idea. But as I admired this, I turned to our next contestant: Gabil. He had led the Third Army Corps in a brilliant aerial performance, and as I praised him over it, he looked down at the ground with a meek expression.

"I remain unworthy, my lord. My failures of leadership caused some of my own to be injured... My incompetence truly shames me."

...Well, in *your* case, I think you had it coming, didn't you? Having that bout of magic-resistance training in the middle of a war... I don't think anyone could ever follow your lead on that one. Or I wouldn't want them to. Ultima gave me a detailed briefing after it was all over, and really, I was amazed at how stupid he acted. She even advised me to punish him over it. Since when had he become such an experiment-loving bastard like that?

Still, thanks to that, it seemed Gabil and his team had unraveled the secret to Dragon Body, a unique skill among dragonewts. I figured that absolved him from facing the full wrath of my anger.

But enough about all that. I switched over to Thought Communication; it'd be counterproductive if I yelled at him in front of everyone. Better to keep things private.

(So we'll talk at length about your decision to conduct an experiment in the middle of battle, but Ultima offered me a suggestion. She said she'd teach you more about magicule management.)

(What?!)

(Demons, you know—they say they can control magicules the way you and I breathe air. She said she'll help you learn some of that, so why don't you have her teach you a lesson or two?)

Maybe being punished would just make Gabil happy, or maybe having Ultima beat him into shape would be better for him. But hell, I'm sure even Ultima knows how to go easy on people. I figured that running the gauntlet with her a bit would help him reflect on what he did. That was the rationale behind my decision.

(My lord, we are still in our infancy. I, Gabil, could hardly be more grateful for being given this opportunity to grow even further! I will make every effort to ensure we live up to your expectations so that all of us may master Dragon Body!)

I thought he'd be reluctant, but his response was surprisingly positive. Guess he's ready for it, then.

Looking back, I kinda miss the days back when Gabil got carried away and had his ass whipped by Gobta. His previously birdbrained personality had settled down a lot now; he's capable of reading the atmosphere around him, and that helps him acquire a certain dignity befitting an experienced warlord. He may still have a lot of work to do, as he said, but he always had the qualities he needed, and between bitter defeats and interacting with Vester and his team, he had gained a depth of thought that he simply didn't have before.

By this point, I could really depend on him. All the experience he had accumulated had helped him truly grow—and that's why I could trust him to be worthy of this power.

"I will grant you my power—and with it, you shall awaken as the newly christened Dracolord!"

So I gave Gabil my souls, setting the table for his awakening and evolution. Unlike Geld, the effect was instant and dramatic. His dark-purple scales acquired more of a reddish hue, and a fiery rush of magicules coursed across his body. But Gabil had no trouble at all enduring it, maintaining full consciousness and controlling the newfound force through sheer power of will. This experiment hadn't been in vain at all—it was bearing real fruit for us.

"Rarrrrrrh! The power is teeming within me! Thank you, Sir Rimuru! From here on in, I shall call myself the Dracolord—and I will use my powers for my lord and my nation!"

Violent lightning shot out from Gabil's body, scorching his very flesh. But in an instant, his body healed, rebuilding itself into a stronger form. I guess it worked—and perhaps thanks to me deigning to call him a lord, magnificent horns sprouted from his temples. Pretty brash of him, I thought, but they looked good. It was a truly remarkable evolution, as dignified as it was power bound, and I was happy to accept it.

So Gabil the Dracolord was born.

It was interesting, though, to see how the Harvest Festival's effects varied from person to person. I immediately fell into a deep sleep against my will, and I could tell Geld was fighting off the same fate right now. But Benimaru still had some extra homework to take care of—and in Gabil's case, it ran from start to finish in the course of a few seconds.

"Sir Gabil! I feel myself strengthening as well!"

"Yes!"

"And me, too. My lord, you've done it again!"

Gleeful voices could be heard across the Third Army Corps columns. They were coming from the hundred-strong members of Team Hiryu. It looked like the lizardmen that comprised the Blue

Numbers had received blessings of their own, too. In fact, all three thousand of them had just evolved into dragonewts before my eyes.

Now Team Hiryu had climbed over the wall to a full A rank, gaining enough fighting skill to be rated alongside mid-ranked demons. It was kind of like having Dragon Body permanently activated, and so the ability itself was now decommissioned for them. They had also lost the skill Scalify, which transformed their skin into dragon scale, but in its place was Dragonskin, a new skill.

I'll let Ultima coach them on controlling their powers, but this new skill really interested me. Basically, it takes in ambient magicules to cover the body in a self-repairing armor. It works on the same principle as the Body Armor skill, but with much more defensive ability. It could regenerate a decent amount of injury as well, which obviated the user from needing any armor at all—nice cost savings there.

What's more, the skill varied from person to person, its strength improving with the power of the user. Gabil's Dragonskin skill gave him the protection of a God-class suit of armor, for example, a perfect shield that deflected pretty much anything. They might still have been dragonewts, but their strength was so high, it was no exaggeration to call them a new race entirely. They still looked pretty lizard-y, not human at all... But that was up to their own motivation, so I didn't really care.

There were a few others I shouldn't omit, either.

Interestingly enough, Soka and the four dragonewt guards serving under her were also affected by Gabil's evolution. These dragonewts were already in constant human form, which meant their natural defense wasn't near that of their peers, but they boasted much greater speed and offensive force. They had the Dragon Body skill, but unlike their friends, they still retained a certain human appearance when it was activated. They could manifest dragon scales and wings when they wanted to, but with Dragon Body, they looked more like dragon-y magic-born than anything. They were the same species as Gabil and the others, but it seemed like they were following a completely different evolutionary path—I wouldn't be surprised if the next evolution made them a different species entirely.

In terms of strength, Soka's team was more powerful than Team Hiryu, to the point where you could call them high-level magicborn, and Soka had enough magicule energy to rank up there with an Arch Demon. Just as I expected, they had made a really significant step forward.

∗

Now let's have them go back in line and get the next lucky winners up onstage.

"Ranga! Hakuro! Testarossa! Ultima! Carrera! Come on up!"

Can't have Gobta without Ranga. I couldn't imagine having any close adviser except Hakuro. And the three demonesses I had serving as observers and information officers spoke for themselves.

Upon my command, Ranga crept out from my shadow. Hakuro stepped up as well, a bit zombielike in his shuffling gait. Testarossa was as graceful as ever; Ultima, light and breezy; and Carrera as regal as a queen. All of them ascended the platform and kneeled before me.

Since they were so nicely lined up, I figured I'd give their rewards in order. First, Ranga. He did a hell of a job saving Gobta.

"Ranga, I can see you have mastered fighting in a team with Gobta. I also thank you for offering him your protection."

"Not at all, my master. I only did what anyone would have done!"

Ha-ha-ha. Cute of him. But I know you're happy to have me praise you, so stop wagging your tail all over the place, could you?

"From this day forward, you may call yourself Star Lord!"

"Yes, my master!"

He accepted it with an appreciative howl, and then the soul corridor opened between us. His evolution began immediately, just like mine, and the Harvest Festival was promptly underway.

"Gnnnhh… Master…"

"Sleepy? Don't force it."

There was no reason to hold back. I put Ranga back in my shadow and let him rest inside. If I had to guess, the other demon wolves would receive their blessings as well—I couldn't wait to see how the evolution would turn out. Ranga, to his credit, quietly fell asleep in my shadow, not letting the power overtake him.

That made it four down. As of that moment, I didn't see anything to worry about, but better keep my head up until the end, I supposed.

Next came Hakuro.

"You have performed your role as Gobta's adviser with an expert hand. I thank you for it."

"Oh, don't be silly. Gobta has matured magnificently. He will hardly need my help at all before long."

"No, no, there's a huge difference between you being present or not. Now, for your reward…"

"One moment, Sir Rimuru. If I may, it's already more than enough that you've heeded my daughter Momiji's wishes."

Oh. Right. I did say that, didn't I? But I wasn't going to accept that.

(That's a different matter. I want Benimaru and Momiji to be happy, too, after all. Besides, as her father, I'm sure you have some mixed feelings about Alvis jumping in, don't you?)

I switched to Thought Communication for this, since it let us talk without taking up much time in front of this audience—really useful stuff.

(I did, yes. But I believe in this young man, Sir Benimaru. And I know, when I look at my daughter's eyes, that her feelings are true. Thus, I am satisfied.)

(Good, then. I have no doubt he can make them both happy.)

Whether they can have a child, only God knows, but…

(So…)

(Well, give me a sec here. It's important that I give credit where credit is due, you know? So I asked Kurobe to forge a masterpiece for you. I hope you'll take it and keep all his labor from going to waste.)

That's right—I had a newly forged sword from Kurobe for him. Kurobe had been improving his skill by leaps and bounds; the workmanship on this piece is nothing short of excellent, making it a Legend-equivalent work of art. Benimaru's blade was also at Kurobe's forge for repairs, by the way. In the previous battle, he wasn't able to tap his full potential due to the difference in weapon performance he faced, and when Kurobe heard that, he was both crestfallen and eager to reforge the blade. "*I'm gonna make it the best blade I can*," he told me, and he's still holed up in his workshop with it. This particular sword wasn't quite up to that level, but Kurobe still put a lot of work into it, and I'm sure Hakuro will love it.

(Ahhh, Kurobe did that…? Well, in that case, I will gladly accept it!)

(Great. Feel free to, then!)

Good, good. If he declined it, I wasn't sure what I was going to do. Modesty is a virtue and all that, but really, I think everyone's being a little *too* reserved up here. Let's go on.

"Do not worry, Hakuro. This is something I've had prepared exclusively for you. Please do not hesitate to take it!"

"I, Hakuro, accept this with my full heart. I promise not to let your kindness go to waste, Sir Rimuru!"

And so Hakuro accepted the sword.

Next up were my demoness pals.

At first, I wasn't totally sure what I'd do with them. If adding to their strength was all I thought about, then evolving these three Demon Peers would be my best bet—but as I told Benimaru and Geld, I opted against it for now. I didn't quite have enough souls for everyone, yes, but more than that, I wasn't entirely sure I could control them afterward. I really had no idea how strong they'd get, so I had to put any evolution on hold.

These three were on the same rank as Diablo, so for now I decided to evolve Diablo first and see how he did. I had my concerns about Diablo, too, in a much different way… But well, best not to worry about it. The way I saw it, Diablo was head and shoulders above the rest of his kin regardless; it was funny to see the range of strength present among the Primal Demons.

The three demonesses were under my direct control, entrusted to Diablo, and so I decided to consider their evolution once Diablo's was complete. Of course, I didn't have enough souls in my collection to evolve all three of them right now. They all seemed to have a good balance going with each other, so evolving one over the other would present some problems, no? It'd be dangerous, I guess you could say. If I didn't evolve them all at the same time, it could lead to serious trouble.

That was why I didn't evolve Carrera alone, despite what Geld suggested. Besides, if you looked at magicule counts alone, Carrera was ahead of Diablo on that tally. Giving her more power seemed like too risky of a bet. Uncontrollable power will be the death of her—and of us, maybe. Her nuclear-class Gravity Collapse magic was already too crazy to contemplate—it could even blow people like Geld away if we weren't careful. Maybe she had it fully under control, but the way she just busted that out without a moment's hesitation made me more than a little anxious. Safety first, and so on—I figured we could wait and see how things went before making a decision on their evolutions.

"Testarossa, Ultima, Carrera—all three of you have done a tremendous job as information officers. The souls you have collected are also being put to good use today. Perhaps you may not like how I'm using what you've collected for other people, but..."

I considered not telling them about the potential for evolution at all, but Testa and her pals really did do a good job collecting those souls. It'd be rude to leave them in the dark, I thought—but they vigorously disagreed.

"What are you talking about, Sir Rimuru?! There's no way we could ever be unhappy with you!"

"Right! We're the ones who can't repay you enough."

"Both of them speak the truth, my lord. We are already fully satisfied. We have been granted bodies—and even names, for that matter. That has been more than enough to strengthen us."

All three of them denied any dissatisfaction with my decision. And yes, maybe they *are* too strong already. All three of them are probably still stronger than the freshly awakened Gabil. I had to agree with them—but they still had a reward coming.

"I'm glad to hear that from you. You make me feel like my heart's never far away from your minds, and I appreciate it. That's why I want you to accept the rewards I've prepared for you."

"Rewards?"

"But…"

"Well…can't say no to that, can we?"

Right? It'd be too much trouble for me if they said no, so I wanted to shut the door on that first thing.

"In recognition of your work, I hereby acknowledge you as full members of my leadership. Your duties will be the same as before, but in times of war, you will be granted partial command authority. I will also grant you new titles."

Testarossa was the Killer Lord. Ultima, the Pain Lord. Carrera, the Menace Lord. I thought up those titles after consulting with a few people. They might sound pretty harsh, I guess, but it's exactly what they were up to during this war. As leaders, their role was to focus on combat, so I thought this was a pretty good fit, actually.

"From this day forward, I grant you permission to call yourselves by those titles. And from now on, I expect you to serve as my close confidants, exactly like the old guard!"

""""As you wish!""""

The three of them bowed their heads in unison. I guess they liked their rewards. *Good thing they didn't complain*, I thought as they filed back to their column.

∗

Okay. Let's keep this pace going.

The next people were the groups that performed well for me in the labyrinth. Bovix and Equix were each given a set of new equipment. Gadora was officially promoted to guardian of Floor 60, which meant he was entrusted with the Demon Colossus. Beretta was thus officially retired as head of the Ten Dungeon Marvels, Gadora taking his place.

In addition, I granted Gadora access to the research facilities dotted across the labyrinth. He'd be working on R & D for us going forward, so now felt like a good opportunity to place my full trust in him. He seemed elated at the news, so I guess it was the right reward. If he steals our research data, well, I'll deal with it then, but I don't think I have much to worry about. He's just a friendly old man, hard to dislike, and I hope he'll do his best as one of us going forward.

That all went without a hitch. Next was the main course. Beretta, the now-retired Dungeon Marvel, and the four Dragon Lords in the labyrinth were not technically working under me. Ramiris was their boss, so I left them out of these proceedings for now.

My attention was currently on "Nine-Head" Kumara, guardian of Floor 90; "Insect Kaiser" Zegion, guardian of Floor 80; "Insect Queen" Apito, floor boss of Floor 79; "Immortal King" Adalmann, guardian of Floor 70; and "Death Paladin" Alberto, advance guardian of Floor 70. A real rogues gallery if I ever saw one. I doubt I had to worry about any of them falling out of control by this point, but let's evolve them one by one.

First up, Kumara. I was giving her the title of Chimera Lord.

Maybe it was because she had gained her revenge in this battle, but she had a much better developed sense of presence now. It's funny to think she was my enemy when we first met—you never do know how things will turn out. Clayman might have been controlling her, but she had now defeated Colonel Kanzis, the man behind it all. I was proud of her for that.

I let her in the labyrinth entirely because Ranga told me she was good at cultivating forests. I was advised to let her guard Floor 90, and that's exactly what I did. If it weren't for that, she might still have been that little fox kit, for all I know. I'd always recognized that she was a powerful young monster, but not even I imagined she'd become a Dungeon Marvel in such a short time. But maybe it was destined to happen after I named her, though, huh? I'd have to thank Ranga for suggesting that.

Anyway, Kumara was now the master of eight different magical beasts. They were serving as the bosses of Floors 82 through 89, each a Calamity-level threat. Together they were called the Eight

Legions, and they looked kind of familiar to me, actually. A few days after I gave her the name Kumara, I decided to check on her during a walk, and Kumara asked me to call her friends by their names, revealing to me this group of adorable little monsters. I had experienced countless failures when it came to naming monsters, so I knew the danger I'd be risking—but all Kumara wanted me to do was call the tail beasts the names she had already given them. I figured that was safe enough, so I casually took the job. (I'm sure it's clear, of course, that I didn't say yes just because it was the most darling little girl asking me with her doe eyes and everything. No way.)

And...well, I didn't think it'd turn out like *this*. I'm starting to suspect that I really *did* "name" them, after all. I can tell you that the eight creatures she showed me certainly didn't fight like that.

Affirmative. Strictly speaking, they are not the same, but rather a similar phenomenon to what existed before. The end result was a strengthening of the bonds between the subject Kumara and her tail beasts.

Ah. I knew it.

I didn't notice at the time, because those mystic beasts didn't go into sleep mode or exhibit any other changes, but the moment I saw them in battle, I thought it could've been true. Those cute little critters, now incredibly vicious and powerful Legions. Talk about your crazy before-and-after transformations. Everyone was shocked, and so was I. Kumara, after all, technically got not one, but *nine* names out of me.

Thanks to that, the Eight Legions each built a stronger bond with her. The power that each one gained through absorbing magicules also fed back to Kumara herself, which led to the overall strength we see today. Well, what's done is done, I guess. Kumara might've been defeated in war if all that didn't happen, so if it all works out in the end, I'm happy.

I poured my souls into Kumara, and she wound up completing her awakening in an instant. The Eight Legions lined up behind her glowed as they merged back into her body. Then nine tails sprouted out of her. Her original one was now a golden color, while the others were a shining silver.

They were all quite beautiful, but the upgrade to Kumara's beauty was even more impressive. She was so filled out and enchanting that it was hard to imagine her as an immature young girl any longer. The magnetism was greater than ever before. Her long hair had changed from its previous dark brown to a golden color, like stalks of wheat in the sunlight, and it ran down her back with a silky sheen.

Was it her beauty that evolved, mainly? No—she had more magicules now, of course, already surpassing the awakened Gabil. I definitely wasn't expecting this. Kumara herself could hold her own in combat, for sure, but it was only when she combined with her Eight Legions to go into chimera mode that she reached the apex of her powers.

Conversely, when Kumara becomes stronger, so do her Eight Legions. Since they're all named, they're connected to my soul, and they *also* receive blessings from Kumara's own evolution... And that, as unfair as it may seem, gets fed back into Kumara, powering her up even more. It was like Kumara monopolized all the power I could give. I sensed some calculated scheming on her part, something very unbecoming of her beauty. That must be why she didn't get along with the much more right-minded Apito too much.

Still, there's no way such a rapid evolution couldn't weigh Kumara down hard. She seemed to be struggling to stay conscious. She was a control risk at this rate, and I didn't want her overdoing it. "Go back and rest," I gently ordered her. She looked a little peeved but meekly listened to me.

Chances are she'd go to sleep like Ranga while she got used to her boosted force. Either way, I looked forward to her growth. I mean, she's already a real looker at this point, but you know what I mean. For now, though, it was back to her guardian realm with her.

✳

The event continued. Zegion and Apito were next, and I wanted to tackle the latter first.

"Apito, you fought a superb battle. That Minitz guy looked like one tough dude, even among the other imperial generals. You demonstrated strength equal to his, and that's something to be proud of."

I didn't really mean for Apito to get as strong as that at first. What I *was* looking for was honey, and as long as her hives produced enough high-quality goods, I was happy. But here she was, Insect Queen and part of the Ten Dungeon Marvels. Kind of odd, really.

"Don't be silly. I am not even close to where I want to be. I have lost all my kin, and even then, that was only enough to fight to a draw."

"No, no, that's not—"

I was trying to deny it, but when I saw Apito's smile, I stopped.

"This time, I was unable to seize complete victory. Thus, I do not see myself as worthy of receiving a reward."

"Well, yeah, but—"

"But if I am allowed to make a wish, would you allow the souls of my brethren who died in battle to reside within me once more?"

Hold on, what? She may not want a reward, but *this* wish seems pretty damn reckless to me! She must have the impression that I'm this omnipotent wonder slime, but she's wrong. I just don't see how that could be—

Report. It is possible.

Oh, I *can*?!

Maybe Raphael's the omnipotent one around here.

"All right. In that case, I will instill the spirits of the dead within you."

Apito's brethren were magical insects we hadn't gotten around to giving Resurrection Bracelets to. I'm not sure if they had "spirits," exactly, but it seemed appropriate.

"Thank you kindly. This pleases me greatly."

Apito didn't qualify for an evolution, but I figured she'd have a blessing coming her way via Zegion's. I was planning to ask what she wanted all along, and she seemed happy with this, so I guessed that was the right approach.

Next came Zegion. He was the strongest among the Marvels, so I considered putting him off for now, but I also felt like there wasn't much need for worry. One look at his calm demeanor told me he didn't seem to be in any danger of going berserk. It's just what I would expect from the most powerful member of the labyrinth. Even Raphael acknowledged his unparalleled combat sense, and his magicule count rivaled Benimaru's. No wonder he was good enough to train under Veldora, learning some wacky fighting moves picked up from manga along the way.

It explained his performance in this past battle, too. Zegion single-handedly defeated the strongest members of the imperial army, hardened soldiers the other Marvels struggled with. Taking them all at once like he did, he'd look like an idiot if he lost... But he crushed them with ease, wasting no time beating even the worst among them. He had definitely proven his might, and really, I think he might be stronger than your average demon lord. Even with my "true demon lord" awakening, I fear he could still beat me if I blew it bad.

And I wanted to awaken this guy...? Suddenly I wasn't so sure about this. Diablo and his kin couldn't beat him, either. Too late for that, huh? Maybe I was creating the equivalent of several awakened demon lords here, but there was no point chewing my fingernails over it now.

I had given souls to five people so far, and the evolution ritual was now well underway—in fact, I'd been starting to feel power flow into me, as of a little while ago. My Food Chain skill was feeding the results of the sleeping recipients' Harvest Festival back to me. It was a massive amount of force, but my body was taking it in without any problem. I guess all this promotion was tapping my reserves.

No problem, then. Momentum is important with this kind of thing, so let's keep this ball rolling, I say. Don't fall back now—keep going! And look at it this way—how strong do you think Zegion will turn out? Isn't that *exciting*? It was for me anyway. The thing is, remember, that thanks to Food Chain, even if there's a chance he'd surpass me, I'd always wind up on top in the end.

Hoping that turned out to actually be true, I continued with the ritual, shelving my worries.

"Your strength astounds me. Honestly, I never thought you would attain these heights."

"It is all thanks to your guidance, Sir Rimuru."

No, that was Veldora mentoring you...

...Hang on. Raphael was lurking in the shadows with this, too, huh? Maybe Zegion thought that was me all along. Correcting him would take too long to explain, though, so let's just go with that.

"Enough modesty. It is your unrelenting efforts that brought you this far. I hope you continue to refine your strength for me—and from this day forward, I hereby grant you the title of Mist Lord!"

"Yes, my lord! Nothing could elate me more!"

Zegion was as reticent as ever, but even I could tell how moved and shaken he was by my words. I was just speaking off the cuff, but it must've sounded like the gospel to him. He must be applying more of a "worship" filter than I thought—but being adored like this isn't such a bad thing, is it? And here I thought I was just protecting a rare insect for the future. I guess it's *me* being protected all along.

There was nothing predictable about his growth. His talents were off the charts. He was basking in a dense cloud of magicules leaking out from Veldora, and he had a training environment where he could be revived after death. Add to that the best training partner anyone could have, and you couldn't ask for much more.

But there was no point quibbling over the details behind the process. He was stronger at the end of it, and that's what mattered. So I granted him my souls. He shook for just a moment, but then his will pushed back the flood of power, bringing it fully under his control. Unlike Gabil, it was pure spirit that tamed it. At this rate, I probably looked pretty gutless for falling asleep for so long. You wouldn't think this was something you could conquer through sheer willpower or guts or whatever... But now I was seeing examples of exactly that, so there wasn't much denying it.

So that was Zegion's evolution, but there was something even more terrifying about it. He had literally willed part of his outer shell to transform into the divine metal of crimson steel. Not only was he demonstrating control over the laws of physics—he had made his exoskeleton into a God-class suit of armor. His own body was a weapon, and in melee combat, I pretty much had to call him the strongest out there. For spiritual life-forms like Zegion, combat strength doesn't necessarily equate to one's social status... But there's no doubting how much of a threat he is. Even now, in the middle of his evolution, it looked like he was already acquiring a litany of other powers. I think we better sit down later and see exactly what all he obtained.

Zegion seemed to be doing a pretty good job suppressing the power coursing into him, but there was no doubting that the Harvest Festival was underway. And as I anticipated, only Apito received any secondary blessings from it. Those two were the only ones I gave aid to by providing my own cell matter, so by definition, Apito is Zegion's only blood relative.

There were loads of other dangerous species in the labyrinth's insect floor, of course, but they had been all but wiped out in this battle. We couldn't resurrect any of them, sadly; we'd just have to wait for them to be naturally replenished. This regrettably included Apito's closer family... But the souls of all these bugs had just been given to her. I wondered what she was planning to do with them, but it looked like she wanted to use them to strengthen herself. We'll see the results once her evolution is all said and done.

Apito's expression wasn't pained in the slightest as she played her role in this event. She remained wholly calm and dignified, like the queen she was. Just like Zegion, I really had to hand it to her. I felt a little bit cowed, even, as I ordered them back to their positions.

....

......

...

Once this celebration ended, Zegion and Apito both returned to their respective labyrinth lairs and wove themselves cocoons where they could complete their evolutions.

Between the blessing from Zegion and the souls from her kin and the bugs serving under her, Apito took in an enormous amount of energy. It caused her own body to break apart inside the cocoon, reconstructing itself to become stronger and more battle-ready. She was literally reborn, and through the unique skill Motherly Queen that she acquired, she created a total of nine insect-type magic-born, each with multiple insectoid traits of their own.

Motherly Queen was the ability to take in the internal biology of any insects she consumed and re-create them as magic-born. These were the first bricks, so to speak, of the new insect hierarchy that would grow over time—with Apito reigning as their one true queen. She was one of the Dungeon Marvels, but she was also a servant of Zegion's—and Zegion wasn't shy with the favors and blessings he gave her. That was more than enough explanation for why Apito went through such an astonishing evolution.

And if Apito evolved this much only through a secondary blessing, it was a given that Zegion would change even further. Although his physical strength was already at the apex of its evolutionary abilities, the amount of magicules in his possession now eclipsed the awakened Clayman's. But what really stole the spotlight was a certain skill he obtained through his evolution.

Apito's Motherly Queen was totally a game-breaking skill, something almost sinful in what it accomplished. It was astounding enough, but Zegion's was on another level. He had acquired the ultimate skill Mephisto, Lord of Illusion, and ultimate is exactly what it was—truly befitting of someone apprenticed to Veldora.

With this power, Zegion was now the undisputed king of the labyrinth. Between that and the insect paradise Apito would soon work to build, the Dungeon now had a king and a queen, and the rule over the realm was absolute.

*

With those two underway, only Adalmann and his faithful assistant remained among the labyrinth dwellers.

There's no doubting Adalmann's intense faith in me, as well as the fact that he's a bit—okay, a *lot*—of a freako. Cut from the same cloth as Diablo, I suppose you could say. It's helped me tap into holy magic, though, so it's not all bad, but...

It turned out that Adalmann was good friends with old man Gadora all along; they had engaged in assorted research together back in the day. That's why he was able to craft the extra skill Holy-Evil Inversion, which neatly eliminated the main weak point that he had. I didn't give it a lot of attention at first, but in a way, this was kind of a genius move. It was a little funny to call him smart despite not having, you know, a brain to think with, but that's how monsters roll, I suppose.

Of course, some monsters really *don't* need a brain—their intellectual makeup resides in their astral or spiritual bodies instead. There are even some supernatural creatures who think with their "hearts," so to speak, instead of any brain organ. Think of it as kind of like people who've gained the Complete Memory skill, such as Shion. All that does is re-create memories, of course, but it opens up the potential for thinking purely with one's soul and astral body... And once you achieve that, it pretty much releases you from a physical life span and punches your ticket to spiritual livelihood. Once that happens, pretty much no physical attack can deal fatal damage, and if your physical body's torn apart, you can regenerate it at will. Only certain special attacks, or weapons graded Legend or higher, would be any kind of threat.

Adalmann hadn't quite reached that point. Wight kings like him are spiritual monsters, yes, but he's still bound by the yoke of his physical body. His thought processes are all contained within his spiritual body so there's no such thing as dying of old age for him—but even so, he cannot continue existing with just his soul and astral body. He was *this* close to becoming a spiritual life-form, but he wasn't quite immortal yet—that kind of thing.

The same was true for his cohort, Alberto the Death Paladin, not to mention the death dragon they kept on their floor. They were all conscious enough to cover for those weaknesses of theirs while fighting, as well. Adalmann specializes in long-distance magic salvos; he supports Alberto on the front line while also providing magical support of his own. The death dragon is always airborne, dumping attacks from above, and if Alberto ever gets too damaged or fatigued, it would immediately take his place as the tank. This teamwork had become a proven winner for them.

Sadly, their opponent *this* time was simply too much for them to handle. There's always someone better than you out there, I suppose. If you're enough of a fighting master to wield Legend-class gear—Hinata's Holy Spirit Armor, for one—then you can basically cancel out any attribute-based attack out there, even the "undead" element. Hakuro was capable of that, for example, and I'm sure he'd make masterful use of the Legend-class sword I gave him, greatly boosting his battle abilities.

...So it's great to have someone like that on *our* side, but it was our foe who carried a Legend-class blade this time. And not just any old foe—it was the top elites among the Imperial Guardians, the great force the Empire boasted. Alberto's sword, whether it was a failed experiment from Kurobe or not, was still an excellent, Unique-class piece of work—but it couldn't hold a candle to a Legend. Alberto was only able to hold his own with an inferior weapon because he was the more skillful fighter. His sword shattered on him in the end, sealing their defeat, but it'd simply be wrong to blame him for that loss. If anything, he deserved praise for putting up such a good fight.

"I'm sure you felt the result was disappointing, but all of you fought brilliantly nonetheless. That goes especially for you, Alberto. Your swordsmanship knows no peer."

"It awes me to hear that, my lord."

"You as well, Adalmann. The next thing I knew, you've fully mastered the magic I taught you. I think we could all learn a thing or two from your unflagging diligence."

I may not look it, but I hate lifting a finger when I don't have to. I only dive into subjects that I have a personal interest in. But since he has a reliable, intelligent partner in Raphael overseeing matters instead of me, I'm sure Adalmann's hard work will prove incredibly valuable to us all.

"Oh, no, I couldn't possibly portray my wisdom as anywhere close to yours, Sir Rimuru."

Not *my* wisdom. Raphael's. Not that I'm gonna point that out.

"No need for modesty, Adalmann. Now, I will grant you yet more power. I hope you will take the needed lessons from this defeat and grow even more for me!"

"Your kind generosity for a defeated servant like me only drives me to strive ever harder! I will work myself to the bone for you, Sir Rimuru!"

He was tearfully choking out the words. I wish he wouldn't phrase it *that* way.

However, Adalmann was also the other awardee here today who turned down my offer at evolution when I mentioned it to him.

"My lord, unlike everyone else here, I am a defeated man, something I cannot forgive myself for. Someone as incompetent as me, potentially reaching the same level of awakening as you... Perhaps, when I am given another opportunity and achieve greater successes than now, I will be better able to accept this lofty honor!"

That's how he put it, but I managed to coax and push him into it anyway.

I mean, honestly, I didn't expect much of anything from him in the first place. Back when Shinji's party stormed their way up to Floor 60, I all but expected the Adalmann trio to go down hard. But now they've far surpassed my expectations. They were just a poor match for Krishna, their opponent this time around; that was all there was to it.

So partly as encouragement to keep him from working himself "to the bone" and so on, I tapped some of my soul supply for Adalmann. It wasn't what we had planned for at all, but the labyrinth was going to remain our final stronghold for a while to come. It's important to shore up its defenses, and Adalmann's evolution was an important part of that.

The labyrinth contained all our vital R & D facilities, and we could even quarantine the entire capital inside it during emergencies. I never even imagined what a boon it'd be when I invited

Ramiris to stay with us. I saw her labyrinth as a personal sandbox, but now it was our most formidable fortress. That was all thanks to Ramiris—and Veldora as well. I made a mental note to express my gratitude to them later on as I addressed Adalmann.

"I know you feel that your performance was below your standards, but you have my utmost esteem nonetheless. I hope you'll prove that I was right with your future efforts!"

"Yes, my lord! I promise I will live up to your lofty expectations!"

So Adalmann's evolution began. He proved to be no exception—an irresistible drowsiness soon descended upon him. I didn't want him suffering thanks to me, so let's keep this evolution ritual going.

"I'll take your word on that, indeed. From this day forward, you may call yourself the Gehenna Lord. May you keep striving to live up to that title!"

"Absolutely, my lord…"

Whew. It's hard to sound all dignified like that for extended periods of time. And I should add, it's hard to come up with titles like this. I was up all night pondering over them. I mean, I don't need to sleep, so I was more bored than anything, but…

…Anyway, I decided to give Adalmann the title of lord, which was quickly beginning to signify the top rank within my hierarchy. We might see more lords in the future, but for now, Adalmann was one of only twelve to be awarded that rank. It made him one of the most powerful military figures in the world, and I'm sure it'd give Adalmann more of a voice in Tempest affairs…assuming I ever gave him the chance to speak up.

Now, Adalmann was hardly the only top performer here. Alberto was still kneeling by Adalmann, who was now visibly fighting his desire to sleep. Behind him, the death dragon was hunched over, trying to make its huge frame as small as possible. They'd both received blessings from their boss's evolution, so casual conversation probably wasn't their first priority.

So I decided to grant Alberto some new battle gear to replace his broken sword. He already had overwhelming sword skills, so with the right weapon in hand, that'd easily be doubled. And while I was at it, I thought, why not give him some of Kurobe's best work to date?

...But then I reconsidered. Among the spoils of war we seized from the enemy were a small cache of Legend-class gear. Caligulio, their enemy's top general, even had some God-class items—extremely rare in the best of situations. It'd be a waste to just hang that stuff up in a museum somewhere. I tried palming it off on Kurobe, but he said he didn't need it, claiming that "I can create my *own* God-class gear by now, sir!" And he was right. Benimaru's own blade was about to be reforged by Kurobe's hands to God-class tier. That much I was assured of, so I decided not to foist this gear on him, after all.

So who's the right recipient here? As Caligulio made clear enough, merely being awakened didn't make you truly worthy of God-class gear. Once you reached that level, the equipment chose the owner, not the other way around—I didn't need a fancy analysis to see that. Something gets called God class, I feel, when after many years, the magisteel inside it evolves into crimson steel and assumes a sort of spiritual existence as a tool—a concept called *tsukumogami* in Japanese. This means the owner has to be worthy of the item in order to wield it, I imagine, and that's just not gonna happen within a human being's life span.

Here, meanwhile, we had a noble soul that had become undead, exposed to endless hardship, and still never lost his skills as an acolyte. Now Alberto was a Death Paladin, and for him the concept of a life span was meaningless. He had been applying himself, studying hard and acquiring sword skills that rivaled Hakuro's. Maybe he'd be the right person for this weapon? I thought so anyway.

Besides, everyone else in my entourage already had their preferred weapons on hand. Some of them even refused to carry anything not made in Kurobe's forge, such was the trust they had in him. Diablo and the three demonesses, meanwhile, could use the skill Create Material to manifest whatever gear they wanted. The results performed in proportion with the skill of the owner, and for the demons, they could easily surpass Legend-level protection. They had zero need to carry any preexisting armor around.

Some people, like Shion, liked pouring magic power into their weapon all the time, out of sheer love. Maybe that's why the long-sword Shion preferred had now evolved into Goriki-maru Version 2, with Legend-class murdering capability, without me even really noticing. Her sword *did* break, didn't it? I'm pretty sure I saw it get cut in half in the battle against Razel, but now it was good as new. Just like Shion herself, the blade had risen from the ashes like a phoenix.

It was more exasperating than surprising, if you ask me. That—and scary. And they say Shion puts a lot of love into her cooking, too, but if so, what the hell does *her* "love" consist of, exactly?! Whatever it was, it could resurrect a shattered sword. Did I really want to consume a meal chock-full of that stuff?

This was turning into a dangerous train of thought. Time to get back to business. Now that I knew owner compatibility was a big issue with battle gear, I decided that I didn't need to give my top brass anything new for the time being. That was a good enough reason in itself, but Raphael was the one who convinced me in the end, assuring me that Alberto was the best person to receive this God-class blade. I nodded, not questioning its judgment one bit, and decided to go ahead with it.

So Alberto would be rewarded with a complete set of God-class gear—a full suit of armor, with a longsword and kite shield thrown in.

"Alberto, your swordsmanship is among the best in the world. In recognition of this, I grant you this battle gear. Please maintain your world-class skill as you continue to shine in the service of Adalmann!"

"Yes, my lord!"

At my cue, Shuna stepped up pushing a wagon with all the gear piled on it. Alberto watched her hand it over to him, visibly shaking with anxiety.

"This... This is..."

He must have noticed the caliber of this stuff at first glance. The astonishment was clear in his quivering voice. I can't blame him—there are only a few known examples of this sort of stuff in existence, making them quite literally the gifts of the gods. Being able to handle gear like this is among the highest honors a knight could receive in this world.

"Do you think you can use this gear?"

I'm not about to take no for an answer. Sensing the pressure from my gaze, Alberto drummed up his fortitude.

"Of course, Sir Rimuru! And I swear I will live up to your dreams...!"

His voice echoed through the coliseum, and I was glad he was so over the moon over it.

The moment he touched the God-class armor, it naturally wrapped itself all around his body. It had no problem accepting him as its new master, apparently. But I did make one miscalculation. Once it gained this true master, the armor's capabilities wildly exceeded anything that I was expecting.

As long as Alberto wielded this gear, he essentially functioned as an incarnated spiritual life-form. That was the true power of God-class equipment—its ability to temporarily upgrade a being with physical form into one with spiritual form instead. And a spiritual life-form is, in so many words, a godlike existence, like Veldora and, well, me, I guess. It doesn't really *feel* that way, but I'm definitely quite close to immortality. I know I won't age anyway, and it seemed pretty likely that I'd never die—not unless I lost my magicules or experienced a core break in my heart.

In other words, spiritual life-forms experienced no natural death, were immune to all kinds of status ailments, and could overcome death itself through sheer power of will. That ability to raise people to the same level as such wondrous supernatural beings was enough to convince anyone that God-class gear was truly extraordinary.

At the same time, I could understand why Raphael recommended Alberto. Benimaru will be evolving into a spiritual life-form on his own, and Ranga and Shion are kind of following in his footsteps, so I'm sure it'll happen to them, too. I didn't think Gabil and Geld were quite there yet, and giving them God-class gear wouldn't change that. Alberto truly was the right man for this stuff, in the right place at the right time—and that was that.

*　　*　　*

And I can't forget about Adalmann's pet dragon, either. His death dragon put in a killer effort, too, so I definitely wanted to award it somehow. I pondered over what to give, but it wasn't long before I had the perfect answer—a name. No better way to make a monster overjoyed than naming it, right? This would come with some danger normally, but I have Raphael with me. I'm sure he'll keep me safe and regulate the magicule flow and all that.

Proposal. In this case, there is already a bond between the subject Adalmann and the death dragon. Rather than creating a soul corridor here, I recommend consuming souls for the purpose of naming it.

Hmm?

That's an unexpected suggestion from Raphael, but if I opt for that, how many souls are we talking about?

Understood. Five thousand. Proceed?
　　Yes
　　No

If it's around five thousand, that does sound like a much safer approach. Raphael had apparently analyzed my souls on hand and figured out a way to convert them into magicules via Belzebuth, Lord of Gluttony. It was guaranteed not to be dangerous at all, I was told, so how about we go with that?

I stood in front of the death dragon, patting its head. It appeared to be pretty nervous about this. Scary-looking, for sure, but still awfully cute.

"I have a reward for you, too, okay? From this day forward, your name is Venti, Dragon Lord of the Underworld!"

The souls were consumed, and the naming was completed. After that, several dramatic changes took place. The gigantic body of the death dragon, well over twenty yards long, began to shrink, and shrink, and shrink, until what I saw before me was a beautiful woman wearing a dark robe.

Uh, who's this? I thought for a moment. But I didn't let it faze me. With monsters, anything goes, really. That's something I've experienced more than I care to admit, and what I've learned as a result is that panic will get me nowhere. I did my best not to show my agitation, maintaining an "of *course* this would happen" attitude as best I could. I think I did a good job, too.

"Ah, my most beloved of beautiful gods! I am awed at the blessings you have bestowed upon my lowly body!"

Oh, sure, yeah. Of *course* you could talk just fine. Also, I just gave you a name, okay? Any blessings you received came from Adalmann, not me. I think we're seeing a mix of effects here, but let's keep that straight, all right?

"Ohhh, how wonderful for you, Death—er, Venti!"

"Yes, Master. Our god has not forsaken me after all!"

"Indeed. Our faith has been duly rewarded."

"It has!"

What a beautiful master-servant relationship. I felt like I was being left in the dust, but hey, good for them.

And so Adalmann and his servants had all received their gifts.

Consuming souls to name monsters is actually pretty darn convenient, isn't it? If you go around naming Dragon Lord–class creatures, there's really no telling how many magicules that'll consume. Even with Raphael overseeing things, I don't have infinite magicules, you know.

Belzebuth had helped me gradually stockpile more and more magicules, but I used nearly the whole supply naming Testarossa and the other demons. I could have tapped Veldora for some assistance, but I don't think he'd like doing that too much, and getting him to change his mood about something requires monumental effort. That's best kept as a last resort, I thought.

I also didn't want myself inadvertently going into sleep mode after an impromptu naming binge. I was running on a much higher

baseline of magicules now, and I had no idea how long I'd need to recover from being tapped out. We *were* still at war here, and this was one dangerous gamble I absolutely had to step away from. With this approach, though, I was home free.

Now, on this topic, I had given a lot of thought about how to reward Ramiris. But how about leveraging this new discovery a little? In other words, I figured she'd be tickled pink if I named the four Dragon Lords for her. They had no real connection to me, but with this soul-based approach, it'd still work just fine. I really gotta hand it to Raphael for pitching the idea to me—and besides, even after all this evolution, I estimated that I'd still have over twenty thousand souls left over.

It's thanks to Ramiris that I was able to retain so many in the first place. In fact, she didn't want any from me at all—"Just take 'em! I ain't got no use for 'em!" I felt kind of bad about that, so I thought this would be a nice, elegant way of paying it forward. Hope she's up for the idea. I'll remember to ask her about it later.

$$*$$

That ended the proceedings for the labyrinth gang. Now this celebration was at its climax—and only two problem children remained. Who, you ask? Well, who else but the toughest nuts of all—Shion and Diablo.

Based on what I had seen so far today, I was convinced nobody was going to go out of control on me. But we can't let our guards down. This is Shion and Diablo, after all, the worst of the worst. If both went on a rampage at the same time, I couldn't even imagine the extent of the damage—and with our top defenders all busy evolving right now, too.

Anyway, let's begin with Shion.

"Shion, I hereby grant you the title of War Lord. Please continue to maintain as much calm decorum as you can, please."

"Of course! You'll never find a woman as calm and mature as me!"

Um, who're you talking about again? Because it sounds like you're talking about yourself there, or something? Now that's what I call high self-esteem! I *have* been impressed with her self-control as of late, but Shion's still got a lot to learn on that front. Best to take a long-term view.

"I'll not comment on that, but make sure you keep consulting with your comrades, protect our nation and all who dwell in it, and prevent yourself from going out of control for me."

With that, I granted Shion her souls.

But... Huh? There was an almost shocking lack of change. Shion looked at me, acting slightly put off. We had a staring contest for a while, but still no sign of transformation. Was that a dud, or what? Boy, is this awkward. Now it's like I haven't given her anything, huh? I suddenly had a crisis on my hands. I haven't prepared anything else for her!

As I was panicking over what to do, something truly unexpected happened. Nothing had changed with Shion, but the members of Team Reborn under her fell to the ground one by one, fast asleep. Then I noticed that a few members of her fan club who styled themselves as her elite guard were rapidly dozing off themselves. It varied from person to person, but it looked like all of them had received blessings from her. Shion seemed completely unaffected. What a strange phenomenon. No point thinking about it too much, though. They're under her direct control, so I guess that's the kind of thing that'll happen. Best to leave that to her.

"Right. Well, Shion, let me know if you sense any abnormalities in your own body."

"Absolutely! By the way, Sir Rimuru, do you have any special rewards prepared like the one you devised for Gobta?"

Shion fidgeted a bit as she asked. Hmm... I had to empathize with her. I'd conducted her ritual like all the others, but to the audience, it must look like I gave her a fancy new title and nothing else. Some people would be glad enough for that... But with Shion, it's not like she needed new weapons or whatever, so...

Something like what I gave Gobta, huh?

"Very well. In that case, I'm going to teach you how to make a very special dish!"

"What?! Are you admitting, then, that I am a better cook than Shuna—?"

"Absolutely *not!*"

How could she ever jump to *that* conclusion? Shuna, listening on next to her, just rolled her eyes in contempt, although my immediate denial quickly restored her sunny disposition. Shion looked less than pleased with me, but when I whispered into her ear that I'd have an expansion installed in the kitchen, she gave me a happy nod and went back to her column.

Team Reborn, meanwhile, was evolving in very interesting ways. They seemed to be turning into spiritual life-forms, in a sense— but with physical bodies, unlike demons by default. Rather close to demons but still primarily physical in nature—and most importantly, they could still breed and produce offspring. It looked like we had a totally new species on our hands. Death-oni, I guess you could say? Shion's oni foundation seemed to be emerging more strongly on them than before, with some of them acquiring her body-enhancing extra skill Divine Force. No one was sprouting any horns, though.

Their magicule counts weren't on the level of Team Hiryu, but given their immortality, it was hard to judge which group was stronger, really. You could've said they evolved from hobgoblins, and anyone would've believed you. The biological processes of these monsters truly baffled me.

And so, despite Shion herself having surprisingly little to show for it, her evolution ritual came to a close.

*

And now we were at the bottom of the list. Diablo. My biggest headache.

He had been visibly fidgeting for a while now, looking at me with this expectant smile. Honestly, he'd probably cause more damage if I stopped the event now than if he went into an evolutionary frenzy. If anyone got in his way here, they were as good as dead.

Well, let's do it.

"Diablo."

"Yes, Sir Rimuru!"

I had nothing but bad feelings about this.

There's little doubting that this evolution will make him the most powerful figure in this nation of monsters I've constructed. I don't mean the strongest of my group—I mean stronger than *me*, no doubt. He *claims* he can't beat Zegion, but I'm sure he was giving himself a handicap somewhere. He overpowered Jiwu and Bernie, both formidable foes, at the same time by himself. Zegion's strength *was* a surprise to me, but Diablo seemed like he was one step ahead.

In other words, he was already my strongest underling. In fact, if Diablo really put his mind to it, he might even outgun *me* in his current state. If you compared him to me back just after I awakened, it wasn't even close. So how was he going to evolve now? I needed to be extremely cautious.

"Diablo, I can think of no title more appropriate for you than Daemon Lord. May you continue to serve as my right-hand man and unite all the demons under our banner!"

Especially *those* three demonesses.

"Keh-heh-heh-heh-heh... I remain as ever at your service, Sir Rimuru!"

Seriously, Diablo. Please. I nodded and performed the ritual.

And so a new fiend was born...

The evolution was over in an instant, it seemed. I suspected another Shion-type dud at first, but I was wrong. He was just exhibiting perfect control over all energy flows and not letting any changes show at all.

Nice one, Diablo. What a masterpiece. Now he had evolved into one of the strongest beings in the entire world. A bit of it was flowing into me through our newly created soul corridor, and *man*, what a fright. I now had a vague idea of the upper limits of his power—and given how Benimaru's and Shion's evolutions were apparently disappointments, Diablo truly had become my most powerful underling. In fact…well, his magicule count was up there with mine, and considering the skills he'd built up, I feared this was no longer someone I could defeat in battle.

Guess that bad feeling I had was pretty accurate. I expected something like this, though, so I wasn't wrought out over it.

"Impressive evolution there, Diablo."

"The compliment is most appreciated, Sir Rimuru."

So we're good? His personality was still the same. If he decided to overthrow me right now, it *would* be pretty funny… And don't tell anyone, but I *would* try fighting to keep my position.

But despite the evolution completing itself, Diablo looked like he was trying to acquire some new ability.

"What're you doing?"

"Ah, well, you see, during the previous battle, I realized the usefulness of ultimate skills, you could say. I was ignoring them before since Guy was bragging up and down to me about them, but now I think I may as well gain one if it's available to me."

"Oh, huh…"

What kind of idiot is this? It's funny how stupid smart people like him can be sometimes. Feels like I'm surrounded by a lot of those types, actually.

"So yes, I thought I'd take this opportunity to learn one so I can brag about it the next time I see him, keh-heh-heh-heh-heh…"

"Uh-huh…"

He hates it when Guy brags to him, but it's okay for him to brag back?

Well, given his attitude up to now, I could easily imagine how much of an ego he copped with everyone besides me. I didn't need Raphael to spell *that* out. But this would be aimed at Guy, not me, so I had nothing to worry about. As long as it wouldn't come back to haunt me, there was no use fretting over the little things.

So it looked like Diablo's demeanor remained as rock-solid as always, and at this rate, I didn't think I needed to worry about a sudden mutiny anytime soon. He had full control over his evolution, even, so there was no reason for me to treat him as anything but the faithful, capable staffer I saw him as before.

*　　*　　*

Incidentally, as I found out later, Diablo's blessings were passed on to his second-in-command, Venom, along with the hundred demons under Venom's direct command. However—and this is just a hunch on my part—I think Diablo found a way to siphon as much energy away from those blessings as possible. I wasn't sure if such a thing was possible, but if Diablo could do it, I wouldn't be surprised in the least. Strength, after all, is earned, not given—I'm sure that's Diablo's line of thought.

Regardless, Venom was showing some real growth. He had undergone an evolution of his own, becoming a full Demon Peer. He still wasn't nearly on the level of Testarossa and friends, though, and even compared to Moss and Veyron, I wouldn't call him all that intimidating. There was no way that someone who had reigned as the strongest for so many years could be defeated by an upstart out of nowhere. Even among Demon Peers, there was a clear ranking in place.

"Well, of course," Venom told me. "I'm still a newcomer, you know; I haven't even been living for a century. I hardly even deserve to be compared to them."

I suppose Venom is something of an uncommon case—a Contemporary-era demon with little experience to his name. Given the unique skill he was born with, however, maybe he was a reincarnate with some crazy story behind his history. He had no memory of his past life, he told me, but would sometimes recall words despite not knowing their meanings. Visiting my nation frequently gave him bouts of déjà vu, apparently. If he *was* a reincarnate, that certainly would make him something special.

But Venom still knew his place in the world. He had evolved to the same level as Testarossa and her friends, but he wasn't letting it get to his head, and he didn't look down on his other colleagues. He knew how much he had evolved, and he had picked up on the gap between himself and the next level. For a demon, experience is far more important than magicule counts.

That was real mature of him, I thought. But he also let me in on a little inside scoop.

"To tell the truth, I did actually challenge Lord Diablo once before—and let me tell you, he made *disgustingly* clear the difference between us!"

He was all smiles as he recalled it, but *man*. Bad move there, dude. I'd expect nothing less from Diablo's closest associate, though. Guess there's a reason why he likes the guy.

Despite the sheer stupidity of that challenge, it sounds like it turned out to be a good thing. Venom learned from the experience, and he never made the same mistake twice. If he ever *did* get carried away again, I'm sure Diablo would rub him out anyway. He had no mercy for people too big for their britches, no matter how close they were to him.

Learning from your mistakes is a valuable skill to have. I look forward to seeing how Venom develops.

As for the rest of the blessing receivers—well, to tell the truth, they were still having their bodies formed in our incubation capsules. All one hundred of them were now reborn as Diable Chevaliers. They couldn't quite match up with Arch Demons, but they were now demonic knights, up there with any other high-level magic-born and capable of killing a Great Demon in one hit.

They were way off the charts, really... But Diablo didn't really care about them at all. So they remained Venom's servants. Diablo preferred to keep himself free and mobile, retaining his position directly under me, and that convinced me most of all that he hadn't changed. No matter how much he evolved and surpassed me, Diablo was still Diablo.

So all my top staff had completed their evolution rituals. I'm glad it went over without any major hiccups.

But the victory celebration wasn't done yet. I continued to call out to people who distinguished themselves in battle, thanking them for their hard work. Then we moved right on from there to a celebratory feast, although one attended only by those still awake. We'd have to wait until next time to assemble the entire gang, but until then, we enjoyed today's party well enough.

I was disappointed, however, to find that Jaine and the Twin Wings weren't joining us. They were quite apologetic but said they had urgent matters to attend to, so they took off in a hurry after the coliseum event ended. Hopefully they'll be able to chill more with us next time they visit.

Right now, however, I'm more concerned about a couple of people getting belligerent under the influence.

"...Sir Benimaru was out of my league anyway. I knew that all along!!"

"No, no, Lady Gobwa, you're quite attractive; trust me on that. But look at *me*! Lady Alvis, the girl of my dreams, takes my hand... and then she freakin' *kills* me! That's beastmen for ya, y'know? They like 'em strong. They want a mate who's at least as powerful as they are... And if you're strong enough, you can have as many women as you want. But *me*, ohhh noooo..."

"Goodness, Sir Phobio, you're more than strong enough. If *I* were stronger, I could've stepped in between those two ladies, but—"

"Hey, you can drop the 'sir' stuff with me. You're plenty strong yourself, Lady Gobwa. You just had some real stiff competition, is all. Not even I could beat them, y'know? It is what it is."

"Sir Phobio...er, Phobio. Please, call me Gobwa, then."

"Sure thing, Gobwa."

"Phobio..."

Whoa, can you *not* do this in public, please? I'm mature enough to not cause a scene over this, but this isn't some private candlelit restaurant, all right?!

Then again, though, two jilted lovers starting to kindle something with each other isn't such a bad thing, is it? Love works in mysterious ways, and so forth. I'll let it slide...

And the night passed along happily, the party in full swing.

So our nation had a set of new lords governing it.

Regulations forbade them from calling themselves demon lords, but we now had nine among us who were practically equivalent to awakened demon lords. Add our three Primal Demons to this, and barring some really exceptional events, I think we were capable of dealing with anything that came our way.

Since these twelve people now had lord epithets, I decided to refer to them collectively as the Twelve Lordly Guardians. Some of them were also part of groups like the Big Four and the Ten Dungeon Marvels, but the *lord* term in their titles took precedence. That's because, unlike those two other groups, I had no plans to replace these twelve anytime soon. Being a lord, in my realm, is a sort of lifelong appointment, since all of them had eternal life in the first place. In the future, I think it'd be ideal if they eventually stepped away from day-to-day duties and only took up their Lordly roles during wars or emergencies.

We had a lot of other great staff on hand, like Rigurd and Rigur and Gobta and Mjöllmile, but *they* were all mortal. We needed to strike a clear difference between how we handled permanent posts and jobs that would go through generational changes. It didn't need to be addressed right this minute, but the time would come soon enough.

The one person on my mind is Gobta. He's a top leader (despite it all), he's surprisingly resourceful, and he's more than reasonably strong in a fight. That transformation team-up with Ranga was a real game changer for him. There was no doubting Ranga's evolution would power him up a lot, but I was sure Gobta could still keep up with him, too.

He really is unique. Despite being named and evolved, his outward appearance didn't change at all. He blathered on about how he "evolved in terms of talent and stuff," but now I'm thinking that might've been the truth. And now, with today's reward, Gobta's position in Tempest has been set in stone. He had been granted a position closer to me than many other top officeholders, and that wasn't lost on everyone looking Gobta's way.

In a surprising way, maybe *that* was the biggest reward I gave out today. It struck me as pretty funny as I watched all my friends enjoy the party.

And one more thing:

Word of what happened today must've spread fast around the world, because somewhere along the line, I had been given the nickname Rimuru the Chaos Creator. This was fine. I decided to go with it. I was fully aware of all the crap I'd been pulling, after all.

The celebration that Jaine attended was a truly astonishing event to witness. One after the other, the demon lord Rimuru was evolving all of his closest staff…into de facto true demon lords.

This… This is impossible! I must be dreaming, aren't I?!

She was too shocked to even speak. She was well aware of how much trouble the demon lord Rimuru could be, but *this* scene was so ridiculous, so beyond reality, that it surpassed the worst of her premonitions.

Jaine's objective in coming here was to ask Rimuru how he intended to handle the Primals. She trusted Rimuru personally, but it took more than personal trust to quell her fears about something as menacing as the Primals. Once they were unleashed, after all, they could easily destroy the entire balance of power worldwide. That much, in fact, was just proven by this war. Nine hundred and forty thousand of the Empire's best were helplessly annihilated. It was quite a stroke of good fortune that Rimuru was allies with them, but there was no guarantee that they'd be able to maintain that relationship forever.

So Jaine came here as an ambassador to scout things out and see how Rimuru was doing. When she greeted him, she found him acting perfectly natural, unchanged from when last they met. So she lodged her complaint with him in somewhat harsh terms, hoping to gauge his thoughts based on his reaction. The results, sadly, were disappointing. He just said "I'm sorry," acting all remorseful as Jaine admonished him. And once the whole story was revealed to her, through Rimuru's assorted excuses and explanations, she realized that Diablo had engineered this demon deluge all by himself.

"So you're certain that Diablo is Noir, the Original Black?"

"Mmm, looks that way, yeah. I didn't know either at first, but for whatever reason, he's been really friendly with me…"

He trailed off, shrugging. It didn't seem to be a lie—apparently he truly *did* become the overlord of a small army of demons without really realizing it. Jaine had enough life experience to know he wasn't pulling an act—and she knew that further griping wouldn't make Rimuru any more capable of doing anything about it. It wasn't even his fault, really. She worried that all this new power would make him more arrogant, but—much to her relief—that turned out to be a nonissue.

But maybe she shouldn't have been so relieved. Maybe she should have warned him more harshly, when she had the chance.

Even if the Primals were a force majeure, as he put it, mass-producing true demon lords like that? The work of true malice—and nothing less!

…No. She was sure Rimuru meant no malice at all. She understood that. This was probably Rimuru hoping he could handle whatever came by himself, instead of causing further trouble for Jaine and her kingdom. Normally she would consider this a hostile act of intimidation, but she was also sure he didn't mean to have it seen that way.

In fact, after the whole Primal thing, maybe he decided there'd be no more keeping secrets from the dwarves. This was just an act of open disclosure, based on sincerity and trust—and if so, Jaine was undeniably partly to blame, too. Maybe if she had instilled some common sense into Rimuru before now, it wouldn't have come to this. Maybe that could've been possible, maybe not—but either way, it was too late now.

The—the whole balance of warpower in the world…

Jaine felt about ready to have a stroke, but she fought through it, musing over what might come next.

The event continued without a hitch, Rimuru's agents gaining new powers one by one—and with them, the armies of monsters who served under them as well. In just a few short hours, Tempest had just massively expanded its capacity for waging war; there was no doubting that fact. Nestled within the Forest of Jura now was a gigantic military state, a threat that the Eastern Empire couldn't even compare against.

Realizing this, Jaine once again rued the fact that she didn't take action earlier. But...

No, it wouldn't have mattered. The last time we deliberated over this issue, our conclusion was "nothing we can do; no point thinking about it." King Gazel put any further debate on hold, but I don't think we'll find some magical solution anytime in the near future. And if not...

Their war with the Empire was far from over. The enemy's armies were still deployed, but Rimuru said he was colluding with them, and soon they'd conspire to storm the imperial capital. Jaine traveled here in the first place because they were supposed to discuss all this at a meeting. But now...

I've never been so confused in my life. This is no longer just about the Empire. I've got to tell King Gazel about the new true demon lords Rimuru has created...

For a moment, Jaine considered pretending that she didn't notice anything. It was little more than trying to escape reality, but it didn't seem like such a bad idea, either. But she had just confronted Gazel a bit ago over keeping quiet about the Primals. She had no right to remain silent about this.

"Dolph, I'm leaving now."

"Oh? Why is that? We have a meeting scheduled for tomorrow, I believe."

"You could save face by attending for me. I'll return via magic. No need for a bodyguard or escort."

"Um, very well..."

Dolph, unable to pick up on flows of magic, had no real idea what was occurring before him. Jaine, jealous of him for that, sighed and fell into a funk as she considered the future.

Despite their unshaken facial expressions, the Twin Wings—Lucia the blonde, Claire the silver-haired—were both intensely distressed.

Here in Tempest, the monster nation, lived a great number of powerful magic-born. They knew that, and they even grew acquainted with a few of them, Geld in particular. They saw them as a threat at first, but now they were united in an alliance. They no longer needed to be so cautious now, no matter how many of their high-level magic-born matched them in skill.

Until now, that is.

They were here on orders to ascertain Tempest's current strength. Now that they were engaged in full-frontal war with the Nasca Namrium Ulmeria United Eastern Empire, the mightiest of human-led nations, Rimuru's army was bound to suffer some casualties. If so, it'd doubtlessly interfere with the construction of the sky city that Frey was so looking forward to. So they were asked to survey the damage and formulate predictions for Tempest's future, organizing reinforcements if need be. That need, it seemed, was wholly nonexistent.

"*Zero* damage, then?"

"It's hard to believe... But judging by how cheerful everyone is, it must be the truth."

It was the most unexpected of reports.

Gladdened to hear that, they decided to attend the victory celebration they were informed of. They didn't expect, however, to bear witness to events that would make their eyes pop out of their skulls.

(This is unthinkable. We take our eyes off him for a moment, and now part of his head staff is as powerful as Lady Frey...?)

(No, look over there. The demon lord Rimuru is about to say something.)

Claire snapped Lucia out of her panicked state just in time for the start of a "ritual" that was as unimaginable as it was appalling. Beyond appalling, even. It was so detached from reality that their minds went completely blank. Clearly, this was no longer a situation only the two of them could debate over.

(We must report back to Lady Frey immediately.)

(Yes, you're right. Let us return home at once.)

With a brief telepathic conversation, they quickly came to a decision. Then they flew back home, immediately telling Frey what had happened.

………

……

…

In a corner of the unfinished keep at the top level of their temporary castle, Frey let out a long, deep sigh.

"What could that slime *possibly* be thinking?"

"What's the matter with you?" replied a man in the room. "You look beautiful when you're all melancholy like that, but I don't think sighing suits you very much."

This was Carillon, and now that both he and Frey were serving as Milim's assistants, they had come to grow deeply acquainted.

"That's the last thing I need to hear right now."

"But really, what happened? Is he struggling against the imperials?"

Carillon looked concerned. Frey just seemed depressed.

"Would that it were the case. Then I'd just obediently send off reinforcements, not a care in the world."

"So what is it? Don't tell me that bum Rimuru pulled off another bout of crazy nonsense."

"…Precisely," Frey declared after a few silent moments. Carillon remained quiet.

"…May I make a suggestion, Carillon?"

"Yeah?"

"It's probably inadvisable to call Milim's best friend a bum."

"Kind of late for *that*, isn't it? *You're* the one who just called him 'that slime.'"

"Are you even listening to me? No need to be so nasty. Don't worry; I don't talk that way to my own staff."

"That's fine, but let's not go off on this tangent forever, shall we? Tell me what's going on."

Frey let out another dejected sigh, her fragrant breath tickling

Carillon's nostrils. It made him feel a little better, but he kept his eyes on Frey, not letting himself be distracted.

"All right. You won't regret asking, will you?"

"Depends on what it is."

"Look..."

"I won't regret it, okay? So quit shouldering it all by yourself. Give me some of it to handle."

"Right. Good. I like that part of you."

Frey smiled, feeling her blues clear up a bit. Then she told Carillon part of the story she heard from her Twin Wings.

"Seriously?"

"I'm always serious. Those two girls would never lie to me."

"So...what, Rimuru now has *seven* more demon lord–class people serving him?!"

"That's right."

"And they're all stronger than me?"

"I couldn't tell you... But those three ladies felt stronger than *me*, at least."

Even before their evolution, their powers put them on equal footing with Frey, according to what she knew. But after Rimuru did... *something* to them, the Twin Wings felt an overwhelming strength boost from them all. Some of them were still in the midst of evolving, according to the report, but their full powers were expected to take hold before long. Frey had to accept that report at face value, but that didn't mean she was fully convinced.

Carillon, after hearing it all, was stunned into silence. "...You're kidding me, right?" he eventually asked.

"Do I look like the sort of person to lie about this?"

"No."

"Well, there you go, then."

Neither Carillon nor Frey had ever exercised the full extent of their strength in front of their own people. But the Twin Wings had served Frey closely for years, and they had at least an idea of their master's true strength. Even if it were mere estimates they were reporting to Frey, this was intelligence ignored at her peril. What's more, nobody serving Frey would dare to offend their master with jokes or lies. Carillon knew that, and he thus had no choice but to accept this story.

What the hell are Phobio and Alvis doing...?

But despite that internal complaint, Carillon knew Phobio was never any good at gauging his opponents' strengths. All kinds of extraordinary things could happen around him, and he'd be totally oblivious.

...But surely Alvis could have noticed? Why haven't I heard anything from her?!

As Carillon stewed over this, Frey spoke up again, as if suddenly recalling something.

"Oh, right. Your understudy Alvis also got engaged to Sir Benimaru, the general overseeing Sir Rimuru's armies. If this marriage goes well, maybe it'll be to our nations' benefit. Sir Rimuru approves, it sounds like, so that's good."

"That bastard actually did it?!"

Alvis had consulted Carillon about it. He advised her to seize Benimaru by force, and at the end of it, Alvis scored a resounding victory. He couldn't help but grin to himself over it.

"It sounds like she'll be his *second* wife, though..."

"Tch. Not the first, huh? Well, as long as she has a kid, it's all good."

"That's rather vulgar of you."

"Hey, don't worry, Frey. To me, you're the only woman I've ever loved."

"Quit playing games with me. In our society, women take multiple husbands. It's the exact opposite of *you* guys. How do you think it'd ever work out?"

The harpy race is almost exclusively female, with procreation reliant on one of the few males or a powerful magic-born for genetic diversity. A queen-type harpy like Frey is capable of expanding her armies through parthenogenesis, or virgin birth—no partner required. With beastmen, on the other hand, it was common for stronger men to maintain relationships with multiple women at once. This weeds out the weak and leads to a stronger race over the years. Both species have the same ultimate goal in mind, but no matter how you looked at it, they were inherently incompatible with each other.

Carillon and Frey, however, fully recognized each other's strength. Thus, although their relationship was very much a tightrope walk, they still managed not to step over that one final line in the sand.

"Well, since I doubt I'll receive a good reply from you right now, I'll just keep on trying to chip away at you, okay? So the question is, what the hell did that Rimuru bastard do?"

He could celebrate Alvis later. For now, Carillon was all business, and Frey was fine with that. They were on friendly terms with Rimuru's nation, and they wanted to keep it that way, but they needed a good grasp of what happened. Then, if possible, they wanted to take things between themselves to the next level, too.

"It reminds me of Clayman's final moments. He was throwing out some crazy powers right then."

"Yeah, the 'awakening' thing Rimuru talked about?"

"What do you think caused it?"

"*Pfft!* He didn't *look* like he was hiding any power. Clayman must've gained it right at that moment."

"And how did that work?"

"Well…"

"Via souls."

"Huh?"

"Clayman said that gathering souls was how he'd awaken to his 'true demon lord' self. If that's really true, there's no way he wasn't actively collecting them."

"Ah. So that's how he tried awakening himself?"

"Probably. Honestly, I've never killed a human being, so I've never even seen a soul before."

"Me neither. I've only fought against my own kind, magic-born, or angels. And we never wanted for much in my nation, so I never took interest in humans."

"Right. But I think that answers the question. It looks like Sir Rimuru found a way to acquire a huge number of souls during the war. Now he's passed them out to the magic-born under him to trigger awakenings."

"That's ridiculous. It's bad enough that would-be demon lords like us are serving someone else, but now all those *other* guys are getting ahead of us? Damn. So how many souls did Rimuru use for this?"

Carillon scratched his head, and Frey turned her eyes toward the city being built beneath them.

"Hey."

"Come to think of it, I didn't tell you how the war turned out, did I? Well, amazingly enough, Tempest's army suffered zero casualties. The Empire, on the other hand, had an army of nine hundred and forty thousand soldiers completely wiped out."

"...Huh?'

"You think I'm lying?"

"N-no..."

"I only *wish* this report was a mistake."

So the demon lord Rimuru had obtained a total of nine hundred and forty thousand souls, and with that kind of number, it'd likely be child's play to elevate seven of your faithful servants to "awakened" status.

And maybe it was more than seven, even. According to the report, head general Benimaru exhibited no change during the ceremony; all he had done was agree to marry Momiji and Alvis. But there was no way Rimuru wouldn't reward his closest associate with some souls. It was more likely that his evolution was delayed for some reason, coming along at a later date instead.

"Wow. So one side totally bustin' up the other, huh? That's hardly even a war any longer. I woulda put up the white flag by now, but what do you think the Empire's gonna do?"

"Who cares about the Empire? They don't matter anymore. The problem is what *we're* going to do."

"Yeah... Well, I've already surrendered myself to Milim. I already thought seeking out power for myself would be seen as treason, so I avoided it... But I guess I never had anything to worry about."

"How so?"

"Rimuru's raised up his staff to his own level now, right? Talk about generous. And looking back, I realized that Milim's probably the same as him."

"True. Us getting awakened probably wouldn't cause her to lose much sleep."

"Right? So why don't we just do what *we* want a little, huh? I think we've maybe been relaxing a little too much lately, but it's hardly too late. We've still got a chance to aim higher."

"We do. I always did like that about you."

Frey and Carillon looked at each other. But just when things started to warm between them—

"Wah-ha-ha-ha-ha! Well said, you two! I can't go awakening people willy-nilly like Rimuru, but I *can* give you guys my special brand of training! And you don't have to worry about death if you're inside the labyrinth, so we can go *all out*, too!"

—Milim barged in, timing impeccable as always.

"Dammit! *You* were here, Milim?! You just *had* to show up when it was gettin' good, too..."

"If I've told you once, I've told you a thousand times—stop sneaking up on us whenever you show up. And I have no interest in training with— *Listen* to me, Milim!"

Carillon and Frey were already whining at her, but Milim paid them no mind. Her ears were equipped with a top-of-the-line feature that shut out anything she didn't want to hear.

"Right! I'll go ask Ramiris to help us out!"

"Wait, wait, wait! I never asked you for training help either!"

"Hold it, Milim! If you won't listen to us, then I've got an idea of my own. How about we have Sir Middray handle all the cooking from now on? Are you okay with that?"

This statement from Frey triggered Milim's sense of danger. It was more than enough to stop her cold. *Nice one, Frey*, Carillon thought as he observed them.

"Uh... All right. But if you wanna train, ask me anytime!"

"Sure. By the way, have you finished up your homework?"

"Ummm... Well, I heard this really neat story I had to check out, so..."

"You haven't, have you?"

Frey smiled at her.

"I... Um, my break's over now, so I'm just gonna head right back."

"That's the spirit. Good girl."

So Milim returned to her homework, Frey and Carillon successfully surviving the crisis. But both of them still had a drive to evolve burning within their hearts. Would that ambition ever be fulfilled? That remained to be seen.

CHAPTER
2

FUTURE
DIRECTIONS

That Time I Got Reincarnated as a Slime

Before I forgot, I decided to go thank Veldora and Ramiris.

For Veldora, I had some new clothing. He always went around topless with a cape, and I saw that as kind of a problem. He didn't seem to mind it much— maybe he thought it was a good look for him—but I thought now was a good time to offer him an alternative in gift form.

"Ohhh, Rimuru! My heartfelt friend and ally! At long last, you have finally grasped how I feel, yes? I've always wanted to wear cooler clothes!"

"Uh, you know you could've asked Shuna anytime, and she would've set you up, right? Like, just go in the wardrobe room, and there's a few outfits you can magically adjust the sizes of."

"Fool! Only a custom-made outfit would be worthy of my time. And if my most trustworthy ally prepared it for me, I'm sure it would be the finest outfit in all the land, would it not?"

Um, I have, like, zero fashion sense, just so you know…

Veldora seemed to be giving way too much credit. I mean, I'm only wearing what the people around here tell me to wear. Looking back, I was horrible with my clothing choices in my previous life as well. I basically got by with business suits outdoors and sweats indoors. Lots of sweats. Comfy, no biggie if you get a stain on them… Perfect.

That was what I based my choices on with Veldora, and surprisingly, it was a bigger hit with him than I had guessed. He was rapidly throwing on every piece of the outfit, right in front of me.

"...Well, I'm glad you're happy with it. Keep up the good work now, all right?"

"Mmm, yes, leave it all to me! Kwah-ha-ha-ha!"

Considering everything I get from him, this was ridiculously cheap compensation. I mean, yes, it's a custom job made from top-of-the-line fabric, but still, you know... Next time I'm free, I'll try thinking of some other way to thank him. But that can wait.

Next up was Ramiris.

"Ramiris, you really saved our necks. Thank you for that."

"Aw, quit actin' like we're strangers or something! I owe you a whole heck of a lot, too, so you scratch my back, I scratch yours, y'know?"

Ramiris looked a little bashful. I wasn't much good at expressing gratitude, either, but it's important to do it when you need to.

"Right, so I thought I'd give you a reward as well."

"Oh, what's that? Did you make me a dress or something, like with my master?"

"If you want something like that, go ask Shuna. She'll set you up. But as for me..."

There was no way I'd ever be caught designing women's clothing. Shuna can tackle that for me. Myself, I had things to name.

"Oh, um, so you're gonna name my cute li'l Dragon Lords?"

"Pretty much, yeah."

"And I'll basically be their mom?"

"Exactly."

"Wow! That's really incredible!"

I was kinda surprised by that, too, actually, but it really did work.

"At the event yesterday, I gave Adalmann's pet the name of Venti. Once I did, she evolved, and now she can turn into a human anytime she wants and speak to us fluently. So I thought maybe you'd like the same for your own Dragon Lords, y'know?"

Those transformation skills threw me for a loop—but if you think about it, dragons taking human form is a pretty common trope in

fantasy fiction, isn't it? It's not completely unexpected. Thus, I figured there was a chance Ramiris's four Dragon Lords could pull that same trick. Then we'd have more staff on hand, and maybe life wouldn't be so stressful for Beretta.

"In that case, name away is what I say!"

Ramiris happily nodded her approval. With her consent, it was time to get started.

"Do you have any ideas for good names?"

"Mmmm... You handle it!"

Guess Ramiris isn't too good at coming up with names. If she was leaving all that to me, then they were probably gonna end up with fantasy game–style names... But maybe that works, actually? They *are* boss monsters, after all, so maybe it's not worth sweating over.

So I had Ramiris go fetch the Dragon Lords and bring them to the labyrinth lord's chambers where Veldora resided. Seeing all four of them lined up before me, it dawned on me that these guys have probably been beaten up by adventuring teams many times over by now. They remained doggedly devoted to their posts, however, so I really wanted some cool names for them. Being a Dragon Lord means having more magicules than even an Arch Demon, but it hadn't been that long since Milim picked them up, so these guys weren't quite as good as they could be. If naming them triggers evolutions, that ought to give them a ton more intelligence—and then they can be smarter, and stronger, than ever before.

With something like this, going with your initial gut feeling is always the best bet. The Fire Dragon Lord became Euros the Draconic Flamelord; the ice one became Zephyros the Draconic Frostlord; the wind one became Notos the Draconic Skylord; and the earth one became Boreas the Draconic Terralord. I was borrowing liberally from Greek mythology; these were the names of the Anemoi, the deities assigned to the winds of each cardinal direction, and I thought these would be perfect for the Dragon Lords.

These names were my creation, but Ramiris would be treated as the one who named them all. That seemed to work without a hitch, much to my relief. Thus, Ramiris and the dragons were now connected by their souls, and I hoped they'd continue to serve her faithfully.

So how did it work out? Well, just as I guessed, the Dragon Lords could all transform into forms close to human—not completely so, though, as they still retained some draconic characteristics. Euros, the Brimstone Dragon Lord, was a beautiful woman with red hair, her auburn skin covered in a dress made of dragon scale, and her tail resembled a flaming whip. Zephyros, the Frostkeep Dragon Lord, was a slender, handsome young man; his elegant, gentle appearance, combined with his long green hair, gave him an almost feminine sort of beauty. Notos, the Skythunder Dragon Lord, looked like a little girl, all cute from a distance but bearing jagged teeth and menacing fangs up close; the size and look were a mismatch for her incredible strength. Finally, Boreas, the Earthshaker Dragon Lord, was a large, muscular man covered in dragon scales, spines growing all over his body.

The four of them looked like they headed some legion of super villains, the combination of horror and beauty they presented resulting in a twisted sort of attractiveness. This shift, however, was just for looks only; they hadn't turned dragonoid like Milim, and their species was still straight-up Dragon Lord. Dragonoids, after all, are spiritual life-forms with a physical body, a sort of mutational offshoot from the True Dragons. Even with all the Dragon Lords' powers, they were still physical by nature, so they weren't going to rank up there with the perfection the True Dragons exuded.

Still, despite the remaining Dragon Lords, I'd call this evolution a big success. Even better, they had acquired more magic force than I anticipated. They all had several times more magicules than pre-evolution, and it looked to me like they'd get close to the awakened Clayman on that front. Not quite a true demon lord, but still, a wonderful leap forward for them. Considering how much some simple names boosted them, I shuddered to think what would've happened if I consumed my own magicules for this. For all I knew, I could've suffered irreparable damage. This whole naming system is really scary, in a way.

All told, I consumed five thousand souls on this job. There's just nothing at all logical about monsters, I realized all over again. But no point pondering over it. Either way, the evolutions of the Dragon Lords, which served as my thank-you gift to Ramiris, were now complete.

By the way, if you're looking strictly at magicule counts, the Ten Dungeon Marvels are all about evenly matched with these Dragon Lords. However, it looks like there's still a major gap in combat power, something you can't express with numbers. Zegion's a good enough illustration of that, but even the other Marvels make the evolved Dragon Lords look kind of weak. Yes, they had strong monster bodies and attacks that leveraged them, plus a bunch of magic. They were undoubtedly vicious, powerful forces... But they'd still lose out to their peers with better combat skills.

A lot of that just came down to lack of battle experience; they didn't really have a firm foundation in combat yet. I'm sure it was frustrating for the Dragon Lords to keep getting whipped all the time during the labyrinth siege. In fact, the moment they evolved and gained language fluency, the first thing they did was ask me for training.

Having a new humanoid form meant they could now master human-style combat, and they now realized that a more refined skill set would get them a lot further than their monster-style techniques. Instead of relying on physical attacks like bites, maulings, and element-driven breath, they'd need to understand their magic better and incorporate it into their fighting. I assumed they wanted to learn how to fight as humans and try working that into their own approaches. They came up with that on their own, and really, that showed some pretty remarkable development already.

"Kwaaaaah-ha-ha-ha! I will gladly take care of them for you!"

Veldora, emboldened after doing such a good job raising Zegion, immediately accepted the trainer role for the Dragon Lords. Thus, their journey began.

In time, some of the Dragon Lords would demonstrate more strength in human form than as dragons. They mastered ways to transform their own claws and scales into weapons and armor—which seemed like kind of a backward way to do it, but oh well—and I assume they liked the results they got from that. I wouldn't discover this until much later, but…yeah, I guess it's just as well.

Three days had passed since Caligulio and his staff were resurrected, and by now, they had regained most of their composure. The shock of being brought back to life by a demon lord was hard to put into words, but somehow, they had managed to accept it as the truth.

The question then became: *What happens to us, going forward?*

For now, they were still living and sleeping in tents. Food was arranged for them, carried in regularly by monsters—skeletons, in fact, but nobody was complaining. These tents were lined up in a barren, hilly area with no real vegetation; the scenery was dreary, but it was neither too hot nor too cold, making it an oddly comfortable space. The death-laden atmosphere of the battlefield and the long rows of graves for the dead weren't any big deal once you got used to them. The people these graves belonged to were out walking and talking in skeleton form anyway, so it'd be silly to fear them. In short, it wasn't an arrangement to wail about at all.

According to what they heard, they had been set up on Floor 70 of the labyrinth. This was all explained to them by a wight king named Adalmann, who oversaw things on this level. Some of the people there had actually fought against him, so nobody doubted who he was. Besides, Adalmann was quite caring of them, treating Caligulio and the others pretty well by POW standards.

"My god, Sir Rimuru, has deemed fit to resurrect you all, and thus, I follow his divine will. He is not the type of person who would take away a life previously given. I will suggest you take your time to think about what you want your future to be like."

Based on that philosophy, Adalmann had let Caligulio and his staff go free. But nobody was suggesting they break their way out of this level. Their lives were already in the hands of the gods, they realized, and so they decided to trust in the demon lord Rimuru. Caligulio agreed with this, and besides, he was confident any escape attempt would end in failure. That's why, taking Adalmann's words to heart, he decided to call his staff together for a meeting.

Nearly a hundred officers were now gathered in a large tent used for military conferences. These were senior staffers, some of the Empire's greatest heroes, but any power they had was well and truly gone now.

"All right, people. First off, allow me to apologize. My incompetence is what put you all in this situation, and for that, I am sincerely sorry."

Caligulio looked at his assembled audience and bowed his head. Nobody there thought the apology was warranted.

"What are you saying, my lord? We are just as guilty as you for not stopping His Majesty."

The staff nodded their agreement to the aide's statement. The senior officers—most notably Krishna—also agreed that Caligulio was far from the only culprit here.

"I am of the same opinion as everyone else. Thanks to our foolishness, we have incurred the wrath of God himself... And by God's mercy, we've been given the opportunity to atone for our sins."

As he phrased it, the Empire's whole invasion was a sin, and Caligulio agreed with him. As overconfident of their military might as they were, they didn't even try to learn much about their enemy. Looking back, Caligulio could hardly believe his own stupidity. The thought that his friends must all be feeling the same way brought an embittered smile to his face.

"Thank you. Hearing that makes me feel a little more at peace with myself. And I swear to God that I will never forget this feeling."

The moment he said the word *God*, the image of the demon lord Rimuru flashed through his mind.

Yes... As far as I'm concerned, Lord Rimuru may as well be my god.

There was no place in the Empire for Caligulio to return to. If he did, he'd take the blame for the loss, and they'd skip the court-martial and jump right to his execution. He had no intention of shirking his responsibilities, but he thought it wrong to throw away the life granted by Rimuru for nothing.

Well... I'll have time to weigh my options there.

It was natural for Caligulio to think about putting his own problems off for later. His face was no longer that of a brute driven solely by self-preservation and greed.

"Now, let's get to the topic at hand. I've gathered you all here today because I want to build consensus on how we should move forward. Sir Adalmann has generously given me the freedom to consult with all of you in this meeting, so let's try to get some work done so his kindness doesn't go to waste."

Once Caligulio said this, the people present exchanged glances and began discussing matters among themselves. That would be unthinkable during a typical military meeting, but Caligulio welcomed it—he wanted honest, unadorned feedback from everyone.

After chatting about it for a while, the group narrowed their thoughts down enough to form two major factions. One thought it best to stay here and retain their current allegiance to their captors; the other argued that they must return to the Empire without delay.

These two sides were deadlocked with each other, and both arguments were wholly understandable. It was only natural that those with families would want to return home, but whether that was possible depended on the intentions of the demon lord Rimuru. Perhaps it'd be doable with further negotiations, but if they made too much of a fuss about it, it could put the demon lord off.

"I would like to believe that he has no interest in executing us for no reason, as Sir Adalmann assures us. But we have to keep in mind that this doesn't mean we're forgiven."

Given the way their lives were saved, their fates were all in the hands of the demon lord. They might've been granted a little freedom, but getting too selfish presented unknown risks.

"...I imagine all of us in this tent would be executed if we came back. But even despite that, I want to make sure that the soldiers who fought so bravely for their country can get home safely. I'd like to appeal directly to Lord Rimuru and ask him for his favor here."

"Perhaps, but keep in mind, we are something akin to hostages right now, and we have no idea whether our nation will pay compensation or not. It's a thorny issue."

Then Major General Minitz, who had been silently listening to everyone's takes so far, spoke up.

"It's not gonna happen. We've never even imagined ourselves as defeated. You know how consistently ruthless we've been in our dealings with hostile nations."

The floor fell silent. The Empire had never accepted anything other than unconditional surrender in the past. It was arrogant of them, but given their constant streak of victories, they had a right to be arrogant. But now that they had suffered a total defeat, they'd have no one to blame for themselves if they were unforgiven. Everybody here understood that—and they knew that even if they could return to the Empire, their future there would look pretty bleak.

Still, some wanted to fulfill their responsibilities to those soldiers with families waiting back home.

"Major General Minitz is right. I wonder what His Majesty the Emperor will think about all this..."

"I hate to say it, but I think our intelligence bureau was far too negligent. How many demon lord–class freaks do they think Tempest even had?!"

For an imperial officer, this remark was wading into taboo territory.

"Hey! Watch your mouth, you! I don't care what happens to the IIB at this point, but the ones you called freaks are the major leaders of this nation, you know."

"Sorry. Slip of the tongue..."

Free speech was welcome here, and there were no monsters in the tent. No one had seen Adalmann since yesterday; Caligulio assumed he was off attending to business somewhere. That's why they were having this conference today... But that didn't mean they could say anything and everything they wanted. They couldn't forget their status as prisoners of war.

"Lord Rimuru seems to be a generous leader to me, but I doubt he'll overlook any bad-mouthing of his staff. Remember that well, everyone, and keep an eye on what you say."

Despite stating that, Caligulio agreed with his officer's voiced opinion. At the very least, the fact that somebody under Rimuru's command could handle magic as intense as Gravity Collapse told volumes about how dangerous this demon lord was. Why didn't the Imperial Information Bureau know anything about them?

I fully understand why he called the IIB negligent. If anything, I wish I said that myself...

But then one audience member uttered something that threw cold water on Caligulio and his officers.

"Are all of you idiots? Listen to me. The IIB was definitely aware of *some* intel, at least."

Bernie, silent until now, suddenly let out that bombshell with a chuckle.

"That's ridiculous! So why did they withhold accurate intelligence from His Majesty?"

"They didn't betray us, did they?!"

The whole group was agitated. Only Minitz and Caligulio remained calm, and Minitz was the first to respond.

"Your name was Bernie, right? The man on an undercover mission not even we were told about?"

"Right," Caligulio added. "Single Digits like you probably would know some top secret information that we weren't aware of. So what was the IIB thinking, and what did they want us to do?"

All eyes focused on Bernie after that question. Everybody on hand wanted to know. The IIB had sworn absolute loyalty to the emperor. It was hard to believe that they would betray anyone—and that meant Emperor Ludora was in a position to anticipate this happening all along.

Bernie snorted at the crowd as he looked around, giving Caligulio and the others sympathetic looks. Then, without hesitation, he dropped another bomb.

"Well, it's exactly what you're all imagining. The emperor knew everything. He was already taking your defeat into consideration."

"That—that's madness..."

"What do you mean by that? Are you saying His Majesty knew we'd be defeated but sent the entire army over anyway?!"

"Impossible! That's far too much of an insult against the emperor!"

The officers were all getting worked up. But someone began to have an inkling of what was going on.

"I see. So we were just throwaway pawns the whole time?"

"No, that's not quite the right way to put it, Minitz. If I had to guess, His Majesty's purpose was—"

"*Pfft!* Keep your mouth shut, Caligulio. If someone needs to take the heat for leaking national-level secrets, let it be me, not you. Listen... All of us right now are dead, me included. And if we are, this won't count as betraying the emperor anyway."

Such was Bernie's resolve. He had lost the powers that promoted him to the Single Digits, even the ultimate force granted to him by the emperor. Now it was time, as a leader, to show a new pathway for everyone.

"Bernie..."

"Sorry, Jiwu. But you know I'm never gonna be *that* loyal to His Majesty. I only served him for one reason—because I knew I could never beat him."

That, too, was Bernie telling the truth.

....

......

...

Bernie, born in the United States of America forty-five years ago, was once an average, freedom-loving student. Somehow he wound up in this world instead, where Gadora discovered him. He was then taken in by Damrada, from whom he learned the art of fighting. This gave him confidence, and somewhere along the line, he became vain enough to think he was among the best in the world. But his confidence was shattered by a single woman serving at Emperor Ludora's side. A beautiful woman—and also a truly monstrous creation. A lofty pinnacle that Bernie would never reach, even if he moved heaven and earth and went through thousands of reincarnations. It was hard to believe such a being even existed, but reality was all too cruel to him.

The woman's name was Velgrynd—one of the Empire's most closely guarded secrets, one that must never be spoken of to outsiders.

One day, Bernie was escorted by Damrada to the emperor's palace, a great honor that fueled his ambitions even further. As a lover of freedom, he detested the idea of an emperor who dominated every aspect of people's lives. He dreamed, however foolishly, that he could overthrow the emperor if he just had a chance. The price of that foolishness was paid in fear, for when Bernie met Velgrynd for the first time that day, he was immediately seized by it, giving in wholeheartedly to it.

As Bernie was gripped by this fear, Emperor Ludora addressed him from beyond the curtain.

"You have the qualifications... The requirements to serve as a vessel. I will lend you my powers. Please keep up the good work."

Ludora's voice sounded entirely free of emotion, as if it was echoing out from some faraway point. The next thing Bernie knew, he was in absolutely no position to defy the emperor any longer.

....

......

...

"His Majesty doesn't care if a million of his elites are wiped out. In fact, that's all part of the plan."

That sentence, by itself, made little sense. But Caligulio knew what it meant.

"...Oh. So he's willing to sacrifice a million officers and enlisted men if it results in someone like me awakening?"

Hearing Caligulio give the correct answer after so little explanation surprised Bernie slightly. But hearing him say "someone like me awakening" made it clear how he knew.

"Ah, so you're awakened, too? Then I think you probably understand it all. Yes, you're right. His Majesty's goal is to build a collection of awakened people to serve as his pawns. If he can gain even one more of them, that's easily worth a million casualties to him."

This was a truth that not even the Empire's senior officers were aware of. From the very beginning, Emperor Ludora expected nothing from his military. The most important thing to him was how many awakened personnel he could collect.

"Quality over quantity sort of thing? So when we took on Veldora three centuries ago and failed..."

Minitz gave Bernie a sharp gaze as he asked the question. Bernie was aloof as always.

"I don't know what happened back then, but if you think about it, doesn't it make sense to you? I can kill every man in this tent by myself... Or I *could* have, I mean. That's how vast the power gap was."

"I see, I see... And that's why it was a given that we'd be defeated, then? The whole strategy was built on the assumption that we'd take horrific losses. I'd like to call it a brilliant move on His Majesty's part, but this time, it was just a disaster."

"Exactly. I'm sure His Majesty didn't expect us to lose *after* your awakening."

Minitz sounded convinced of it, Caligulio bitterly listening on.

"Well... I'm sorry I wasn't good enough."

He mumbled it out, his tone self-deriding, but Bernie denied it.

"It's all right. It's not that you weren't up to the challenge. We just matched up poorly against our opponent."

"Yeah. There was nothing we could do against that."

Jiwu nodded her agreement. She and Bernie had both lost to Diablo, the same demon who defeated Caligulio. If they couldn't beat a freak of nature like that, they assumed Caligulio couldn't, either.

"So you're saying Tempest's strength was beyond what the IIB projected?"

"Looks that way, yeah. The plan was to use the demon lord Rimuru as a stepping-stone to gain more pawns for us, but we blew our chances because we misjudged our opponent's strength."

Bernie couldn't help but laugh, as inappropriate as that was considering all the personnel lost. But he still wished he could rub this in the emperor's face someday.

"...Well, Bernie, you were trying to use us as a diversion so you could stage your sneak attack, I suppose, but it failed. What are you gonna do now?"

"Ha! I told you. I'll take the heat for it, okay?"

"What do you mean?" Minitz calmly asked. A few moments passed, everyone in the tent silently waiting for Bernie's answer.

"...Let me get one thing straight with you folks first. Like I just said, you guys are all already dead. I don't mean that metaphorically; I mean you're dead as far as His Majesty is concerned."

"Mm-hmm. Is it trouble for him if we stay alive like this?"

"That's not quite the way to put it. The emperor has no use for soldiers who've been deprived of their powers and have zero chance of awakening. And if he has no use for you, then he has no reason to protect you, either."

"I suppose not, no."

"Think of it on that basis, and there's a real good chance they won't accept any prisoners if Tempest offers them. And not just that—if the surviving soldiers return home, it'll spread antiwar sentiment across the Empire. Do you think that's in line with His Majesty's will?"

"Doubtful."

Minitz sighed. Now he understood what Bernie wanted to say.

"And since we're no longer important to His Majesty, we're just a third wheel to the IIB?"

"You got it."

"And they'll seek out and deal with anyone who tries to return home?"

"Definitely."

And then they'd pin the blame on Tempest to stir up the anger and vengeance of their people, likely. Bernie was confident that's what the IIB would do, and that was the story he was giving the tent now.

"...But we're talking seven hundred thousand people. It'd be impossible."

"The people who underwent enhancement surgery didn't lose that much power. If we fight back, we'd be fighting against our own side!"

Minitz raised a hand to quiet the startled officers.

"...Do you have an idea of who might be capable of that?"

Most of the audience thought the idea was ridiculous. But Minitz remained coolheaded. Caligulio, remembering what happened when he was awakened, remained silent. With *that* kind of power, he concluded, it wasn't so impossible at all.

"Could the Single Digits do it?"

"If that's a yes-no question, then the answer is yes. But that's just armchair theorizing. If a single person has absolute power, that's good for offense but not for defense. If the enemy swarms you with huge numbers, then inevitably you'll have areas you can't fully defend. At the same time, it's also not a suitable approach if you're pursuing a fleeing enemy. If they scatter in all directions, you'll inevitably miss out on some."

In this case, it'd be necessary for the Empire to take all of them out with no survivors whatsoever. Bernie didn't know anyone who'd be capable of that...with one exception.

"Now, common sense dictates that this is impossible, right? But it's not. The Empire's got an absolute freak of nature who can pull that off."

Bernie recalled the figure in his mind. It made him shiver. The beauty, and the horror, could only be understood by those who've had an encounter. Bernie was one of them, and that fact made him very unhappy.

"...Someone that makes a Single Digit like you quake in their boots? It appears that I'm gravely mistaken here."

Minitz sat back in his seat and looked up at the ceiling.

"Me too. I joined the military because I dreamed of ruling the world in the name of the Empire. But now..."

Now everything was being decided in a place that had nothing to do with the military. These power struggles were being played by someone else, and there was no room for the non-awakened to butt in.

"Foolish of us, wasn't it?"

"Yeah. What a farce."

Caligulio and Minitz exchanged glances, both looking ready to cry. And not just them—all the other officers in the tent looked like they had just woken up from a dream, and they weren't happy about it. *It's so pathetic*, Bernie thought. Everyone would've been a lot happier if they didn't know the truth, but then they wouldn't have been convinced about their situation. That's why Bernie laid it all bare for them, leaving nothing behind.

"So do you see now? You understand the situation you're in? If you go back home, there'll be nothing but despair waiting for you. You gotta stay here as prisoners and just wait until the war's over."

"Sir Bernie, what are *you* going to do?"

"I'm going back to the Empire. The war's not gonna end anytime soon at this rate, so Lord Rimuru is probably gonna try negotiating with the Empire... And he'll need a guide for that, won't he?"

And that guide would almost certainly be disappeared. The current, powerless Bernie would absolutely be assassinated. But he was determined to do it.

Now everyone was silent. Here and now, they understood all too well that the demon lord Rimuru had an iron grip on all of their fates.

●

After expressing my gratitude to Veldora and Ramiris, I decided to go to Floor 70 of the labyrinth.

Adalmann, following yesterday's evolution ritual, had fallen into a deep sleep. His Harvest Festival was underway, but his castle was still fully wrecked, so we dragged him to a guest room up top and had him sleep there. Alberto and Venti were put into their own quarters as well, and I was sure they'd all be waking up soon enough.

But the imperial prisoners of war were a problem for me. Adalmann was taking care of them, and it wouldn't be good to leave them unattended. Besides, I was hoping they were calm enough by now to give me some more information about the Empire. It was a good opportunity for that anyway, so I decided to go and check on them. I had my two secretaries accompanying me, and I figured that'd be enough to keep me safe through anything.

"You didn't have to go do this yourself, Sir Rimuru..."

"Oh, you wanna do it for me, then?"

"Yes! Go down there and talk to them!"

"Keh... Keh-heh-heh-heh-heh. Right! Off we go, then!"

Diablo never changes, does he? And maybe that's true for Shion, too. There's no way they'd voluntarily go down there. *I'd never let Shion do this alone*, I thought as she hugged me close to her chest. It was odd that they were both fine the day after the evolution ritual, though. Shion was still unchanged after a full twenty-four hours, and Diablo was completely back to his usual self.

"So did you manage to acquire any new abilities?"

"Keh-heh-heh-heh-heh! Well, thanks to you, Sir Rimuru, I've finally succeeded in obtaining an ultimate skill! Now I don't have to sit there and fume while Guy annoys me with his bragging."

I'm sure Guy found Diablo far more annoying than the other way around. Like, I'm totally confident about that.

"Well, if that was so frustrating for you, you should've acquired one on your own. I'm sure you could've figured out an ultimate skill without my help, Diablo."

"No, no, I couldn't have. If I gained the skill after Guy told me about his, it'd be like I was copying him. It would look terrible."

I don't get it. This isn't about who's copying whom, you know. If there's something useful out there, why don't you just have him teach it to you? Or am I thinking about this all wrong?

"Heh. How narrow-minded of you, Diablo. Better to ask than go astray, as I think they say—and ever since Sir Rimuru taught me that, I've always striven to listen to what people have to say. Gobichi has taught me the true essence of cooking as well, and now I've acquired full mastery of my craft!"

Shion seemed awfully smug about that, but personally, I think Gobichi just wanted to get away from her. I really wish Gobichi wouldn't go giving Shion this strange confidence of hers, too. He needs to step up and take care of her to the bitter end, you know?

"Oh, was that the reason why Sir Gobichi was hospitalized a bit ago? If he had to put up with *your* cooking all the time, no wonder he fell ill."

Yeahhhh… Maybe I shouldn't be chiding Gobichi, after all. But Diablo's gone through some tough times on this front as well, and Shuna doesn't even dare taste test anything Shion creates. So who'll deal with Shion's cooking? It's gonna have to be Benimaru, isn't it? Yeah. It's his responsibility to educate Shion, and I'll make sure that's clear with him. And I'm not saying that just because I want to needle the newlywed or anything. Please don't misunderstand me here.

Shion got us all derailed, but as we chatted on, we reached our destination in no time. Once we were transported over to the hilly area of Floor 70, we were greeted by some people who shot up and saluted the moment they saw us. I'm not sure that's really the appropriate thing to do with the demon lord of an enemy nation, but Diablo and Shion seemed satisfied with it, so I didn't quibble.

"Lord Rimuru has graced us with his presence! Summon Lord Caligulio at once!"

And with that, the soldiers started jogging to and fro, forming a column that led directly to a single tent. Caligulio was conducting a military conference in there, according to the people guiding the way for us.

Inside the tent were a hundred or so important-looking people. They all saluted, on their feet and demonstrating impeccable posture. Getting this treatment from the top brass surprised me a little. I mean, I'm the king of their enemy, and I'm in slime form right now, too. But nobody was looking down on me, and I guess Raphael's suggestion was more successful than expected. It's only natural, I suppose, if you think about it. If someone kills you and then brings you back to life, it's probably wise to fully submit to them. If *I* ran into someone like that, you can bet I wouldn't defy them.

Convinced of this, I sat down on the seat at the head of the table I was guided to. I needed to be dignified here, so I changed over to human form, with Shion and Diablo behind me. Shion looked a little disappointed to not have me in her arms, but getting preoccupied with that was pointless, so I looked around the room and began to speak.

"All right, folks. Having all the big shots in one place is kinda helpful to me, actually."

""""Yes, my lord!""""

They all bowed their heads at once. It was gonna be hard to talk with them like this, so I asked them to sit down before I began.

"Relax, guys, okay? I've got something I want to discuss."

I gave them a warm smile. Hopefully this would ease their minds a little and enable us to have a nice, pleasant chitchat.

"Adalmann is busy with other matters at the moment, so he might not be able to come back for a while. So I was wondering if you guys had any requests for me right now."

"That is too kind of you, my lord. We are always well taken care of here, so please, do not concern yourself about our plights."

Eesh! So formal! Caligulio provided the answer for the rest of them, but this treatment was just beyond stuffy. Then again, they've lost the war, so I suppose this would be normal of them anyway.

"Well, great, then. So regarding our plans for the future…"

"Yes, my lord! There is actually something we would all like you to do on that matter!"

They had a request after all, huh? I was fine with that, as long as it wasn't anything too unreasonable. Then Caligulio gave me quite a surprise.

"We are hoping that we could be taken care of within this country for the time being, so if possible, we'd like to ask for your continued kindness…"

Um…?

I pressed for more details. According to Caligulio, they were actually discussing their future direction when I stopped in. The conclusion they came to was that, if they returned to the Empire, it was very likely they'd all be killed.

"Whoa, whoa, are you guys crazy? What kinda country kills the soldiers that fought for it just because they lost?"

I couldn't help but blurt that out.

"But I think that's exactly what will happen."

Bernie, of all people, replied first. He was calm and logical now; it was hard to believe this was the same guy who attacked us. As he explained, nobody here could say that this grisly fate wasn't possible for them.

"Hmm… So they'd sacrifice a million to awaken just one person? You've got to be kidding…"

"It's the truth, my lord."

"Well, hang on. If that's true, then isn't it weird how they held off on a military invasion for so long because they feared that Veldora's seal was broken? Maybe we had that wrong, and they were actually waiting for his return?"

"I'm afraid that not even I can understand Emperor Ludora's thoughts on the matter. However, Lord Rimuru, I humbly believe that your observation is correct."

Is this really Bernie? He was so polite that it seemed like a whole other person.

But that's the deal here, huh? This guy Ludora's true objective wasn't just to win this war. He was going to pit the generals and soldiers of this Empire against an enemy powerful enough to weed out the losers from those who'd be awakened by the experience. The sheer scale of this was too much for regular people to even comprehend.

Report. It is an interesting idea.

Stop that, dumbass! There's *nothing* interesting about using human beings as test subjects. Raphael *does* act up like this sometimes, doesn't it?

Zegion was a successful example of such experimentation. For all I know, maybe I'm being the guinea pig for some other experiment of Raphael's.

Negative. There is no confirmation of such a situation.

Oh, really? I mean, I believe you, but...

Anyway, that could wait. The question was whether to accept Caligulio's request.

"You know, though, it costs money to feed all you guys. When we're talking seven hundred thousand of you, that means importing food from other nations, too, so..."

If they're likely going to be killed back home, I'm a little hesitant to just kick them out of Tempest. But honestly speaking, there's no reason for us to take care of them. I'm only responsible for my own people. These guys—well, I'd *like* them to make the most of their lives, but I can't do everything, you know? If we take in an influx of seven hundred thousand trained military personnel, our neighbors to the west aren't gonna keep quiet about that, Blumund especially. In fact, it could even lead to needless blood being spilled. Still...it'd be kinda cold to just tell them to go home. I already saved their lives once, so I guess I should take responsibility for them right to the end.

No other option, really, besides taking care of them. But I wasn't gonna do it for free.

"In our nation, you know, we have a credo that only those who put in the work deserve to have food on the table. If we're gonna feed you, we need you to work for it, but are you okay with that?"

The room had awaited my response with bated breath. Once I finished speaking, they all looked delighted.

"Absolutely, my lord!"

"Order anything you want from us!"

They sure were motivated, even though I didn't tell them what they'd be doing yet. Either way, I'd allow them to stay here, then. I had assumed that prisoners of war didn't mean much to the Empire. There were no Geneva Conventions here, no rules that warring states were expected to follow. The way Bernie described it, these POWs wouldn't be much of a bargaining chip for negotiating a cease-fire. If so, better to just commit and accept them as a labor force.

The length of their stay was still to be determined, but they'll be working for us until at least the end of the war. They may not be too useful if their stay here's too short, but we'll have to wait and see how that pans out. Hopefully they'll prove useful for something or other anyway. The officers here didn't seem to have any intention of defying me, at least. Maybe I could just leave them to Geld and have him take advantage... But he's in an evolutionary sleep right now and unavailable for a little while. So what can they do until he wakes up?

"By the way, are you guys any good at public-works projects?"

It often comes as a surprise that a military would be full of people good at engineering. In my previous life, it was a well-known fact that when a warlord of ye olde Japan wanted to build a castle, his samurai were the ones who oversaw the construction. Even in modern times, Japan's Self-Defense Forces played a huge role in things like disaster relief; the news would talk about how active they were in overseas aid projects and so on.

Similarly, the engineers over in Dwargon have some pretty high-tech talent. They're not the most glamorous soldiers, but they're quite useful. It's no exaggeration to say that Kaijin, ex-leader of the dwarven Engineering Division, literally laid the foundation for that whole kingdom. So there's always been that link between the military and civil engineering, but...

"Oh, of course! I'm proud to inform you that the Empire's technological capabilities are the best in the world!"

Good. In that case, let's see what they can do.

"All right. Here's your first task, then—you see that destroyed castle out there? I want you guys to restore it to its former glory for me. I'll work out the supplies for it, but I want you guys to handle everything else, from design on up. Can you do that?"

Since they destroyed it and all, I thought it'd be nice if they could fix it up as well.

Caligulio eagerly nodded at me. "As you wish," he said, looking supremely confident. A few men, presumably his staff, immediately got to work with all the swiftness of a well-oiled machine; they looked like people ready to do the job. Once Adalmann wakes up, he could send some skeletons over to help out, and I think we could get this thing rebuilt in the not-too-distant future.

Now the imperial army had a job.

*

Time for my other objective—intel gathering. I thought we needed to go into some depth today, so I took a few of Caligulio's staffers familiar with imperial matters and asked them to join me in one of our conference halls. I wanted to hold a meeting with them and the members of my cabinet who were still awake, so we could talk about what we'd do with the Empire next.

At this point, the Empire was presumably still unaware that Caligulio's force was defeated. Yuuki might've received reports from

Misha and Laplace, but worrying about leaks from them seemed unwarranted to me.

Besides, we're already aware of the Empire's current maneuvers. I told Luminus about the three hundred airships traveling over the sea toward them. *"Hmph!"* she'd replied. *"Watch me turn the tables on them all!"* I doubted Luminus herself would take action, but we had a treaty, and she'd promised to guard against the imperial forces coming from the north. The Holy Empire of Lubelius, as the world's religious headquarters, churns out a ton of paladins, and apparently they had their own standing force as well. Between that and the hidden threat that was the vampires, I felt fine leaving things in their hands. If Luminus got in any danger, the one-hundred-fifty-thousand-strong Western Deployment could step up, too; Testarossa had them standing by, ready to respond at a moment's notice.

Most of all, though, Hinata was part of the team intercepting the airships. They were truly prepared for anything, but we still can't let our guard down. I looked at my assembled group and announced the start of the meeting.

The following seventeen people were seated in the hall:

- My secretaries, Shion and Diablo.
- Benimaru, my supreme general, and Rigurd and Kaijin, my assistants in political affairs.
- Gabil and Gobta, my two corps leaders.
- Hakuro, my adviser; Soei, my intelligence officer; and Gadora, too, as a material witness of sorts.
- The three demonesses—Testarossa, Ultima, and Carrera.
- On the imperial side, there were Caligulio himself, Minitz, and Bernie and Jiwu.

Including myself, we had eighteen people in here.

We started with introductions, and of course, the imperials were utterly stunned when they found out the three demonesses were all Primals. Man, were those stares painful to endure. Sorry, guys. It's Diablo's fault, not mine. I could already anticipate the complaints coming my way, so I decided to pretend nothing happened and get down to business.

"Um, so if there's stuff you can't share with me, that's cool, okay? Just tell me whatever you can."

With that, I used Argos, the Eye of God, to put up a display showing the airship squadron in flight. Caligulio would be explaining the current state of the Empire to us, as we agreed upon beforehand. The imperials looked pretty upset about the video on the large surveillance screen, but Caligulio kept his composure and promptly began his briefing.

I already knew a bit about the situation over there from Gadora. That old man didn't seem to care at all about betraying the Empire, but Caligulio was a soldier. There might be some things he can't talk about, and we'll just have to follow up on that later. I told him what I knew in advance, so I'd be having him provide his briefing based on that.

"Very well. In that case, I will begin."

He was even more brisk and businesslike than I anticipated.

The Armored Division that Caligulio led had a department called the Flying Combat Corps, which boasted four hundred state-of-the-art airships. Three hundred of them were flying to northern Englesia, carrying full troop loads. Each one could carry up to four hundred people, and a crew of fifty was enough to fly one, so that meant a maximum of three hundred and fifty passengers. All this was just as Gadora explained to me.

These ships were transporting the Magical Beast Division led by one General Gradim, a force of thirty thousand in all. However, it was actually more like sixty thousand, since each division member was partnered with a magical beast of their own. They were also joined by support personnel providing logistical services; they had a major general named Zamdo commanding them, but they were probably noncombatants who shouldn't be counted in military numbers.

"It is a tad embarrassing to talk about this here, but most of the troops sent to Englesia are still novices. They can operate an airship just fine, but in an actual combat situation, their performance is likely going to suffer. Normally they would be conducting R & D for us, so I hope you can show them some mercy..."

As Caligulio explained, the Empire had deployed all its war-power to Tempest, so he gave his rival Gradim nothing but noncombatant personnel. The support staff numbered around thirty thousand in all, but there were hardly wizards or the like; most were sorcerers, a level below. Beyond that, the rest were airship operators and maintenance techs, and Caligulio asked me to take them prisoner instead of killing them, if possible.

"Of all the brazen things to say! You invaded another country, and now that it looks like you'll lose, you want us to save them without killing anyone?"

Shion was enraged over this. It made Caligulio turn pale as he apologized. I tried to quiet her down a bit, but really, I thought she was right. Caligulio understood that well enough, too, which explained why he was so apologetic about it. But:

"Well, what happens over there isn't in our jurisdiction. Depending on how things go, I might have to disappoint you there."

"Yes, I understand that, of course. Please do as you wish, Lord Rimuru."

I'll consider his request if I think it's possible, but I can't make any promises. My resurrection magic isn't a cure-all—sometimes it doesn't work if the conditions aren't right. And depending on how Luminus reacts to this, I may not be in any position to intervene anyway. I had heard that Gradim's Magical Beast Division is a pretty considerable threat, and there's no guarantee that they won't deal serious damage to Hinata and her troops. If that happens, there won't be any time for mercy. We've got a ton of defensive capability, so I don't think we'd ever be defeated, but there are never any absolutes in war, so I can't make guarantees like that lightly.

So that was the end of that. Now we had to talk about Dwargon's eastern city.

*

I switched the Eye of God over to a shot of an army some sixty thousand strong. They were deployed and looking pretty relaxed, no tension in the air whatsoever. The imperial officers were shocked all over again, but I pressed on with my briefing.

"At present, Yuuki and I have somewhat reluctantly joined together in an alliance. This might look like a tense standoff, but it's actually just kind of a big performance."

Minitz snorted at this. "Well, look at that. If part of our army was compromised from the start, we had practically no chance of winning, did we?"

Caligulio nodded. "Yeah. And the moment my Armored Division and Gradim's Magical Beast Division are wiped out, they'll turn their claws toward the imperial capital, and then...checkmate, eh?"

They exchanged embittered looks. Now they knew they were defeated both in strength and in strategy. But not everyone was on the same page.

"I don't think so. The emperor still has people in the capital who'll protect him. I know I've said this many times before, but an awakened soldier is a literal one-man army. I'm sure they would've foreseen the possibility that Yuuki would rebel against them."

It was kind of weird hearing Bernie talk like this. My image of him as Masayuki's long-suffering flunky was still too strong in my mind; this seemed like someone totally different.

"Is this the *real* you I'm seeing here, Bernie?"

"Ah... No, the real me is more how I was when I was traveling with Masayuki."

I asked the question on reflex, but Bernie was honest enough to provide an answer. So his current attitude is him in "military" mode, but he's usually a lot more informal, huh? He also informed me that he's originally from the United States and is forty-five years old; he was originally an average student like any other, so the Bernie I saw before me was all the result of his education in this world. That much probably doesn't matter to anyone besides himself, although it did make me feel a little affinity for him.

"But you're probably right. I heard that there's someone in the Empire who could potentially kill me. And it's totally expected that a cornered mouse can find a way to turn the tables on the cat."

The "quality over quantity" dynamic in this world was tough to wrap your head around. No matter how big an army you assembled, they could still be defeated by one single person if they're unlucky. That's how *we* won, too, so we needed to consider being in the opposite position as well.

"In that case, why don't I travel over there and show this someone a thing or two?!"

Shion's hand was already on her giant sword. We had zero guarantee that she could win, so I had to turn down that request.

"Keh-heh-heh-heh-heh... In that case, allow me to—"

"Denied."

I don't even want to imagine a scenario where Diablo lost, but still, no. My policy here is to wait and see until we can create a situation where we're totally sure we can win. That much, as I reminded everyone in the room, I wanted to be thorough with.

Intelligence is really the most important thing, though, isn't it? I can't even count the number of failures we've had because of lack of information. We gotta keep our ears open right now, so we don't fall into the same trap again.

"So you guys were sticking with Masayuki because it let you get close to me without attracting suspicion, right? Honestly, I had no idea at all. And the timing of that attack was incredibly dangerous for me."

I was talking to Bernie and Jiwu. They might've been acting on Damrada's orders, but it really was a perfect strategy, one not even Raphael picked up on. I had to applaud them for that, enemy or not. I'm sure they had opportunities to target me before then, but it couldn't have been easy for them to keep their maximum fighting skills under wraps until that one critical moment. We had the upper hand this time, maybe, but things could've easily gone the other way, and the emperor would've gotten exactly what he wanted. Tempest without Benimaru and me would fall into total disarray, and the Empire would've instantly overrun it.

"My pride got the best of me there. I was laboring under the assumption that the labyrinth is always safe. I need to remember that, during war, there is always another danger to consider."

"Me as well. I will be sure to more thoroughly vet anyone who gets close to Sir Rimuru."

Benimaru and Soei must've been hung up about that, but I can't pin this on them alone. They had always been way more vigilant than I ever was, anticipating every potential eventuality. I just didn't have my ears up for danger at all, and that was something I needed to improve on.

"Sir Damrada was the one who ordered us to protect Masayuki. He never told me what for, and I don't think that order could've leaked out anywhere."

"Me neither. We didn't receive our orders at the same time; it was through different channels so we wouldn't know each other's real identities. I didn't know Bernie was a Single Digit until the assassination order came for you, Lord Rimuru."

Now Bernie and Jiwu were a full part of the conversation. I made it clear they had a right to remain silent, so I appreciated their willingness to talk for me. But something about these statements bothered me.

"Do you mean you didn't know or that you didn't remember until just then?"

"No, I've never met another Single Digit besides myself. I only learned Jiwu was one as well when I got that order."

"Same here. I don't think any of them know each other's true identity except for the commander and vice commander."

That was a surprise. The Empire's best forces don't even know each other at all? Why are they leaving them in the dark like that?

Understood. Presumably it is for the purpose of preventing treachery.

Mmm... If they don't know each other's identities, they can't conspire to overthrow their bosses. That's just *beyond* thorough. It shows how careful they are to protect the emperor's safety, I guess.

"I can understand that, I suppose, but it strikes me as pretty wasteful and inefficient. If you two were acquainted, you could've been working together against me from the very beginning."

My statement elicited a chuckle from Gadora. "Sir Rimuru, may I speak frankly and with the utmost of respect for you?"

"Sure, of course. Anything's welcome."

"Very well. If I may, Sir Rimuru, you possess a great deal of intelligence, but I fear that you are not very careful at times. I know this man Damrada very well, and I'll inform you that he's a cunning fellow. He doesn't even trust his own subordinates, and for him, caution is his lifelong mantra."

Sounds like Raphael was right—they arranged it that way to prevent any conspiracies. I knew Damrada was one of the three leaders of Cerberus and a man who trusted money and nothing else, but I guess he was that way with everything in his life, huh? And he was one of the highest-ranking Single Digits as well?

"I've never met him before, but he sounds like a pretty bad guy. Given his approach to killing Gadora, I figured he had to be a Single Digit... And if he was in a position to give orders to you two, Bernie and Jiwu, does that mean Damrada's the head of the group?"

"No," Gadora replied. "Damrada is likely the vice commander. I am all but certain the commander is Tatsuya Kondo."

Right. The director of the Imperial Intelligence Bureau and one of the people Gadora had his eye on. Gadora said he didn't know him very well, but despite the lack of information, he seemed fairly certain about that based on Damrada's true identity. Having all this exposed left the imperials in the room despondent.

Bernie and Jiwu were giving me all sorts of useful info; they must've figured there's no point hiding it any longer. They said Gadora was right—that Damrada is the vice commander of the Imperial Guardians, ranked Number Two in the whole Empire. We weren't sure if Kondo was the leader yet, but there's no doubting that Damrada's still way up there in the hierarchy.

Good job, Gadora, I thought as I listened to them.

"And to tell the truth, the attack on Lord Rimuru wasn't a command from Sir Damrada but actually a secret order from Commander Kondo."

"It was for me, too. It was weird, I thought, because it overrode our orders to guard Masayuki."

Jiwu explained to me that she had prepared a backstory for herself where her home village was rescued by Masayuki. That way, he'd instantly trust her, and then she'd be "repaying the favor" by guarding him.

"Well, if you were going to blow your covers at the same time, wouldn't it have been better to work together from the start?"

"...I agree with you, yes. I believe he was using Masayuki to keep from arousing your suspicion, because it certainly was the perfect opportunity to kill you..."

Looking back on it, Bernie realized that he had some questions about the whole thing. Assuming there were no lies in their tale, and considering the overall situation, it might have been that Damrada and the commander had different objectives. Damrada organized this entire undercover operation; it'd be odd for him to order its total abandonment. Maybe it was a sacrifice made to improve their chances of success, but even so, I was sure there could've been another way. I thought it was natural for Bernie and Jiwu to wonder about that—and to suspect some underlying reason for it.

"By the way, have any of you Empire guys ever seen Emperor Ludora's face?"

The question suddenly occurred to me, so I asked it. Only Gadora raised his hand.

"You're kidding me. You don't know what the man you serve looks like?"

Benimaru sounded pretty surprised.

"Well, Boss, *you* don't act much like any other ruler," Kaijin said. "You're social enough to go eating and drinking around town, and you're always willing to chat with anyone who wants to. That's just weird!"

"Oh, come on!"

"Hey, no disrespect intended. King Gazel has that side to him, too, although he's a bit stricter with his behavior than you. But you know, royals and nobles kinda like a little more...*prestige* in their lives, right? And I think a good number of them prefer keeping their faces away from the little folk."

"Huh..."

"What Sir Kaijin said makes sense to me," noted Rigurd, "but I'm still not sure I really understand it. That is to say, hiding your face from the people who're supposed to be guarding you, even... Isn't that a little too excessive?"

"Well, yeah, even I thought that was going way too far," Kaijin agreed.

"It *is* weird, innit?"

"Not weird," Hakuro said to Gobta, "so much as abnormal. Um, Bernie, was it? May I ask you a question?"

"What do you want to know?"

"Why is it that the emperor's own guardians don't even know what he looks like? How are you meant to guard him, then?"

Being exposed to that sharp gaze of Hakuro's made Bernie sit back up, attempting to rally himself. "Well, it's simple. Only people ranked sixth or greater have seen His Majesty in person. Our commander and vice commander are often out on other business, but the remaining four accompany our emperor at all times."

The members of this quartet were apparently referred to as the Four Knights, and all of them were so formidable that, as far as Bernie and Jiwu knew, none of them had been replaced in many, many years.

"So the two of you weren't quite as trusted as those four, then? Are you inferior to these Four Knights in ability as well?"

Hakuro certainly wasn't shying away from the tough questions. It seemed to frustrate Bernie a little.

"You...could take it that way, yes. Trying to defeat any of those four would be an uphill battle for me. Plus, His Majesty is also attended to by the juggernaut we discussed before—the fearsome Imperial Marshal, someone I'd never have a chance against. In fact, I'm not sure the rest of the Single Digits together could even score a victory against this menace."

There's that so-called juggernaut again.

So far, we know about Kondo, Damrada, the Four Knights, and this Marshal figure, huh? That makes seven, and if you add Bernie and Jiwu to that, you've got nine people—one for each "single digit," so to speak. But hang on—if the cutoff for access to the emperor was Single Digit Number Six, then the Marshal must not be a ranked member, technically. That means there's still one more unknown Single Digit out there—in other words, eight people I better stay on my guard for in all. And if Kondo wasn't actually the commander, that'd be one more figure to add to the mix. Worrying, indeed.

Learning about that was good and all, but I wanted to ascertain something else first.

"You know, I heard from Gadora that Masayuki and Emperor Ludora look exactly alike."

Gadora nodded. The rest of the meeting hall considered this for a few moments.

"And Damrada ordered you to protect Masayuki, right? And he arranged things so that both of you would be in the dark about each other and nobody would suspect anything. But after all that trouble, you received an order that abandoned the entire setup. Is it me, or are Damrada and the Single Digit commander working against each other here?"

I was pretty sure about this by now, so I went ahead and said it out loud. If I had to guess, it seemed likely Damrada really *was* trying to keep Masayuki safe. Why? I don't know, but the fact that he and the emperor are spitting images of each other must have something to do with it.

"But you said you were using Masayuki, right?"

"Right. I had no idea why we were asked to protect him, keep in mind. That's why I didn't question the commander's order at all."

"Me neither. Sir Damrada never explained his reasoning at all."

They were using Masayuki to get closer to me. If Damrada ordered them to do so, it would've made sense—but then the commander had to stick their neck in. This brought up another question I had to ask.

"So do you think the commander's aware of Masayuki's resemblance to the emperor?"

"Hmm… That's a good question," Gadora said. "But if the commander is Kondo, as I believe he is, then he most certainly would have known."

"We do know this man Kondo, although I can't surmise what his situation was at the time. The stories say he's a very sly man, who has an iron grip on all the intelligence the Empire has."

"Yes, in his capacity as head of the IIB, he's been called a mysterious figure stalking the halls of information. The IIB and military have never been on very friendly terms with each other, and I had a hard time dealing with him, too. We had tried launching hostilities against him several times, but they all ended in failure. That alone is proof that he's far from ordinary."

Funny how Caligulio was trying to fudge the details, only to have Minitz reveal everything anyway. It was clear that, to the imperial military, Kondo was seen as a wild card and a threat—and if he could get the better of someone as talented as Minitz, he was a force to be reckoned with.

"*I* could certainly never beat him anyway."

Old man Gadora, despite appearances, is no slouch in battle. By my estimation, he might rank up there with a Saint in strength. His magicule count isn't all that high, but he more than makes up for it with his casting skills. If someone like him claims he can't win, then Kondo must be at least Saint level, a titan up there with Hinata or King Gazel. Besides, Bernie and Jiwu were Saints as well, and Caligulio went and got himself awakened. Without an ultimate skill to call his own, Gadora probably couldn't have beaten any of them.

So now I knew that Kondo's a danger in a fight and a master of spycraft. And he must have known about Masayuki, I imagine.

"But if Kondo was aware of Masayuki," I said, "perhaps he had different intentions from Damrada, huh? Bernie and Jiwu's attack was so massive, it's clear they didn't really care if Masayuki lived or died. That's totally at odds with Damrada's order."

"Well..."

Bernie had a bit of trouble picking his words.

"...To tell the truth, what the commander told us exactly was to get rid of Masayuki as well, since he'd no longer be useful."

Such was their orders, but after traveling together and building something of an attachment, they were both hesitant to just kill the guy. Hence they decided to put off discussing his fate until they were finished with me. If they could hide him somewhere, then perfect; if not, the idea they had was to magically erase his memories instead.

Anyway, it was all crystal clear to me now.

"So we know that something's definitely up with Masayuki. I know he's not gonna like this, but I think he'll need to be kept under guard for a little while. Can I have you handle that, Soei?"

"Yes, sir."

Right. I knew I could count on him.

"Let's assume that Damrada and the commander have different agendas, then. One of them wants to protect Masayuki; the other one wants him dead. We don't know why yet, of course, but clearly there's a conflict here."

"Yes. And if we can find a way to take advantage of this, it could be a great windfall for us."

"I don't think it'll be that easy... But the fact that our enemy isn't a monolith is itself good news."

You think so? I guess. If you're having trouble distinguishing friend from foe, then you have to assume everybody's a foe. But let's get some more information before we decide on matters.

✳

Now that I knew what was going on with Bernie and Jiwu, I wanted to talk about the factions within the Empire. Not the military, exactly, but the other higher-ups with access to ultimate skills.

"All right. Can you tell me more about the Single Digits?"

Bernie obliged. "Sure. There are only nine Single Digits at any given time. For someone stronger to take up a position, it's quite likely someone else would need to be forcibly kicked out of their rank."

Hmm. Meaning that there's not that much difference in strength among the top Single Digits?

"You mean that it's possible for, say, numbers nine and ten to swap spots?"

"No," he said with a shake of his head. "Rank number eleven is a sort of auxiliary Single Digit, while number ten is a substitute. If someone drops out of the Single Digits, one of those two can take their place, but only on a temporary basis."

So there was a pretty insurmountable gap between ninth and tenth, then? Sounds like the clincher is whether you've got an ultimate skill. Only if you're awakened, and that awakening nets you an ultimate, would you be considered for the Single Digits. Bernie, by the way, is ranked seventh, with Jiwu coming in ninth—which means I had to look out for numbers one through six, number eight, and this Marshal guy, too.

Meanwhile, the two of them didn't know much about Damrada's faction. They didn't even know who besides themselves were Single Digits, so I doubted they were lying about that. But I wanted to know more about other people anyway, so hopefully they could give me something useful.

"Number ten, the substitute, is kept on call within Empire territory at all times, so they can spring into action the moment something comes up. Meanwhile, Imperial Knights ranked eleventh or below are assigned to groups of three and tasked with solving Empire-level cases and crises."

As Bernie put it, Number Ten was a pretty powerful guy as well—no ultimate skill, but still maybe as strong as an awakened demon lord. With the remaining ninety Imperial Knights, you saw a pretty big talent gap between the twenties and the ranks below that, but even so, you had to be at least Enlightened class to become a member. Some of the people up top could rank pretty close to Saint level. If the Eastern Empire wanted to boost the Imperial Guardians' overall strength, they'd likely have to stage a war pitting them against multiple demon lords at once.

"Are you kidding me?" Minitz countered. "They want to wage war against someone who defeated us without losing a single soldier?"

"Yeah. The fact that a hundred Imperial Guardians are more of a threat than a million-strong army sure gives me pause, though."

"Well," Bernie said with a sigh, "that's how it is. The imperial army serves mostly as a visual threat to people, after all. The

Empire needs a visible, public sort of deterrent for the unwitting fools who can't comprehend what *real* strength is."

I could tell he was talking about more than a threat to the nations in the west. It applied to the Empire's own subjects as well, people who paid taxes in exchange for guaranteed safety. If the Empire told them a hundred people were all they really needed to defend the land, that'd make anyone uneasy. In this case, quantity truly *did* mean something important—after all, offense is one thing, but when defending, you need numbers. The more bases you have to maintain, the more personnel you need to defend them. In that sense, the Empire's policy actually seems pretty sound.

"You know, in the past, the main purpose of our standing army was defense. We'd use only our elite forces to attack other nations and sap their will to fight. Once their work was done, we'd send the army over to establish rule in the name of the emperor. At some point, however, we began to dispatch our army first. I've always wondered why they did that, actually. It never occurred to me that it was so they could 'manufacture' more awakened people..."

Gadora seemed convinced. In fact, this sounded like a pretty important secret to me. Now I think I'm beginning to see Emperor Ludora's objectives.

"So victory wasn't the point of this whole invasion in the first place, was it? And Sir Caligulio *did* become awakened, along with several others whom I think came close. I think Emperor Ludora's true mission was to add more fighting pawns to his collection."

Benimaru must've reached the same conclusion I did. And Bernie was getting more talkative, too.

"You're right. There were several people in this invasion deemed likely to awaken—not just General Caligulio, but also Major General Minitz, Colonel Kanzis, and Krishna and a few others, too. My orders specified that I should work with the newly awakened to find an escape route once the dust settled... But really, this is the first time I've seen the commander's plans go *this* haywire."

He accompanied that with a little chuckle, but I sure wasn't laughing. If *that* many people awakened on us, we would've had more than just a tough battle on our hands. Besides, now that we knew the Empire was trying to awaken more of its troops, we had to admit that our assumptions about them were completely wrong. I thought they went to war because they were confident about beating us and the Western Nations, after all. Raphael agreed with me on that, and it certainly seemed logical to me, but...

...Report. Definitive conclusion failed due to a lack of information. This will be redefined later to achieve perfection.

I felt a hint of embarrassment from Raphael there. But asking it to read *that* deep was far too much to hope for, and I wasn't about to do that. So no harm, no foul this time, I'd say—just as long as we can use this experience for next time.

Acknowledged. I will review the information so nothing is overlooked.

Great. I'm counting on you, okay? Really.

I'll need Raphael as a reference on the Empire's future movements. For now, though, let's discuss our takes on these new revelations.

"So Ludora was collecting awakened people for his group of elite fighters. I don't like admitting it much, but it seems like he can grant them ultimate skills, like he did with Bernie and Jiwu. Then you've got my group, the Octagram, and the assorted champions of the Western Nations. The emperor's trying to gather enough people to crush them all at once and conquer the world, isn't he?"

Benimaru and Diablo both agreed.

"It's quite a headache, but it sounds right to me. And that's why any non-awakened soldiers mean next to nothing for him."

"Mmm, yes. Humans are inherently weak creatures, but possessing even one ultimate skill could put them on more equal footing with the likes of us."

"Tough to admit, isn't it?"

"I am not enjoying the thought, no."

"Hey, it's fine, right? If those skills are *that* useful, then we can just learn them, too, and we're good."

"It'd make fighting far less interesting, wouldn't it?"

"Keh-heh-heh-heh-heh... That's rather backward thinking, isn't it, Testarossa? If our foe fails to possess such powers, then there's no need to use them, is there? That was the thought process behind the ultimate skill I procured for myself, after all."

"What?"

"Hey, that's not fair!"

"Quit getting a leg up on us like that!"

"Ah, such delicious jealousy from the have-nots! I used to ignore Guy instead of letting him taste my envy, I'll have you know."

Diablo's a pretty selfish guy, isn't he? I thought he was backing me up here, but now this conversation's going in stranger and stranger directions. If we don't stop this, Testarossa and her friends are gonna start acting *real* dangerous before long.

"Getting back to the topic," Rigurd said, "is it safe to assume that you think the Empire's objective is to weed out the strong from the weak, Sir Rimuru?"

"Yeah, I'm with the boss on that one. This world's full of people with superhuman force, starting with King Gazel and continuing on with Hinata and Her Excellency, Emperor Elmesia. Keeping these giants protected was what kept the balance of power in the world stable. And if they can build enough numbers to break that balance, well, that's when the *real* fun begins, ain't it?"

Rigurd and Kaijin both got me perfectly.

"Aha. So they pitted strong against strong, surrounding their allies with people who can assist them. That way, the weak wouldn't get in their way."

"Wow. Pretty awful. But at least the weak don't have much work to do."

"Yes, it'd be a blessing for the weak if it only took the strong to settle wars. But accepting all these sacrifices in order to create more strongmen truly does go against my aesthetic senses..."

Hearing Gabil's and my other friends' reactions made Caligulio and Minitz wince a bit. They were both neck-deep in that whole scene, and now the sheer madness of the operation was probably sinking in. Plus, I think Hakuro was right just now. War really *should* be fought only by people eager to fight. It's crazy to get weaker people involved… But of course, the world doesn't always work that way.

"By the way," Gadora said, "I seem to recall that kid Yuuki saying that the demon lord Guy wasn't happy to see the Empire gaining strength. They say he's the strongest demon lord of all, so I found it rather odd that he'd be so concerned."

Certainly, if they had ultimate skills on hand, maybe they had what it took to hurt Guy. It's only natural for him to be wary.

"Guy's objective is to unite the world under the rule of the demon lords, after all. The Empire is directly clashing against that, so it's far more than just a conflict of interest between them. But…"

"That's odd, though. How can someone as arrogant as Guy allow the Empire to keep existing?"

"The stronger the opponent, the more engaging the fight, after all. But Guy's being surprisingly slow to act. If he was able to, I imagine he would have promptly gone out himself to lay waste to all those fools…"

Diablo, Ultima, and Carrera all had their questions. Testarossa had the answer.

"Oh, that's easy. It's because Lady Velgrynd lives in their territory, and if he messes with the Empire, he might get on her bad side. That's why I was similarly on my best behavior in imperial lands."

Caligulio gave her a surprised look.

"*That* was your best behavior?" Minitz muttered softly.

I don't know what Testarossa was up to over there, but it's none of my business. I don't want to start being assigned blame for events that happened way before my time, so I let it slide.

The name Velgrynd piqued my curiosity. Could that be—?

"Hmm. Surprising. Blanc—er, Lady Testarossa, showing respect for the Flame Dragon from the Divine Aerie of Fire?"

Minitz was clearly trying to change the subject as rapidly as possible—Testarossa's "come again?" smile probably unnerved him. But now I was convinced I knew who Velgrynd was. Here we had a True Dragon, one of four in the world; Veldora's flame-wrangling elder sister. So *that* was the Empire's ace in the hole…

"I wouldn't call it respect, no. The relationship between our kind and the True Dragons was...somewhat complicated. But since our master, Sir Rimuru, and Sir Veldora are both on our side, it'd only be natural to pay our respects to his sister as well, wouldn't it?"

Um, so if it wasn't for their current relationship with Veldora and me, the demonesses wouldn't show any respect at all for True Dragons?

"Hang on, Testarossa. So you stayed on your 'best behavior' because you couldn't beat Velgrynd? Or could even Guy beat her?"

"Strictly speaking, no, I could not. Guy I cannot speak for, but victory would have been impossible for me. It's not a matter of strength, though. The True Dragons are immortal beings; there's no overcoming that unfair advantage."

Testarossa was the epitome of unfairness in battle, I thought, but now she was using that term for this True Dragon. What could Velgrynd be like, even? I just hope none of this talk gets back to Veldora, though. I could already hear his haughty laughter in my mind.

"Sure. So maybe not even a True Dragon's a threat for Guy, but he still can't fully destroy them, huh?"

"Hmm... I don't know. Not with magic, at least."

If you can't kill them, it doesn't count as a win—that seemed to be the standard for demons, and if it was, there was never any beating a True Dragon. And I think Veldora told me before about how his race can always resurrect themselves after death. A demon could be eliminated by crushing their heart core, but in the case of True Dragons, they'd still come back to life anyway, although their personality and part of their memories would be reset, I guess. Maybe some True Dragons can retain those memories, though, like some demons can. If so, that'd render them truly immortal.

"I see. And if the Empire has someone like that for us, we can't afford to make any ill-advised moves."

What Velgrynd was to Guy I couldn't say, but to us, she was absolutely a threat. But when I voiced that concern, Caligulio shot me a confused look—and then he, Minitz, Jiwu, and Bernie spoke up in order.

"If I may, my lord... As far as I know, the Empire has enshrined

Lady Velgrynd as its official guardian dragon. If you look back in history as well, this dragon has protected us from attack by the angels. However…"

"However, she stays with the Empire only because they offer her tribute. It's merely a whim on her part."

"She is a beautiful, noble dragon of crimson, and she symbolizes the prosperity of the Empire as a whole. We in the Single Digits are granted an audience with her after His Majesty accepts us. There, we have her learn our names and appearances, and we swear that we will never defy her."

"Yes, I went through the same ceremony. I'd have to be insane to defy her. No one could ever win that battle."

So the Empire and Velgrynd were connected, but not in such a way that the Empire could ask her for any favors, I guess. Also, something about Bernie's reaction bothered me a bit. More than a bit, actually. A whole lot.

"Hey, um, you don't have to answer this if you don't want to, but you said that nobody could beat the Marshal, right? But who would win in a fight between that guy and Velgrynd?"

"…Sorry?"

"Let me rephrase that. In your dealings with them both, have you ever gotten, like, a similar vibe from the two of them, or that kind of thing?"

"Are you…?"

Bernie understood what I was getting at. He attempted to laugh it off but failed. I also noticed Jiwu going pale next to him, lost in thought. Now I was sure of it. This Marshal was actually Velgrynd the Flame Dragon… And there was no doubt that she was the reason why the demon lord Guy hadn't attacked the Empire. That—and the Empire might have had some other threat that rivals this dragon—otherwise, Velgrynd alone seemed like too weak a reason for Guy to sit on his hands.

I turned toward our big screen and let out a sigh.

"Well, great. So if we make any kind of misstep, we'll incur the wrath of Velgrynd, huh? Send out an army, and she could annihilate the whole thing in one go. In that case, working with Yuuki's force to invade the Empire would be incredibly reckless."

Intelligence gathering really *is* important. Becoming aware of Velgrynd at this point prevented me from stepping on a huge landmine. I wanted to win peace from the Empire, but staging a reverse invasion right now would be a fool's errand.

"But if Sir Veldora's sister is our enemy," Benimaru said, "I'm not sure anyone among us would be capable of defeating her. Perhaps we could have Sir Veldora intervene on our behalf?"

It sounded a bit like a cop-out, but give the question some calm thought, and that's the logical conclusion. True Dragons are an existence beyond gods, even, and anyone who thinks they could fight and win against one simply isn't facing reality.

"Ooh, I dunno about that. I hesitate to get Veldora involved in our personal affairs."

I didn't want to ask Veldora for this—I'm sure he'd be reluctant to fight his own sister, for one. But that just made our next move more difficult to work out.

"I will need to inform my boy Yuuki about this, I think. He can hardly keep his army deployed out there forever."

"Good point. We're gonna have to rework our entire strategy now, so we'll need to get in touch with Yuuki ASAP."

Hmm. I pondered over this. But then my problem child Diablo dropped another bombshell.

"This sounds like a problem for Guy as well, so I've reached out to him. I think he'll arrive here shortly, so why don't we listen to what *he* has to say?"

Huh?

I couldn't help but fix Diablo with a cold, sullen stare. He gave me a bashful look back, which almost made me want to kill him. Right when I was troubled the most, this idiot goes way the hell out of line like this...

"You called him?"

"Yes!"

No, *not* "yes"!

But I couldn't ignore reality, so I adjourned the meeting and began getting ready for Guy's visit.

*

Guy was clearly in a foul mood from the moment he arrived.

"Hey. I'm here. You got a lot of guts callin' me all this way, you know."

Yeah, really. But can you say that to Diablo, please, not me?

Guy plopped down roughly on his chair. He had been taken to our more luxurious reception room in the guest house to avoid offending him any further, but maybe that was premature of me. This was a house that we only opened up to the chosen few—royalty, nobility, that sort of thing. If he started taking his frustrations out on our furnishings, we'd be eating a lot of money in damages.

The decor in here was selected by Mjöllmile, who always had a good eye for that kinda thing; he imported fixtures from all over the world, and some of them were as artistic as they were valuable. It all matched with my tastes as well, so most of the pieces were more quietly elegant than "I'm rich"-type fancy. That Japanese sense of *wabi-sabi*, or quiet, simple refinement. Mjöllmile did a great job sticking to that theme, I think. Rigurd and his kin were still too inexperienced to reach this level of good taste; they never got to interact with artwork before, so understanding the quality of things would take them some more time. But Rigurd also said "It's so relaxing, being in here" when he paid it a visit, so maybe we have matching tastes, after all.

Regardless, if Guy starts getting violent, I'll deal with it then. We didn't have anywhere else suitable enough for entertaining him, so maybe at least a little damage was inevitable. There was no way I'd do something as suicidal as entertain the world's strongest demon lord in a bare-bones waiting room.

His chair was creaking ominously already. It was another first-rate piece of furniture, carved from fragrant wood. A soft sofa is always nice, but there's nothing like a good wooden chair that can adjust itself to virtually any body type. It makes you feel like you're surrounded by lush, inviting force, at peace with nature.

If he broke it, I'd have him pay for it—but now I was doubly glad I dismissed everybody else from the meeting.

The imperial group was back on Floor 70 for the time being, Gabil escorting them down; he'd be watching over them while Adalmann was absent. Soei was busy arranging for Masayuki's security, while Rigurd was touching base with the relevant authorities to ensure the city was running fine while quarantined in the labyrinth. Kaijin, after conferring with Vester, was having him inform King Gazel of our meeting and its results; I didn't want to hide anything from him, so we'd be in touch later. Gadora, meanwhile, was reaching out to Yuuki, reasoning that he needed to know about the current situation as they worked out a future course of action. Gobta and Hakuro were on standby in a nearby room, along with the three demonesses, just in case something flared up. It'd be safer to keep them out of Guy's sight, because who knows *what* would happen if you mixed them all together, so that was what I decided to do.

So there were four of us in the reception room—Diablo (the original perpetrator), Benimaru, Shion, and me. Guy had brought along three women of his own. One, seated next to him, had a face that reminded me of Milim's. Her white hair possessed a brilliant sheen, her eyes a deep blue that seemed to absorb anyone who gazed into them. She was surprisingly beautiful, but depending on how you looked at her, she could also be mistaken for a child. It was strange—and given how she casually sat next to Guy, they must have been on equal footing, and I knew only a small number of people like that. If I had to guess...

"This is the first time you met, isn't it? Lemme introduce you, Rimuru. This is Velzard, Veldora's elder sister. The Ice Dragon is probably a more suitable name for her, but either way, don't forget it."

"A pleasure to meet you, Sir Rimuru. I am Velzard. Perhaps you've heard the name Velzard the Ice Dragon before? I knew you were taking care of my brother for me, so I've been meaning to say hello to you."

Well, I was right. She was Veldora's sister, one of the four all-powerful True Dragons—Velzard the Ice Dragon, in the flesh. That graceful bow to me was so beautiful; just seeing her sit so gracefully on her chair was a sight to behold. She seemed to enjoy the scent of the wood, too... But as elegant as her smile was, it still sent a cold sweat running down my back.

Hanging out with Veldora all the time made me think I was used to handling True Dragons, but this lady was just bad news. The danger was just palpable; it would have been more appropriate to call her a being from another dimension. Veldora had only recently grown capable of controlling his aura with decent precision. I figured he had it down perfectly, but seeing Velzard before me, I understood just how naive I was. This woman made aura control look incredibly natural. I couldn't sense any of it at all, which showed just how well she could handle it. If she didn't introduce herself as such, I never would've known she was a True Dragon. In fact, I may've even thought she was a normal human being. There was no hiding that beauty and dominance, though, so I never would've looked down on her.

"Ah, hello. My name is Rimuru, and maybe I don't look it, but I'm demon-lording it up around here. Your brother's been a ton of help to me."

Why do I always sound like such a putz whenever I introduce myself to people? And why does Raphael always clam up at times like these? It was so absurd, I thought, but I still tried to keep smiling.

"Aw, how humble of you! There's no need to be so protective of him."

Velzard let out a pleasant, high-pitched laugh. As soon as she did, her mature atmosphere dissipated, and the impression she made resembled a cute little girl's. Honestly, she looks like she's high school age and no older—she really *is* related to Milim. Thankfully, that smile did a lot to ease the heavy atmosphere.

Then we all introduced each other. The other two women in Guy's entourage were Mizeri the Original Green, whom I met before, and Raine the Original Blue, whom I hadn't. They were in their "dark maid" uniforms as usual, standing behind Guy with flawless posture. They were the same rank of demon as Diablo, but looking at the prudent step back they took, it sure didn't seem that way. They *were* Primals, though, the strongest of demons and nothing a mere Demon Peer could compare to.

Better be careful I don't exhibit any bad manners around them, I thought as I carefully wrapped up the intros. Benimaru, seated next to me, was the picture of politeness, but I was nervous through Shion's entire greeting. With Diablo, I felt like someone trying to dismantle a live bomb. I wondered why I decided to take *this* group in, but it was too late to do anything about it.

✳

Once we were all seated, I asked Shuna, who guided everyone in here, to make some tea for us. She did so without any sign of agitation, a seasoned pro when it came to hospitality. And not just her— all our servants were doing their jobs as usual, as if it didn't matter who they were serving. Real professionals, all of them, and I'm sure I was watching Vester's strict training bear fruit here.

After taking a sip of Shuna's tea, I got down to business.

"So the reason I invited you here is because I wanted to ask you something, Guy."

"Oh?"

"Um, so the Empire invaded my country, and I defeated them and stuff. I was thinking about staging an invasion of my own, but then I heard the Empire has Velgrynd—er, Velzard's younger sister, I suppose. And judging from everything else I've heard, it sounds like there's some manner of connection between you and the Empire as well...?"

"Huh. Smart of you to notice."

Guy flashed me an excited grin. I had the worst feeling about all this. I really wish I didn't have to delve any deeper, but things weren't gonna work out that way.

"So you wanted to interfere with the Empire's attempts at powering up their army, right? That's why you let Yuuki live, too, I bet.

I'm sure you didn't want the Western Nations to fall, but it wasn't only that, yes? You called it a game, but who are you playing this game with?"

I pretended that this was just casual curiosity on my part. In reality, though, a lot hinged on this. If the Empire boasted both Velgrynd and some other threat equal to her, I needed to know about it. If we attacked while still oblivious to this, there was an excellent chance some of my friends would've died. So I asked him, my eyes staring right into Guy's.

"Heh-heh-heh… Good, good. If you've picked up on that much, why don't I tell you the whole thing?"

Nice to see Guy wasn't interested in lording it over me here. Scary, too, in a way. I listened on.

"To tell the truth, I have a bet going with a certain guy I know. This guy has a habit of going on about these crazy ideals of his, and I wanna present him with a little reality check. So we agreed that we'd never directly fight each other, but to use only the pieces we have on hand."

In other words, they'd be letting other people do the fighting—and whoever defeated all their opponent's pawns first wins.

"What kind of pieces are these…?"

I already had my hunches about this, actually.

"Heh. They're you guys."

Yeah. Thought so. I kinda wish he'd stop treating me as his game piece, but no point complaining about that here. Let's just work through this and get as much useful information as we can.

"So is the person you're playing in this game the imperial emperor?"

I was sure of it already but still felt I should check just in case. Guy had Velzard at his side, so it followed that the person with Velgrynd at their side was Guy's opponent. That may not necessarily have been the emperor, though, so I wanted Guy to confirm it for me.

"You got it. Emperor Ludora is an admitted rival of mine."

He had no intention of hiding it. In fact, he sounded happy to tell me. And if *rival* is the word he chose, should I assume Ludora is just as strong as Guy? I really can't win against him, can I? And there's nothing I hate more than playing a game where I've got no apparent path to victory.

"If I could say something…"

As I held my head in my hands, Benimaru was bold enough to speak up in Guy's presence.

"Sure."

"Then, I'd like to ask—what are the conditions for victory in this game? Do we have to defeat Emperor Ludora, or do we just have to subdue all his pieces? I'd like to have more exact guidance."

Ah yes, that *is* important. I assumed beating Ludora was my only way out, but if beating his pawns—in other words, neutralizing the Empire's force—was all that mattered, I liked my chances a lot more. We'd still have a lot of nasty dudes to fight, but that still beat tangling with someone on Guy's level.

"Keh-heh-heh-heh-heh… Perhaps eliminating Guy would be another way to win the—"

""Are you *that* stupid?!""

Guy and I shouted in unison. Honestly, Diablo just exhausts me. He must have exhausted Guy as well, because we wound up giving each other knowing looks. I didn't expect to establish a rapport with him this way, so thanks, Diablo. I seriously can't have you offending him right now, so my rating of you just plummeted straight for the basement, but thanks.

"So," I said after advising Diablo to shut up for a while, "how would you answer Benimaru's question, Guy?"

Guy, instead of answering, looked straight at me. The moment his lips curled upward into a grin, my sense of danger went into overdrive.

"Rimuruuuu…"

Oh, man. I got the worst premonition right then. In fact, it was beyond a premonition. Now I understood when Mjöllmile looked a little confused the first few times I called him Mollie. I'm sure I'm making the same face right now.

"You know, I have a favor I'd like to ask of you…"

"No."

"Well, hear me out."

I wish he'd hear *me* out first. But this is Guy we're talking about. It'd never be smart to anger someone with this much potential for violence, so I had no choice but to listen on. Mjöllmile always heeded my requests, no matter how confused he looked about them, but I had absolutely no intention of honoring Guy's.

"Basically, I want you to stop that bastard Ludora. I'm not saying you have to defeat him, but just do something about all his pieces and help me win this, okay?"

He couldn't have looked eviler if he tried. Then he stood up and walked behind me, rubbing my shoulders as he continued.

"You'll do that for me, won't you?"

He started applying more force.

This is coercion, isn't it?

"If I say yes, what's in it for me?"

If this was one of those offers I couldn't refuse, I at least wanted to negotiate a better deal. Maybe this was suicidal against someone like Guy, but I decided to work him as much as I could.

"You know that the world balance I've been maintaining is now thoroughly wrecked because of you, right? What do you think about that?"

"Sorry."

In an instant, I was completely defeated. I was trying my best to build a new balance right now, but I'm certain that it was me who took most of the power from Guy's side. To put it more bluntly, bringing Testarossa and the other demonesses under my wing was a bad idea. If I turned down Guy's requests at this point, I was opening myself up to the risk of being seen as an enemy.

So my hands thoroughly tied, I gave up and accepted the offer.

∗

Just as Guy returned to his seat, there was a knock on the door. It opened to reveal Shuna, the aroma of tea drifting in the air and dispelling the tension. She also had some slices of cake on a tray, so we took a break. I've already decided there's no escape for me, so I

promise this isn't me procrastinating on my problems. Shuna had more tea and cake in the next room over, so my two secretaries and his two maids went over there. I thought they'd gripe about that, but they were surprisingly obedient about it.

I took a sip of Shuna's tea. It had a soft, gentle flavor. Testarossa's tea was all but complete perfection, but this was rather tasty as well, in a comforting way.

"Huh. This is pretty good, isn't it?"

I was glad to hear Guy was satisfied.

"Oh, you're right. And this cake is more than just a bunch of sugar—there's so many layers of depth to it. The tea has a lovely, full-bodied aroma, but the bitterness only serves to enhance the sweetness."

Velzard seemed to like it, too. That's a relief.

"Yeah. This room's got some nice decoration, too, doesn't it? I really dig furnishings like these."

I wasn't expecting to hear that from Guy. A tyrant like him would've been the last person in the world, I thought, to understand stuff like *wabi-sabi*. Guess I really need to stop judging people on preconceived notions like that. They say that the warlord Oda Nobunaga was into this sort of look as well. He liked to spend time in tea rooms where he didn't have to worry about his social status; maybe he valued the ability to reflect on matters over some tea that way. I'm just making all that up, but still, I guess showing Guy in here was the right move, after all.

Feeling a little more at ease, I decided to elicit some more feedback.

"Oh, yeah? I'm glad you like it. You're actually the first people I've entertained in here. It's the most extravagant reception room we have, so I only show it off to people I wanna impress."

"Yeah? Trying to make yourself look good around me?"

"I sure am. Can't really be a demon lord if I didn't, y'know? If I was willing to abandon all my pride, I'd just spend my life sneaking around in the shadows instead. Which would've been fun, maybe, but…"

Right. So a quick jab to start. Show him that I wasn't at his total mercy before I heard him out. Depending on his reaction, I'd adjust how I dealt with him. But Guy just laughed at how much I was overcompensating.

"Ah-ha-ha! Trying to feel out the likes of *me*, eh? Hilarious!"

It wasn't, but at least I knew I was still wrapped around his finger now.

"Yeah, thanks."

"But no, no worries. What I want from you, you know, it'll help you guys as well, all right? I just want you to keep the war going and destroy the Empire."

Guy paused to take a graceful sip of his tea. He's totally in his element here, like some kind of fairy-tale king. I mean, demon lords pretty much *are* kings (or queens) in this world, but regardless. But how Guy-like to throw me a fastball straight down the middle like that, huh?

"In other words, you want me to reduce Ludora's pawns to zero without killing him? Given your apparent reluctance to answer Benimaru's question, I'm assuming it's something like that."

"Wellll, you know, there aren't any real strict rules for determining a winner in this game. The only actual rule we have is that players can't meddle with each other directly."

"So if the opponent admits defeat, or dies, or it's impossible to continue the game itself—any of those conditions will count as a win?"

"I suppose so." Guy nodded, taking another sip.

As he put it, he and the emperor had been duking it out for over two thousand years. Not *directly* fighting, mind you—they had a few scrapes before then, but once Milim was born, and Veldanava the Star-King Dragon perished, they began exercising a little more restraint. Whenever they had a battle, the impact on the world was just too great—they could no longer throw everything they had into the conflict. It was a wild story, but one look at Guy in front of me, and I knew he wasn't fibbing.

So the game continued to the present day, Guy building up his pawn count while maintaining the world's balance. A lot of his monsters enjoyed incredibly long life spans, and he was patiently waiting for them to evolve over time. But nobody, not even his fellow

Octagram members, knew Guy's true intentions. Not even Milim, he claimed, was aware of the game between him and Ludora.

"Then why're you telling *me*?!"

"Mmm? Why do you think? You're the first person in all these years to push Ludora this far."

Guy didn't need me to inform him that the imperial army had been annihilated. With all the gigantic magic spells we were tossing around, I'd be shocked if he didn't notice, but...

"Killing them all was absolutely the correct answer, though. You kept Ludora from earning any more pieces for himself."

Sounds like Guy knew Ludora's objective here, too. Thanks to him, I now had a fully accurate version of the story. The emperor, in so many words, was giving his elite soldiers a trial to endure—a crushing defeat, where the survivors would (hopefully) evolve for him. The basic idea was to gin up an excuse for war the citizenry would accept, expose his army to a lethal threat, and get as many survivors evolved as he could. He had proof it'd work, too, because the failed imperial expedition against Veldora long ago produced a certain number of Enlightened.

Guy had taken a similar approach. Non-awakened, to him, were useless as pawns, and so he tacitly accepted conflicts between demon lords. The more true demon lords that got awakened, the more of an upper hand he'd have in the game. That was the whole basis for his strategy, and after that, it was just a matter of timing. Once he was absolutely certain he was above his opponent, that's when he'd stake it all. It had proven to be surprisingly difficult, however, what with all the obstacles in the way... So they had kept on playing up to now, with no winner decided.

For both Guy and Ludora, it was a grandiose operation, one that seemed to stretch across countless generations. For most life on this world, it was nothing but an annoyance, but for the two of them, it was probably just a way to fill their free time.

"And this time, too, if even a few dozen people could've survived an encounter with Veldora, some of them were bound to be awakened. I'm sure that's what Ludora assumed."

So I didn't even register in Ludora's mind, then? That must've made me one hell of a game piece for Guy. It's a little frustrating, but that's the reality here.

"And you want me to use this current opening to attack the Empire?"

"Well, I'll leave the method up to you. And I know this goes without saying, but merely *posing* as a superpower is pointless."

I'm sure he's right. A show of force was no threat to these guys. It'd just lead to more casualties without offering any strategic advantage. So forget about me sending a massive army or anything.

"If you happen to know this, is there anyone in Ludora's forces we should be particularly on guard for?"

"Ah, I dunno. My focus has always been on how well I can train my own hand in this game. If I'm the *strongest*, after all, then it doesn't matter how weak or strong the other guy is, right?"

Just the kind of arrogance I'd expect from a tyrant like him. This is the type of guy who never bothers looking at his opponent's discards in a poker game—then, just when you think you beat him, away he goes with a full house like it was nothing. Masayuki, too, was the sort of guy who could draw a royal flush straight off the deck; I wouldn't want to sit at a card table with either of them. But all this "game" talk's getting me sidetracked.

"Well, either way, I think we need to get things crystal clear with the Empire—and soon. That's based on my own credo, though, not because you asked me to."

We couldn't put this problem off any longer. We needed to open dialogue with Emperor Ludora at once... And if we did, it'd be smarter to come in with as much of an advantage as we could.

"You're not planning to travel there yourself, are you, Sir Rimuru?"

Benimaru looked a bit put off. But I wasn't bending.

"What else can I do? I can't leave Yuuki out to dry. I want to join up with him instead, and then we can hopefully work out peace on our terms."

"Wouldn't that be dangerous?"

"It's gonna be dangerous no matter what I do. Let's say that someone else goes out there and signs a peace treaty. Would you trust in that at all?"

I sure couldn't. It'd clearly be a conspiracy to catch me off guard—and then, while I'm out walking in the woods or whatever, they'd send out their assassins to get me. I'd have to be on guard at all times, and that's gonna majorly crimp the life of leisure I'm tryin' to build here. I certainly don't want *that* to happen, so I needed to settle this matter for good.

"That's a fair point. Who will guard you?"

"You, of course."

Benimaru gave this a half grin.

"That is fine by me."

He certainly seemed confident. I knew I could rely on him.

Seeing this exchange made Guy chuckle. "Ah-ha-ha! You're a funny guy, but so's your associate over there. I sense something a bit odd about him, too. Maybe he's still got some room to evolve, hmm?"

"He might, yeah. Benimaru's already the most trusted of my inner circle."

"Oh? What—and not Diablo?"

"Yeah, he's strong, but…you know, kind of a handful…"

"I hear you."

This felt like heartfelt sympathy from Guy. That—and also him treating me as a friend. I could tell from his reaction that he's got a lot of problems of his own.

"Now, there's one thing I wanna confirm with you…"

"What is it?"

"Ludora's got the ability to confer ultimate skills on other people, right?"

Guy gave me a thoughtful look, eyes squinting. "Well spotted. Yes, Ludora's got quite the remarkable little trick there, lending his powers to others like that."

Thought so.

"And do you know how this 'lending' works, exactly?"

This was important. If Guy knew the terms of this deal, it'd help us narrow down the list of people in the Empire we had to watch out for. Right now, that list couldn't have been more than ten people by my estimation, but I didn't want to work entirely on assumptions.

"Ahhh, don't worry. That power's not omnipotent or anything. He can only hand out powers for a limited time, and they're degraded versions, too. As for who qualifies... Well, I know you have to be awakened to receive the power, at least. That—and there's some other restrictions, too, that I'm not fully aware of. It's really not as much of a threat as it sounds like."

It was a real Hail Mary of a question, but he gave a remarkably quick, succinct answer. That's just about all the intel I need, I think.

But...like, it'd really take someone like Guy to say that passing out ultimate skills "isn't a threat," you know? I was starting to think Milim and Guy were cut from the same cloth. These differences in perception were needlessly complicating my job.

Watching Guy as he tucked into his slice of cake, I couldn't help but resent him a little. Seeing him talk about world-altering battle while enjoying a fancy-pants teatime snack annoyed me, and the way he treated me like yesterday's news once I accepted his request was similarly irritating.

...But wait a second. We're supposed to be talking about some important stuff here... Or so I think, at least. But despite that, our little private chat seemed to be at its end, somehow. Disgusted, I stabbed my fork into my cake. Nothing like a little sugar to get the brain going. Time to sort out everything I've learned without letting Guy get under my skin too much.

*

It was quiet, the air calm and peaceful. But despite our business being over, there was no sign that Guy was leaving.

Skillfully, Shuna poured a refill into Guy's empty teacup. She had a separate pot on hand for serving, so the remaining tea leaves wouldn't get used up too quickly.

"*Man*, you're good, you know that? None of the chuckleheads working for *me* could do any of this."

"I'm flattered, my lord."

Benimaru looked a little worried, but Shuna was unfazed, retaining her wits and not letting Guy bowl her over.

"Hey, you think I could have Mizeri and Raine train under you for a little while?"

"Train?"

"Yeah. I want you to teach 'em how to bake cakes like this."

They cooked for us at the Walpurgis council, actually, and I thought it was a pretty nice spread—but when it came to desserts, Shuna had a clear edge. She was neck and neck with Mr. Yoshida in the race to invent new taste-tempting offerings, so she was polishing up her skills by leaps and bounds.

I accepted this as normal, but Guy's reaction reminded me of how much of a luxury this was. Like, ever since I came to this world, I'd been doing pretty much whatever I wanted—something that only hit home with me now. Re-creating the things I used to love, striving to make all my favorite foods available over here... But no matter how much passion and skill you had, some recipes just couldn't be re-created without the right ingredients. Even a chef as outstanding as Mr. Yoshida couldn't have made this cake we're enjoying without the high-quality liqueurs we're producing in Tempest. Better remember to be grateful for that.

Anyway, what answer should I give Guy? I thought about just telling him to come over here and buy from us, but no need to be that stingy. So I decided to teach them only the recipes we've developed ourselves, keeping Mr. Yoshida's inventions a guarded secret.

"Shuna, could you teach this recipe to the two women in the adjacent room later?"

"I would be glad to!"

"You'll need our quality ingredients to make it, keep in mind, but maybe we can cut you a deal on them later."

We refined our sugar to keep any impurities from mixing in. We had a machine for that and everything—my sweet tooth, combined with the technical skills of Kaijin and his team, was producing quality that didn't suffer at all from what I knew in Japan. We weren't cranking out enough to put on the market, but it allowed us to indulge, at least. Maybe we could add a couple sacks to our production quotas and pass them on to Guy.

"You're okay with that?"

"Sure."

And I meant that. I wasn't giving away our tech, but if we had buyers for our product, I wasn't going to hoard it. Having Guy invite himself into our nation whenever he wanted might cause some grief, I feared... But aides like Mizeri knew how to activate and run transport gates, so I was sure we could just send our goods through there once we finished making them.

That—and I had some other thoughts, too. If Guy found us useful, keep in mind, that all but guaranteed our security as a country. The deeper our ties with foreign nations, the more it connected to our own safety. Two countries needing each other meant that they couldn't rattle the saber too casually. A regional economic zone is as good as a strong military alliance in my book; that was my pet theory.

I also didn't want any trouble with Guy, so the more cards in our hand, the better. This was, after all, the first time I had ever paid so much attention to a potential opponent. (Or maybe the second time after my initial encounter with Veldora?) Putting aside the question of whether I could beat him, fighting would lead to more than just needless hassle. There'd be real harm done, and barring some unforeseen emergency, I intended to respect Guy's intentions. Maybe he'd use and abuse me sometimes (like today), but I'd just have to put up with it. I have my limits, but...

Now that I had "enjoyed" several conversations with Guy, I was starting to realize that he wasn't quite the blockheaded despot I thought he was. He was surprisingly rational and understanding, too, and his dealings with Diablo demonstrated that he wasn't afraid of getting his hands dirty. I'd like to hope he saw us as useful enough that he wouldn't make any unreasonable demands.

So um, you mind going home soon?

But my tiny little wish was soon crushed.

"Hold on. Before I leave, there's one thing I need to ask."

What? Is there something we haven't covered yet?

"Yes?"

"Why did Diablo evolve?"

Da-dummm!!

I thought he didn't notice, but I guess I was kidding myself. I *hate* dealing with people as perceptive as he is.

"Well, um…"

Now what? What kind of response would Guy be willing to accept, even?!

"And not just Diablo, either, huh? It took a while to scope out what was happening over in your labyrinth, but how come you got all those guys down there at 'true demon lord' strength, hmm?"

Guy's lips were smiling, but his eyes sure as hell weren't. I guess cheap excuses weren't going to work…

Understood. You could frame it as experimentation with your Belzebuth skill, and that should be acceptable.

God is good!

Right, let's do that. That's the Raphael I know. I can always count on the dude at times like these.

"So you know, I've been experimenting with my powers a little bit lately, to see if I can beef up our forces for the battle against the Empire. As I did, I discovered that one of my skills has a pretty interesting side effect I can take advantage of."

"Oh? What kind of side effect?"

I dunno.

Tell me, Raphael!!

Understood. The effect of reverting souls into pure energy and granting them to those capable of awakening. Call it forced evolution, and that should be enough explanation for the subject Guy Crimson.

Oh. That *is* what I did, isn't it? That whole evolution ritual harnessed the power of Belzebuth, not Raphael. This was the unvarnished truth, even; I wouldn't be lying or hiding anything from Guy. This might just be the way to go, actually.

"Belzebuth, you see, can take people's souls and convert them back into energy. Then I can grant that 'soul energy' to other people, you see. If they're not qualified for it, it won't do anything at all, but—"

"Uh-huh. So if someone has the seed for it, they can get awakened that way? Wow."

Guy seemed convinced. I suppose he could tell I wasn't lying to him anyway. Raphael saved my bacon once again.

"Yeah, well, with wars in this world, individual strength is a lot more important than vast numbers, right? So it's a given that I'll want to enhance my team's individual skills."

"Yes, that makes perfect sense. By the way, I've been thinking this for a while... But you're pretty abnormal, aren't you?"

"Huh? No I'm not."

"No, I mean...slimes don't usually *talk*, you know? And I've been letting that slide, but then you won over Veldora somehow; you built up this whole town... It's just not normal, by any stretch of the imagination. Are you a reincarnate, maybe? You are, aren'tcha?"

"Hmm? Oh, you didn't know? Yeah, I died in a different world from here, and then I got reborn as a slime with my mind intact."

"Seriously?"

"Seriously."

We stared at each other. No, really, he *didn't know*? I thought we had broken this down ages ago. I'd been pretty public with this fact, and it was a famous story over in the Western Nations, too. I thought for sure that Guy would've heard it somewhere or other. Maybe it's not always a good idea to assume the other party knows everything you think they do—not that I misspoke or anything, but it was something to watch out for. Don't want to give out too much information just because I want to keep the conversation going.

"It's really true?"

"Yes, it certainly is."

"Sir Rimuru never lies."

Why is he so doubtful about this? Now he's turning to Benimaru and Shuna for confirmation, the bastard.

"*Ahhh*-ha-ha-ha-ha-ha! Wowww! I always assumed you were a pretty screwy monster, but *that's* the story behind you, huh? Simply being reincarnated between worlds is a rarity in itself, but *you* got reborn as a monster? Man, talk about a bad break."

Guy let out another belly laugh. I didn't see it as all *that* funny.

"But now it all makes sense. If you traveled between worlds in soul form and still managed to keep your mind intact, well, no wonder you've got such a toughened heart core to ya. It explains why you're picky about retaining a human form, too...and maybe why you evolved so insanely fast and got those ultimate skills."

So in short, I'm a stubborn old ass, huh? Well, maybe. I like to think I'm pretty thick-skinned, not to brag. Never give up, never lose heart, always think positive—that's what I live by.

"It's that convincing to you, huh?"

"Yep. You always struck me as a shady guy, but now I think I can really trust you, after all."

That's just rude, isn't it? But I'll forgive it. I can't beat him in battle anyway... And I certainly don't want him all suspicious and hostile around me. Again, the power of positive thinking.

"Well, I'm glad we got that cleared up, and I think I've asked you about everything I need to. So I imagine you'll be heading—"

"Oh, can I get some more of this?"

"Certainly."

I was about to push Guy back home when he interrupted me and brazenly demanded a second slice of cake. Shuna immediately sprang into action, and it'd be weird if only he was eating, so I asked for another slice, too. Stress eating isn't a good habit to acquire, but I just wanted some sugar to perk me up. But Guy got in my way yet again.

"So, Rimuru, let's go back to what I was asking."

I had a gut feeling that this was going to be painful.

"Huh? Asking about what?"

"You awakening your team members here. Because it sounded to *me* like you could share some of your power with my servants, too, but what do you think? Sound possible, or what?"

Dammit... This dude's just like me, isn't he? Incredibly shrewd, trying to take advantage of anything useful... Making me think the conversation is over, only to pull the "just one more thing" killer blow. Not that I'm *this* blatant about it... Or maybe I am?

No point pondering that, though. Guy needs an answer, and for that—

Understood. It is possible.

Oh. The guy answered me before I even thought of the question. That made me feel a little sad, somehow. I could almost feel it thinking *I'm getting sick of dealing with you.*

Understood. There is no such intention.

Something about this exchange made me think it's incredibly angry at me. Better not prod it any further. Raphael's all I have to rely on, so if it gave up on me, I'd be at the end of my rope.

Right. Now for a more serious question. If I built a soul corridor between myself and Guy's "servants" (whoever they are), would that still work?

Affirmative. Forced intervention is now possible even if you do not share a common soul lineage with the monster in question. The target must not resist the connection, but as long as it is qualified to awaken, an infusion of energy is capable of inciting evolution.

Roger that.

This just leaves one problem—how many of my souls it'd consume. I don't know how many people he wanted me to awaken, but if I don't have the goods, we're getting nowhere here.

"I don't think it'll be a problem, no. Can't be sure unless I try, but I'm reasonably sure it'll be fine. But I don't have enough energy left to pass out to other people, though."

This was my attempt at nimbly turning Guy down without angering him. I actually had just over one hundred thousand souls left, but Guy couldn't have any way of knowing that. Surely he'd give up now.

"Right. So as long as you have souls to provide, you can do it, then?"

"Uhhh..."

He's *not* giving up?

"Because you know, I once gave Mizeri about ten thousand of my own souls. It didn't trigger anything at all, though. No sign of her awakening or anything. So I thought I was just wasting my time with that approach."

He can just pass on souls as is like that? These demons are pretty clever, aren't they? But that wouldn't cause an awakening?

Understood. In order to incite an evolution, the requisite souls must be converted into the required form to be compatible with the target. Simply giving away souls is unlikely to have the desired effect. Furthermore, granting souls to other people is a highly inefficient use of energy, producing only about 10 percent of the anticipated value.

Aha.

So in order to make a would-be demon lord take root, you needed to give it the right sun and water and stuff? And of course, knowing how to do that is different from actually pulling it off. So would it be better to wait for his servants to spontaneously evolve, then?

Negative. A monster named by a higher-level being has its very nature altered. Even if it has souls it acquired on its own, that is unlikely to cause an awakening.

So once they're named, that's the end of the evolution process. It's hard enough for someone to qualify for an awakening, but *that* sounds like quite the unexpected pitfall to me. The vast majority of monsters never qualify at all; naming is a much more likely method of powering up, so maybe it's the same thing in the end.

Anyway, being named changes the nature of a monster to the point that it's no longer able to extract the appropriate energy from the souls they acquire. Guy seems to be unaware of this, so I guess Raphael strikes again. Truly, it's the smartest teacher I ever had in my life.

...

Oops. I was sincere with that praise, but maybe Raphael took it as me making fun of it. But I had my answer, so let's just move on.

"Mizeri, huh? Did you try it with Raine or anyone else? And actually, you were the one who named them, right?"

"That's right. Again, well spotted."

"Well, there's your problem right there."

"Oh?"

"When they're named by a higher-level life-form, that changes their nature enough that it won't work, it looks like."

"...Mmm. That sort of thing, huh? So it's a waste of time no matter how many souls I give them. But you've got a way to adapt the soul energy so it'll work on the target?"

I had to take a crash course from Raphael to figure all this out, but Guy was picking up on it super rapidly. Everything he said was right on the money, too.

"My approach ought to, yeah."

"Okay. I wanna ask you a favor."

Here we go. Now I was really starting to understand Guy's personality. When he starts to use that wheedling voice of his, he must think there's no way I'll say no. I'd really like to slap a denial on him, but I'd be too afraid to try it. I value my life too much for that these days, so I'll just play along for now.

"Um, just so you know, all the souls in the world won't evolve someone if they don't qualify for the right."

"No problem there. Both of them meet the requirements just fine. You think you can awaken them for me?"

The way Guy was talking, his two maids were total garbage, useless in their current states. His evaluation standards are so weird. Based on what I heard, Mizeri and Raine are Primals on the same level as Testarossa and her gang. But he's just slamming them like this instead? And considering one of my own secretaries made a sport out of egging Guy on, I was getting more and more nervous by the moment.

Ah, well. Now it boils down to whether I have the souls I need.

"Okay, so it's only Mizeri and Raine you'd like to have awakened?"

"Yeah. How many souls is that gonna take?"

For a self-awakening, it was ten thousand; for a servant of mine in my soul lineage, it was a cool one hundred thousand, ten times as much. If I was working with unrelated third parties this time, I'm sure it'd be even more inefficient. So as for the number—

Understood. Five hundred thousand souls.

Five hundred thousand? So a quarter million each?! Twenty-five times more than usual—and over twice as many as a "soul lineage" job... It seemed like a ton, but if that's Raphael's quote, it has to be true.

"I think five hundred thousand would be enough for the two of them."

"Huh? That's all? Well, shoot, I got enough in me right now, then. I won't even have to kill any more humans."

He *has* them? And like, what was he gonna do if he didn't?!

"Oh, you do? That's, um, good."

A dry chuckle was about all I could let out. I might've been begging Guy to stop right now if the numbers didn't work out. I'm glad I didn't have to, but considering all the casualties lately, I kinda had mixed feelings about this. The difference in how we value souls— and all that. I secretly prayed we didn't have any more conflicts of interest going forward.

Benimaru and Shuna listened in on all this, worried looks on their faces. I decided there was no reason to hide my conversation with Guy from them.

"Well, if you could grab our guests for me, then..."

I had Shion and Diablo join us as well.

Guy was in an elated mood as he enjoyed his cake. Slice number three. Glad he likes it.

As soon as he handed me his half-million souls, he started acting like his work was done here. I already confirmed with Raphael that everything was set to go, but was it petty of me to be less than overjoyed about all this?

I pondered this a little as Shuna brought the two maids back in for me.

"You amaze me again, Sir Rimuru. That cake was excellent."

"Yes, and we're thrilled that you're willing to share the recipe so freely with us."

Mizeri was gushing; Raine was meekly appreciative. They must've gotten the message, and they were behaving perfectly kindly around Shuna. If *this* was enough to satisfy them, I really wished we didn't have to play these dumb world-war games. The world was so full of surprises to explore! And besides, these two seemed like perfect maids to me. They didn't have the world-destroying sense of taste that Shion did, and I was sure they'd hone their skills in no time.

Before that, though, I had an evolution ritual to perform.

"I am glad to hear that... And if we can continue to work in tandem, nothing would make me happier."

Cooperation is so key, in my opinion. I'd like them to understand that cooperation isn't a one-way street, but...

"Rimuru's about to give both of you more power, girls. You need to be more thankful to him."

So should you, man.

Swallowing the thought before I said it out loud, I smiled at the two girls.

"Now, a word of caution about this. Once I complete the evolution, you might suddenly get extremely sleepy. This is called the Harvest Festival, and it's perfectly normal, but you might be too catatonic to travel much for up to a few days. In the meantime, you can feel free to stay with us."

Guy and his entourage had traveled via Mizeri's transport gate to a spot just outside the labyrinth. I then obtained Ramiris's permission to let them inside, but once the evolution was complete, I didn't think either of them were gonna be on their feet for a while. I doubted Guy was the type of boss who was thoughtful enough to bring them back home with him, so I intended to set them up with some lodging.

And besides...

"Are you sure?"

"Of course. So perhaps you two could send Guy and Velzard back home while you're still awake?"

That was my aim. Our negotiations were over, and I really wished Guy would leave already.

"Huh? Ahhh, I don't wanna impugn on you *that* much. We'll take the two of them back with us, so just go ahead and start infusing, could you?"

Wha?!

Guy's unexpected reply almost made me audibly yelp. And not just me—Mizeri and Raine themselves looked just as astonished. Their reaction told me what I already assumed: Guy actually lifting a finger to do something for them was unprecedented.

Clearly, he had an agenda of some kind. An agenda that, quite frankly, I found incredibly annoying. I didn't want Guy to see my power in action; I wanted him the hell out of here. Then it occurred to me. It always struck me that Guy and I had a lot of similarities, but maybe we were even more identical than I thought. I mean, if I were him, of *course* I'd want to observe what went on and see if I could copy it. Even if I couldn't, I still wanted as much info as I could get, so I could counteract it if need be. Based on that, it was very like Guy was thinking the same thing—and in that case, I was all the more motivated not to reveal my hand to him.

Or has he already spotted me out?

Understood. There is not a problem. As instructed, only Belzebuth will be brought to the forefront, so the rest will be kept fully hidden.

Sweet. Just leave it to Raphael, and I could even pull the wool over Guy's eyes. Not that I can let my guard down yet. I just didn't want him learning any more about me, you know?

"No, no, there's no need to be shy! We've got tons of extra rooms, so you just get going on your way, okay?"

I wasn't gonna negotiate. Guy was absolutely trying to stick around so he could observe my powers. I wasn't about to expose my hand for no good reason. I've got to do whatever it takes to get Guy out of this place...

We exchanged polite smiles, even as intense psychological warfare erupted below the surface. Just as it did, the door to the room was almost blown off its hinges.

"Rimuru! I was looking for you! The surveillance feed's gone silent over in the Control Center. I want you to restore it for us."

"Yeah! I'm pitchin' in to help monitor the world, too, y'know!"

Veldora and Ramiris certainly seemed to be enjoying themselves. But we were in the middle of a very important conversation, so I wished they'd pick up on that a bit. Besides, the Control Center's meant for waging wars, all right? It's not your personal playroom. And yes, we *are* still at war, but I think you guys are just using that screen to search for neat new spots to visit.

...I had a lot I wanted to say, but I had no right to complain. It was all my doing, besides. *"Once the war's over,"* I blurted out the other day, *"why don't we go out and have some fun?"* They had been arguing over where to go ever since.

They've never traveled much around the world, despite how ponderously long they've lived, and I guess they caught the travel bug thanks to me. That's why they made a routine out of using my Eye of God to bump around the world and take in the scenery when they had free time. This surveillance magic never used much energy, so we could keep it constantly active—and what's more, changing the viewpoint was something anyone could do without much training. The Eye couldn't cover every spot in the world, but it still had a wide range. Abuse it too much, though, and the magic effect would temporarily wear off.

"I'll head down there later, okay? Just sit tight and wait a second."

Guess I'll have to lecture them later about keeping quiet when I'm entertaining guests. As their guardian, that's my job. I mean, I wanted to do some travel research, too—or I mean, it was important that I gave them a good education about the world. But anyway, I was busy negotiating with Guy, so I tried to kick them out. However:

"Oh, hello there, Guy. Got some business with Rimuru, huh?"

Ramiris noticed Guy in the room. Veldora's eyes were elsewhere.

"Looks like you're having fun, Veldora."

"Gahhh?! Wha-wha—?! Why are you here, my sister...?!"

"Here I thought you've matured a bit, but you're as boisterous as ever, aren't you? Great job taking human form, though. Looking pretty good for someone who just broke out of their seal, too."

"I... I'm glad you are well..."

The fun was apparently over for Veldora. Now he was stiff as a board. Velzard was being perfectly nice to him, but for my friend, it must've looked different.

"But I'd love to spend some time talking with you. It's been so long!"

"I, er... Well, I'm sure you're a busy person, my sister, and I have work of my own to attend to. I'm afraid I do not have much free time..."

"Oh, no need to worry about that. I think Guy and Sir Rimuru have a lot to talk about still, so why don't we have a nice, *extended* chat?"

Velzard's emphasis was clearly on the word *extended*. She completely ignored Veldora's claim of work obligations, and now he was looking to me for assistance. I gave him a brisk nod back. Good luck, man.

"Could we borrow a nearby room, Sir Rimuru?"

She flashed me a beautiful smile, and how I was going to say no to that? I can't!

"Of course. I'm sure you've got a lot of catching up to do, so take your time!"

I had no choice. Farewell, Veldora. We'll never forget your gallantry!

He looked pretty bent out of shape over not getting any help from me. Then, with a quick hand movement, he grabbed hold of Ramiris.

"Wh-whoa, Master! This isn't any of my business!"

"Please! Don't leave me alone!"

The pathetic display convinced me. Veldora must be ill at ease around his sister Velzard. Or maybe more terrified of her...?

In my previous life, I had a friend who didn't like his big sister too much, either. "*She's such a dictator,*" he'd complain to me, eyes glowing with enlightenment—and I guess that applies to True Dragons, too. (I also had friends who'd whine at each other about how annoying their little sisters were, but I only had one elder brother, so I couldn't join in. I'm sure it was the same kinda deal with both sister types, and Veldora was starting to remind me of them.)

Then something occurred to me. A while back, Veldora and I were arguing over where we should go for a trip, and he was dead set against traveling north, like I suggested. He said it was too cold for him and so forth, but that seemed unnatural to me. There couldn't be any way the cold would affect him. Looking back, though, maybe he knew Velzard was there?

As I watched Veldora, begging not to go as he held the door in a death grip, I couldn't help but feel sorry for him. Maybe I had it all wrong. I fully intended to abandon him since I didn't want to get burned, but let's lend him a bit of a hand. If it didn't work out, I thought, I'd just relent and that'd be that.

"Hey, Guy... You live north of Englesia, right?"

"Mm? Ah yes, you call it the Tundral Waste down here. Pretty cold."

"Yes," Velzard said, standing up and turning to me as she kept a firm grasp on Veldora's shoulders. "I don't suppress my magical force up there, so no life can survive in the region. Guy doesn't like the weak, so I did that to keep everyone else from blundering near him."

Good, good. Let's keep it going.

"So if I had to guess, Velzard, your power involves cold and ice?"

"...Not exactly, no. But in terms of the effects it produces, I can see if people think so."

Perfect. No doubt about it, then. It's funny to think that Veldora, as boundlessly confident and fearless as he was, still had a weakness like this.

"You have trouble dealing with Velzard, don't you, Veldora?"

"D-do not say such ridiculous things! There is nothing I have trouble dealing with!"

What a time to act like a tough guy. It's only causing you more damage, you know.

"Right? Of course not. After all, I took care of you for a long time, didn't I?"

There was not the slightest cloudiness to Velzard's warm smile. Not once did she ever suspect her brother might dislike her.

"When Veldora was just born, you know, whenever he went on a rampage, I promptly destroyed and rehabilitated him. Then, when he did it again after being reborn, I'd stop him, calm him down, maybe give him a gentle lecture or two. He had a few developmental problems—he couldn't turn human, that kind of thing—so he'd always cause far too much damage. If I didn't clean up after him, he would have grown even more out of control."

Velzard told me about all the things she did in the past, framing them as sisterly acts of kindness. I dare anyone to listen to it all without bursting into tears.

"Veldora... You've been through so much..."

"You see that, Rimuru? Do you *see* that?!"

No wonder he preferred being away from her. What she did was devious—and the worst part was that she meant no malice at all. If we didn't unravel this misunderstanding or assumption on Velzard's part, Veldora might spend his entire life fearing her. But Veldora wasn't helping his case much, either—that tough act made it impossible for him to defy her. He needs to drop that false courage, or he'll never get along with people...or True Dragons, I guess. Whatever.

"Velzard, I don't mean to meddle too much, but I feel that Veldora might have a few hang-ups when it comes to you."

"Oh? Why is that?"

"Well, long story short, you're overdoing it. Instead of just forcibly lecturing him without listening to his side of the story, if you gave him more guidance about what's right and wrong, he'll learn it more naturally that way. Veldora's capable of listening to reason, after all. So instead of resorting to violence, can you just tell him how you really feel instead? If you want, we can even put you up here for the night."

Velzard considered this for a few moments, then sighed and nodded. Whew. Glad she accepted it.

"R-Rimuru…"

"Aw, isn't that great, Master? Can you let go of me now?"

"Very well. Looking back, I'm not sure I ever really considered Veldora's thoughts. Perhaps we can take this opportunity to have a nice, long talk?"

So she was gonna talk his ear off regardless. Uh-huh.

"All… All right. Go easy on me, please."

Veldora regained his composure, too, in a resigned sort of way. Hopefully this can help alleviate the rift a little bit. He exited the room (voluntarily this time), but he was still clutching Ramiris in his hand. I'll pretend I didn't see that.

"H-hey! Wait! This is none of my business!"

I think I maybe heard that plea from somewhere, but it disappeared once the door shut. I must've been hearing things. Time to focus on Guy again.

∗

Veldora's exit made the room suddenly feel very quiet.

"Right," Guy muttered. I nervously swallowed as I anticipated his next words.

"Well, it sounds like Velzard will be staying here for a bit, so I think I'll stay overnight as well."

"Sure. I'll have a room ready for the three of them, so don't worry about that."

"Huh? The three of who?"

"Oh, aren't you leaving?"

I sure wish he was. But I'd be left disappointed.

"What are you, stupid? We're pals, aren't we? So let's hang out today. Get these two evolved for me already."

Grrr. He certainly was a persuasive speaker, but I hated letting him have his way like this.

"No, no, I'll be glad to give you the royal treatment when things are less urgent, so for today—"

"Didn't you say a moment ago that you have lots of extra rooms? I don't need the 'royal treatment' today, so just set me up with whatever's free right now. I wanted to try that 'tempura' thing you were talking about earlier, so you mind hooking me up?"

Welp, I lost. After all this, I had no possible pretense for saying no. It meant revealing what I considered to be one of my most powerful moves, but it beat refusing and stoking his anger.

"...All right. I'll get you the best room we have out of what's available... And I'll arrange for a tempura dinner tonight."

I nodded briefly at Shuna.

"Absolutely. I will start preparing at once."

With a sweet smile and a perfectly polite bow, she left. Haruna silently took her place, standing by in one corner of the room. Her sheer unobtrusiveness demonstrated how skilled she was as a maid. Mizeri and Raine looked impressed as well, so I had to assume she was top-notch by international standards, too.

Guy, meanwhile, looked extremely satisfied with himself over beating me. It sucked, but I'd just have to admit defeat for now—but the moment I had that thought, the previously silent Diablo finally opened his mouth.

"Keh-heh-heh-heh-heh... I see. You'll be staying over tonight, Guy?"

"Hmm? Yeah, but—"

"Ah-ha. Then you'll have plenty of free time on your hands?"

"What are you...?"

"No, no, I just thought this would be a lovely opportunity for us."

"An opportunity? For what?"

"I needed to finish the story I was telling you earlier, you know. And you bragged about your ultimate ability to me a long time ago, didn't you? Well, I wanted to ask you about that in more detail today, so..."

Whoaaa! Nice one, Diablo. Now the tables were turned—Guy was on the ropes! I can't let this chance pass me by!

"Well, in *that* case, Diablo, why don't you take Guy here over to the inner chamber? You guys can chat your heads off the whole rest of the day!"

"Thank you very much, Sir Rimuru. I cannot tell you how much I appreciate your kindness."

As soon as he said it, Diablo put his hand around Guy's shoulder.

"Huh? Ah! Wait!"

"No, I cannot wait to sit down with you. Let's go."

Guy was kind of like a house of cards if you poked him the right way, huh? All it took was Diablo's quiet insistence to ferry him right out of the room. He can be so unexpectedly useful sometimes.

Now that Guy was gone, I could finally use my powers at peace. I didn't know when they'd come back, so let's get this ritual over with fast. I wasted no time pouring my souls into Mizeri and Raine, inciting the evolution.

Report. The prescribed amount of one hundred thousand souls has been reached. The subject Mizeri's evolution has begun.

Um? That's odd. Guy gave me half a million souls—

Moving on to the incitement of the subject Raine's evolution... Successful.

I was down only two hundred thousand souls.

Huh?

So as long as they're qualified to evolve, they can do it even if we're not linked soul to soul?

...Hey, wait a minute! That's not even the issue. You got three hundred thousand souls you didn't use here! Don't tell me...?!

Report. I have mastered the knack behind this, so the necessary number turned out lower than expected.

Oh, you got the knack down, huh?

...Wait, what? No! That's no excuse! I received a zillion more souls than that! He's never gonna buy that!

Understood. The subjects Testarossa, Ultima, and Carrera were included in the required amount.

What the hell're you doing to me?! Raphael's gone crazy on me! How fearless can you even get? Are you seriously trying to get one up on the demon lord Guy Crimson?!

...Wait. Dude. If he finds out, *I'm* the one who's gonna pay for it, man!!

Understood. It is not a problem.

No, it is. It's a *lot* of problems. Seriously, I'm kind of afraid of you right now. Acting all fearless like this is *so* frightening.

Negative. This is simply the result of my information particle-handling skills performing better than expected. Any surplus can be considered extra remuneration.

You think so, huh? Because I think you're *reeeeeally* stretching it, but...

Seriously, this is scaring me more than trying to run a scam against the yakuza. If Guy ever found out, he could disassemble me into a pile of broken atoms, and I'd have no reason to complain. I don't sweat, so I wasn't betraying any of my agitation on my face, but inside me I had cold sweat falling like a rainstorm. For the first time in a while, I'm actually glad I'm a slime.

So we partied it up that night.

Guy looked a little miffed with me, but he never did complain. In fact, he thanked me.

"There's a lot I could say about today's events, but I'm tired out for now. It looks like the evolution took place without a hitch, and for that, I thank you."

He really *did* look exhausted. I wonder why? Diablo, meanwhile, was a stark contrast in how energetic he was. Weird.

"No, no, you're quite welcome."

Not getting involved was the smart bet here. I pretended not to notice anything as I left that sleeping dog to himself.

The food seemed to be to his liking, and the hot spring bath gave him what looked like a sorely needed recharge. Velzard was in a good mood after chatting with Veldora, and for an unplanned social evening like this, I thought we did pretty darn well.

"I'll be back."

"We'll do our best to entertain you then."

"I do look forward to that. We live in a very cold place, so that hot spring was so soothing to me."

"Well, I'm glad you liked it, too. We can't wait to have you back."

"How polite of you! I'd love to see Veldora again before long, so we'll be sure to take a few days next time."

Speaking of Veldora, he wasn't currently with us. That's because he was prone on his bed, thoroughly battered and unable to move after going a couple rounds with Velzard.

"Hee-hee-hee... Kwah-ha-ha-ha! Tell him I went a bit easy on him this time, but don't expect any mercy when I return."

"You sure you want me to tell him that?"

"...Sorry."

She seemed to be apologizing in an ever-so-wispy voice, but I'm a kind slime, so I pretended not to hear. Hey, I'm sure Velzard didn't *mean* to kick his ass, and I'm sure Veldora will be good as new in a few days. Really, I hadn't seen him take any wounds since that whole Chronoa incident, so it was a helpful reminder of just how strong True Dragons really were.

Veldora had another big sister over in the Empire. We have to figure out how to deal with her, so I think I'll have Raphael give me the rundown on how True Dragons fight each other later on.

*

After giving me some valuable information to work with, Guy and his crew finally left. I'll be using that info as a reference as I resume our deliberations on the next course of action.

As I resolved to do this, I saw someone jogging up to me in a tizzy. It was Mjöllmile.

"Ah, Sir Rimuru! I was wondering where you were. I've been looking all over!"

"Why the urgency?"

"You'll know when you hear this: Big Mama's here, and she wants to see you."

"Big Mama?!"

I promptly rushed over to a certain inn in a prime spot of town. Big Mama always stayed there on her visits.

This was a nickname, of course, one shared only between Mollie and me. We gave it to her because bandying her real name around was bound to cause us trouble. It was Elmesia El-Ru Thalion, the Heavenly Emperor of the Sorcerous Dynasty of Thalion.

Among the Three Pranksters—the name we three gave ourselves— she was known as El. I was Rim, Mollie was Gar, and she was El. She led the group, I was second-in-command, and Gar was our minion henchman. We had a lot of fun with this, you could say.

If El wanted to see me this urgently, I had to drop everything for her. I'm *pretty* sure she's aware we're fighting a war right now, though...

"We told El that we're at war, didn't we?"

"Oh, of course. In fact, she told me herself that she'd save her next visit for when things settled down."

Mollie here has actually known Elmesia longer than I have, sitting in for me when I'm busy and negotiating over this and that— both in public and private.

"Public" here meant official diplomatic relations with Thalion, and I was pretty much hands-off with that stuff, leaving it wholly to Mollie and Rigurd's circle. They oversaw construction progress, established trade regulations, set up tariffs and other logistical matters, discussed security for merchants and visitors from both our nations... Anything and everything had to be looked over with a fine-tooth comb until they were mutually acceptable to us all. It was a daunting task, but they did their best at it without complaint.

"Private," meanwhile, was more about the fun debauchery we got up to as the Three Pranksters. "Debauchery" might sound a little shady, and indeed, our little side hustles weren't the kind of things your mother would approve of.

What were they, exactly? Well, basically we were attempting to take full control of our newborn (and gigantic) economic trade zone.
....
......
...

At first, the three of us were simply drinking buddies. We were discussing business matters at the bar before long, however, and the next thing I knew, this had ballooned into sensitive matters concerning the management of our nations. It's on me for having such a big mouth, but Mollie's equally as guilty for not stopping me. Besides, it's not like us two were the only ones blabbering away; Elmesia leaked out a lot of secrets to us as well.

It's little wonder we all let our guard down. All three of us were blaming it on the alcohol, essentially. Benders can be real scary.

This relationship was, of course, totally confidential—just a secret between the three of us. It'd have to be, because if word got out about these talks, we'd be subjected to a whole lot of vitriol. I'm sure my staff would be silently applying pressure on me to stop, and Mollie would probably develop an ulcer from all the criticism. I bet even Elmesia would become the target of some sarcastic remarks from Erald.

So we were a tight-knit secret society, the Three Pranksters, and by this point, our friendship had transcended our positions in society.

This arrangement began in earnest, if I recall, around when we won the battle against the Rossos.

Right when that clan was on the decline, the Western Nations' criminal underground circles were all but decimated. Nobody was providing any cohesion, and things were starting to break down into factional warfare. I wasn't about to abide by this, so I asked Testarossa to help keep the peace over there; that prevented things from getting out of hand, but we couldn't keep things as is for long.

Only when the local police—or military, really—couldn't handle matters did we provide some secret assistance to them. That, however, brought up the issue of how to deal with the criminals we caught. The reason local militias couldn't handle these cases was because of the inevitable reprisals they would trigger. In some cases, local or regional government leaders were the ones committing the crimes, and the authorities would be hesitant to act in situations like that. They couldn't let crimes go unchecked, of course, but if they pursued them too much, it could potentially lead to insurrection, even. In a lot of cases, the local state had no choice but to keep silent and not intervene.

It was all pretty troubling, so one night I was whining about it to Elmesia during one of her stops at our inn.

"I was rather hoping we could discuss something more fun than that," she said at first, clearly reluctant... But as she listened on, she gradually opened up to me, leaning forward and asking for more details. Essentially, the way I painted things, it could be beneficial to not just me, but her, too. In other words, I was telling another what-if fairy tale to hold her interest.

Crime and the economy are inexorably linked. If the gap between rich and poor widens, that leads to resentment and could even affect national order. It's why organized crime grows so huge; they serve as a receptacle for the poor, and after a certain point, they could wreck the entire power balance of the nation. Mollie, it should be said, was originally one of those underworld bosses, and I suppose his familiarity with matters let him grasp my point immediately.

What poor people need is a place to belong. We had to provide jobs available to anyone so they won't turn to crime, no matter how far they've fallen. Oftentimes, this would be where the military comes in—they've got tons of positions to fill, and they're always looking for people to fill them. But if the country itself is poor, sometimes not even that functions properly. So we wanted to provide a little under-the-table help to them.

"First off, we'll create our own crime outfit. We've already laid the groundwork for this by absorbing all the groups we've crushed in each nation... And I'm thinking about taking out all the ones we've let survive for now, too."

It might've been a bunch of drunken nonsense, but it did succeed in grabbing Elmesia's attention.

"I see… No, there's no group in the Western Nations that can complete with Cerberus. And I think a lot of people would swear their loyalties to this new group as long as they're guaranteed food, clothing, and shelter."

Elmesia hadn't been too enthusiastic so far. But what I said next proved to be the deciding factor.

"Right? So we could take care of the poor that way. Next we'll tackle the wealthy."

"Hmm?"

"Now that Granville is dead, the Rossos are going to fall—and fall fast. They might still have a lot of power, but you know they're going to do nothing but weaken over time. So I'm trying to move another project along to serve as a replacement."

"A project? Let me hear more about it."

"Well, you know it. The idea you mentioned before, about having Blumund function as a concentrated industrial hub. Sir Fuze is making preparations for me along those lines, and he's already secured the necessary personnel, I understand."

Mjöllmile and I had already consulted with each other on this grand concept. It's important that we coordinate our interests with our neighboring countries, after all, if we want to spread friendship and prosperity.

"We could combine the Dwarven Kingdom's industry, Farminus's agricultural output, and Thalion's industry as well. We'll need to fine-tune things so we're not competing against each other, but we could have all this industry flow right into Blumund—and then they could serve as a window into all that Western Nations territory."

"Ah yes, Erald *did* report to me about that. So you were actually planning to go through with it?"

"Of course. Why not?"

"All right. But, Rim, how will you profit from it?"

"Profit's secondary here."

"Hmm?"

"Just kidding! But that's what we're trying to do. Taking control of core technology, releasing it to the world, you know. And

I'm thinking we could build a really big educational institution and attract talented students from all over the world. Establish ourselves as a major tourist destination, then skim off the top behind the scenes!"

"Wah-ha-ha-ha-ha! And don't forget about your patents concept! This wonderful system where money keeps flowing in without having to do any work! I understand it well enough, but it could take time to get other people to use it."

"...Mmm, I see. So your idea is to create new products that require this core technology, then secure the intellectual property rights?"

"You're so quick on the uptake, El! I'm glad for that. But don't go copying the idea off me, okay?"

"First come, first served, is it? But no, no—I won't copy it, but let me in on some of the action instead!"

"Wah-ha-ha-ha-ha! Pitch in for us, El, and this project is already as good as done!"

"Oh, Gar, you give me far too much credit! You're right, of course, but..."

And so we laughed into our beer mugs all night.

The next day, we gave each other bleary looks, everyone wondering if we said too much.

"Hey, so about yesterday's chat..."

"Yes, I recall it. You said some things you probably shouldn't have, didn't you?"

"Yeah..."

"If—if you could find it in you to keep it a secret... We can't afford to have the project shudder to a halt at this point..."

"Oh, stop worrying, Gar. Maybe the drinks were talking for me, but I'm a woman who keeps her promises."

And so through a failed attempt at fraternization through getting blasted, we were now all on the same wavelength.

We pushed on with plans at a steady clip from that point forward. When you had the leaders of two superpowers on the same page, things went fast.

Our inroads into the Western Nations criminal underground

were progressing at a pace that would've easily surprised the outside observer. In just a few months, we had finished unifying all the region's crime groups. Thus, a brand-new secret society was born, one we called REG—the Three Wise Drunks. The group's members had no idea about the origins of that name, but that was certainly not our problem.

What's more important is how the project's moving along. The poor people facing oppression in their local regions were quickly taken in by the mysterious "REG" outfit, and after a month or two of examination, the right people were selected for the right jobs. Any outstanding talents, we decided, would be invited to my nation for further study.

All the little details behind this were being overseen by Glenda Attley, one of the former Three Battlesages who was still serving under Soei. She said she'd gladly take any job, dirty or not, and now she was acting every bit like a mob boss. Working beneath her were Girard, ex-leader of the Sons of the Veldt mercenary group, and Ayn, the elementalist who once worked for him. These were two pretty notorious names around the Western Nations, with the type of leadership skills that naturally attracted the seedier elements of the local population. This underworld fame served them well as they carried out Glenda's orders.

Most people seemed to assume this trio was the Three Wise Drunks being referred to. We really *were* just three drunken idiots, but people were misinterpreting it as being "drunk on dreams" or other fancy stuff like that, so I'd keep the truth to myself.

So that's what we had cooking underground. Now let's examine our activities as public figures. For this effort, we decided it was better to create two organizations that would compete against each other, instead of a single monolith that'd be too vulnerable to corruption.

The first one is a new company founded by Mollie, mostly comprised of educated staff from Blumund and engaging in commercial business in tandem with the Council. This we named the Four Nations Trade Alliance, chaired by a representative from Tempest with a board of executives from Blumund, Farminus, and Dwargon as well. Mollie was installed as CEO, ensuring I'd always have a hand in its affairs.

The second group was a coalition of Western Nations trade groups that Elmesia would work behind the scenes to form. Doran, monarch of the kingdom that bears his name, would be lent money to establish the firm under his banner, which would allow it to absorb the surviving members of the Rosso family. Essentially, we were setting up a playing field for everyone who's particularly hostile to us, but it attracted a lot more people than expected.

The firm was named the Western General Trade Company, with one of Doran's sons serving as president—Prince Figaro Ros Doran, a descendant of the Rossos, who possessed all the intelligence and talent that name conferred. The prince and his father were the only people who knew about Elmesia's involvement; they agreed to play along in exchange for her protection. "In the Rosso family," Doran reportedly said upon hearing of the plan, "you need a flexible mind to survive. If the world's most powerful demon lord and someone with as much influence on the world as the Heavenly Emperor are forming a team, deciding not to take part would surely spell our doom."

If you're gonna credit the Rossos for anything, praise them for how seriously they took their contracts. As long as we both fulfilled our side of the contract, we could trust this relationship to stay unchanged for the foreseeable future.

It's also worth adding that between Elmesia's shares and mine, we controlled 61 percent of the Western General Trade Company. Elmesia was the top shareholder, so if Figaro decided to betray us, the firm would collapse right then and there. "Not that someone as talented as him would do something that stupid," Elmesia told me, and I was apt to agree with her. So Figaro was accepted as our trusted president for the time being.

Thus, we had two different companies kicking off at the same time. These two firms were ostensibly competitors in the same field, conducting price wars and scrambling to secure exclusive distributors. But this was all legal, healthy competition, with no use of force involved.

Some of the staff occasionally took the cowardly approach and tried tapping organized crime to lend them a hand, although for *some reason*, it always backfired on them. The REG group informed me of some pretty wild stories related to this. I deliberately didn't try to stop any would-be criminals, but I hoped it was clear to people that if they went too far, they'd be the ones to pay for it. It was a shame that some ne'er-do-wells would resort to extreme measures, but at least both companies were bursting with motivation.

They were also growing much faster than expected. In just a few months, they had developed into stable organizations, with positions established in a multitude of specific fields and a firm hierarchy in place. Right now, when we were under imperial attack, I heard they were enjoying quite a bit of war-based demand for their goods. I wondered if this was a bit *too* opportunistic of them, but since I was taking in their profits as a shareholder, I decided to call it a necessary evil and leave it at that. It wouldn't do to regulate *everything*, after all, and that goes double when it's my own interests at stake.

And so in relatively short time, we were on our way to seizing the local trade community for ourselves.

....

......

...

If Elmesia had stopped by here without advance notice, there must've been some kind of emergency. Maybe Prince Figaro skipped town on us after all? We had countermeasures in place for that scenario, but it'd mean I'd have to give up some of my shares, so it'd make sense if Elmesia wanted to come over to discuss that.

✳

At the inn, I was taken to a detached townhome Elmesia was occupying.

"Thanks for waiting for me. How's it going, El?"

No point speculating any further. Time to ask what she wanted to talk about. She *did* look pretty miffed about something, not even trying to hide her depression as she stared right at me.

"Oh, um, something upsetting you?"

"'Upsetting' would be the *kindest* way of putting it! Do you have any idea what you have done?!"

Um, what? Oh, man, she sounds legit pissed. And this didn't seem to be any "Wise Drunk" business after all...

"How do you mean?"

"Sit down."

"Uh, sure."

Not wanting to anger the sharp-eyed Elmesia any further, I meekly kneeled down on the tatami-mat floor. Mollie was doing the same next to me, and this seating position was clearly making his legs cramp up.

"Rim, is it true that you've been evolving some of your people?"

H-how does she know *that*?! I gave Mollie a quick side glance; he shook his head back to indicate he didn't know, either. So where did the leak come from?

"My boy Gazel gave me an urgent message. He said he wasn't sure whether to tell me but decided to in the end. Honest of him, isn't it?"

To Elmesia, even a sly old fox like Gazel was still her "boy." But that's what happened? I wasn't really hiding what I did, so I shouldn't be that shocked, but the sheer speed was pretty unexpected.

"Well, the Eastern Empire's a lot more dangerous than I thought, so I wanted to get ourselves powered up as best I could. I didn't think hiding it was a good idea, so I invited Jaine to witness it."

"Oh... So it's true...?"

She stood up, turned her back to me, and looked out a window. There was something sad—sorrowful, in a way—about the sight.

"...Why are you talking like it's somebody *else's* business?!"

Then she whacked me on the head with the folding fan she took out from her pocket.

"N-no, I didn't mean it like that..."

I was just trying to lighten the mood here a little. Sheesh.

"What do you even want to *do* with an army that powerful?"

"Huh? It's not that I wanna *do* anything, really. I'm trying to build a country that's fun to live in."

"And Gazel tells me you have more Primals serving you than just Diablo now?"

"Yeah. Sorry, I thought I told you. I wasn't aware of it myself until a little while ago. You know Testarossa, don't you, El? I always thought she was really talented, but it turns out she's a Primal, too, I guess. So there's her and two more, Carrera and Ultima, and they're serving as heads of our supreme court and chief prosecutor, respectively."

When I finished explaining matters, Elmesia began to visibly shake.

"And *that* is the truth as well?" She groaned. Then she sat down in front of me, gazing straight into my eyes as she asked me directly, "Are you trying to destroy the world?"

"Huh? No way."

"Because from *my* viewpoint, that's the only thing this could be!"

Now she was shouting. I hurriedly began making excuses, Mollie joining my side, as we verbally sparred for the next half hour or so.

"So you're telling me that Guy and Ludora are playing a game, using their respective pieces to decide on a winner?"

"Right, exactly!"

"Is that true, Gar?"

"I, um, I can't say I am that well-informed on the situation, either... But really, I'm not entirely certain this is something I should be listening in on, is it?"

"Well, no, it's not, but too late for that, right?"

"If I may, I'm not entirely sure 'too late for that' is much comfort for me..."

Yeah. Guess I totally dragged him into this, didn't I? Sorry about that. But given the relationship we have, I'm sure Mollie will forgive me soon enough.

"*Haaah*... I think I understand now. If Guy was cajoling you, you were certainly in no position to turn him down, were you...?"

Yes! Precisely! Guy was threatening me—let's phrase it like that.

"Indeed. It's painful for *me* to accept as well."

I was beginning to take on Mollie's manner of speech, but either way, we were finally starting to appease her.

Elmesia sighed again; either her anger was gone or she was scrambling to regain her composure.

"So what are you going to do?"

"What do you mean?"

"You're not going to resign yourself to being a pawn in Guy's game, are you?"

"I think I am, actually."

"Why?"

"Well, I've been thinking..."

She seemed to have no idea *what* I was thinking. So I tried to give her more insight.

It seemed a given that the Empire still had some powerhouses—people of unknown ability—in store for us. Trying to avoid a fight was one potential option, but I thought it'd only postpone the problem. I'd have to live in hiding all the time, on constant lookout for imperial assassins. There'd no doubt be a few skirmishes with them, and no matter how well I defended myself, there were bound to be casualties.

To prevent that from happening, I wanted to keep the initiative on my side. To the Empire, war is something of a ritual devised to create awakened people—and if so, I'd have to keep fending them off for ages to come. Ignoring them would just give them more time to build their army up.

"So that's the decision I've made. There's no point in padding my numbers, so I'm just gonna march right over with my main force and negotiate a peace deal. If we can get rid of Ludora's pawns while we're there, hopefully Guy will take care of the rest for us."

I really couldn't rely on Guy at all, so I wasn't expecting *that* much from him. But then the question became who to take with me.

"Are you going to be all right, Sir Rimuru?"

"Whoa, Mollie, who do you think I am? I may not look it, but I'm part of the Octagram, you know. Whether it's an emperor or his personal guard, I ain't losing sleep over any of their guys!"

"Ah, yes indeed! Truly, you are like a goddess to—"

"Hmm? Goddess?"

This guy's still looking at me that way? One glare from me made him rethink his words.

"—I mean, truly you are a demon lord we can all trust in!"

"Yes, well...um...just leave it all to me, then! Ha-ha-ha!"

"Wah-ha-ha-ha-ha!"

We both laughed our heads off.

I knew this wasn't what he wanted to hear after this, but if things *really* went south over there, I was planning to turn tail and run back home. I'd have to pretty much become a shut-in, and I was prepared for that, so I didn't bother dwelling on the idea much.

"Hmmm. So can you specify to me whether you planned to simply defeat Emperor Ludora's guard or kill them all outright?"

I wasn't a fan of any questions that assumed I'd be victorious, but I already had an answer to this one.

"I'll avoid killing as much as I can. Based on the game's rules for victory, Guy wins once I neutralize everybody except for Ludora, after all. Once I reach that point, I don't think it's a matter for me any longer."

Elmesia gave that a satisfied nod.

"All right. Do your best not to disappoint me, then. If worse comes to worst, I will take care of matters in your nation."

Please don't say such ominous things to me!

"No need to worry! I'm not into sacrificing myself nobly for the greater good, y'know! My motto's for everybody to have fun together, so no way am I gonna get killed over this."

"Good," she replied with a breezy smile. "But remember this as well: If you die, it will put this world fully in ruins. You are the only one who can tame monsters like Diablo and his Primals. The other creatures you evolved to demon lord level may not all agree with each other. If a conflict arises, it will inevitably erupt into war. Do you understand that? You can't just cast off what you're trying to do when you're not even done yet. Never forget that."

That was Elmesia's heartfelt advice to me.

"I know. I get you. I really do."

I swore it to her, my face dead serious.

*　　*　　*

The game was now in its final stages. Just a few more turns, and our victory would be set in stone. One wrong move, though, and the entire board would be flipped upside down.

We need to be calm—and careful. The first thing's to contact Yuuki and discuss how we'll deal with Emperor Ludora. Then, the day after that, we'll set off for the Empire.

It was a record of battles, a heavenly game continuing on for many years—a game between the demon lords and the Heroes, with supremacy over the planet hanging in the balance.

But to Velgrynd the Flame Dragon, it was a game with no meaning. She had no interest in it, nor did she care who won in the end. Why go through all this trouble, she reasoned, when the two sides could just fight it out directly to determine the better player? Of course, Guy and Ludora had tried that many times and never settled upon a victor, and that's where this game came from. The only rule: No direct confrontation.

There was no point complaining about it, but that didn't mean Velgrynd enjoyed it very much. Besides, if she was being honest, she felt this whole game put her side at a disadvantage. The only pawn Guy had who could defeat Ludora was Velzard—as long as they could do something about her, Ludora was the winner. But the same was true of Guy; only Velgrynd had a chance of beating that demon lord. The thing is, Velgrynd herself thought it'd be a difficult slog at best. Velzard had a concrete chance of winning against Ludora, but Velgrynd just didn't feel fully prepared against Guy. Hence, she thought, they were the underdogs to start with.

What a pain...

She meant that.

Velgrynd was never a fan of scheming behind the scenes; spending hundreds of years meticulously preparing for everything was simply out of her wheelhouse. So she left all that to Ludora, simply following his orders. As long as Ludora wanted to win this, she would spare no effort to pitch in. If he wanted her to fight, she would—she'd figure out what to do against Velzard, and she'd make sure they won.

Guy was undoubtedly the strongest of demon lords, and Velgrynd's sister, Velzard the Ice Dragon, was the worst possible match in battle for Velgrynd. They were basically natural enemies, and a head-to-head battle against her would be difficult to win. If the two True Dragons fought each other, they'd take each other down at best—at worst, it'd mean reincarnation and going back to the drawing board for Velgrynd.

But even that was being too optimistic, perhaps. Velgrynd's element was heat; Velzard's, ice. Two polar opposites, one symbolizing acceleration, the other shuddering to a stop. If they fought for keeps, the outcome would be disastrous. Neither would survive; both would fall. In other words, there was a good chance both Velgrynd and Velzard would disappear entirely. The sisters would be reincarnated, but their current selves would fade to nothing—they'd inherit their memories, probably, but they'd still be different people.

That scared Velgrynd. She didn't mind fading away like that, but she didn't want to lose her love for Ludora. Clinging to something as trivial as love—it made her laugh at herself.

"Complete victory," as she defined it, meant both she and Ludora were safe. That's why they needed some insurance… But that insurance was proving difficult to handle.

What a load of trouble he is. Apparently, he lucked out enough to break the seal, so why hasn't he even come to see me?

Velgrynd was peeved at the "insurance" that was Veldora; it never occurred to her that he might be afraid of her. The Veldora she knew would have begun a worldwide rampage long ago… But for reasons known only to him, he was currently buddying up with a newly christened demon lord. When Velgrynd heard that he even participated in the most recent Walpurgis council, she suspected years of being imprisoned in a seal had driven him insane.

Still, it was hard to believe that Veldora, as much of a fan of large-scale mayhem as he was, would sit silently in front of a million-strong army. She was sure he'd step out and make himself known, but instead she was shocked. Veldora was still holed up in the depths of the labyrinth, refusing to show himself. That was completely unexpected.

He's always done what he pleases… But why hasn't he shown up this time?

Veldora was extremely protective of his territory, just as he was in the last imperial invasion. Anyone who infiltrated the Forest of Jura, Velgrynd assumed, would unavoidably have an encounter with its guardian dragon. That, in turn, was precisely what Ludora wanted. To him, a strong army was nowhere near as important as a few individuals who had transcended their limits—and last time as well, the few who survived were successfully evolved.

Only those who hold on to hope under extreme circumstances—hatred, fear, despair—can break through the shell of humanity and reach the next level. Even if it literally annihilates an army of one million, it'd all be worth it if it awakened a few people. Such were Ludora's thoughts, and Velgrynd saw the wisdom in that. That was why Ludora never gave the IIB's more detailed reports to his army. He wanted to mislead their commanders so they'd be more motivated than ever to fight.

To Velgrynd, the sheer confidence of every corps commander was almost farcical to see. There was very little chance—none at all, in fact—that this mission would work out. An army enhanced through "science" or whatever had no hope of beating Veldora. Thus, once again, there would be unthinkable amounts of death… But that's what gave her hope.

Hee-hee-hee… I wonder how many survivors will awaken this time. The more people who receive Ludora's powers, the better a chance we'll have to win. I'm looking forward to it.

Yet despite Velgrynd's anticipation, the results of this invasion left her speechless.

*

"They were *all* wiped out?"

"*Pfft*. I was surprised myself... But you as well, eh? Quite a while since I've seen *that* look on your face."

"Don't make light of this. Neither of us was expecting a defeat so huge that absolutely no one's left alive. That means your aim to get even one single awakened has failed."

The idea was to give as much experience to their soldiers and officers as possible, raising them up to be at least Imperial Knight material. Those were the people who'd become awakened in operations like this. That was the hidden objective of it all, but instead, they had zero survivors.

Claiming the attack on Veldora turned out better than this was, if anything, underselling the issue. Only through interacting with the greatest strength in the world, experiencing the despair that wrought, and living to tell the tale could a human being enhance their chances of evolution. That was why they organized this gigantic army for the invasion—but if nobody survived, then it was all for naught.

As if that wasn't enough, all the Imperial Knights they had sent on undercover missions into the forest had gone silent as well. They had consumed a large number of valuable game pieces in this—a major loss with no gain in return.

"Well, that's how it goes."

Velgrynd was less than happy with Ludora's nonchalant reply, but one look at his eyes, and her anger disappeared. The sheer frustration in his gaze was too intense to bear for long. She could tell he felt the same way she did.

So she switched gears. It didn't matter to her if they lost an entire army. They'd have no complaints if some awakened came out of it, but even failures like this one were no great problem. However, they couldn't afford to ignore the adversary that engineered this loss. If a million imperial troops were literally wiped off the map, their opponents' strength was no laughing matter, either. They needed to be 100 percent sure who did this.

"Do you think *he* did it again?" Velgrynd asked, regaining her composure.

She had seen no sign of violence from Veldora at all, but they had reports that the Storm Dragon destroyed an army of twenty thousand over in Farmus. The IIB didn't have any operatives in that rural nation, so they couldn't learn more about that incident, but this time was different. They *should* have had a full grasp of the situation, and the files would be coming to Velgrynd, addressed to the Marshal, in short order.

If Ludora found out about this defeat before her, it was only because he had the power to do so. She was eager to get a viewpoint from this man she trusted so immensely. If she had to guess, her fun-loving brother would never miss the opportunity to go on a rampage. If a million soldiers were attacking his turf, Veldora would have to come out—and then they could gauge just how much power he had. She assumed they'd find out if he truly could control his aura now, to the point that they couldn't even spot his presence.

To Velgrynd, her brother's growth was a joy to behold. He might be a fool, but she still cherished him. But he was also a handful to deal with. She had to recruit him to their side at all costs, lest he join Guy's side instead. Velgrynd was always looking for ways to make that happen. Learning about his growth was vitally important to her.

But:

"He didn't. Amazingly enough, not even I am able to gain much in the way of detail."

Ludora told Velgrynd everything he knew—the major failures of the opening battles; the legions entering the labyrinth who still hadn't been heard from; the awe-inspiring magic that wiped out the rest of their forces; and Caligulio's awakening in the final battle. That—and the exact way the Armored Corps found themselves defeated, as if he was there to watch it himself.

"You're kidding me."

"It's true. All four of the remaining Primals are aiding the demon lord Rimuru's camp. If they decide to throw everything they have into battle, your brother hardly needs to lift a finger."

"Then the balance of this game has utterly collapsed. I wonder if Guy is just as upset about this? Or is it exactly what he wanted?"

"Good question. If this is what Guy has been after all along, it's time for us to admit we're at a huge disadvantage in this battle."

Ludora chuckled. They had spent years upon years building their strength, preparing for the best possible moment to strike—steadily, never rushing anything. And now, in the blink of an eye, someone else had acquired an unimaginable amount of strength. This was Rimuru, the Newbie, the smallest of little specks they never even noticed before. It was time to admit as much. And Velgrynd, sensing that, began kindling a burning desire to fight this threat.

"But you haven't been able to fully grasp the scene inside the labyrinth?"

"Heh-heh... You got it. Annoyingly enough, not even my power can break Ramiris's own."

It made sense to Velgrynd. The Labyrinth Master had been all but impenetrable—not exactly an impartial referee for this game, but definitely not someone involved with the pieces on the board. Until now. Now she was completely favoring the demon lord Rimuru. Regardless of how their game with Guy turns out, she was planning to set up shop in the Forest of Jura that the Empire just attempted to invade.

Ramiris did not have any great power herself. She seemed negligible enough to Velgrynd, someone who'd never have any effect on the game. But her Mazecraft skill was likely capable of shutting out all information between the labyrinth and the outside world. That, she now realized as she rolled her eyes, was going to be cumbersome.

"But didn't Ramiris lose her power as the Arbitrator?"

"She certainly did. I neglected her since she was no threat to us, but her labyrinth may just be the greatest hiding place in the world. We could see into it through Bernie's and Jiwu's eyes until now, but..."

"But now you can't, out of nowhere?"

Ludora nodded. "I'm sure this was a ploy to catch me off guard."

"I suppose it was. This is certainly more troubling than I thought..."

Velgrynd understood just how serious this was. Basically, they had no idea what happened inside the labyrinth. Normally, she'd default to assuming Veldora did something, but now she felt there was more to it than that.

"The main issue here is that Rimuru's apparently stuck some powerful compatriots of his inside the labyrinth as well. Your brother is the highest ranking among them, but who can say how much this newcomer has tamed him…?"

"The Veldora I know would never meekly take orders from someone else. And while *you* may be another matter, I doubt Rimuru could bind him down with a skill of any sort."

Their reports indicated he was working in tandem with the demon lord Rimuru, but Veldora was never the type to do other people's bidding. He openly defied Velgrynd—and Velzard, his other sister—all the time. She felt safe assuming that no one could subdue him by force.

So did the demon lord prepare something that could actually make Veldora his lapdog? Velgrynd tried to imagine what it could be but gave up.

If such a thing existed, we wouldn't have gone through all this trouble over the years. Perhaps I could ask the demon lord Rimuru himself?

"Best to hear it from the demon lord, I'd say."

Velgrynd's muttering made Ludora laugh out loud. "Ha! I'm glad you've come to the same conclusion I did."

This demon lord Rimuru could no longer be ignored by either of them. Given that he'd already tamed Primals, it was safe to assume that Veldora was similarly at his beck and call. If that were the case, they'd need to figure out how to wrest Veldora from Guy's camp first.

"If we're going to make a move, now might be a good time for it. Guy has no doubt let his guard down now that our first advance failed. A demon lord as patient as he would no doubt expect us to retreat and wait for our next chance."

"Good point. He's always been careful with his movements, never taking major risks. Perhaps a quicker move is better advised here. We have little time to lose anyway."

Velgrynd was delighted. Finally, Ludora was looking to settle matters with Guy. They would no longer bide their time, and she could use this opportunity to seize control of Veldora in short order. Perhaps their momentum could also crush the newcomer demon lord Rimuru, too, bringing them toward an all-or-nothing confrontation with Guy.

"Heh-heh-heh... Allow me to handle this, then. I'll go out there, kick some ass, and then you can come over and lay the groundwork. I believe in you, Ludora."

"Of course. And if we can just get our hands on Veldora, the rest will take care of itself. Tatsuya's come up with a rather interesting plan as well, so I think we can make up for this debacle very shortly."

Even the nightmarish Primals would be no match for a True Dragon like Velgrynd in a head-on matchup. If they defied her, she'd smash them to the ground so they didn't cause needless trouble later.

There may be others in the camp who'd cause problems for us... But if I'm out on the battlefield, it's all moot anyway.

Now Velgrynd was exuding confidence.

"Well! How about we make those fools shed some blood to warm up?"

Their attention was turned toward a group of people arrogant enough to defy Ludora, a band they had allowed to go free so far. That would end today. Anyone who plotted a coup against the emperor would see no possible outcome except death. That was why Velgrynd made the suggestion, but Ludora just grinned and shook his head.

"I'd rather keep them alive than kill them."

"Oh? That's uncommon to hear from you. I thought you'd be kind enough to grant them a painless death."

"No, I need them for Tatsuya's proposal, you see. He was hoping to set off another big battle over here, in order to attract Guy's attention."

"Hmm. Rather like Kondo, isn't it? I'd never even think about using imperial traitors against our enemies."

"Don't like it? Well, I wouldn't call Tatsuya's plan very humane, certainly... But I do believe it makes logical sense."

Velgrynd gave this a vague nod. No matter how outlandishly cruel this plan was, it didn't matter to her. She just wanted to give the traitors divine punishment with her own two hands.

Here was a True Dragon who loved Ludora, but she certainly didn't love humans at all. She didn't have a vendetta against them—no desire to kill them down to the last man—but anyone foolish enough to betray the emperor needed to die.

Well, all right. If it'll help Ludora, I will let them go for now.

With that, Velgrynd moved on.

"So what's Kondo's plan, exactly?"

"I'll talk about that in a moment, but first, we need to review our current strategy."

Velgrynd immediately knew what he meant.

"Ah, right. With things how they are, a two-pronged strategy is kind of pointless."

"Exactly. Let's withdraw for now. We can always attack Luminus later."

"Yes, once you and I persuade Veldora to join us, everything else is bound to come together, too. But I'll call Gradim and his forces back as well, just in case we run into any resistance."

"Would you mind?"

"Not at all. For now, let's keep the rebels subjugated and take down Dwargon while we're at it. That should be enough to fully distract Guy."

With that, their scheming was over. Velgrynd stood up. It had been millennia since she had waded into the game. And now the table was set for a tragedy that would later be called the Red Purge.

That Time I Got Reincarnated as a Slime

The darkness in the imperial capital ran deep and black. Advances in science had given the city natural gas-powered streetlights to illuminate its streets, but even so, there were still many back alleys hidden from the public eye. The city was still developing, but it would be quite a while before all the darkness inside was eradicated.

Now Misha was quietly walking in the dark where she was born and raised, and here, it gave her mind comfort instead of fear. That's just how she was.

In the days since she finished her report to Yuuki, Misha had kept hidden in the shadows, busily preparing for the upcoming coup. The imperial army was currently out on an invasion; it'd be dangerous for an officer like Misha to be seen in public. Desertion was punishable by death—and also described what she was doing pretty well at the moment. But she strode on with confidence, not a hint of fear on her face. It made evident just how confident she was in her knowledge of the city's darkness.

Besides, despite her preference for staying behind the scenes, Misha was an excellent fighter—not as good as Vega or Damrada but certainly a talented boss all the same. She was an expert at intel gathering, priding herself at outclassing Dwargon's and Blumund's agents. That was why she felt sure she could hide from the Imperial

Intelligence Bureau, and she had stayed alive in the capital well enough up to now.

Now she was heading for her usual destination... But tonight, that seemed to be a mistake. She hadn't been careless at all, but nonetheless, a man appeared to block her way.

His name was Tatsuya Kondo, the "figure stalking the halls of information" in the IIB. Damrada hadn't confirmed it with her, but he was also likely the commander of the Imperial Guardians. At the very least, there was no doubt that Misha could ever hope to beat him one-on-one.

"Where are you going this time of night?" Kondo asked, his cold voice particularly resonant.

Misha smiled, even as she internally chided herself. "Oh, it's you, Lieutenant Kondo! Are you working late tonight?"

Despite any misgivings, she acted perfectly serene with him. But for her, the situation couldn't get much worse right now.

I can't believe he sniffed me out in this remote nook of such a vast city... What a monster. No way could I beat him, either. And my escorts won't even buy any time for me.

Kondo had appeared without warning, but he seemed to be alone. That didn't give Misha much optimism. She searched for a way, any way, to get out.

"You're Misha, aren't you? Staff officer for Commander Caligulio? Why are you back in the capital during a wartime operation?"

His tone was dead serious.

"It was so scary, Lieutenant Kondo! I was actually asked by Lord Caligulio to go on a secret mission back to the capital."

She had to deceive him somehow. At the same time, she searched her surroundings for other people, keeping her guard up. There was no one else in this cramped alleyway, which was fine, but her bodyguards had apparently disappeared on her.

Did they already take care of them? How outclassed are we anyway? I didn't even notice a fight...

In an instant, Misha gauged the situation. They did not know each other personally, but there was no way Kondo wasn't aware of Misha. She didn't know how he saw her, but it didn't seem like words alone would get her through this. Her guards were dispatched without a moment's hesitation. Deception, she assumed, was out of the question.

So she decided to ask for help from Damrada, whom she was planning to meet up ahead. But then an unpleasant thought entered her mind.

How did they find out where I was? Sir Yuuki decided to trust Damrada… But can I do the same?

It was Damrada who arranged this meeting place for them; they were supposed to work out the details of the top secret conference they'd have with the demon lord Rimuru tomorrow.

Not good… Not good at all. There's a chance Damrada double-crossed us…as much as I hate to think it. Sir Yuuki trusts him, and besides, I owe Damrada as well.

Misha and Damrada had known each other for over twenty years. They were both leaders of Cerberus, and she felt she knew more about him than even Yuuki. That's why this was all so confusing for her. He knew Damrada to be coldhearted—rational. Based on what he told her, he had no apparent reason to stab Misha in the back. She not only wanted to believe that—after listening to Yuuki explain matters, she was convinced of it. So now wasn't the time for hesitation. She had to believe in her friends until the end.

So her mind made up, Misha looked at Kondo.

"My gratitude goes out to the great Emperor Ludora for the good fortune of meeting you here."

"Oh?"

"It was you, Lieutenant, wasn't it? The guy who took out my pursuers? I knew I wouldn't be able to take on that many opponents by myself."

"Ah. Proceeding with that script, then?"

"Oh, are you suspicious of me? Even after I've been desperately trying to get back from that hellhole to bring you my information at all costs?"

Misha boldly continued the performance, approaching Kondo and sidling up to his chest. This was Misha the Lover's specialty—using her feminine charms to ensnare unwitting men. It was powered by a combination of Curse Perfume and the illusory magic Charm, and it worked on the mind of the target, stimulating their base instincts while inhibiting their thought processes in order to make them fall in love with her. Their dependence on Misha would grow further if she was closer to them—physically and emotionally. Once she had it all in place, she'd have as much control over the target as she wanted.

She was using this on Caligulio as well; by her estimation, a few more embraces, and he'd be hers for the taking. And not just Caligulio, either—a litany of men had fallen for her wiles. As far as she knew, it had never failed before. It was the most powerful card she had to play, because even if she never had a chance in battle, she was sure any opponent would succumb to lust for her.

So Misha placed her supple hands around Kondo's back, pushing her ample breasts against him. Then she gauged his reaction. She could sense him slackening a little. She giggled.

Hee-hee! Good. He pretends to be this stuck-up bastard, but even Kondo's still a man, huh?

This was going better than she anticipated. Maybe this would work out, after all.

"Hey, why don't we go someplace else, huh? A room where we can relax, maybe."

She whispered the words, her lips close to his ear. Kondo's right hand moved a bit. "Very well," she could hear him whisper back.

This is going well. My best bet is to meet up with Damrada at our rendezvous point. Even if that doesn't work out, I can have Kondo sleep with me, and then he'll become my captive—

It was the last thought Misha would ever have. With a dry *bang*, Misha collapsed to the ground, the left side of her head bleeding profusely all over the street.

Somewhere along the line, Kondo had produced a Nambu semi-automatic handgun. The smoke rising from the muzzle made it clear this was the murder weapon that had shot Misha in the temple. He put it away, expression frozen, as if nothing untoward had happened.

His unique skill Decipherer, which read the thoughts of anyone he came in contact with, had already collected all relevant information. Misha's objective, Yuuki's plans, the fate of the imperial troops staging the invasion—it took him less than a second to read all that. But despite the devastating truths just revealed to him, Kondo's face remained frozen. Instead, looking almost bored, he spoke into the darkness.

"...A coup? What a deranged idea. And yet you claim you're not betraying His Majesty?"

From the darkness, where nobody should have been, emerged a lone man. Instead of answering Kondo's question, he walked up to the crumpled figure of Misha. It was Damrada.

"Kondo, you didn't have to kill her, did you? With the right education, she could have been of great help to His Majesty."

"No, there was no chance of that. Apply a ranking to her skills, and she would be lucky to reach thirty-seven or so. She might have had a chance if she could reach the teens, at least, but no woman of her caliber could ever serve His Majesty. Besides," Kondo coldly spat, "I was completely exposed, and she couldn't penetrate my defenses."

Damrada shrugged. If Kondo said so, he must have been right. There was no point arguing. All he had were mixed feelings over the fate of Misha, one of his friends.

He kneeled next to her, holding out his left hand to the left side of her head. A soft light closed the wound. He pushed Misha's protruding eyeball back into its socket, pulling both eyelids down. Finally, he wiped her face clean, trying his best to restore at least some of her beauty. He couldn't bring the dead back to life, but at least he wanted her to rest in peace.

"Why waste your time? Leave her, and the body will be disposed of before sunrise," said Kondo. "Just answer my questions, please."

"I can't put my emotions aside the way you can."

"You're too soft."

"*You're* just crazy. How can you act so thoroughly emotionless at such a young age?"

"I don't have any emotions. End of story."

"That's ridiculous—"

"I have seen hell in my time. It was Emperor Ludora who saved me from that hell. If you're switching sides on me, you won't receive any mercy."

"I am ever His Majesty's faithful servant. I could never betray him."

"We'll see about that. Remember, you're under my spell at the moment. If you want me to trust you, better prove it by your actions."

Then Kondo walked away, never looking back. Damrada took one final glance at Misha, then left the scene himself. Nights lasted a long time in the imperial capital. There was still work left to be done.

Not long after, agents from the Intelligence Bureau disposed of Misha's body, leaving not a trace behind. The darkness of the capital's nights was so deep it could bury even these events, as if they had never happened at all.

●

Upon receiving Yuuki's instructions, Kagali immediately went on the move. If they were going to carry out this coup, careful preparation was absolutely essential. Messengers were instantly dispatched, and within a few days, all the major players from around the world were gathered in one place.

Nearly thirty of them were now at Yuuki's mansion in the imperial capital, faithful agents who all swore absolute loyalty to the man. Some, like Vega, were embedded in other imperial corps and couldn't participate; the people here composed around half of Yuuki's executive staff. The coup itself had been in the works for some time, and the attendees were all eagerly awaiting Yuuki's speech, feeling that the time was near.

They were all quite capable, climbing the ranks on their own strengths and making names for themselves in the military. Their loyalty to Emperor Ludora was nonexistent from the start. Some were even excited at the concept of engineering an Empire-wide revolution. There were visitors from other worlds, halflings with strange and unusual skills, superhumans subjected to cruel body-enhancement experiments, and first-rate adventurers raised by Yuuki himself. There were even enslaved warriors collected by Damrada, as well as magic-born under Misha's protection.

What they were faithful to the most was violence—and that's exactly where the Composite Division shone the most.

A large meeting room was opened to them all, located upstairs above the grand atrium floor. Yuuki came in with Kagali just as everyone took their seats.

"Hey there, guys. Great to see you all here."

He was all smiles, speaking in his usual cheerful tone as he greeted them.

"Tomorrow, I have a meeting planned with the demon lord Rimuru. I'm having Misha bring over Damrada as well, so we'll discuss more details once he arrives."

This instantly caused an uproar.

"Weren't we staging this coup by ourselves?"

"The demon lord is too cunning and unpredictable. Are you sure we can trust him?"

"No, wait. Aren't we at war right now? Rimuru can't just slip out of that and slink over here."

Voices shouted out from across the hall. Yuuki's smile just broadened.

"The imperial army has been annihilated, you know. Rimuru killed all nine hundred and forty thousand troops who invaded the forest."

"That's insane!"

"It's too fast. Calculate the travel times, and it's only been a few days since we engaged them…"

It was far too much for the audience to believe. Yuuki quieted them down with a laugh.

"If we're going to overthrow the empire, we need fighting power. That's why I've decided to join forces with Rimuru."

The audience began to understand Yuuki's words, even if they didn't agree with them. The more intelligent among them had shifted their attention to whether this intel was reliable or not.

"Is this information Lady Misha brought back?"

Many Cerberus members were among the group, aware of Misha's presence in the military.

"You got it. If we hadn't allied with them beforehand, I think they would've killed Misha long ago."

"Lady Misha did that?!"

"Astounding..."

She may have done mostly undercover work, but she was also a well-known figure, a truly appropriate leader for Cerberus. Everybody in here attained their positions in life through their own efforts alone, so they knew how to assess their peers fairly. They had a lot of trust in Yuuki that way, oddly—they knew he'd never value someone inferior in ability.

"Well...in that case, I welcome this alliance. I'm not too happy about how you kept this to yourself until now, but I'm sure you had your reasons for it, eh, Boss?"

"Not really any major reason, but yeah. It's just that I lost to Guy, and he made me promise him something."

"Guy? You don't mean Guy Crimson, do you?!"

"You fought the Lord of Darkness? That's way out of line, Boss!"

"Impossible. I'm amazed you survived."

Now the audience was in an uproar for another reason. Yuuki quieted them down again.

"I'm sure you all have your opinions, but I don't have time to explain everything. For now, you'll all gonna have to accept it, and I hope you'll be patient with me on this. Instead, I'd like to discuss the arrangements we'll make at tomorrow's meeting and how we'll conduct our operations afterward."

The only official forces remaining in the capital were the IIB and a force of new recruits. The top-ranking IIB personnel were a threat, perhaps, but their rank and filers didn't really count as a military force. The new recruits formed a vast army, numbering a good hundred thousand, but they had no real skill. They were just fill-ins, not even worth considering in this coup attempt. There were also around twenty thousand guards serving as police, but in terms of their equipment, they were no match for a military. The difference in gear was so vast, it'd be like a grown-up taking on a five-year-old. At best, they could stop their coup for a short period of time.

But the most powerful forces of all, the Imperial Guardians, were still at the disposal of the emperor.

"The IIB has Guardians mingled in among them, too. So technically speaking, it's really only the Guardians who we need to worry about."

"Right, yes. I've run into them in ranking duels before, but the guys up top really do pack a punch."

"Oh, quit patting yourself on the back. For all we know, there are traitors like us among the Guardians, no?"

"Could be. Me, the only thing I have faith in is power. I'm not going to swear allegiance to some emperor who swaggers around like a fancy lad all the time!"

Scattered laughter broke out. They had allies among the Guardians. Reaffirming that fact just now, everyone realized just how much of an advantage they had.

The joke was told by a somewhat small man, known for his arrogant attitude. His name was Arius, and he was an otherworlder— not summoned, but a "visitor," one who made the journey by chance.

"So will the demon lord Rimuru's forces be ready for this by tomorrow?"

The black-haired girl asking this question was Mai Furuki, a high school teen over in Japan who was then summoned and picked up by Yuuki back when he still led the Free Guild. Thanks to the support Yuuki offered, she held deep, admiring trust for him.

"Good question. If they're bringing an army, it'll take a while no matter how fast they are. Not unless they're flying over— Hey, they ain't gonna fly into the capital, are they?"

Now a large, muscular man was chiming in—Tornewot, a former slave fighter. If he hadn't caught Damrada's attention, he might've spent his whole life toiling in the mines until he collapsed. Thrown into the army, Tornewot received an education, something he took intense pride in. Despite his bulky build, he was quite an intelligent man, enough so that he had been appointed a staff officer in the Composite Division.

"Perhaps, but flight magic consumes spiritual force. That won't be a problem for a demon lord, maybe, but I don't know if his rank-and-file monsters can all fly."

Tornewot's question was answered by Alia, a petite magic-caster who also wore the heavy armor of a fighter. She was nowhere near as young as she looked—in fact, she was an apprentice of Gadora's, and she had also undergone body-enhancement surgery, making her a unique figure in this crew.

"I don't mean *that*," Tornewot countered. "Whether the Empire's main force is away or not, they've got a surveillance network covering the skies above the capital. If a large army comes in from the air, they're gonna get noticed no matter how far away they land."

Alia's face reddened a bit. It was a surprisingly accurate observation, and being shown up like this was a tad embarrassing. By magic-caster standards, she was unusually short-tempered and too quick to speak without thinking matters over.

"Hey, it's important to keep an exchange of ideas going here. Analyzing things from different angles could help us see things differently, after all."

Yuuki quickly interceded, guiding the chatter back to the main topic.

"Rimuru has contacted me through old man Gadora to say that only a small number of them will be coming tomorrow."

The contact came through a Gadora-engineered anonymous magical call. Even if the IIB was listening in, it was all encrypted and impossible to decipher. Gadora outlined the main points of it to Yuuki, and according to him, the roster they'd send tomorrow was still undecided. Rimuru was definitely coming... But who would escort him?

Sounds like Rimuru's decided a show of force won't work on Ludora, too. Quality over quantity, huh? I bet he'll bring nothing but his top brass over, then.

Maybe about ten or so at most, Yuuki reasoned.

"They're underestimating the Empire that much? Or are they making fools out of their allies?"

The question was lodged by a slender beauty, stretching herself out—not a question so much as just stating what was on her mind. This was Orca, a warrior, and she might've appeared a bit airheaded at first. Despite that, she was an extraordinary talent with a number of hidden skills.

"Wrong on both counts, Orca. Like I said, it takes a lot of time to ready a large army—delays pop up in so many different ways. I'm sure he decided it was better to work with a small team of elites."

Tornewot stepped up to explain matters again. Yuuki smiled, glad to be spared the trouble.

"Exactly. That's why we need to work out our own direction now."

If Rimuru was only bringing his best fighters, that brought up the question of who would pit themselves against whom.

"I'm gonna ask Rimuru what he thinks at the meeting tomorrow, so we need to put our thoughts together. For example, what are we gonna do with Emperor Ludora?"

It might've been pretty arrogant of Yuuki to say that. Defeat wasn't even on his mind; only victory was in his future. Discussing their treatment of the emperor before the coup had even succeeded was a tad abnormal, after all. But no one pointed this out. Even Tornewot, always ready with a verbal jab, grinned and waited for Yuuki to continue.

"The Dwarven Kingdom is aware of our activities as well, so the currently deployed Composite Division forces are free to head off to the capital without worrying about their rear. If all they have to deal with are the imperial forces left in the capital, it'll be easy, right?"

"It sounds that way. The Guardians are the only threat?"

"That's right," responded Yuuki, still smiling. He knew the true threat was elsewhere—an unknown entity known simply as the Marshal. And if you thought about why Guy let Yuuki live in the first place...

Why did Rimuru take action this time? He's a pacifist at heart. I figured he'd hate to attack other countries out of nowhere...

Perhaps he just didn't want to have any regrets. But Yuuki felt that couldn't be the only reason. So he mentally put the pieces together—and then he saw a hint of Guy's shadow behind Rimuru as well. If that was the case, he concluded, perhaps there was a monster in the Empire that could be a worthy opponent for even Guy.

"Depending on how things work out, we might have to kill the emperor, won't we?"

"Not so fast, Arius."

"Yeah, don't reserve the right for yourself!"

The crowd here was so excited now that they were openly talking about the emperor's upcoming murder. Yuuki agreed it was too early to discuss his treatment, but he was glad to see everyone so revved up in advance.

In fact, they'd be discussing Ludora's fate at the meeting tomorrow. Gadora was opposed to killing him, and Damrada's loyalty was still squarely aimed at the emperor. They were both important collaborators on this, and Yuuki hated to clash with them. Plus, there was a healthy chance this "monster" Guy was so wary of was Ludora himself—and if so, it'd be suicidal for Yuuki to make any careless moves.

Let's wait and see how this turns out, he concluded. *No need to put myself in the hot seat for no good reason. I could always have Rimuru take the emperor, too.*

They'd be saving strategic details for after Damrada's arrival, but Yuuki already had a draft outline ready for their approval. First, the main part of the Composite Division would overrun and capture the capital. Any Imperial Guardians who got in the way would be taken care of by those present in this room. Yuuki expected big things from them all; they were no less capable than the Guardians themselves. Maybe they couldn't take the top-ranked ones, but they still had a numerical advantage. If multiple allies swarmed on one, that should make up the difference.

The big guys like Ludora and the Marshal could be left for Rimuru, considering he was kind enough to join their fight and all. That's what Rimuru was probably aiming to do anyway, so he was sure the demon lord would accept that.

Meanwhile, no imperial reinforcements would come from anywhere to defend the capital. Out of their three major armies, the Armored

Division was destroyed by Rimuru; the rest of the Composite Division would join them once the trend was clear; and the Magical Beast Division was way up in the clouds over distant lands. Even if they found out and rushed over at full speed, it'd all be over by then.

Now that the plan had progressed this far, it was all but a sure bet. Yuuki wasn't about to hurry matters, but he was sure victory was imminent. Still, he still couldn't shake the uneasy feeling that he was missing something. What could it be—?

"Pardon my lateness," boomed a calm voice that echoed across the heated meeting hall. The moment it did, everyone shrank back, as if showered with ice-cold water.

"*There* you are, Damrada."

He was finally here.

$*$

Today Damrada was dressed in his military uniform, a rarity considering his usual merchant's disguise. That was when Yuuki began to worry.

"Where's Misha?"

"She's dead."

The hall fell silent. Everyone went on guard, sensing something disturbing. They had all been in many life-threatening situations in their time, so they were sensitive to the signs.

"What do you mean, Damrada?"

"I mean exactly what I said. She was killed by Kondo a moment ago."

The instant he heard the news, Yuuki felt the lingering uneasiness in his chest explode. That uneasy feeling that he had overlooked something... Now he knew what it was.

He and Damrada hadn't known each other for long, but their relationship ran deep. They'd shared in countless evil machinations that could never be revealed to the public. It was his assistance that helped Yuuki take down the Echidna Club, once the overlords of organized crime. They then established Cerberus together, with Damrada working tirelessly to build it up.

That's what Yuuki thought, but maybe he had it all wrong. In fact, everything was going exactly how the Empire wanted it. Cerberus was built from a core group that Damrada recruited for the purpose. Its mission was to weed out the talented from the incompetent, and its network was spread around the world to find and bring in new potential talent. Protecting lost otherworlders was part of that. And they hadn't started this just recently—it had been going on for a while, even back when the Echidna Club was dominant.

In a way, didn't it mean that Yuuki himself was discovered by Damrada in the same manner? He was in the business of scouting strong prospects and bringing them under his wing, and as he worked on that, Damrada discovered Yuuki. If Damrada himself emerged from his undercover position, he'd be too conspicuous, after all. Yuuki was just selected as a charismatic public figure.

He thought he was using Damrada, but it was the other way around. But that didn't mean Damrada double-crossed him. His loyalty was genuine. Perhaps someone had manipulated Damrada in order to make the ever-suspicious Yuuki trust in him—thinking about it that way, it seemed to answer all the questions he had up to now.

Picking up on all this, Yuuki let out an exhausted sigh.

"Well, you sure put one over on me. So when did this all begin?"

"…? What do you mean?"

Damrada sounded indifferent. He used the same tone as always… But now Yuuki was positive something was off. Damrada didn't seem to be playing dumb; he honestly didn't understand this question. The man himself, in other words, didn't even realize he was being manipulated.

No wonder, huh? If he didn't realize it was happening, he wouldn't know to keep an eye out for it.

Yuuki recalled their last meeting. Damrada had insisted he didn't betray anyone, and Yuuki felt that was the truth. Maybe something had been done to him after that, even. If he could trust his own instincts, it seemed that Damrada's manipulation happened only recently.

Right. I'm the one who decided to trust him, and I'm not going to say anything about that now. The important thing is: What does whoever sent Damrada here want from us?

Someone was controlling him. That much Yuuki was certain of now, and based on that, he surmised that they were in a very delicate situation. For all he knew, they'd fully surround his mansion in the time it took to deal with Damrada.

Yuuki was lost in thought, Kagali quietly analyzing the situation herself. But the revved-up audience was enraged by Damrada's behavior.

"How dare you disrespect Sir Yuuki!" Alia shouted, denouncing him.

"Damrada," Tornewot said, "what are you thinking? Are you here to betray us all?"

"Betray?" Damrada aloofly replied. "What a strange thing to accuse me of. From beginning to end, my allegiance for His Majesty, the Emperor Ludora, has been unwavering."

"*Tch!* That's *called* betraying us!" Arius spat.

Damrada was notorious for being corrupted by money, a fact that some of his companions looked down upon him for. Some even openly talked behind his back about how he'd surely betray them all for the right price. That's why the group here was more angered than surprised by this revelation.

Tornewot was the first among them to act, lifting Damrada up by his shirt and shouting at him.

"Quit screwing with us! You found me! You said that I should live for the greater good instead of die in the mines. I was so grateful to you. So why did you do this to me— *Nngh?!*"

This was actually Tornewot's attempt to protect Damrada. Before anyone else could act, he wanted to confront his benefactor himself and figure out what was going on. But to Damrada, this was probably unwelcome attention. With a gentle squeeze of Tornewot's wrist, he flicked his hand back, manipulating his muscle tension to reverse the hold on him.

"Tornewot, do you remember what I said to you?"

His eyes were so cold that they chilled the normally levelheaded Tornewot to the core. "Wh-what?" he replied, grabbing his wrist.

"I told you to be strong for the greater good, didn't I? And *this* power is all you have to show for it?"

All his force converged on a single point. It made Tornewot's wrist creak...and then shatter, all in an instant.

"You... What did you do to my wrist...?"

With that groan, Tornewot backed away from Damrada, rubbing his wrist as he used one of the healing potions he always kept on hand. Damrada stood there at ease, refraining from a second attack, but there was nothing off guard about him. In a world where some monsters can repair broken bones in an instant, you could never let up until you were sure your opponent was neutralized. A failure to realize this would be lethal.

Yuuki narrowed his eyes toward Damrada. He knew this man was powerful. You didn't get to rank that high among the Single Digits without being able to outclass a room full of champions like these. The question was: Did he possess an ultimate skill or not? And if so, how good was he at using it?

Will my Anti-Skill work on it? That's the thing.

Depending on the answer, he may have to kill Damrada. He needed to know, so he didn't dare stop anyone from confronting him.

"You're the emperor's dog, aren't you?!" shouted Arius. "I thought you were just a money-grubbing bastard, but you tricked us all! Why would a coward like you just walk in here alone and expose yourself?!"

Then things began to unfold.

"He's right, Damrada. I owe you a great debt... So I'm going to make your death painless."

Now Tornewot was ready to challenge him with everything he had.

"Too late."

But despite Tornewot grabbing the battle mace hanging from his belt and heaving it up with both hands, Damrada had no problem ducking the strike. In a clean, natural movement, he dived toward Tornewot's chest and gently pushed out the palm of his right hand. Despite the light, airy move, it hit its target with a deep, heavy impact.

This was Spiral Penetrator, a type of *fa jin* martial arts move that strikes its opponent with focused, explosive force. This fighting spirit is given directional kinetic energy that penetrates both armor and muscle, destroying the target from the inside out. Its power is proportional to the amount of infused fighting spirit, and if Damrada was the one focusing it, he could count on it having the lethal force of a tank round.

"*Gnhh!*"

His opponent crouched down, coughing up blood, legs too weak to stand back up. How could he? That single blow had just destroyed all of Tornewot's internal organs.

"It… It's crazy… You were *that* strong…"

"Well, well, well. Judging a book by its cover? The classic move of a conceited pile of muscle, supported by a massive ego. Were you laboring under the assumption that you outgunned me just because I hired you as a guard?"

"*Ngh…*"

"I asked you to be strong. Humans are no fools. They don't need to rely on arcane, esoteric abilities—they can become as strong as they want, if they train hard enough. Just like I did."

Then Damrada shot his leg backward, executing a roundhouse without looking behind him. The attacker aiming for his blind spot, unable to react in time, promptly died of a broken neck.

Damrada made it look like stepping on an ant, but this was Arius, a man whose strength even Yuuki praised. He possessed the unique skill Murderer coupled with the twin skills of Silent Movement and Conceal Presence, the perfect combination for assassination missions. This made him a natural killer, one good enough to rank Number Forty-Four in the imperial hierarchy. But despite his specialty in antipersonnel ops, Damrada wasted no time at all dispatching him.

"As I think I've just shown, leaning on your abilities is not good enough. When push comes to shove, the thing you can rely on the most is your well-trained body and mind. If you ask me, all of you here are useless."

He was choosing harsh words, and those in the room who'd never been ridiculed by even their martial-arts instructors were indignant as they heard them. It was like he was trying to teach the weak a lesson here, and it infuriated them. They all glowered at Damrada, eyes blazing with murderous intent.

In the midst of all this, Yuuki was still calmly, silently observing. Now he had his conclusion.

I knew it. Damrada didn't betray us—someone was controlling him. Someone on the emperor's side, maybe, considering Arius's position in the Imperial Guardians. He didn't kill Tornewot, but against Arius, he showed no mercy at all—that's all the proof I needed. So Damrada still has his free will, but he can't do anything that'd be inconvenient for whoever's ruling over him. Is that it?

Whatever controlled Damrada must have been a very powerful force, indeed. Nonetheless, Damrada was still attempting to find a way to communicate his current situation to Yuuki. Based on that, Yuuki tried to work out the best solution.

"Okay, guys, eyes over here! Switch to a retreat operation right now! I'm leaving all authority to Kagali, so all of you drop every- thing and regroup with the Composite Division."

"Boss? We don't have to run away. Let's take care of this traitor, and then we can rise to action right now—"

"No."

Yuuki immediately rejected Alia's suggestion. He still had his usual carefree smile on, but his eyes weren't so jovial as he scanned the room.

"Damrada's stalling for time. That's why he's going on and on like this. It's what he's been allowed to do, okay?"

"Allowed to do?" Kagali asked.

Yuuki nodded. "Right. Damrada didn't double-cross us. Some- one's controlling his mind, and that someone's trying to wipe us out right here."

This revelation was met with mixed reactions, but it did help his comrades regain their sense of judgment. Holding back the desire to kill Damrada, they focused their gazes on Kagali, the second-in-command.

She had come to the same conclusion Yuuki did. She knew they were in a critical situation; the alarm bells in her mind told her so. Now, with Yuuki's instructions given, she knew what she had to do. Things were urgent, and she knew it was no time to argue with him.

"We'll abandon this place and head for the Composite Division's encampment."

"But what about Sir Yuuki?"

"Oh, don't worry about me. I doubt Damrada would let me leave anyway, so I'm gonna have to deal with him here. You guys get going."

Yuuki turned his back to the crowd so he could face Damrada.

"We're off," Kagali ordered.

""""Roger!""""

Everyone realized what they had to do. Whether Damrada betrayed them or not didn't matter now—once they saw Yuuki turn around, they knew he was ready for anything. The time for debate was over. Right now, as all the superpowers in the room knew, job one was just to survive.

Alia carried the fallen Tornewot. The sight of a dainty little girl picking up a musclebound giant was chuckle-inducing, but no one was laughing. A healer cast some magic on Tornewot as they joined the line of fleeing rebels—and then, in perfectly orderly fashion, they all blended into the darkness of the night.

A few minutes later, Yuuki and Damrada were the only ones left in the vast meeting hall.

"It's too late to run away now, I think. You always did blow the landing that way, Sir Yuuki. I think you're underestimating the IIB here."

"Maybe I am. But if I struggle hard enough, maybe I can find a way out of this, y'know?"

"Don't make me laugh. This isn't a children's game, you know."

"Of course not. I'm always serious."

"Including with your fairy-tale dreams of conquering the world?"

"Hell yeah! And you're the same, aren't you?"

Damrada gave that a chuckle. "Yes," he bellowed from the bottom of his heart, "exactly!"

                                    *   *   *

Yuuki Kagurazaka was, to Damrada, a good boss. He still had a childish mind that caused him to make immature decisions at times, but he also had his coolheaded side. He was incredibly calculating in personality, and no matter how things turned out, life was certainly never boring under him.

That's why Damrada trusted him. He trusted that, right now, he must realize that Kondo was controlling him like a puppet.

....

......

...

At the same time, Damrada's loyalty to Emperor Ludora was completely genuine. He recognized and approved of Yuuki, but his feelings for Ludora were something completely different. They weren't comparable at all.

To Damrada, Emperor Ludora was everything—and right now, he was acting in accordance with his promise to Ludora. Fulfilling that promise was what he pinned his whole life on. He knew Ludora longer than Kondo had, and it was admittedly careless of him to think Kondo wouldn't touch him. He was aware that he was under suspicion. That's why he had been so careful. But it seemed that Kondo was even more dangerous than Damrada thought.

Immediately after he said his final goodbyes to Misha, Damrada's will was put under Kondo's control. How he did it, Damrada couldn't say—but no matter what he tried, he was unable to break it. His consciousness remained fully intact, but every aspect of his actions was now dictated by Kondo.

....

......

...

I had no idea that bastard Kondo would take over my own body, too. Anyone will tell you how cautious he is, but I didn't think he'd take matters this far. Sir Yuuki has truly outdone himself.

If he couldn't deactivate this body control on his own, the only hope left was to rely on Yuuki. He'd need to make Yuuki aware of his situation, but that posed a major challenge. No matter how you looked at it, this was clearly Damrada betraying the entire movement. It was just asking too much, and Damrada himself was about to give up on the idea.

But Yuuki noticed it. He did an incredible job. It moved Damrada deeply, even as he could only say what Kondo allowed him to.

"Allow me, Sir Yuuki, to show you the abilities of the vice commander of the Imperial Guardians."

The restrictions were permission-based; they put blocks on what Damrada could do. But despite that, Damrada tried to relay as much information as he could to Yuuki. Providing his rank was one such attempt. He had to let Yuuki know as much as he could give him, and after that, Yuuki could utilize it as he pleased. Convinced this was the right way, Damrada decided to pin his hopes on Yuuki.

If he kills me after that, it'll all be over. The promise I made to Emperor Ludora will be taken on by Sir Yuuki, I assume. A pity I can't see it with my own eyes, but...

He was sure that Yuuki would carry on his will. If Yuuki ever wanted to fulfill his lofty ambitions, he'd have to carry out Damrada's objectives as well. He didn't have high hopes, but they were hopes nonetheless.

"Oh, don't worry about that. I still have work for you to do, y'know. I'll help you out of this."

"Ha-ha-ha! If that's the kind of infantile nonsense you've got for me, you don't stand a chance."

Controlled or not, nothing could erase the joyful feeling welling up from his heart. And so just as that heart desired, Damrada unleashed his emotions...

●

Over thirty warriors were running along the main thoroughfare of the imperial capital. Led by Kagali, they were attempting to flee the city at night, just as Yuuki ordered them, to regroup with the Composite Division. The division was camped near the Empire's border with the Dwarven Kingdom, over three hundred miles southwest of the capital; merchant caravans would need over ten days to travel that distance.

Those with enough magic force could use one of the transport gates laid out around the city, a first-rate piece of magical technology that allowed travel between supported cities in an instant. But they couldn't push a hundred people through at once, and given their importance, they were kept under heavy guard. Storming one this late at night would obviously lead to warfare.

Thus, without hesitation, Kagali decided to go it on her own. Rather than stir up trouble here, she decided that strengthening her forces' position came first. Everyone in this group was far more powerful than your average human being; if they kept running without any breaks, they could reach their destination in a few hours.

"Are you all right, Lady Kagali?"

"Yes, everything's fine. Thanks for your concern, Teare."

Kagali nodded at Teare, a young masked woman who was running next to her.

As the former demon lord Kazalim, Kagali spent years in only her spiritual body after Leon defeated her. She was not a spiritual life-form yet, and it took everything she had to maintain her sense of presence. But she made it through, and thanks to Yuuki, she finally obtained a homunculus body for herself—one she had no problem training to become as matchlessly powerful as she was before. Thanks to that, she was now equivalent to a high-level magic-born in fighting strength, one who'd never lag behind the rest of this group.

"Oh? Well, good, then. Would've been nice if Laplace were here right now..."

"Yes, I'm sure he could've beaten Damrada, even."

"Hoh-hoh-hoh! Well, our boss is no pushover, either. I'm sure he'll be back with us shortly...after he wins!"

"You said it!"

"Yep! He absolutely will."

Kagali flashed a smile, but inwardly, she knew her panic was growing. Those alarm bells were still going off, making her anxiety balloon in size.

...This is not good. Not good at all.

It was an instinctive hunch; Kagali couldn't count the number of times it had saved her life. She knew she had to do something about it, even if she had no real evidence yet. So she turned toward Teare and Footman, her most trusted companions here.

"Contact Laplace for me."

"What?"

"Tell him to come back here."

It was no problem for Teare and Footman to contact Laplace via Telepathy. No matter how separated they were, the clowns were always connected to each other.

"Laplace is on a messenger run, but..."

"I don't care. Hurry up!"

The alarm bells only Kagali could hear began to ring louder. There was no time to explain, she decided. Leaving Teare behind, she moved on to her next order.

"Everyone, disperse! Survival's your top priority! Take any measures you see fit to—?!"

She was ordering them to find their own ways back to the Composite Division, but she never had the chance. As she now realized it was already too late.

"What a surprise. I thought I eliminated any sign of my presence. You did well to notice me."

A man in a military uniform emerged from the darkness. It was Lieutenant Kondo—and with him, a group of operatives silently rappelling down the buildings lining the main street. There were about fifty in all, but each one exuded a presence that was nothing short of overwhelming.

"Imperial Guardians..."

"That's right. Cease your futile resistance and surrender at once. If you do, I'll give you the honor of dying for His Majesty the Emperor."

"So you admit it then, Lieutenant? You're the commander of the Imperial Guardians?"

Kondo's expression remained blank. He neither confirmed nor denied it, but to Kagali, that was enough.

Kagali's group crowded together, keeping careful watch of the knights surrounding them. Combat was no longer avoidable. Each one of them was armed to the teeth, covered head to toe in Legend-class armor. Perhaps both sides were evenly matched, but the difference in gear was as clear as day. It was a dizzying disadvantage to have, but none of Yuuki's troops would give up at this point.

"Ha! Let's do it, huh? This'll just save us time later!"

"Right. Let's see what the Guardians can *really* do!"

Tornewot had been at death's door a few minutes ago, but now he was keyed up, and Alia was following his lead. As superpowered as they all were, they had no intention of admitting defeat without attempting anything.

In the meantime, Kagali was desperately analyzing the situation. The probability of them all surviving this was practically zero. At this stage, the only tactical victory they could gain was to transport as many comrades over to the Composite Division camp as possible. To achieve that, they'd need to buy some time—until Yuuki could defeat Damrada; until Laplace could return to pitch in. Time, precious time, was what Kagali realized they needed the most.

Well… I hope one of the two make it in time, but let's see what happens.

She took a step toward Kondo.

"Oh? You want to be my opponent?"

"Yes. I want to see for myself what the head of the Guardians is capable of."

Kagali understood that her own strength was far below Kondo's. But her objective was to serve herself up as a decoy.

Even if I can't win, if I can at least carve out some time…

With that thought in mind, she steeled herself, facing Kondo. The lieutenant, on the other hand, seemed all but oblivious to her, sighing at the sight of the combat beginning around him.

"I detest waste. I have no intention of putting up with your stalling attempts. And you need to understand that 'wanting it more' won't help you win a war."

"You think? Because I think if you pray enough, you might just see a miracle."

"*Hmph.* Imagine, an ex–demon lord raving so incoherently."

Kagali sneered back. Only a very few companions were supposed to know that she used to be a demon lord—but Kondo just blared it out for the world to hear. To put it another way, he must have decided it was too insignificant to keep a secret.

"You're really looking down on me, aren't you?"

"I'm not intending to. But let me tell you something else. I imagine you're trying to regroup with the Composite Division, but don't bother. His Majesty himself has just organized a force and set out to defeat them."

"What?"

The emperor going off to battle was an extremely unusual state of affairs. But what caught Kagali's attention more was the "force" being organized.

"What did you expect? Only the strong matter to us. If you swear loyalty to His Majesty, then fine. But a bunch of minnows with no chance to evolve? No, thank you."

"What do you mean…?"

"Am I not getting through to you? The only reason you're being kept alive right now is because you still have the potential to evolve. All of this is going according to His Majesty's plan."

"Don't give me that! Are you saying you knew our entire scheme?!"

Kagali was furious. Kondo just gave her a resentful look.

"What a silly question. Or did you think you were pulling the wool over our eyes here in the capital?"

A dim, angry flame lit itself in Kagali's heart—the flame of humiliation. With her unique skill Schemer, Kagali had formulated a wealth of plans, succeeding in most of them. She had made a number of mistakes recently, mostly in relation to Rimuru, but she was proud to be Yuuki's close confidant and chief strategist. But Kondo just sniffed at all that.

"How dare a mere human like you talk that way…"

"A mere human? Do you mean Yuuki Kagurazaka?"

The wave of intense anger, like a rush of blood to her head, nearly blinded Kagali. But she could see that this was just Kondo executing his plan. If she let her anger get the better of her, it'd cost her a potentially winnable battle.

As proof of that, Footman was now attacking Kondo like a berserker, perhaps inspired by Kagali's anger. He was the most powerful attacker among the clowns, and now he was unleashing massive missiles of magic, not sparing a moment to consider the damage to the city. Kondo avoided them without much of a fuss, but now sirens were going off; there would be panic in the streets before long.

At this rate, the rebels would have to deal with Guardians, security forces, and curious onlookers, all at the same time. Kagali saw no reason now to mind her manners. They'd have to treat anyone in their way as enemies and blow them away—but Kondo and his men were just as aware of that. Why was Kondo allowing this to happen, then? Kagali wasn't sure.

Stay calm. Chill out. He's just trying to piss me off...

She had seen through his scheme, and all she had to do was not play along. So she stifled her anger... But then, out of nowhere, she felt a great unease, as if she had overlooked something serious.

Wait... Damrada was under someone's control. If that was Kondo's doing...

Both Footman and Teare were now joining the battle. Around them, Yuuki's comrades were in a pitched battle to the death against the Guardians. Not even that was enough to change Kondo's expression. He was now holding a revolver in his hand, produced from parts unknown, and a sword was in his left. That was his approach against Footman and Teare, both outclassing a demon lord in force, and he still seemed fully relaxed.

They had expected him to be powerful, but this was beyond all expectations. *He must outclass Damrada*, Kagali sensed, realizing all over again how much of a threat this was.

He had his gun out, but he didn't show any intention to shoot, engaging Footman and Teare with his sword alone. Even Kagali could tell that it was a masterful weapon—but what she didn't know was that, despite appearing to be a standard-issue sword from the

Imperial Japanese Navy, the blade itself was a work of art, boasting a beautiful, rippled streak along the edge that was mesmerizing to look at. It was a family heirloom, handed down through Kondo's family for generations; no cheap imitation an amateur would bandy around.

This was, of course, not the kind of weapon you'd wield with one hand—but Kondo was doing just that, holding the lower part of the hilt with his left. It was hard to believe he'd normally carry it this way, suggesting that he wasn't demonstrating his true ability with it yet.

This man is a menace. He's taking both of them on, and he's not even trying to fight seriously yet... But why, though? If he wanted to kill them, he'd be far more engaged than this. If he's not, then maybe he sees some kind of value to us? In other words...

Then Kagali arrived at the answer.

"Look out!" she immediately shouted. "Kondo might be able to control people somehow!"

"Heh. You're right."

She thought he'd deny it, but he didn't. It was unnerving.

So he's just revealing his hand? ...No, there's no point denying it if we already suspect as much. If he affirms it, though, that makes us warier of him. I don't get it. Why...?

Now Kagali wasn't sure what to believe. Kondo's behavior was beyond her understanding; she couldn't figure out her next move. If fighting wasn't going to bring them victory, it should've been best to stick to the original stall-for-time strategy, she thought. But she had no clue why Kondo was just going along with it.

...No! It's just not right! He said he wasn't going to put up with our attempts at stalling, so why...? Ah! Wait! That's what he meant!

It was only then that Kagali realized just how much of a menace Kondo truly was. Everything he said had intrinsic meaning to it, she realized. And through the lies he had weaved, he was fully controlling every aspect of this fight they had.

"*You're* stalling for time, too..."

"Oh, you've finally noticed? You see how I'm helping you with your silly attempts at buying time now?"

"Ngh!"

"It's too easy to decipher the thoughts of someone like you, you see."

Despite her attempts at remaining calm, Kondo's taunts were hitting home.

"Don't give me that—"

"Do you know why they call me the mysterious figure stalking the halls of information?"

"..."

"You said it yourself, didn't you? You just said I could control other people. So why don't you also see that it's simple for me to obtain information from the people under my control?"

What is he talking about? an astonished Kagali wondered. It sounded too amateurish to be a lie... But if it were true, it was a tremendously important secret to leak out. It was hard to believe that such a careful man would do something to expose his own hand like that.

"This is a hassle for me as well, you know. Not even I know everything. The plan was to make contact with you all on the outskirts of the city. We'd hardly want collateral damage inside the capital, and going easy on you in battle like this is more trouble than it's worth."

"Going easy?!"

"Hoh-hoh-hoh! You think that little of us, do you?"

Kondo's statement elicited further enraged excitement from Teare and Footman. They were being taken in by his scheme, and Kagali knew how bad an idea that was. Her agitation grew.

"Calm down, you two! Don't let his words disturb you!"

She tried to stop them from going too out of control. Kondo shot her a glance, looking less than amused. Then, after a quick glance at his revolver, he put it back on his belt, for reasons only he knew.

"What a pain. Come on. Allow me to neutralize you as a threat without killing you."

The moment he grasped his sword with both hands, the atmosphere changed completely. Now his aura was something only a true master could achieve.

"Teare, allow me to take over here. Let's go, human!"

The two of them together struck such a presence that even those fighting around them felt pressured into stopping.

Kondo kept his sword high, pointed up in the air, as he quietly gauged his foe. Footman, meanwhile, seemed to be ignoring any semblance of defense. His aura coursed across his body, shooting him forward like a gigantic bullet. He pinballed around, showing amazing agility for his well-nourished body. Then, accelerating with every bounce off the ground, he jumped around the vicinity of Kondo, erratically hopping from landing point to landing point and growing faster all the time.

"Hohhhhh-hoh-hoh-hoh! Try to follow me, if you can!"

Convinced he was exercising his full potential, Footman unleashed his finishing move on Kondo. The secret to his battle technique was the unique skill Amplifier, and that, in essence, is what it did. Whether the movement took wave form or existed as mass, he could accelerate it at will. Simply bouncing off something sped up his body, and he could amplify his weight as well, giving himself mass far greater than how he looked. The sheer kinetic energy this generated could likely tear any enemy to pieces.

"Take this—Angry Splatter!"

With absolute confidence and destructive power on his side, Footman lunged for Kondo. But without the slightest change of expression, Kondo unleashed a skill of his own.

"I've just executed Thundering Universe. You had best consider it an honor."

The quiet announcement was heard only after it was all over. In a single instant, Footman's arms and legs had been severed. The action was far too quick to catch with the naked eye. It'd be absolutely impossible to pull off were it not for the awe-inspiring difference in ability at play.

His head was still attached, but there was now blood spurting out from a gaping wound across his neck. Not even that would be enough to kill Footman, but he was understandably out of this battle.

"And you're Teare, aren't you? Bind his arms and legs, and stop the bleeding out of his neck while you're at it. I can't have him dying on me yet."

The order was given flatly, without emotion. The revolver was back in his right hand again; he was back to his original style. His body language indicated that he wasn't interested in fighting anybody else.

"What...? What are you thinking...?!"

"I'm not going to kill any of you. Especially you, Kagali—or the ex–demon lord Kazalim, I should say. You have a lot of value to us. We can't afford to have you dead."

"Come on. You think I'm going to do that after what you've done?"

"Heh. I'm not asking for forgiveness. Didn't I tell you that I can control other people?"

How loathsome of a man was he, even? Kagali eyed him hatefully. His manner of speaking irritated her to no end. She thought she had the right idea about all this, but she couldn't shake the feeling that she didn't. Every word Kondo uttered got on her nerves.

Then a red burst of light emerged from Kondo's handgun. Seeing this, Kondo smiled a little—a tiny, easily overlooked smile. Kagali was amazed he could smile at all... But at the same time, she sensed the biggest alarm bell yet.

He... It was true? He really was stalling?!

It was far too late to realize that. She abhorred being toyed with for this long, but still Kagali searched for the best way out of this. It was clear Kondo had all his cards in order, although she didn't know what they were. It was impossible to escape; even buying any more time was a challenge.

And so there was just one choice to take. All Kagali could do was strike at the source of this danger, the calamity about to befall her friends. In other words, a suicide strike.

Death, she determined, was the best way to prevent information leaks. As a walking dead, though, Kagali would not truly cease to exist. She'd lose her physical body, yes, but as long as she inhabited someone else, she'd survive. Footman and Teare would realize what she meant to do, no doubt—they were walking dead as well, and just like Kagali, literally dying was unlikely. If all of them advanced upon Kondo at the same time, they'd fulfill their objective without revealing their intentions to him. Even if they all lost their bodies, they'd be able to escape and avoid the worst-case scenario. Such was Kagali's decision, the best chip she had to play right now.

But how annoying! Sir Yuuki went through all this trouble to obtain my body. It took a while for me to settle in, too... Although it beats losing it all anyway. I hate to involve Footman and Teare in this, but I'll see that they receive stronger bodies next time.

Her mind was made up. Laplace, she believed, would help clean up later. Kondo was just too strong—unexpectedly so. Based on her current assessment, Kagali believed he and Laplace were an even match...that or Kondo had a slight advantage. Even if he made it here, and they fought together, that still wouldn't assure victory. It'd be foolish to put Laplace in danger as well, she reasoned.

What she wondered about was just how Kondo managed to take over other people's minds. She wanted to flee after finding that out, but that might just be too greedy of her. So putting aside her doubts, she sprang into action.

"Well, just look at how much this human's toyed with us, huh? Footman, Teare, stop playing with him, and let's give him everything we've got. And *you'll* get to see the full powers of the one they used to call a demon lord!"

Kagali stretched out her aura across her body, exercising power beyond all her limits. A borrowed body like this one had no chance of withstanding this; it'd be lucky to survive another few minutes. But this way, at least, she could settle this without Kondo thinking she chose to end her own life.

Footman and Teare, seeing Kagali's move, immediately understood her plans.

"Hoh-hoh-hoh! It'll take more than blowing my limbs off to stop me!"

"Yeah! And I'm still in this, too! I haven't gone all out in ages upon ages, either. It's so exciting!"

Footman, following Kagali's lead, balled up his body and started bouncing around. Teare began unleashing her aura as well, blowing it up into a massive presence in the middle of the capital. If Kondo could be convinced this was a suicide strike aimed at taking both sides out, the strategy would be a success.

But despite the situation he was in, Kondo didn't even bat an eye. He remained calm and measured as he sheathed his sword and spot-checked his revolver. Then, as casual as can be, he immediately rained all over Kagali's parade.

"So I understand that walking dead can survive in spiritual form alone?"

It was a statement they ignored at their peril. Among their companions, only Yuuki knew the trio's exact species. It was highly confidential intel, something not even Damrada was aware of. Nobody, not even Kondo, could've possibly known about it.

"Wh-why do you...?"

"War is something that fully ends before it begins, one could say. The Armored Division was wiped out because they underestimated the enemy and skimped on information gathering. If you simply run wild without any precise intelligence to go on, you're all but guaranteeing your own defeat. Don't you agree?"

"..."

"And by the way, I have to say that your comrade in arms was tremendously disappointing as well. I had him all set up at the exact right timing, and then some upstart demon lord completely bowls him over. Hardly a demon lord at all, I'd say. It makes me laugh."

"...What?"

"But him losing was more convenient in the end, I suppose. I have a basic grasp of what went on over there, and it led to the creation of someone far more fascinating than Clayman anyway."

"What the hell do you mean by *that*...?!"

Kagali exploded with anger. Any shred of remaining calm was thrown out the window. Her hatred for the man before her, Lieutenant Kondo, made her forget everything else. This was no less than a full confession that Kondo had total control over Clayman.

Looking back, Clayman had clearly lost his mind over time, a trend that progressed for at least several decades according to Laplace. Kagali assumed it was just the stress of becoming a demon lord, chiding herself for being overprotective of him—but if it was all Kondo's doing, that was a different story. It meant that Kondo had a hand in virtually every failure in her plans, and that was hard to forgive. Worst of all, it was Kondo's manipulation that sent her beloved Clayman to his demise...

He has to pay. I'll never let this pass.

Her anger was nothing she or anyone else could control. Footman, sensitive to this, also picked up on it...and thus amplified it further. In the end, ironically, that was exactly what Kondo was hoping for—or aiming for, even.

"Getting emotional in the middle of battle? What a novice mistake. If that's all the resolve you have, no wonder it was so easy to lead you to a trap like this."

With that, Kondo pulled the trigger.

"Ah!"

There was a small *bang*. Kagali jumped back. There was no blood; this was a very special bullet, affecting not the body, but the mind. It was called a Dominion Bullet, a treasure granted by Emperor Ludora, and it was one of Kondo's secret techniques. Each bullet contained a part of Ludora's own power, making it capable of enthralling and controlling others. However, it worked on just one person at a time, and it was very likely not to work against those with strong mental fortitudes.

Kondo had an ample supply, but he still had to be very careful about how he used them—if a shot missed the mark, it'd both expose his hand to the enemy and cost him control over whoever he last shot with a Dominion Bullet. Using one to take over a demon lord's mind required targeting them while asleep or in an agitated state—blinded by lust or by negative emotions like anger or grief. Once they were in the right condition, he could fire a Dominion Bullet to gain full control.

"Well, it took long enough, but we're still sticking to the plan. Kagali, order your cohorts to cease hostilities immediately. You're a careful person, so I assume you've implanted a locking curse on the summoned?"

"Yes, Sir Kondo."

"Drop the 'sir,' please. 'Lieutenant' is fine."

"Yes, Lieutenant Kondo. As you wish."

Thus, Kagali fell into Kondo's hands. And just as Kondo predicted, the souls of Yuuki's comrades all had a locking curse etched on them. The same was also true of Teare and Footman, and thus they could not disobey the words of their commander Kagali.

Not everyone on hand had this locking curse, but it was quickly clear just how doomed they were. Better, they reasoned, to be captured than try to resist this horde.

Silence returned to the darkness of the capital.

"If you want to hate anyone, hate yourselves for being so powerless. Everyone has their own sense of what makes right, but only when integrated into a stronger will can it be acted upon. The same is true for one's ideals. Your ambitions all vanished in the face of His Majesty's just cause. Nothing more and nothing less."

This was the one true rule—survival of the fittest. Kondo was well aware of it.

"Of course, those who are not prepared to be crushed in the end aren't even qualified to have ambitions at all. That does not apply to you... So I'll be sure to remember your disappointments for you."

Kondo himself lived with a certain resolve. That's why he never made fun of Kagali and her friends for what they attempted. If he lost, as he knew and understood from experience, he'd suffer the exact same fate.

Yuuki and Damrada were deep in a fierce battle, exchanging one blow, then another for what seemed like the millionth time.

Without hesitation, Damrada aimed a spinning back blow at a pressure point on Yuuki's face. It was blocked with a palm; Yuuki attempted to gain control of Damrada's wrist, but he was denied as his opponent unleashed a chop to hold him back. Yuuki, anticipating this, twisted his upper body back as he executed a double kick.

But Damrada was quick to pick up on it, sinking down and sweeping with his leg—then his opponent jumped up, perhaps reading this counter in advance, and tried to take his head off with a spinning kick. However, Yuuki's leg cut through thin air; Damrada was back on his feet a safe distance away.

It was a sophisticated, refined exchange of martial arts that went beyond the scope of what human beings could maneuver. They kept rattling them off, again and again, at a pace so regular that they almost seemed to be in a training session. But they were going too fast for the normal human eye to follow. The lack of spectators was a pity, but then again, they'd have trouble rounding up an audience with the skills required to watch and appreciate them.

Here was a battle between dedicated masters, fought only with their own well-honed bodies. But that wasn't all that was taking place. Yuuki was also trying to communicate with Damrada—not with speech, but through Telepathy. Damrada, in turn, was trying to help Yuuki with that. That's why there was so much unnecessary physical contact; when they went hand-against-hand for an instant, that's when they were exchanging messages.

(Wow, we're finally connected, huh? I didn't expect you to gain an ultimate skill as well, Damrada. You had no idea how much trouble I had opening a Telepathy link to you. Have you had this since we met, perhaps?)

(It was borrowed, Sir Yuuki, but yes, I've been in possession of it for as long as we've known each other. I don't use it very often, however, so I doubt you would have noticed.)

Yuuki couldn't help but snicker at this. When he awakened to his own ultimate skill, only then did he realize the mind-boggling difference between them and regular unique skills. Still, there was something in Damrada's reply that he couldn't gloss over.

(Borrowed? What do you mean?)

Skills like these were, by nature, acquired by yourself. Some people could craft them like Yuuki, but they couldn't just be conjured out of nothing. They were using their own desires to change the form of the power within their soul. It wasn't something that could be "borrowed."

(I mean exactly what I said. My power was granted to me by His Majesty.)

(Is that even possible?)

(I understand your skepticism, but you have me as a witness to it. You'll have to accept that it is possible, yes.)

(I see. Fair point.)

Having it phrased that way, Yuuki had no choice but to accept it. That naturally led to his next question.

(So can he just pass on skills to anybody he wants?)

(Oh, no.) Damrada smiled. (The average person does not have the capacity to obtain even a unique skill, much less an ultimate one. Simply accepting that power requires an enormous amount of energy. You'd need to be completely remade, the way otherworlders are, to pull it off.)

(Well, that's a relief. I was worried the emperor was holding a closeout sale on ultimate skills.)

(Ha-ha-ha! No, he hasn't managed that yet. It's one of his objectives, however.)

Yuuki could accept that.

(And that's why he's gathering all these strong people?)

(Precisely. Humans, too, can evolve after enough training. Their entire species changes, and they become Enlightened. As a Saint, Sir Yuuki, I believe you know the process?)

(Pretty much, yeah.)

He had a general understanding. Humans can go from Enlightened to Sainthood, and that took more than regular old training. Even the Ten Great Saints, deemed the strongest in the Western Nations, had just two real Saints among them—Hinata and Saare.

(Only upon becoming Enlightened can one break free from the framework of humanity, where they must live among their own kind. They remain an individual but also gain the ability to connect with the world at large. Those who reach that stage here become Imperial Guardians, having passed the minimum requirements His Majesty has put in place.)

(Being Enlightened's the minimum requirement?)

(Yes, that's right. If you fought against Guy, Sir Yuuki, then you understood just how strong he was, I assume? Even a Saint could never beat him.)

(Yeah, I'll grant you that.)

Guy was simply unassailable. That much was made perfectly clear, taking him on. No half-assed attempt would even touch him.

(If you want to defeat Guy, as an absolute minimum, you must awaken to the ultimate in force.)

(An ultimate skill, in other words?)

It made sense to Yuuki. That came across more strongly to him, now that he had an ultimate skill of his own. The only way to tackle someone with an ultimate was to break out an ultimate of your own.

(Exactly. His Majesty is familiar with this as well. That is why he grants trials to those who are Enlightened, to help them awaken further and become vessels worthy enough of the ultimate skill he can give them.)

(Sounds pretty crazy. But if I were him, I'd do the same thing, I guess.)

(I'm glad you understand so quickly.)

Yuuki and Damrada smiled at each other. It might be completely illogical to the average person, but Yuuki saw the reasoning behind it. Once you had the methodology down, it could allow you to collect a large number of people with ultimate skills. He disliked how someone else beat him to the idea, but he had to admit to its charms. The only problem with it was that it required someone as uniquely qualified as Ludora to engineer.

(The fact that Ludora can grant ultimate powers at all is just amazing.)

(Hee-hee-hee... Yes, it proves his greatness beyond any doubt. And if you become a Saint under his tutelage, His Majesty will grant you the ultimate skill Alternative.)

Damrada's telepathic voice sounded proud to Yuuki. He could feel the respect Damrada held for Emperor Ludora, and it made him laugh a little. Damrada might have been loyal to Yuuki still, but his feelings for the emperor were a different matter. Yuuki knew this was the case, although he really wished Damrada hid it a little more. Of course, he normally never made that kind of mistake, so Yuuki assumed he was acting this way on purpose right now.

(So is Ludora waging this war in order to awaken more of his knights?)

(I suppose he would be. Our previous war was stymied by interference from Veldora, but that was a blessing in disguise. A few people evolved into Enlightened in the process, so we gained even more power than we lost.)

Talk about patience, an impressed—and jealous—Yuuki thought.

So the two of them shared thoughts with each other through Telepathy as they fought, or sparred, or whatever. Finally, Yuuki managed to break through the last of Damrada's psychological barriers.

(Oh, here we go. I found the core of the power controlling you.)

(Ah, wonderful to hear. Do you think you can remove it?)

(Yeah, no problems there. But if I do, won't Kondo find out?)

(I imagine he will, yes, but I'm not sure I care.)

(Well, here we go, then.)

They hadn't been sparring for no reason. Damrada knew about Yuuki's Anti-Skill ability, and he believed it could overcome the thrall that Kondo put upon him. Yuuki was aware of that as well, and without any further instruction, he had spent the past while probing Damrada. Now he would use the new power awakened in him to bring his friend back to normal.

Mammon, Lord of Greed—the ultimate skill Yuuki had acquired—specialized in seizing things. It contained the ability Lifestealer, for example, which sapped energy on contact. Using it allowed Yuuki to deal damage simply by punching and having it blocked. The exact type of energy taken—magical, physical—depended on the opponent, but whatever it was, Yuuki could take it and use it for himself.

Lifestealer didn't work on Damrada, however. He had too much strength, and even under Kondo's control, he still maintained that strength in the best possible condition. Regardless of his mind's intentions, his body was doing the best it could to interfere with Yuuki. That was thanks to Alternative, the ultimate gift provided by the emperor. This skill protected his very soul, an impenetrable psychological barrier that nullified any kind of spiritual attack. This was combined with absolute physical destructive skills that could penetrate all defenses. Put them together, and Damrada had become an undefeated champion in every way.

Kondo was able to control him because the Dominion Bullets the emperor gave him were devised to be higher level than Alternative. If Damrada had learned Alternative naturally instead of receiving it as a gift, his body never would've been taken over. It was a real obstacle, and Yuuki had to use Anti-Skill to the hilt to break down the barriers. In time, though, he found the Dominion Bullet lodged in his soul, and once he had Damrada's permission, he instantly focused his power on it.

"Lifestealer!"

The bottom of Yuuki's palm struck Damrada's chest.

The precisely controlled blow shattered only the bullet and nothing else. It seemed so anticlimactic, but now Damrada was free once more.

"Thank you, Sir Yuuki."

"Yeah. Hope you can stop relying on others like that for a while. I'm worried about Kagali's group, though. I gotta go, but what're you gonna do?"

"Let me join you. I need to speak with the demon lord Rimuru tomorrow regardless. We'll be proceeding with the coup right after that, so it'd be too dangerous to return to where Kondo is."

"True. No need to try patching things up now, is there?"

Yuuki laughed; Damrada joined him.

"Ready to go, then?"

"By all means."

He turned around and headed for the door, Damrada nodding and following along. But just then:

"So why were you playing with this outside element instead of taking care of him, Damrada? You weren't seriously planning to betray His Majesty, were you?"

The cold voice made Yuuki too nervous to move. The real crisis was only beginning...

*

Without a sound, before anyone knew what happened, she was standing right there. Her presence was overwhelmingly strong, her hair blue, her face beautiful. It'd be the first time they met, but Yuuki felt he already knew this figure from somewhere. The figure of the one on the other side of the curtain, seated next to the emperor—the Marshal.

"L-Lady Velgrynd...!"

Damrada's whisper sounded bizarrely loud.

Velgrynd? Does he mean...?!

At that moment, Yuuki realized his face was too tensed up to move. A True Dragon, the strongest creature in the world—now she was before him, their powers beyond compare.

This sure ain't good. I didn't sense this when I saw Veldora, but with her, it's not even a question of winning or losing. Fighting someone like her head-on would just be suicide.

But despite that realization, Yuuki refused to give up. If a head-on confrontation was doomed to fail, simply find a back door—and Yuuki had the perfect special move for that. Play his cards right, he thought, and victory seemed possible enough.

"I never would've guessed Her Excellency the Marshal was a True Dragon all along. Now I understand why Guy hasn't made a move yet."

"My. How unusual for a human. I admire you for not losing your nerve around me."

"Thanks. And by the way, it'd be really great if you could let me go. What do you think?"

"That's fine by me. *I* don't have any business with you... My dear husband does."

Velgrynd took a step back... And only then did Yuuki notice the other man present. His eyes opened wide. Standing next to Velgrynd was a man in an extravagant outfit that was no doubt worth an astronomical amount of money. Yuuki knew his face well.

"...Masayuki? Nah, no way it's him. Or...?"

To Yuuki, this man had to be Masayuki's identical twin—but he noticed a few differences. The most notable one was the hair color. The man before him had shining blond hair, and while Masayuki usually dyed his blond, his natural color was the standard black of most Japanese people.

Looking more closely, he could sense differences in the eyes, too. Masayuki's were always either darting around or just kind of blank, unthinking, but *this* man looked like he could see through everything. It almost felt like those eyes could consume you if you weren't careful. No way were they the same person.

…Guess not, huh?

Now reasonably sure of that, Yuuki then realized who the man really was. If Velgrynd called him her husband, that left only one candidate.

"…Emperor Ludora?"

"That's right, Sir Yuuki. This is His Majesty, Emperor Ludora, the ruler standing at the peak of the Empire."

Damrada provided the reply. He was on his knees already, not even caring if he got his clothes dirty; he urgently wanted to prove to Ludora that he bore no animosity. Yuuki couldn't blame him. He knew how much more Ludora meant to him. The real issue at hand: Why was Ludora here at all?

"Well, color me shocked. Why is Your Eminence in a meeting hall like this? Are you bored, or…?"

"No, I am quite a busy man," the emperor replied, unaffected by Yuuki's teasing. "My game against Guy is in the closing stages. I have no time to trifle with other matters."

This seemed to astound Damrada. He never thought that Ludora would actually address someone lower than himself, and he never thought Velgrynd would allow it.

"Oh? Well, you better stop bumping around my place, then—"

"Enough nonsense. I want you to join me. Agree to it, and I'll let you keep your free will."

It was an order, one from far above, delivered to a lowly worm on the ground. Yuuki hated this type of person more than anything else, but for some reason, he felt like he just couldn't resist.

Is this Thought Guidance in action? It resembles the brand of dominance Maribel tried on me, but far stronger...

The power annoyed him greatly. But since Yuuki had Anti-Skill handy, he could cancel out any skill-driven order on him. Or he should've been able to.

No! This isn't any simple power like that!

Yuuki shivered as he came to that realization. It took a mighty effort not to fall to his knees. This was pure charisma, the unimaginable supremacy of a ruler capable of subjugating anything he sees. He resisted it with all his might.

"*Pft...* Not bad. I wasn't expecting you to break out this cheat code on me from the very start..."

He spat on the floor in anger, a little blood mixed in. It was usually Yuuki dominating encounters like these from the start, and he hated having his style copied like this. But he was still in the clear. He was angry, and that emotion was proof that Ludora's control on him was broken. With a bold smile, he looked his way, only to find the emperor giving him a quizzical look of his own.

"What's wrong? Strange to find your power doesn't work on me, huh?"

"No—"

Ludora turned toward Velgrynd, troubled. She responded with light giggling, which didn't make Ludora feel any better.

"Don't bother, Ludora. When this kid was exposed to your presence, he mistook it for a mental attack. You have to use a lighter touch, or you'll break him before he can even join you."

"What, this won't work?"

"No. You don't have enough people in your life you speak to on equal terms. That makes it hard for you to control your strength."

Velgrynd seemed to thoroughly enjoy how puzzled Ludora was. Yuuki, hearing all this, trembled in humiliation.

Are you kidding me?! Do I not even register to them? Let's take that smug attitude and rip it apart right now!

"That's fine," he said, regaining his composure. "I'll admit it. You guys are definitely the greatest rulers the world's ever known.

But you know, if you have all that power and *still* can't conquer the entire world, then to me, you could hardly *be* more incompetent."

As usual, he kicked things off with provocation. Velgrynd responded first.

"Hmm. Brash of you. How about we kill him after all, Ludora? Bringing this kid into the fold wouldn't make that much difference strength-wise against Guy. Why keep him around just so he can sass us like this?"

But Ludora was more magnanimous than that.

"Oh, don't say that. Maybe you see him as insignificant, but give him the right education, and he can grow to become a tremendously useful pawn. And isn't a little defiance now and then a nice change of pace? A cat, after all, is just as cute if it refuses to sidle up to you. I like him."

It was Ludora's way of completely degrading Yuuki. He snorted at it. Taunting Ludora wouldn't accomplish much if it did nothing to bother him. It was time to break out the big guns. With Velgrynd around, Yuuki couldn't waste a lot of time. He'd have to tap his greatest weapon from the get-go and use the momentum from it to subdue the True Dragon.

Yuuki steeled himself.

"You want me to join you? Fine, but I'm not about to serve someone weaker than me. If you want me around, you're gonna have to show me some *real* power!"

As soon as he shouted it, Yuuki began to act. No time for small talk; no point in putting on a performance. The ultimate skill Mammon converted the size of one's desires into actual power, and Yuuki knew he was a greedy man. It was only natural, he thought, that he awakened to the power he took from Maribel. That was why he firmly believed that a skill as outlandishly unfair as Mammon made him the strongest in the entire world.

So who would he target first? It had to be Ludora. He'd take control of the emperor, using him as a hostage against Velgrynd. If that let him survive this crisis, this whole day would be a blessing in disguise. Such bullish optimism was Yuuki's driving force, and it had brought him great success so far—and this time, too, he'd make a huge leap forward.

It was the only thought in his mind as he started running. In another few steps, he was within punching range. In less time than the blinking of an eye, Yuuki's hand was about to touch Ludora.

He activated Life Absorb, one of Mammon's subskills, in his right hand, combining it with Anti-Skill. This fearsome combo allowed him to penetrate through any barriers his target might have covering him. This was what Lifestealer was meant for, and unlike with Damrada, Yuuki didn't care if this attack was lethal or not. If Ludora died, it only meant he had Velgrynd alone to deal with. Escaping two strong opponents would be a formidable challenge, but a single one was far more manageable.

If he survived, though, that's where Yuuki's left hand came in. It was infused with Heart Control, a terrifying power that acted on the target's emotions and even affected their memories. It was a dominating force, one even more vicious and irresistible than Maribel's own greed.

Yuuki planned to use this one-two punch to blaze a path through this. But the plan was quickly shattered.

"You will *not* lay a hand on Ludora in my presence."

Yuuki was running his body to the absolute upper limits of speed, but not even he could keep Velgrynd from stepping between him and the emperor. Then, without breaking a sweat, she swatted Yuuki's right hand away.

He was stunned. Having his hand blocked was a surprise, but even more astounding was the sheer amount of energy that flowed from Velgrynd. It was a raging torrent, enough to make Yuuki vomit blood. In a single exchange, his body was infused with far more magicules than he could ever hope to withstand.

Instantly, he realized the danger, forcibly twisting his body to get away. If he reacted even a moment later, his body would have been completely destroyed. It wasn't that Velgrynd *did* anything to him, exactly—quite the opposite. All she did was push Yuuki's hand away. The damage was more self-destructive, in a way. He had activated Lifestealer, and then he used it to absorb far more energy than he could control.

As blood flowed from his mouth, eyes, and nose, Yuuki thought over what just happened.

That... That's insane. How beyond my allowable limit was that?! I'm at a point where I can take in dozens of high-level elementals without issue, and I got all filled up in a single instant? How crazy are True Dragons anyway?!

Yuuki wanted to complain to the gods about it. Velgrynd was nobody to trifle with. Despite all the energy taken from her, she acted like she was in no pain at all. Yuuki's attack wasn't even worth defending in her eyes.

Now he realized how impossible this was.

Dammit! I had no idea there was this much difference. No wonder I barely register with them.

They were undeniably on the same level as Guy. Realizing that, Yuuki now knew just how lofty the great heights of the world truly were. It was an impossible gap to traverse, and he only knew it because of the ultimate ability he awakened to. Staging any kind of attack against them would be suicide. He had no choice but to wait for his enemy to make a move.

"I'd advise you not to try anything rash, please. I've come to you on my own volition. And indeed, why don't I respond to your request to see my power?"

"That's a bad habit to indulge, Ludora. Leave that to me. I don't want you getting hurt."

"Hee-hee! Well, *that* won't be very convincing, now will it?"

This was stirring the pot, nothing more. Yuuki wasn't about to let them take all his favorite party tricks away from him.

"Ha-ha-ha! Glad you know what I'm talking about. Realistically speaking, I think I've already lost. But I'm not a quitter, you know. Don't expect me to give up *that* easy."

He knew he was being a sore loser, but Yuuki decided to grandstand a bit anyway. Now that he knew there was no way to beat Velgrynd, all he needed to protect now was his dignity. Even if it got him killed, he wanted to have things his way right to the very end.

Infused with a new drive, he glared at Ludora. The emperor responded with a curious smile.

"Very well. Let me take you on. I will tell you in advance that domination is a strong suit of mine. If you can endure it, you win, and you may go wherever you wish."

The unexpected offer made Yuuki steel his eyes. Ludora clearly meant it. He really didn't mind letting Yuuki go. And while Yuuki couldn't read his intentions here, Ludora saw this confrontation in rather simple terms. Yuuki could gain experience through this—experience that would give him even stronger powers. Once that was done, they could talk it over again... And then he'd have Yuuki in his hands.

The two of them were completely different in ability. That's why Yuuki found Ludora so creepy—and why his taunts enraged him.

Domination's his strong suit? Well, it's the same for me. I'm gonna bet it all on this Mammon skill...

Ludora looked at him, bemused and excited about his first match in a long time. If Yuuki could withstand his domination skills, this might prove to be one treacherous ally, indeed. He was aware of the possibility, but he still chose to engage him.

If this is enough to crush me, well, that's as far as my ideals will take me.

Defeat wasn't even on his mind. And if Yuuki merely pretended to obey him, that was not the end of the world, either. Taming pawns like that, he was sure, was the only way he could truly become the world's sole dominant ruler. And Velgrynd had known him for a long time. She didn't need it spelled out to know what he was thinking. That's why she knew how useless it was to chide him for this.

"All right. If you lose, then I'll make sure to avenge you."

She took a step back.

"You hardly need to worry," Ludora replied, chuckling as he stepped forward. Yuuki followed suit, ignoring his screaming aches and pains as he stood up.

"Your group certainly is interesting, though. No wonder Guy praised you all as the jokers disrupting this whole game."

"...How did you know that?"

"Heh. I just received a report from Tatsuya about them. The Moderate Jesters, I think they're called? Well, *their* leader's fallen into our hands, too. And I'll also tell you this—everything about you is now fully known to me. Keep that in mind as you challenge me."

Tatsuya was Lieutenant Kondo's given name. Ludora must have

had some way to keep in contact with him, and he must've reported on defeating Kagali just now. Realizing all this, Yuuki let out a sigh of disgust. Everything from his unique constitution to the fight and subsequent conversations he had with Guy had been leaked. Yuuki had told everyone he trusted about his ultimate skill. Damrada had faithfully kept it a secret, but now all that was meaningless. Kagali was Yuuki's closest confidant, and naturally, she knew all his secrets.

Oh, man. I'm dead. So they know absolutely everything about me...?

Suddenly Yuuki had an urge to throw it all away. His mind told him that he was out of ideas, but his pride would never allow him to retreat at this point. But most of all:

Then Kagali isn't dead? Ludora's got some kind of domination skill, and if I had to guess, Kondo's got something close to that. In which case, instead of trying to run...

In an instant, he formulated a plan. It had a very low chance of success, but it made him feel better than taking things on with zero strategy.

"Well, how kind of you to say. But all that ease is gonna be your downfall!"

"That's fine. I tend to believe I've won only when I've surpassed my opponent's full strength. So please, by all means, give it *your* all as well. I don't want you having any regrets."

Ludora took another step forward. Then he assumed a fighting stance—a unique one, no weapons involved. He was a swordsman by training, as proven by the longsword on his belt, but he intended to defeat Yuuki purely by domination, as promised.

Yuuki had already seen through Ludora's personality. He had a firm, honest disposition, one not befitting a ruler at all, and now he was sincerely aiming to battle Yuuki. That's what made him so easy to read.

Honestly, winning here in the primary definition of the term is impossible. Even if I pull something off against Ludora, Velgrynd's still here. If I can't escape, then the best I can hope for is to cancel out Ludora's domination?

But Ludora had to be expecting that—and what's more, he had

total confidence that he could take control of Yuuki. And so the only option Yuuki had left was...

"Bring it on, Ludora!"

...betting everything on the slightest of probabilities.

"Regalia Dominion!"

With a balletic move, Ludora sprang into action, instantly closing the distance between himself and Yuuki. Once he was in range, he began activating his "imperial domination," the very pinnacle of powers offered by his ultimate skill Michael, Lord of Justice. Unlike the imitation he proffered to Kondo, this skill had no limitations, and its powers were an order of magnitude greater. Even among ultimate skills, there were still subclassifications in rank—and for someone as recently awakened as Yuuki, there was no way to resist this one.

Ludora stood there, as dignified as could be. Yuuki collapsed on the spot. The winner and loser seemed clear now, but the outcome remained unknown.

"Are you sure you won't kill him? People like him, you know—they'll pretend to obey you, and then they'll wait for just the right moment to strike."

"That's fine. That's what makes it so fun. I'm letting him off the hook as a reward for resisting my dominance."

Despite it all, Ludora's confidence remained unshakable. His absolute dominance was assured in his mind, and he didn't doubt his victory for a moment.

"All right, then..."

Ludora, the victor, boldly smiled. Then he turned toward Damrada, who was staying politely silent in a corner of a room, and addressed him like an old friend.

"Forgive me, Damrada, but I cannot have you getting in my way just yet."

"As you wish, Your Majesty..."

That was all it took for the two of them to be on the same page.

"When he wakes up, please take care of him for me."

"Yes, Your Majesty."

Satisfied with that reply, Ludora left with Velgrynd in tow. He had only just begun tightening the reins on his government, and now that he was on the move, a new era was about to begin. Not even the capital would escape the waves of upheaval—and even though it was the middle of the night, the sky turned red as a rain of pure crimson began to fall.

CHAPTER
4

THE RED PURGE

That Time I Got Reincarnated as a Slime

The Armed Nation of Dwargon's east city was currently weathering a blockade of up to sixty thousand people. But it was all a cover. Beneath the surface, both sides had made it clear that they were allied, the commanders all taking great pains to ensure that no unfortunate accidents took place.

With that in mind, the mood among the lower-ranked soldiers was light. Camping tents had been set up across the area, each filled with idle chatter—but there was still a modicum of tension shared by everyone, even the rank and file. That indicated the surprisingly high level of training every member of the army had received.

It was no wonder that morale was high. After all, their superiors were currently engaged in their final meeting—one where the dream of overthrowing the Empire and building a new nation would come to a head.

Everyone was looking forward to it, and everyone had their eyes on the capital in anticipation. That was why most of them noticed it at the same time.

"It's red..."

"Is the capital aflame?"

"What happened? Wait—did they find out?!"

On this most critical of days, something was happening over

in the imperial capital, and nobody thought it was a coincidence. Everyone knew that something had happened to their leaders.

"Should we send out a recon team?"

"No, we need to organize our troops and march."

"Don't be stupid! If we do that, it'll completely expose us as traitors!"

Having all their superiors away from the force meant there was no one to take command. The Composite Division, already derided as a motley crew in the best of times, quickly lost cohesion. The one who finally brought them back in order was a person who had silently closed his eyes before then. His name was Zero, a man Yuuki named as corps vice commander, and he was the highest-ranked person on the field.

"Silence! I will not allow anyone to act without permission! We will stay here and wait for Sir Yuuki and the others to return. That will remain our policy."

With Zero's declaration, those wavering in their opinions fell back in line. Nobody knew what the right answer was, so for now, they decided to follow orders. But not even that could alleviate the anxiety... And those anxieties came true in the worst possible fashion.

"Good evening, you oblivious fools. I know it's a lovely night tonight, but that doesn't mean you should all get *too* excited."

The woman walked along the street totally carefree, with the ease of a vacationing tourist. It was Velgrynd, her blue hair as beautiful as always.

"Wha...? Who are you?"

The soldiers on the far edges of the street shouted at her. If she was calling out to uniformed soldiers, she couldn't have been an innocent civilian—and even before that, anyone who didn't recognize Velgrynd's utterly unusual presence could never survive in the Composite Division.

So they began confirming her identity, sending messages out to their superiors, as they moved to surround her. One soldier, a man with decent confidence in his fighting skill, stepped forward.

"Whoa there, lady. I don't know who you are, but I wouldn't be picking a fight with *this* many people if I were you. We may not look all fancy, but we're in the Composite Division, the strongest army of the Empire—"

"It really *is* funny, isn't it, the weak calling themselves the strongest? I was willing to let it slide if it kept morale high, but perhaps we should've stopped allowing it at the division level."

"What?!"

Velgrynd's words were those of someone at the highest reaches of society—someone giving orders from far above anyone else in the military hierarchy. It was more than enough for even the raw recruits to know they were dealing with someone dangerous. Zero, as vice commander, was no exception. When he heard this intruder was alone, he shipped himself over to see who it was—and once he heard the subsequent reports, he upped his pace toward the scene. Now Velgrynd was before him.

"M-Marshal..."

He had never seen the Marshal's face, but the presence she exuded was undoubtedly that of the overwhelming figure seated on the other side of the curtain.

"Ah, so there are some more intelligent ones among you as well? Good. I was told not to kill all of you, but just to have some fun until Kondo and the others arrive."

With that signal, the tragedy began.

Gazel was having a depressing day. The war was still dragging along, which was a headache by itself. But more than that, Jaine's report made him feel like his stomach was going to rupture.

Making true demon lords out of those serving him... What could possibly have gotten into Rimuru?!

He heaved a heavy sigh.

Calling them true demon lords was something of a misnomer. *Demon lord* was a title, not a species, and it literally meant a lord who ruled over monsters within a set territory. *True demon lord*, however, described the status of a monster, one awakened and evolved into that state. The threat they posed would be on the upper end of Disaster class, but it wouldn't rate a Calamity.

…Not that there are enough Disaster-class threats to merit dividing them into "upper" or "lower" classes…, thought Gazel.

The Disaster class was essentially reserved for demon lords, so right now it consisted of only eight known examples. Now, however, Rimuru had people working for him who were at least as powerful as those high-end menaces. Just thinking about it gave the Heroic King a headache.

For now, Gazel sent a griping missive to Elmesia about it. He couldn't stand to be the only one suffering, so he decided to have her share in the distress a bit. That—and his government decided to continue observing Rimuru and his band until further problems arose. It was just kicking the ball down the road, he knew, but there was nothing else they could do. If "further problems" ever came up, it'd be the beginning of a war for the survival of humanity.

"And I *truly* don't want that." Gazel sighed.

But the bad news wouldn't stop coming.

"Urgent news, Your Majesty! The Composite Division is on the move! They're engaged in battle with an unknown enemy."

The voice was calm, but Gazel sensed a panic atypical of his dark agents. Before more details came in, he immediately sent out word to assemble Dolph and the rest of his advisers. A few minutes later:

"No doubt about it. That enemy's nothing regular people can handle. It's a monster, an unimaginable monster who could even take down demon lords."

"A True Dragon?"

"Yeah. I've never seen one before. She took the form of a person, but there's no doubting her identity as Velgrynd."

Gazel was on a magical call to Vaughn, admiral paladin and supreme commander of Dwargon's military, who was currently stationed by the east city. He had him send visuals so everyone could grasp the situation.

The worst-case scenario always happens when you least expect it—a fact Gazel was all too aware of now. The sky was burning. There was a woman, a cold beauty, and crowds of powerful soldiers fallen around her. The flames were mesmerizing but also vigorous enough to awe everyone who saw them.

But the true horror only came after that. Velgrynd, visible through the surveillance crystal ball, looked over at Gazel and his team. He thought it was a coincidence at first, but the moment he did, the crystal ball shattered.

"She was watching *us*, too…?"

"I—I can't believe it. How is that possible…?"

"You're kidding! How far away do you think we are from there?"

"It's the truth. She must have sensed the magic and traced it back to the caster, but it's incredible to see her impacting the magic's destination as well. It'd be impossible for me or any other humanoid."

Gazel listened to his advisers in silence. Based on this, they were clearly dealing with an enemy. But who? He couldn't possibly hear her, but it was like she was whispering *No, don't you peep on me* into his ear.

A True Dragon? More like true monster.

Now Gazel knew what the word *strongest* really meant.

He was familiar with the rumors of a connection between the Empire and Velgrynd. They had no way to confirm them, but he had played through a lot of scenarios in his mind so that they'd be able to withstand attack. Now, however, Gazel realized it was all just an illusion.

It was unclear why the Empire had sent Velgrynd on the move at this point. Gazel thought and thought, but he couldn't understand what Emperor Ludora was thinking. There was only one thing he could do.

"I'm going into battle as well."

"Your Majesty," bellowed Dolph, "it's too unsafe!"

"But there is no other choice," replied Jaine. "Abandoning Vaughn right now will do nothing to save Dwargon. You will need to prepare yourself, too, Dolph."

There was little Dolph could say in return. He had no intention of just letting Vaughn die, and as he now realized, admonishing Gazel would do nothing to change the situation.

"I will make preparations to leave as soon as possible," said Dolph.

"Very good."

Gazel gravely nodded and closed his eyes. They had a lot of work to do. All their allied nations would need to be informed, and they'd have to give instructions on what to do with the remaining citizens in the area. If Gazel and his men were victorious, then great—but if they were defeated, what then? There was nowhere else for people to run to, no way of survival except to become imperial vassals. It meant the fall of the nation of Dwargon, and if Gazel wanted to avoid that, he couldn't afford to lose.

"The east city will not have enough room for our entire army, I imagine. I'll let the old guard handle command while the rest of the army marches on the ground. See to that for me, Jaine."

"Very well. But what do you intend to do, King Gazel?"

"I'm going on ahead. If you're late to this, don't expect a place at the table."

Gazel revealed a bold smile, playing the role of a strong king to ease everyone's anxiety. The army was to be mobilized as quickly as possible, but Gazel's group wouldn't wait for them. Dolph and his Pegasus Knights would be the king's only companions.

As Gazel flew across the sky, a thought occurred to him.

Is this why Rimuru gave his underlings all that power? So they could survive this? If so, I have to say he's as naive as ever.

He laughed at this revelation, thinking about the ex-training partner that couldn't throw away his ideals. His smile was nothing he could hold back.

"Is something wrong, my lord?"

"No, just a passing fantasy."

"I beg your pardon?"

"Heh-heh! Now, of all times, I started thinking about Rimuru. It made me wonder if things could work out *this* time, too."

Gazel laughed. He thought he was being overly optimistic, but it beat the opposite end of the spectrum.

"Indeed." Dolph smiled back. "It was the case with Charybdis as well. Lord Rimuru can simply boggle the mind at times. I was amazed at the connection he had with the demon lord Milim."

"Well, if you're going to bring *that* up, you should also mention the hardships I've faced monitoring him. People assuming that everything I report back to them is a lie is growing tiresome."

Henrietta usually kept her mouth shut, but even she had some sass in her at times. Gazel and Dolph couldn't hide their surprise.

"Hee-hee-hee! Sorry. I'll try to avoid assuming that next time."

"Even *you* have some complaints about your job, eh, Henrietta?"

"Of *course* I do!"

"Wah-ha-ha-ha-ha-ha! In that case, Henrietta, tell Rimuru that next time you see him. Why, he's a pain to me as well! I trust you two firmly, but Rimuru's behavior is simply too asinine to believe. When I heard the report from Jaine, I began to question her sanity."

"Ha-ha… It was one fearsome report, yes."

"Normally, I'm the one giving those reports, so it was nice seeing it unfold as a spectator this time."

The venom Henrietta was spitting made both Gazel and Dolph laugh, their voices echoing through the sky.

"I will mention that I've sent a report of our activities to Lord Rimuru…along with some measured complaining."

"Did you?"

Gazel nodded and turned his head forward. The anxiety was gone now, replaced with his usual heroic flair as he flew toward the battleground.

Going back in time a little bit…

It was the day after Elmesia's and my little drinking party, and the sun was already way up in the sky.

"Up early, aren't you, Sir Rimuru?"

"I'm sorry."

Shuna's so scary when she's smiling. I decided to beat her to the punch with an apology. First I get drunk, then I enjoy a little nap—I worked hard to regain those luxuries, so I don't see why I have to be yelled at about it.

"So did you come to a conclusion?" she asked, staring at me as she sighed.

"Um, about what?"

"You were troubled about it last night as well, weren't you? I am worried you're about to do something rash again, and I'm far from the only one."

When she said that, I couldn't help but feel a little jittery. Don't worry. I'm not doing anything rash here. If it doesn't work out, I'll run, and then I'll bitch at Guy and make him do something about it. First, though, I had to try a little.

"Hey, we'll figure it out, okay? I'll be safe with it like I always am."

My cheerful reply didn't remove Shuna's anxious expression. It's hard to fool her, what with her unique skill Parser and all—or maybe it was too obvious to even require that.

I mean, you know, I didn't really *want* to do anything dangerous. I was taking a "safety first" approach, but we had no idea about our enemy's strength. Lieutenant Kondo, Velgrynd, and Emperor Ludora were fearsome opponents, no matter how you sliced it. Winning may not be a possibility—and for all I know, I might even be killed on the spot. I was trying to think of ways to avoid that outcome, but not even Raphael had an answer this time.

If we don't know, though, we'll just go for it. My only choice was to throw in the maximum amount of warpower I had and reduce the danger as much as possible. And so...

"You know, I deliberated a lot over who I'd take with me. This time around, I'm going with my A team only. I'm sorry to say this, but if you don't have enough strength to pitch in, I think you're just gonna slow us down."

"...All right. My brother's been bragging all morning about how he's going with you."

I suppose my thoughts were obvious from the start. I had been engaged with Elmesia since the previous morning, so I didn't tell everyone about my conversation with Guy yet—but Shuna's smile seemed to indicate that she understood it all. I smiled back, realizing how there was never any tricking her. Then she gave me her report in her usual, natural voice.

"That fishy little sneak Laplace slinked in here last night. He said he had a message for you, but he gave us no advance warning, so we've been keeping him waiting for the time being."

Rather abrupt change of subject there. But it didn't seem like anything too important to me. If it was a real emergency, Gadora or someone would've contacted me. Probably a message from Yuuki, but what could it be?

"I guess I'll see him, although I'm not crazy about the idea."

"I'd much prefer to shoo him away, but he *is* an ally, more or less. I'll show him to a reception room."

Shuna wasn't a fan of Laplace, either, it looked like. That was rare for her; she wasn't one to be so frank about her likes and dislikes, but clearly those clowns irked her. I guessed she couldn't ever truly forgive Laplace and his crew for destroying their ogre homeland. He and I were allies, but I'd need to keep that in mind.

"While I'm talking to Laplace," I ordered Shuna, "I'd like you to summon all the cabinet staff who're awake to our meeting hall." I had a lot of things to think about, but I could worry about them all after our war with the Empire was over. Banishing all doubt from my mind, I decided to take care of the immediate problem first.

Twenty people, including myself, were gathered in the meeting hall. There was Rigurd and the four elders beneath him—Rugurd, Regurd, Rogurd, and Lilina. I also had Kaijin, Vester, and Mjöllmile in here. Representing the Twelve Lordly Guardians were Benimaru, Shion, Diablo, Gabil, Testarossa, Ultima, and Carrera. Soei, Hakuro, Gobta, and (for good measure) Gadora rounded out the pack.

I planned to ask Gadora to guide me around the Empire. Even I had to admit it wasn't gonna be an easy job, but honestly, he'd be the least affected out of us all if something went wrong, so I wanted him to play his part. Speaking of which, Bernie volunteered to guide us as well, but I rejected the offer. He had lost all his powers, and he'd be nothing but a liability to us. Gadora alone would do.

Anyway.

Feels like I was just having meetings all the time, but no point complaining about that now. Our country had grown too big for me to call all the shots myself. Of course, as I say that, this meeting's mainly about me dictating to everyone what I've decided to do, but still.

As usual, Shuna served tea to everyone. Once she quietly left the room, I began speaking.

"I've called all of you in today to inform you about my decisions for the final battle against the Empire. Before that, though... Come on in."

I already decided who I'd be taking with me, so there was no point hurrying this. Instead, I decided to introduce Laplace, our messenger, to everyone.

As expected, Laplace had news concerning our plans to fight together. The army blockading Dwargon's east city would be attacking the imperial capital soon, and they wanted us to join them, basically. Guy had already told me about that, and I had no objections—but the conclusion I came to was that this would be a war between the elites on both sides, not a war of armies. I didn't want to see any civilian casualties, so in the end, I decided I had to discuss the details with Yuuki first. That's why I chose to bring the clown into this meeting on short notice.

I had already spoken with Yuuki via Laplace. The date had been set for the following afternoon. This I explained to everyone in the room—I really wish Laplace could've done that for me, but people had a lot of trust problems with him, so I rejected the idea. Trust, I was reminded all over again, really is important.

"Hello, hello! My name's Laplace, and I'm the vice president of a group of, ah, helpful ladies 'n' gents we like to call the Moderate Jesters. I'm here today 'cause Yuuki sent me, y'see."

Oh, man. Is it impossible for him *not* to act suspicious? And why did he choose this moment to dance a little jig to himself? But he was still here as a messenger, so I couldn't just boot him out.

I wasn't the only one annoyed by this, either. Soei looked like he was about to kill him. I know how he feels, but he'll have to be patient.

"Soei, put that kunai blade away, please."

"...Yes, sir."

Gotta be careful with him, too, I see. He meekly sat back down for me, but I couldn't let my guard down yet. Let's just get this intro over with.

"Yeah, so Mr. Laplace here is our point of contact for Yuuki at the moment."

"Just Laplace is fine, y'know."

"Oh, is it? Then, great. Anyway, we've set up a meeting with Yuuki for tomorrow. It's a bit of a rush, I know, but Laplace is apparently gonna transport me over there, so we don't have to worry about travel time. The main question at hand is: Who's going with me?"

Finally, I got down to business.

"Mm-hmm. So I can only carry up to six people in all. Assumin' that you and I are must-haves, d'you mind tellin' me the other four you'll bring, Lord Rimuru?"

I wanted to deploy as much force as I possibly could, but even in the best case, I wouldn't have all my top people on hand. Ranga was still asleep in my shadow, and Geld had yet to wake up as well. The labyrinth gang—Kumara, Zegion, and Adalmann—had reportedly all holed up in their respective domains, showing no sign of stirring. The length of everyone's evolutionary slumber seemed to vary a lot; I guess that's just how the cookie crumbles. So I looked over who was available one more time.

"Benimaru, I'd like you to come with me, but how're you feeling?"

"What, does he have a cold or somethin'?" Laplace asked, a wary look in his eyes. I'm sure he'll find out soon enough anyway, but I wasn't feeling nice enough to explain it all for him.

"I'm feeling fine. Best shape of my life, actually."

Benimaru flashed a heroic smile, retaining his coolness and completely ignoring Laplace. He's much more capable than I'll ever be, a fact that occasionally amazes me at times like this.

I gave him a closer look as I internally praised him—only to find that he had changed species while I wasn't paying attention. He must've worked things out with Momiji and Alvis, so to speak, and now the evolution was complete. In fact, according to what I heard later, Benimaru had spent two nights with each of his new wives in turn. I don't know if I should congratulate him on weathering that…or just sit here, seething in all my jealousy.

Now he had abandoned his physical body, only to reincarnate and become a fully spiritual life-form. The name of his species was Flamesoul Ogre, a type of elemental soul. Like True Dragons, he retained both the holy and evil attributes, making him something like a chaos elemental, a stripped-down version of a True Dragon.

Both True Dragons and chaos elementals could take the form of various attributes, with "flame" being an upgraded version of "fire."

The natural family of elements consists of earth, water, fire, wind, and space—the five major attributes, as they're called. The rule of thumb is that fire beats earth, water beats fire, wind beats water, space beats wind, and earth beats space. Picture it as fire scorching earth, water extinguishing fire, wind scattering water, space blockading wind, and earth occupying space, and there you have the conflicts in a nutshell.

In addition to these five major attributes, you also have the two opposing attributes of light and darkness—as well as "time," which exists over all the other ones and cannot be restrained by any of them.

Elemental spirits like Ifrit are bound by these physical laws… Or to put it another way, they're the embodiments of the laws governing the world, and apparently there are eight types of these embodiments. The light and dark attributes are somewhat special, with light being derived from angels—and darkness from demons. The angels and demons I know of so far could be called elemental spirits, technically, if you trace their roots. Someone like Diablo could tell me more if I asked, but I'm not that interested, and it's not like I could do much with the knowledge anyway.

The key takeaway here is that there are eight kinds of elemental souls, each higher up than elemental spirits. The highest ranked among them are the True Dragons, and currently, only four are known to exist. Veldanava, the Star-King Dragon, is probably associated with the space and earth elements, judging by the name, and maybe more as well. Velzard the Ice Dragon is likely water-based;

Velgrynd the Flame Dragon is almost certainly fire-based; and our own Veldora rules over not just water and wind, but space as well—a pretty big deal, despite how he acts.

So the True Dragons stand at the pinnacle of all elemental souls, and it's safe to say that Benimaru had evolved into a similar existence. Flamesoul Ogres are spiritual life-forms, but they also have physical bodies that let them properly interact with the material world. With their infinite life span, calling people like him god-ogres wouldn't be pushing it at all.

It's a very special evolution that Benimaru pulled off, and I was impressed. His magicule count received a major boost as well—it was now several times what Carillon boasted, I think. It probably wouldn't max out quite at Luminus's level, but I still thought Benimaru was decent competition. At this rate, I was reasonably sure he could fight the Single Digits at an even keel—or maybe better.

"All right! In that case, Benimaru, you're my first choice. As for person number two..."

Gadora was already on the list, so I had two picks left. I was planning to take Shion and Diablo as well, which brought me very neatly up to four.

"...I'm going to have Gadora serve as our guide, and after that, I'll bring my secretaries Shion and Diablo."

So Laplace would be taking me, Gadora, Benimaru, Shion, and Diablo.

"You can count on me, Sir Rimuru! You will be completely safe and sound around me!"

Shion was beaming. I'm not so sure about the "safe and sound" part. I had a lot of concerns, in fact, but Shion's a bodyguard I knew I could rely on. She defeated a superior opponent in Razul, and when it came to battle, I couldn't leave her off the list.

"Keh-heh-heh-heh-heh... I don't know what kind of scheme Guy may be hatching, but putting you through all this hardship is simply outrageous. With you by my side, I assure you that I will put an end to all your worries!"

Confident as always. But I saw no reason not to hold him up to that. Diablo's good at his job, and it's times like these that I want to rely on him.

We might be an elite team on this mission, but we couldn't rest on our laurels. The others here would be following soon; I'd have them join us in the Empire later on. But before I could outline all that, one attendee was already expressing her dissatisfaction.

"If you could, Sir Rimuru, I humbly suggest that I would be better suited to serve as a guide. I hope you'll consider having me accompany you."

It was Testarossa. She *was* born in the Empire, I suppose, and she probably knew a lot about its geography. She was proving to be a talented diplomatic officer, gifted in negotiation, and there was certainly no complaining about her fighting strength—hell, she might even have been stronger than me. The only real advantage Gadora had over her is his acquaintance with Yuuki, so if you think about it, I could probably get along without him. Gadora's pretty strong (especially for his age), but he couldn't hold a candle to Testarossa—and I still had a slight nagging fear that he wouldn't think twice about double-crossing us.

With that in mind, I didn't want to have any regrets no matter what I decided on, but at the same time, I did feel a little bad for her. Maybe I should take the hint.

"All right. In that case, maybe I should replace Gadora with you, then?"

"It would truly be an honor."

Testarossa gave me a beautiful, almost blinding smile. Gadora didn't seem to mind either way, fortunately, so let's go with that.

"Righto," interjected Laplace. "Looks like you've made up your mind, so I'm gonna go prep. Lemme know when you're all set."

"Sure, but what are you prepping for?"

Laplace gave me an awkward look.

"Well, um, you know..."

"He's prepping for a trip to our hot spring. He's been going between there and our dining hall since yesterday, using our recreational facilities like they belong to him."

Soei sounded pretty pissed about it. Good thing I was having Laplace surveilled.

"Ha-ha-ha! You got me, I guess. Don't be such a stick in the mud, Soei!"

As if we'd never notice. He really does have a lot of guts, doesn't he?

"You were paying the bills for that, right?"

"Hey, I'm a guest here, ya know? I'll pay you back with the work I'll be doing for y'all, so how 'bout we treat it as on the house for now?"

"Guts" ain't the half of it.

"Laplace…"

"Hey, hey, hey, it's not my fault this country's such a charmer from start to finish! It's the most advanced in the world, no two ways about it! Paradise, even. Who *wouldn't* wanna kick back and relax while they're here?!"

Now he was laying it on thick about how great Tempest was. Receiving such effusive praise wasn't exactly off-putting, no. I figured maybe Laplace wasn't so bad, after all.

"He's distracting you, Sir Rimuru!"

"Don't worry, Benimaru. He might try to put one over on Sir Rimuru, but I'm keeping a careful watch over him at all times."

Oops.

Benimaru and Shion snapped me out of it. I cleared my throat.

"Well, keep it in moderation, all right?"

"Oh, of course, of course! So yeah, I'll see you guys in a bit, okay?"

Then Laplace gleefully skipped out of the meeting hall. *What a free spirit*, I thought as we moved on to the next topic.

*

"If it'll be only five of you in enemy territory, don't you think that's a little too dangerous?"

"I firmly agree. If anything happens to Sir Rimuru, we would never recover, no matter how many battles we win."

"Indeed. I certainly understand that a vast army isn't what we need in this final clash, but if things go awry, someone needs to serve as a shield for Sir Rimuru."

Soei, Gabil, and Hakuro, in that order, all expressed their opposition to my plans. They discreetly kept quiet about it while Laplace was around, but now they made their grievances clear with me.

"Master Hakuro's right, y'know. And if push comes to shove, I'm prepared to take the heat for Sir Rimuru, too. I'd kinda be a meat shield, y'know?"

"Gobta."

"Ah!"

A meat shield? I couldn't help but imagine that in action. I really wish I didn't.

"Hakuro, stop teaching stuff like that to Gobta."

"Of course. I just thought, though, it is quite important to teach him how to prepare for such eventualities."

I understood what Hakuro was getting at. It was just that my heart didn't agree with it.

"I mean, I'm glad all of you are concerned for me, but *you're* all really important to me, too. I don't want to kick this off with a strategy that assumes we'll have to take casualties. If we want to avoid that, I think we should pool all our resources together for this effort."

"Quite true. Perhaps we are a little ahead of ourselves."

I'm not sure I was convincing too many people. Even Benimaru and the rest seem to be on Hakuro's side. If I were them, maybe I'd feel the same way. Still, though… I appreciate the thought, but I still don't want anyone to die here. Maybe it's selfish of me, but I want to put my own feelings first.

"Anyway, I'm not gonna run a strategy that demands any loss of life. Let's stick with that assumption as we discuss the final stages of our war against the Empire."

Everyone nodded at my words. They seemed ready to participate in this discussion, regardless of their personal feelings.

"If I could begin, Sir Rimuru…"

"Yes, Soei?"

"I have a Replication of mine undercover within the Empire.

There's been a number of obstacles preventing me from reaching the capital just yet. But it does seem that their security network is looser than usual. I was thinking of using Shadow Motion to meet with you once Laplace organizes the transport. Would that be all right?"

I see. That's reassuring, actually. Soei always serves me well as my shadow, and that really hits home with situations like this. He's a great fighter, too, and taking a closer look at him, *he* went and evolved on me as well.

No longer an oni, he was now a species known as Darksoul Ogre; apparently it was a blessing he received in conjunction with Benimaru's evolution. He was raised as Benimaru's shadow back in their ogre homelands, the yin to his yang, and while there was a definite hierarchy to their relationship, they were still fast friends. A natural counterpart to Benimaru, in other words, and that was why Benimaru's awakening affected him so much. The system behind this evolution must've seen Soei as his subordinate, but that wasn't a problem—they still treated each other the same.

Darksoul Ogres are chaos elementals bearing the darkness attribute. Just like Benimaru, Soei was now a spiritual life-form with a physical body. Kind of a servant deity for Benimaru, then? His magicule count was medium-size, not colossally high; it was nothing compared to Benimaru's but still higher than Clayman's in his half-awakened state. That's enough strength for me, and I was sure he could be a good match for ex–demon lords like Carillon or Frey.

Maybe that boost in strength was what allowed him to skirt the Empire's security so far? Well, either way, fine by me. I was just glad to have Soei along—but that also brought Masayuki's protection into question.

"That's a very reassuring offer, Soei. But what about Masayuki?"

"I will have a Replication of mine continue monitoring him. If something happens, I think I can handle it well enough."

He sounded confident.

"In that case," added Diablo, "perhaps I could install Venom as a companion for Masayuki? If we keep it a secret from the boy, I think Venom could play the role of a monitor and bodyguard at the same time. That would lighten Soei's load, and it'd also provide some extra insurance."

Ooh, good idea. Venom had a very sensible, un-demonlike personality, and he'd been getting along strength-wise, too. I felt like he and Masayuki would get along well—maybe they could even become good friends. It sounded like a real neat idea.

"That means your second-in-command would be unavailable, keep in mind."

"Keh-heh-heh-heh-heh... That will not be a problem. With Testarossa and the others around, my own work will not be affected at all."

Sounds great, then.

"Are you good with that, Soei?"

"It would be more certain, perhaps, to provide a visible bodyguard rather than monitor him from the shadows. I would be able to save the energy that Replication consumes as well."

Excellent. Let's do it.

"All right, let's go in that direction, then."

"Yes, my lord!"

"I'll get on it right away."

So Venom would be Masayuki's escort, and Soei would instead join us on-site. The only thing left to decide is whether to deploy our army—and how.

"Now, as we fight alongside Dwargon, do you think we'd need a show of force for the Empire?"

Our First and Third Army Corps returned home with us once they finished retrieving all the bodies. Their full manpower was stationed here in Rimuru, our capital city. The Second Army Corps, meanwhile, couldn't be deployed because Geld, their leader, was still taking his evolution nap. Which meant...

"Sir Rimuru, is this where we may come in?"

"Whoa, wait a sec! We're shipping out first!"

Gabil I expected, but it was rare to see Gobta so enthusiastic about stuff like this. But unlike last time, I felt like relying on strength in numbers was too risky. If we were fighting a massive army, I wouldn't attempt a large assault that'd get too many of my allies involved, but this time, we were a bit like a SWAT team. They might decide to carpet-bomb us with nuclear magic or expose us to even more drastic measures. Armies waging magic battle tend to rely on the power of their legion magic, with teams of elites slinging attacks before that magic's broken—but if the opponent's above a certain level of strength, the soldiers at the end of the line are just dead weight.

"What do you think, Hakuro?"

"Hoh-hoh-hoh! I know exactly what you're thinking, Sir Rimuru, and I see it as the right thing to think."

"Okay. No novices, then. And we shouldn't take any low-ranking soldiers in either?"

"I believe that's best for minimizing casualties, yes."

"And so…"

"So it'll just be the Goblin Riders from my corps?"

"And Team Hiryu from mine will be readied for combat!"

Sounds like it. The Goblin Riders ranked an A for their overall teamwork. They served as excellent decoys in the war so far, and I didn't think anyone could beat them that easily. When it came to fleeing, they were all but unbeatable, so I didn't see any issues there. Also, following Gabil's awakening, every member of Team Hiryu was now past A in rank. I'm a little concerned about the control they had over their powers, but—ah, they oughtta be okay.

"All right. Gobta and Gabil, I want you to start prepping along those lines… Oh, wait a second."

I was about to set it in stone when I remembered something else important.

"Gobta, can you guys call upon your starwolf partners right now?"

"Huh?"

"Like, Ranga hasn't finished the awakening process yet, so all the other wolves under him are still sleeping, too, right?"

"*Ohhh!*"

Guess that's a no, then.

"Right. You'll stay here on standby, then."

"B-but…"

"Don't tell me you aren't aware of your limitations, Gobta."

"…Sorry."

Gobta was visibly mopey about this, but I couldn't do much about it, sadly. The Goblin Riders' main advantages stemmed from the high mobility of their starwolf mounts. Each Rider may have ranked an A-plus no problem, but I still couldn't afford to take them along on this.

"Hey, it's not your fault. Hook up with Rigur and focus on security within our own borders, all right?"

"Yes, sir!"

So with some regrets, Gobta's army had to stay here. Which meant our only other deployable troops were…

"How's Team Kurenai doing, Benimaru?"

"No problems there. Every one of them's achieved a rank of A."

Perfect. They had an excellent commander in Gobwa, and some of them had even evolved into ogre mages during the blessing process. They ought to be reliable enough if we send them out.

"Soei, how about Team Kurayami?"

"They are deployed across the land, gathering intelligence and gauging the enemy. I can call them back if necessary…"

"No, keep them working behind the scenes."

"Very well."

No need to demand them back here. The importance of their intelligence ops went without question, so let's have them keep that up.

"That just leaves Team Reborn…"

"I'd love to deploy them, Sir Rimuru! They're ready and willing to play a more active role at any moment!"

"Hmm, yeah…"

Shion's awakening brought about no special changes in her, but Team Reborn's fighting power had grown a lot, with some members achieving an A rank. They were hard to kill, which was a big advantage, so I figured they'd be okay in this battle—but Team Reborn was at its most effective only when Shion was with them. If nobody was around to command them, they'd be rudderless. It'd be less risky, I thought, to keep them back home like Gobta's force.

"…Nah, I think we'll leave them."

"Oh no!"

"Team Reborn's more of a bodyguard force than an army, you know? I'd feel safer if you're with me instead, Shion."

"Ah, I see!"

Shion readily accepted that.

So now we had our deployment fully worked out. Team Hiryu had a hundred members—Team Kurenai, three hundred. That was four hundred people ranked A or higher in all, making for an excellent little fighting division. They may not have been the largest, but no one would ever doubt their battle skill.

Still, this wasn't quite enough to reassure me.

"Now, Ultima and Carrera, I have a job for you two."

"Oh, absolutely! Anything you like!"

"What is it, my lord?"

"Ultima, I want you to continue accompanying Gabil's force as an intelligence officer. Carrera, I'll be assigning you support duty for Gobwa this time, not Geld."

"Oh... The lizards again?"

"Understood. I'll try to be as discreet as possible in my post."

Their replies weren't exactly filling me with confidence. Ultima seemed to have a beef or two with Gabil, and frankly, I didn't believe Carrera could keep a low profile doing much of anything.

"Heavens, Ultima! Do you have some issues with my force, perhaps?"

"Yes! Lots of them! Like, the way you guys act creeps me out. It's kind of hard to figure out what makes you tick, from a common-sense perspective."

"Ha-ha-ha! No need to worry about that! When it comes to battle, we always take things fully seriously!"

"And you call experimenting with the hostile fire of enemies in the middle of war being serious?"

"Don't be silly! It's wise to try every possible tactic in order to gain an advantage in battle. Experimentation is part of that, and it's something all of us should take seriously, I think!"

"No, it's something you should finish up *before* battle begins! Why do I even have to lecture you about this?!"

I suppose having a beef or two with him is understandable. From what I was hearing, Ultima seemed to be in the right, too.

"I'm sorry, but do you think you could put up with it this time, at least?"

"If those are your orders, Sir Rimuru, I'll do my best with them! I was thinking that I'd need to teach them a lot of things anyway, so I'll try to see this as a good opportunity and stuff."

Even with that resentful glare, Ultima was as cute as always as she evaluated Gabil. They may not get along well, but I felt like I could leave Gabil in her care.

"And, Carrera, well, you don't have to worry about keeping a low profile too much."

"Oh?"

She was bound to start bashing heads in battle anyway, so trying to be "discreet" here seemed pretty absurd to me. Instead, I just wanted Carrera to think a little more about the right time and place for that kinda thing.

"The number one rule I want you to remember is to keep your allies safe from damage. Beyond that, just keep quiet until the fighting starts, all right?"

"Sure! That sounds simple enough!"

Is it?

I wouldn't make any more demands, I promised her, as long as she absolutely abided by that one. Hopefully this would help everything work out, but...

"Hakuro, could you accompany Gobwa as well?"

"Certainly."

"Try to rein in Carrera for me, okay?"

Hakuro nodded, sniggering a bit.

We had our deployment all sorted out—or so I thought, before Gadora raised his hand.

"Sir Rimuru, if I may be so bold, I'd like to discuss something else with you."

"What's that?"

"I think it might be a good idea to include the Demon Colossus in this war."

Aha.

Getting it out of the labyrinth is a bit of a problem, but even if it breaks, it won't lead to any human casualties. With Gadora taking control of it, I was sure he could get out safely if need be. He had both a Resurrection Bracelet and an emergency-return spell in his arsenal, after all. No matter what kind of raging battlefield we threw him into, we wouldn't need to worry about him, which was a big advantage. But did we really want to reveal the Colossus's combat capabilities to the world?

"Vester, what do you think?"

I asked Vester for his opinion. He replied with a defiant grin as he pushed his glasses up his nose.

"It might be the perfect occasion for the big unveiling, actually. I've already given a detailed report on it to King Gazel, and he's been eager to see it in action for a while. I'd like to collect data from it in all kinds of conditions, so it'd be interesting for me to see how it performs on an actual battlefield."

Vester really is a scientist, isn't he? The value of a weapon is determined by how powerful it is—you gotta fire it off in public *sometime*, even if it's just for a show of force. From that standpoint, maybe this battle would be a nice place for a demonstration. That's what Vester thinks, I presume.

Certainly, the Demon Colossus was best suited for close-up warfare. It wasn't a weapon of mass destruction that way, but it'd be killer for intimidating opponents, sapping their will to fight. If I was letting the three demonesses out on the battlefield, it'd be morally wrong for me to turn this down.

"But if the enemy seized it from us, wouldn't that be a serious technology leak?"

"Oh, I promise we won't make *that* mistake!"

"Well, if that happens, we'll just develop an even better golem next time. There's no single endpoint to technology, after all. Still, just in case, it has been equipped with a self-destruct mechanism, so there's no need to worry about any leaks."

Hold on. He was making this out to be a nice, happy story, but there was one part of it I couldn't ignore.

"A self-destruct mechanism?"

"That's right. Sir Veldora was quite insistent on having one in there. I thought he was joking at first, but I have to hand it to him—he must have anticipated a situation like that."

No. He definitely didn't. I had a feeling Veldora was behind it; it was the kind of harebrained thing either he or Ramiris would come up with, given all the manga I've been feeding them. I really wish they'd stop obsessing over useless crap like this. Still, better to have it than not, at least.

"All right. In that case, I don't care too much if it breaks down or falls into enemy hands, but don't be reckless with it, all right?"

"So we can bring it out?!"

"Yep, you're clear to go. And Gadora, we may or may not need you in battle, but I'd still like you on hand in case of emergency."

"By all means, Sir Rimuru. And personally, I don't want to be too cruel toward my former colleagues. The way I see it, the Demon Colossus will come into play only if they break out some new weapon we're not aware of!"

Sounds safe enough to leave to him, then. Gadora's quick on his feet, so he might decide to switch sides again if defeat starts looking inevitable for us. Maybe he was angling to position himself outside our labyrinth just in case it came to that—that seemed plausible to me, but it wouldn't be right to voice that yet. We needed to be optimistic for now and keep Gadora away from any second thoughts. In other words, all we needed was an undeniable, overwhelming victory against the Empire, and we were good.

So the final lineup, with Gadora included after all, was now set in place.

＊

It was evening by the time the meeting ended. Once it adjourned, each of us began to prepare for tomorrow... Although for me, that meant relaxing a bit in our dining hall.

Tomorrow I'd be giving a pep talk for my personal entourage in the morning, and then we'd all head off via the transport spell. In the afternoon, I'd confer with Yuuki; Laplace was going to take me to him, so we'd have plenty of time to spare. This would just be a day trip for me, so I didn't have a whole lot to prep for. I certainly didn't need to bring a gift for Yuuki or whatnot; I figured we should keep things casual.

"Are you sure you should be so blithe about this?"

"Ahhh, I bet it's fine. And what about you? You sure you should be leaving Momiji and Alvis alone right now?"

Benimaru was with me in the dining hall. Being a newlywed and all, I wanted him to have as much relaxing home time as possible. That was why I asked about his wives, but Benimaru just chuckled at me.

"They told me they're taking a cooking lesson from Shuna today. I heard they have an informal agreement not to try to one-up each other, but thanks to that, they've shooed me away from the house for now..."

Whoa. Not exactly the happiest, most carefree way to kick off a marriage, is it? I wondered if they could keep things up like that, but it's not on me to comment on other people's family lives.

"I—I see," I said, sagely nodding in agreement as Diablo excitedly brought a meal over to us—like a real butler, for a change. I mean, it still felt weird having a Primal demon serving as my butler, but he seemed to enjoy every minute of it, and I wasn't about to shoot him down. I was used to this treatment now, besides, and I wasn't about to change my mind.

"Thank you very much."

"No, no, this is part of my job as well, so..."

You think so, huh? Well, if you're happy, I'm happy.

"I have this as well for you, Sir Rimuru."

Shion was there, pouring me a glass of wine. She didn't make it herself, of course, so it was perfectly safe and nonlethal to drink, but something about her presence made me really uncomfortable. This was a simple meal of fried pork cutlets and rice, after all, so I really didn't need this five-star service. Having Diablo and Shion standing behind me just added to my fatigue.

"Here, why don't you guys sit down and eat with us?"

"What a kind thing to say."

"Oh, no, I'm already full, so don't worry about me!"

"Yes, Shion's been sampling the wares in the kitchen, after all."

"Damn you, Diablo!"

Eesh. They were at each other's throats over every little thing. It seemed pointless to give them any more attention, so Benimaru and I let them be and enjoyed our meal.

"So do you intend to fully trust Yuuki, then?"

"Not from the heart, no. That's kind of asking a lot. But right now, I kind of *have* to, you know? And I want to, also."

"Then I will follow your lead, Sir Rimuru. Our entire strategy, after all, assumes that we can trust him."

"And what if he turns traitor?"

"That would be…trouble. But we can manage, I imagine."

"Mmm. Well, sorry for the trouble in advance."

"I'm always ready and willing."

Something about Benimaru's smile really encourages me. In war, you always have to trust your allies—your friends. Let any doubt seep into your mind, and that throws your chances of success at any operation into uncertainty. If Yuuki betrays us, we'd pay an enormous toll for that, so it's certainly a difficult choice I'm being forced to make. But I decided to trust Yuuki, and now that I made that decision, there was no point worrying over it.

"I was wondering, by the way… Do you even *need* to eat now?"

I posed the question to Benimaru, who was tucking into his meal right alongside me.

"In terms of 'need,' the answer is no."

"Ah. I thought so."

"But the same applies to you, doesn't it, Rimuru? I'm just glad I didn't lose my sense of taste."

"Oh, I hear you. When I lost the three main desires all human beings have, I thought the world was gonna end, honestly. I went through a lot of hard work to regain my appetite and need to sleep, so I'm really enjoying every day now."

"I'm sure. I was worried about the possibility as well, but I'm the same as always on that front, so I can't complain."

We nodded at each other. Then something occurred to me.

"Oh, so all three of your major needs are still there?"

"Yes, fortunately. All of them."

"Even sleep?"

"I don't need to sleep, but meditation puts me in a sleep state. It still helps me recover from fatigue as well."

Wow. So I had to go through all that work in order to sleep, but he gets to keep that from the start? And it even gives him a lot of benefits I don't get to enjoy. But what I was even more interested in…

"And your sex drive?"

I lowered my voice as I asked it. Benimaru nodded back, looking a little embarrassed.

"Aw, what the hell? I thought you couldn't evolve because you won't be able to have children then."

"That's right. But both Momiji and Alvis are pregnant right now."

"Well, congratulations—but wait, did you keep your sex drive *after* the evolution?!"

"I assumed it would disappear as well, but whether I'm fertile or not, it's still there, yes. Looks like I won't be leaving them lonely, after all."

I was just too jealous. Keeping functionality I never had in the first place… Talk about a perfect evolution. God dammit, why can't *I* have that…?

"Gee, that's greeeeeeat."

"Yes… Hey, why are you taking my food?!"

"Shut up, you traitor!"

My jealousy finally ignited as I took Benimaru's dish away.

All I got left to enjoy is food, but look at you, *you bastard!*

Could anyone have faulted me for thinking that way?

Anyway, we continued to enjoy ourselves well into the night— the usual scene, kind of. But all that was about to end abruptly.

*

"H-holy smokes! Guys! Somethin' really awful's happened, apparently, so I gotta get back, like, right now!"

Laplace was shouting as he stormed into the dining hall. He wasn't alone.

"Bad news, Sir Rimuru! We just received a call in the name of King Gazel. It informed us that Velgrynd has appeared before the Composite Force, and they're requesting immediate support!"

Vester's eyes were bloodshot. Surprised, I rose from my seat.

"Okay, assemble the group I'm leaving with ASAP!"

"Right away."

Benimaru promptly sprang into action. They'd all be here in short order.

"Laplace, give me just a little bit. We'll join you."

"W-well, if ya want, but..."

I wondered if Laplace's panic was just an act—some scheme to lure us in and trap us. But upon hearing Vester's report, I saw that it wasn't the case. Something major was going down in the Empire, something not even Laplace was informed of. It was important to stay calm.

"I know this is a big deal, but don't panic. We're in an alliance, remember. You'd be a lot more useful bringing all of us than going back alone, won't you?"

"Useful?"

If the enemy's strongest fighter is right in front of the Composite Division, maybe we could consider this an opportunity. Reportedly someone attacked Yuuki as well, but if we can beat all of them now, it'd give us a decisive advantage in our negotiations. With that in mind, I decided to ask Laplace for more details.

"So what happened, exactly?"

After a few moments of hesitation, Laplace answered me.

"Well, Teare reached out to me. She said our team's president, Lady Kagali, was callin' for me, 'cause Kondo and his team were attacking them."

Ah, Lieutenant Kondo. One of the guys on my "watch out for" list. Probably good to team up with Laplace and beat him up now. But what I wondered about is whether Yuuki's force wasn't able to fend these guys off—and why.

"What's Yuuki doing, then? Did he lose, too?"

"Well, it sounds like Damrada's takin' him on."

"Damrada? The Cerberus leader who's actually vice commander of the Imperial Guardians, right? So he turned traitor on Yuuki?"

I was under the impression he was on Yuuki's side. But he's not? I've never met him, so I can't guess at his motivations.

"That I don't know. Teare and Footman keep on changin' their stories. But for now, it's clear he was fightin' the boss."

Hmm. Hard to say much. But one thing's for sure—a lot of enemies are on the field, and they're dispersed all over the place. Job one was to gain an accurate bead on the situation. Not wanting to waste any time, I deployed Argos, the Eye of God, on the spot. We already had the coordinates, giving me a pinpoint view of the Composite Division's encampment. I projected it on the dining hall wall.

"Wow," muttered someone in the room.

There we saw a beautiful woman, a lustrous smile. Her most notable trait was her blue hair, tied up in buns on top of her head. She had on a dress I'd describe as similar to a *qipao*, plus a military jacket draped over her shoulders. She was standing alone, as if strolling through an empty field, except there was a large army of sixty thousand troops behind her—or at least, the vestiges of an army. Those were dead bodies in the air, huh?

We could see pillars of crimson connecting heaven and earth—a high-gravity force field.

"Gravity Collapse, huh? What a drag, stealing my greatest trick like that."

Carrera was taking this pretty lightly, but her expression was dead serious. I could see why. The magic this woman, presumably Velgrynd, had broken out was even more precise than the spell Carrera cast. She perfectly specified the range of it, keeping it at bay and under control. There were no other traces of destruction in the area, showing that her spell affected the gravity and nothing else.

"So she used gravity to send the troops flying without damaging anything else?"

"That's right, my lord. And even more vexing to me, there's not even a single grain of sand caught up in it. The only thing it's blowing into the sky are whoever she sees as an enemy."

Is that possible? I guess it must be. We were seeing it happen here, so there was no point doubting it.

"We're going to fight her?"

"Keh-heh-heh-heh-heh… She is every bit the elder sister of Sir Veldora, is she not? How fascinating. I've always wanted to have a serious fight with one of them."

Diablo was bold as always, but honestly, I didn't see any way that he'd win.

Negative. If we challenge her with all our strength, we have a chance to win.

Great to hear, but the all-hands-on-deck approach was a non-starter for me. There'd definitely be casualties then, so I'd prefer to avoid battle if I could. So would going after Emperor Ludora be a better bet than Velgrynd? If I could have Guy and Ludora settle their game, we could bring this battle to an end and avoid any unnecessary sacrifice.

"But I don't understand. Why isn't she completing the spell fully?"

"Perhaps she doesn't like destroying nature, unlike us."

"I doubt it. Look at that. There's a pile of corpses with the blood all drained from them."

Testarossa pointed at one corner of the screen. She was right—we could see multiple corpses in a pile. I used a split screen effect to focus on the spot, and there, near the pile, we saw a man in a military outfit and a woman I was familiar with.

"…Is that Kagali? Yuuki's secretary?"

"She's the head of the Moderate Jesters. She created us. God dammit! I don't wanna believe it, but it's true. Footman 'n' Teare told me as much through Telepathy, but I guess Kondo really was controlling Lady Kagali."

"Controlling? You mean mind control?"

"Yeah. And worst of all, Teare and Footman can't defy Lady Kagali's orders at all. Our Telepathy got cut off a bit ago, and I bet it's 'cause she ordered them to stop."

That sucks. I think it's awful to take away a person's free will like that... But that's not the pressing issue. We're in serious trouble.

"So how far does Kagali's thrall or whatever extend if she's being mind-controlled? Are *you* all right?"

I couldn't really tell since he was wearing a mask, but Laplace really did look frustrated. If he was as helpless as Teare and Footman against his leader's orders, that was a major problem.

"Nah, I'm fine. Lady Kagali created me, it's true, but I'm the only one who ain't obliged to follow her orders. The bigger deal right now is that most of the folks Yuuki's gathered have a locking curse on 'em. Their top leaders are gonna be the main problem in that case, but judgin' by how the army's lookin' right now, I don't see much point worrying about 'em."

Yeah, it looked like Yuuki's force was done for. Even if there were survivors, none of them could ever escape that magic. It seemed like a few people were still safely outside its influence, but after seeing this tragedy unfold, they'd mostly lost their will to fight. Locking curse or not, I doubted we could count on them for much. Given all that, Laplace's safety was actually pretty darn good news.

"Well, I'm glad you're okay, at least."

"Ah, don't bother. This is it for all our friends."

He sounded unaffected, his voice flat, but I doubted he was too serene. Watching his friends get manipulated like this had to be infuriating. That much, I'm sure, was genuine.

Instead of saying anything, I patted Laplace on the shoulder. He gave me a surprised look.

"But isn't it too early to give up?" I asked, trying to sound naturally cheerful. "Kagali's not dead or anything. If that guy Kondo is controlling her, we can just defeat the source to bring her back to normal. I'm sure Yuuki's still fighting, too, so let's get over there and help them rise back up."

Some of it might've been empty consolation, but it beats being all pessimistic about this. We can always wallow in despair later. What can we do right now? That's what's important.

"You're a funny guy, ya know that? Sayin' the same kinda things my boss does. It's humans who persecuted and exiled us, and now it's humans who're gonna help us, huh? ...What a pain."

I thought I could detect Laplace smiling beneath his mask. I *am* a monster, you know... But yeah, slime or not, I used to be human. Maybe it's not worth bringing up, but...

"Hey, mind if I ask ya something?"

"What is it?"

"What do you wanna *do* as a demon lord?"

Oh, that? Well, my answer's been the same for a while. Ever since I was reincarnated into this world, I've only had one ambition.

"I'm gonna make it so we can all live happily together. That's why I've created this town, this nation, and built relationships with all these other nations. Beyond that, I'd like to value diversity and get along with everyone who shares in my tastes and interests."

"Yer not thinkin' about takin' over the world or whatever?"

"Huh? Nah. Too much work."

"What?! But if you conquer the world, you can do whatever ya want with it!"

"Yeah, but I'd get all bored, y'know? The more ideas you come up with, the more possibilities that'll open up—and the more fun you'll have creating fun stuff you never thought possible. Right?"

Laplace puzzled over my impassioned plea. Then he started waving his hands, as if in panic.

"That's crazy, man! What d'you mean, 'fun stuff'? I wasn't talkin' about that. I was talkin' about you takin' over the world!"

He doesn't get it, does he?

"Well, what, if I got to do whatever I wanted, does that mean it's okay for me to execute mind control on people? Or do you think it's better to be controlled like Kagali is right now?"

"N-no, but..."

"I think it's important that we preserve the rights to free speech, thought, and expression. That connects to respect for basic human rights overall. It creates diversity, and it's the driving force for all kinds of cultural development."

"Huh?! That's just gonna create more selfish bastards, ain't it?

You can't get people on the same page that way. How're you s'posed to steer a country like that?"

He had a point. The greatest weakness of democracy, I think, lies in how to separate national interests from the feelings of individuals. But that counts as diversity, too.

"It's fine. We can figure out how to do it together later. I'm basically a selfish bastard, too, and I sure don't want this nation to go in a direction I'm not on board for."

I'm perfectly fine being a big talker and nothing else. "Reign, do not rule," as the saying goes. I'll do what I've always done, and luckily for me, I have a lot of role models in this world. Luminus's way of using religion as a cover for her rule and Elmesia's positioning herself as absolute ruler up top were both helpful references... Still, I have a long way to go, so I didn't need to decide who I'd be right this minute.

"But that's why political issues and stuff can wait. Right now, what's more important is cultural development. Entertainment, you see? Without that, developing this country is pointless."

This was a really key point, one I hoped would show up on the exams in our future history classes. If I wanted people to lead interesting lives, we needed to produce a ton of entertainment. That's why I didn't want any restrictions on people's ideas or speech.

Laplace stared at me in puzzlement as I explained this. "I don't get it. It's beyond my understanding. He... I mean, the boss... He promised me he'd conquer the world and make it a good place to live. That's why I believed in 'im... In Yuuki. But what the hell's up with you?"

"What do you mean?"

"You're just mockin' him, ain't ya? With that namby-pamby stuff."

"I'm not mocking him, dude. I'm just saying that world domination doesn't sound as fun as you think... And it's a lot *harder* than you think, too."

That finally silenced Laplace for a bit. Then:

"...Yeah. I know that."

He sat limply on the floor, his head turned toward the magical screen. There we saw that pile of bodies, Kagali standing in front of it.

"You asked what we were doin' over there earlier, huh? Well, I'll tell ya. The biggest secret out there, but I'll tell ya. I think you know that we're all walking dead, but I'm gonna tell you about how she's gonna increase our numbers."

Oh? Wait, this *does* sound important.

"Whoa, calm down. This isn't something you should be talking about in our dining hall, is it?"

"Ah, who cares? Now ain't the time for that. Y'see, we were created by Lady Kagali's hand. That's what she was capable of as Curse Lord—gatherin' up the corpses of the dead and their lingering grudges to create a powerful magic-born. It's called Dead Birthday, a kinda forbidden curse magic."

We call it a dining hall, but technically it's reserved for cabinet-class officials. No civilians were in here, though I have to say, Laplace was really taking the plunge, huh? Revealing classified secrets in a place like this. The only people left were Benimaru (back from delivering orders), Soei, Diablo, Shion, Hakuro, the three demonesses, and Vester, who had been watching the video feed with us. Gabil had also returned from giving orders at some point. This was serious stuff, but fortunately nobody was here who I didn't want listening in on it.

"Oh my, that spell name certainly brings back memories."

"You know it, Diablo?"

It was useful having such a magic nerd like Diablo around. Good thing he was familiar with this.

"The body I received from you, Sir Rimuru, was forged through an application of Dead Birthday. In my case, the body didn't come with a soul, but it was perfect for incarnating myself within. The original intent of the spell is to take at least ten thousand corpses, join them together, and take their powers for yourself."

It was an inhumane kind of dark magic, a forbidden curse if I ever saw one. Of course, I'm kind of a serial soul stealer myself, but let's ignore that for now.

"So if Kagali here is trying to make their power her own, does she want to imbue the resulting body with the will of someone in particular?"

"It depends, but I think it's safe to assume so."

"Yeah, Diablo's right. Footman, Teare, and Clayman are all

survivors from where Sir Kazalim came from. Once they lost their homeland, they resorted to these forbidden arts so they'd never forget the humiliation."

Sounds like my hunch was correct, then. Which means that if they complete this spell, it'd be a pretty bad scene.

"There are, or were, around sixty thousand people in the Composite Force. If ya got *that* much material to work with, y'know, you could probably create at least ten walking dead at Clayman's level."

"Whoa, whoa, whoa…"

"And what's more, those sixty thousand contain a lot of really strong folks. And unlike Footman 'n' Teare, they're gonna offer just a ton of easily controllable power, y'know?"

I asked Laplace to expand on that, which he did with visible disgust. As he put it, Footman and Teare were still emotionally immature because they were swallowed up by the vast amounts of power running through them. When Kazalim created his first walking dead, he wasn't too adept at allocating the right amount of power and souls to the right target. As a result, he gave those two far more power than they could hope to withstand. Then, learning from his mistakes, Kazalim created Clayman, which became a resounding success.

That being said, Teare and Footman weren't exactly failures. Their immature minds led to some delays in intellectual growth, but they still wielded a lot of power. In fact, the pre-evolved Geld would probably have his work cut out for him against Footman. In light of that, in terms of fighting ability alone, they were an even greater success than Clayman himself.

If you were to create power-oriented walking dead from a group of sixty thousand corpses, Laplace estimated, the results would be condensed down to six or seven people. This is an Empire that didn't bat an eye at sacrificing a million troops to create even one awakened person; I'm sure they lost no sleep at all over doing this.

"…Man, we were all kids back then, y'know? And Teare still *is* a kid, pretty much, and that goes without sayin' for Footman, too. Only Clayman ever really grew up, but then he went 'n' got himself killed through his own stupid antics. Still, though, I don't think we did you guys wrong at all, huh? Survival of the fittest, 'n' all that. Only natural to wanna test someone out if you don't trust 'em, and we sure don't give a crap about sacrificin' others if it'll expand our own powers. That's how I see it anyway. So ya still wanna join forces with me?"

He didn't have to tell me any of this, but he did. There was no point trying to deliberately agitate us with this—in fact, it'd be a really bad move. But if he was going through with this anyway...

"Don't kid yourself. I will never forgive you for inciting the orcs and destroying our orcish homeland. But Sir Rimuru has decided to join forces with you, and I am in no position to refuse it."

"Benimaru is right. Just thinking about what happened to everyone in our homeland breaks my heart. But there is nothing I could do to you that would make me feel better. Only when we have a world where everyone can live in happiness—the world Sir Rimuru desires—will I lose my regrets."

"Heh. I'm sure you're trying to monopolize all the blame so we can take out our frustrations on you alone, but don't kid yourself. We'll need more than that to erase our anger. It's nothing small enough to be alleviated through torturing the likes of you."

"Yes, quite so. As you say, survival of the fittest is all that matters—and our inexperience at the time, most of all, was the culprit. I'm sure you've cried over your own inexperience at times, haven't you? And if you have, I'm sure you understand how we feel."

Benimaru, Shion, Soei, and Hakuro—the four of them loathed Laplace and his band, but they were still swallowing their pride so we could all fight together. It's just that they couldn't forgive Laplace's gang for what they did, but they're trying to work through it. These ogres sure can be generous sometimes—I noticed that back when Geld first joined us, and I'm seeing it now.

"All right? We haven't forgiven you, and I sure don't trust you completely, either, but for now we're allies. So let's forget our differences and just fight together, okay?"

"...Yeah. And you too, right? I wanna save the boss and my president. So lend me a hand, won't ya?"

Laplace bowed his head deeply. For once, he was being sincere, not at all his usual aloof self. If this was an act, I'd lose faith in other people for good. For now, at least, I wanted to trust him.

∗

Laplace's request was met with nods of approval from Benimaru and the others. His gestures toward us all were so determined, I suppose it tugged at our heartstrings.

"Right. Then we'll head over with the six of us as planned and rescue Yuuki."

"Sounds good. Let's save that bum so he can give us a proper apology."

Benimaru was certainly motivated.

Of course, this *is* Yuuki we're talking about. Knowing him, I'm pretty confident he'd beat Damrada and emerge without even a scratch. The real problem is how to deal with Velgrynd, though. But just as I was about to offer some instructions about that, Shion surprised me.

"So this Kondo man is the mastermind behind all this? If he's capable of controlling the likes of Kagali, then perhaps Clayman was being controlled, too."

"""" """"

We all fell silent. Benimaru was frozen in surprise, while Laplace just muttered, "The hell?"

"Keh... Keh-heh-heh... The first secretary says some rather interesting things..."

Diablo could try laughing it off as much as he wanted, but— perhaps remembering how things were back then—realized there was nothing inherently wrong with what she said. "It's possible," Hakuro even added.

No, guys, it's definitely more natural to believe that. According to Laplace, Yuuki had given orders to Clayman to lie low and not cause trouble. The whole bit with the orcs was one thing, but Clayman's descent into insanity after that wasn't at all what Yuuki wanted from him.

Affirmative. Based on the newly obtained information, I have redefined the situation as this: The subject Clayman exhibited some unexplainable behavior, but if he was being influenced by Kondo and other people, it begins to make more sense. The clear answer is that the Empire stood to gain the most from him.

Yeah, that's what I'm thinking.

"...So you're saying that we had to go through that stuff with Clayman because of Kondo's intentions?"

"Shit."

"Watch your mouth, Benimaru, or else I'll tell Shuna."

"I will. So don't, okay?"

Ignoring Benimaru and Shion's back-and-forth...

"I hate to say it, but I have to agree with Shion. I tried to perform an analysis of his criminal psychology, but there was something unclear about Clayman's behavior. I saw signs that he was in a hurry to move his forces for some reason, even though he should have acted more cautiously. I, at first, thought it was merely his stupidity in action, but it would make sense if there was a third party intervening."

Whoa. Diablo's got the same opinion as Raphael. Guess there's no doubting it now.

"I don't know what the truth is, but let's assume Kondo controlled Clayman and act based on that. If you're paired up with Kondo, be aware of the possibility that he'll try to take over your mind!"

""""Yes, Sir Rimuru!""""

I might be wasting my time with that warning, but it's better than saying nothing.

Anyway, we really do need to watch for this Kondo guy. If we're not careful, he might be an even greater threat than Velgrynd. So I had everyone keep Kondo in mind so we were all prepared.

Now, let's summarize our plan.

"Gabil, I want you and your team to answer King Gazel's request for help. Don't try fighting Velgrynd, though. She's enough of a danger for you and the other leaders, but she'll massacre your soldiers, probably."

"That is very clear to me, my lord. Not even I would ever dare to challenge a True Dragon."

"Hoh-hoh-hoh! No, we're no match for her."

Gabil and Hakuro seemed to understand that well enough. The purpose of sending their reinforcements was mainly to buy time; once we rescued Yuuki, we'd then be handling Velgrynd ourselves.

"But should we leave them to that ceremony?" Ultima asked. She was referring to the Dead Birthday thing Kagali was working on, I supposed.

"I wouldn't worry about that," Diablo informed me. "It takes a great deal of time before that forbidden spell is triggered, at least two hours per walking dead created—and more than that if you are stuffing more energy into it."

It hadn't even been an hour since the ritual began. We'd first have to meet with Yuuki, then beat Emperor Ludora, and then if we hurried back...

"Uh-uh. Diablo's right if we're talkin' about the usual procedure, but Lady Kagali's usin' a kind of workaround."

"A workaround... Wait! Ah, right, Velgrynd is helping her."

Diablo seemed to get what this meant. But no one else did, and we really didn't have time for long-winded explanations any longer.

"Okay, so how much time do we have?"

"Keh-heh-heh-heh-heh... At worst, they could create several walking dead in two hours."

Two hours, huh? Could we defeat Emperor Ludora in just that amount of time? ...Ah, no point worrying over it. We just have to do it, and that's that.

I looked toward Laplace.

"And you're the strongest of her creations so far, right? Better than Clayman anyway. And despite the others being geared for strength or whatever, you sure seem stronger than them."

"Well, I was specially made, y'see."

"Okay. Well, my group's ignoring Kagali's spell, then."

"Ah... Are you sure about that?"

Gabil seemed surprised.

"Yeah. Think about it, Gabil. Laplace is pretty strong, but he's not an insurmountable opponent. The other two, I'm sure all of you could beat easily."

That was how I saw it. Laplace may be hiding his strength, but he can't fool my eyes. Basically, it didn't feel to me that he had awakened to an ultimate skill. Gabil would have a tough time, but I think Soei's an even match for him. So if Kagali could create walking dead as good as Laplace, that'd be a drag, but anything less than that seemed pretty manageable to me. We can't just leave them be—they could become a threat if left to grow up—but I don't see this as something I absolutely had to intervene in.

"If Velgrynd is contributing to this spell, then all the better for us. If possible, try to prod her so she can't concentrate on it. If you can't, then you can just leave her. I mean, no point stirring up that hornet's nest."

Gabil and Hakuro exchanged a glance, then nodded, seemingly convinced. And also, just in case:

"If she decides to turn on you guys or King Gazel, then I want Ultima and Carrera to take her on."

I figured as the most powerful of all my staff, Ultima and Carrera could buy time even against someone like Velgrynd. I could ignore whatever happened with Kagali's ritual, but if Velgrynd makes a move, the whole army would be decimated. I had to avoid that, so that's why I gave the order.

"Aw, thanks for counting on us! Sir Veldora's sister or not, I'm not gonna give her any quarter!"

"Yeah. We'll see if we can win once we feel her out. I got one heck of a winning streak going, you know, so I'm gonna get as much enjoyment out of this as I can."

It sounded like I could count on Ultima and Carrera for this. I'll just pretend that I didn't hear about the loss to Zegion.

So I thought we had a plan, but:

"One moment, please. I think Ultima and Carrera alone will not be enough against Lady Velgrynd. I know this is rude of me after offering to guide you, but I was wondering if I could tackle her as well."

Now Testarossa was throwing her hat into the ring. This was a bit troublesome to me. It was an appealing proposal, but if we were striking the core of the imperial capital, I wanted to attempt it with as much firepower as I could gather. This was an emperor even Guy recognized as a worthy rival, and he had at least four Single Digits guarding him. If we were taking on someone *that* high up, I really didn't want to lose Testarossa. At the same time, though, if she could buy some time with Velgrynd for us, that'd be pretty helpful as well.

So maybe I should take Gadora, then—

"Allow me to take her place, if you could. It will help us buy at least a little bit of time, and I think it would improve our chances."

That was Soei making the offer, and it sounded like a reasonable one. At the very least, it seemed better than taking Gadora. With Benimaru, Shion, Soei, and Diablo, I felt decently sure we could take on pretty much anybody.

"Okay, let's go with that. Don't disappoint me, Soei."

"Yes, my lord!"

The main purpose of Gabil's team was to buy time and, if possible, eliminate enemy forces, Kondo included. If things went really awry, that was where the demonesses came in. That, I thought, was about the best we could do.

"Right. That settles it, then. And again, Gabil, don't have your team get killed before we get back."

""""Yes, sir!"""""

And so our policy was somewhat hurriedly decided upon.

It was at this moment that Vester, who had been watching the screen the whole time, hoarsely shouted out:

"Whoa! King Gazel has arrived, it looks like!"

I looked myself, and there I saw the Pegasus Knights flying in from up high.

"Let's hurry. Rendezvous with Gazel's team before they take damage and tell them about our strategy!"

"Leave it to me! I promise you that I, Gabil, will perform this lofty task with sheerly the utmost of brilliance!!"

"Great. Now, everybody, let's get moving!"

I gave out the order—and then one long, long night began for us.

After teleporting Gabil's group away, we joined Laplace on our way to the imperial capital. I would be taking human form from the start, so I could deal with whatever came our way.

"Okay, we're here. This is our secret base over in— Ah, where's *this*?"

It was magic that took us here, but Laplace immediately began acting strange. Even at this point, I was having a terribly bad premonition.

Looking around, I found ourselves in a vast hall, like none in my own nation. It was lined with intricately carved columns and covered with expensive-looking carpet. I could almost mistake it for a royal audience chamber in an imperial castle, but there was something not quite right about it.

"Dude…"

"W-wait! No! Usually, when I do this thing, it always takes me to the right place! This ain't never happened before!"

Laplace looked pretty panicky as I glared at him. He didn't seem to be lying, but if he wasn't, what the hell was going on here?

After a few more swivels of my head, I saw a raised platform about fifty yards away. Something resembling a king's throne was on it, so I guessed it really was some royal chamber. An important-looking person was seated on the chair, and next to him was a beautiful blue-haired woman. There was no mistaking the distinctive buns her hair was tied into. It had to be Velgrynd herself.

"Velgrynd?! Wait, wasn't she on the battlefield just now? She can't be here, too, can she?"

"Teleportation could get her here in time, but that doesn't seem to be the case."

Benimaru looked just as confused as I was, and Soei and Shion weren't much different.

"Are we surrounded, then? It appears to be a trap."

Diablo broke the bad news to us. I noticed it about the same time he did—dozens of other people were in this chamber, and they all seemed powerful to me.

"Damn you, Laplace, you were trying ensnare us the whole time—"

Soei wasted no time confronting our would-be traitor, but he was the last thing on Laplace's mind.

"That's loony. You interfered with my spell?! That's... How's that even possible...?"

Laplace was completely befuddled. Guess he wasn't expecting this either; this didn't strike me as a trap on his part.

As we warily eyed the circumstances we were in, a man approached us.

"Hey, Laplace! Thanks so much for coming. I couldn't be happier to see you tricking the demon lord Rimuru and his friends like this."

It was Yuuki, dressed in his imperial military uniform and smiling.

"B-Boss?! Wait, wait, wait. What's goin' on?"

"Ah-ha-ha! You can quit the act now. Once we get rid of the demon lord in here, we win, right?"

Yuuki's words instantly enraged Shion and Soei—but Benimaru, and surprisingly Diablo as well, remained calm as they listened to him and Laplace speak. It was impressive to see, actually.

(You guys believed Laplace, too?)

(Oh, er, no. I was thinking of running him through once those two let their guards down.)

(Hey!)

(Keh-heh-heh-heh-heh... Well said, Sir Benimaru. Kill before you show any external sign of it. The classic rule.)

What kind of mafia gang am I running here?! There's no "classic rule" like that in *my* country!

Dumbfounded, I persuaded them to wait and see how things unfolded. At the same time, I tried to appease Soei and Shion, who were practically oozing with murderous rage. In the meantime, the argument between Yuuki and Laplace had grown rather heated. Laplace was all but begging for his life, swearing up and down that he meant none of this.

"Please believe me, guys! This time, I promise, I didn't mean to do nothin' against any of you!"

The more desperate he got, of course, the more suspicious it made him look. Yuuki really painted him into a corner here, I had to admit. Feeling sorry for Laplace, I decided to end this charade.

"Hey, calm down," I said, patting him on the shoulder a couple times. "That guy's Yuuki, but he's also *not* Yuuki, is he?"

"Huh?"

"Unfortunately, I have to assume that Kondo's controlling him."

Maybe Damrada beat him; maybe Kondo sneaked up on him during the fight. Either way, having a mind-control expert among the enemy was really starting to make things complicated. If I didn't believe that, we would've been stabbing at each other's throats by now.

"Ohhh! Right, yeah! Like, it's fun to fool other folks, but when *I'm* the fool, man, does it grind my gears!"

Gotta love that personality. Finding out I trusted him pepped him right up, it looked like. But it didn't improve our predicament at all. We were still surrounded, and we were still in crisis mode.

"*Tsh...* Didn't expect you to see through it *that* easily. Here I was hoping you'd be so lost and confused that you'd turn your blades on each other."

Brainwashed or not, Yuuki was just as mean-spirited as ever. I'm sure that's how he is at the core, and I like to think I'm mature enough to not let it bother me.

"Your Majesty, I regret to inform you that my strategy has failed."

"Ahhh, it was just a silly sideshow anyway. Very good. Now, before battle begins, I was hoping we could have a little chat."

Once Yuuki addressed the person sitting on the platform, the figure stood up and began to walk. Yuuki meekly moved to the side to clear the way for him—clearly he was now a loyal vassal of Emperor Ludora. I couldn't completely dismiss the idea that it was all an act, but I'd better not be too optimistic about that.

Velgrynd followed Ludora, as if accompanying him. She looked like a normal human being, apart from her sheer beauty, but clearly that was for camouflage purposes. Myself, I could see it. She had encased herself and the man in front of her in a thin barrier that shut off all possible interaction with the other side.

"What intimidation. I highly doubt she's a fake."

"I agree. Up close, it's amazing just looking at her," Benimaru replied, nodding at my words.

But not everyone reacted like us.

"You think so? I've trained with Sir Veldora often, so the feeling's familiar to me. Not that I've ever defeated him..."

Shion... You've been training with him, too? And by "training," she must mean actual battle in the labyrinth. If they were fighting to the death in there, I could only hope she got some good results from it. But if you can't win, it's kind of meaningless, isn't it? It wasn't really a boast, but it wasn't her being a sore loser, either.

"Yes, a very impressive barrier. But like Shion said, I don't see that much of a difference between her and Sir Veldora."

Diablo's opinion seemed closer to Shion's. Did this mean they thought Velgrynd wasn't anything special, or was Veldora actually a lot more impressive than I believed? I wasn't sure, but even the normally confident Diablo couldn't guarantee a victory for us. That was important. Diablo, despite it all, never lied to me, so he wouldn't claim he could do something that he can't—and I knew what that meant.

"I'm sure this wasn't quite in your plans, but I thought a meeting between two heads of state would prove rather interesting."

Ludora smiled as he addressed me. Wow, he really *is* Masayuki's lost twin. His hair was an almost shining blond, though, and he styled it a bit differently. That—and he had blue eyes versus Masayuki's brown. Actually, there were a lot of little differences, but somehow, the two of them projected the exact same vibe.

And actually, I recalled something odd Masayuki said recently.

"I've been worried about my hair lately."

"What, are you balding?"

"Yeah, the stress and all... No, of course not! I've been noticing that my hair's getting lighter in color lately. It's gone from black to more brownish."

"Hmm. Maybe you're losing melanin or something?"

"You think so? I hope I'm not worrying about it too much..."

You know, the sort of self-image problem every young man goes through. Or that was how I saw it, but for some reason, it popped back into my mind right then. It was a concern, but not one I should've been thinking about immediately.

Ludora was now right in front of me.

"You're right. We weren't planning to come out here. But there *is* something I wanted to talk to you about."

"Wonderful. Why don't you have a seat?"

Ludora waved his hand. Two chairs appeared before us. Some kind of magic trick? I don't know how it worked, but it didn't seem like a chintzy trap or whatever. Atmosphere was key here, so I sat down without hesitation, Benimaru standing by my right side and Diablo insisting on the left. Shion swiftly took her place right behind me, and Soei was next to her. Laplace, now seeming *very* out of place, looked around a little before sliding into a spot to Shion's left.

Once everyone took their locations, we were greeted by Velgrynd's teasing voice.

"Oh, you're sitting down first? Rather questionable manners."

Manners? I don't know jack about those. He told me to sit down, so I did.

"No need for that, Velgrynd. He didn't do anything wrong. If he's a demon lord, then he, too, has a land he rules over. He and I are equals, I think."

That's a real-life emperor for you. He sounded like he meant it, too. How generous.

"Well, if you're fine with it, I have no complaints."

Velgrynd also seemed rather easily convinced. I guess she didn't *really* care much. I wish she'd stop threatening me like that.

So Ludora sat on the opposite chair, Velgrynd casually standing to his right. Behind him were four guards lined in a row, armed with God-class gear—the Four Knights Bernie told me about, I assumed. Finally, standing to Ludora's left was a man dressed in an all-black uniform. He didn't look Japanese to me, so I guessed he was Damrada. Yuuki had the nerve to stand next to him, making his position in this hierarchy clear. I had no hesitation considering him an enemy now.

Still, this meant that all the Empire's top people except Kondo were here. I brought all my high-ranking officials as well, but we were at a serious numerical disadvantage right now. The Empire had several dozen top-ranking members of the Imperial Guardians here, including five Single Digits, and even Velgrynd was on hand. To be honest, I had serious doubts about our chances in a fight. Plus, they even had Yuuki. It's no exaggeration to say this was a crisis like none before.

I guessed from Ludora's words that this state of affairs wasn't Laplace's fault; it had all been a setup from the beginning. Funny to think how unnerving it is to have everything go your enemy's way like this... But I kept up my bold demeanor, not revealing what I felt inside.

"Well, guess you got one up on me today, huh? I considered the possibility that people would be expecting us, but I didn't quite anticipate this."

That was a lie. We were aiming for a surprise attack on their elite forces, so I thought we were about to seize the initiative here.

"Ha-ha-ha! No need to be so modest. It was just as unexpected for me. I thought the Armored Division I sent would be defeated, but the fact that there were no survivors and no awakened stemming from it was beyond any of my estimations."

Well, there was one, but Diablo killed him. I wasn't about to tell him that, but really, whoever devised that plan was a real genius, in my opinion. Pretty inhumane, maybe, but still.

"So who came up with that strategy anyway?" I lightly asked, not expecting an answer. But then, rather surprisingly, Ludora told me everything out of his own mouth.

As he explained, the plan was drawn up by Lieutenant Kondo. That I expected. But it turned out the plan was a lot crazier than I thought:

- First, they'd awaken a few people from the invasion forces; after that, they would pretend to back away in defeat.
- If we gave chase, the Composite Division would intercept us. However, since there was a possibility this division had already

turned traitor to the Empire, they would be treated as an enemy force as well.

- Once they were certain about the betrayal, everyone would be eliminated all at once. The Marshal would take on that role.

However, that plan kind of fell apart on step one, so Kondo made some major alterations:

- Ensnare and capture Yuuki's group, after letting them run free for so long. Even based on what they knew from the demon lord Clayman, Yuuki's betrayal was pretty much confirmed by this point.
- Kill off Yuuki's group, confirm what he was scheming to do, and make final adjustments based on that.
- That left sixty thousand people in the gathered Composite Division, who would then be sacrificed to produce magic-born.
- At this point, the Marshal would go into battle and make a flashy display to attract the attention of Guy and the rest.
- Any would-be troublemakers would be rounded up and killed all at once. That's why they needed to concentrate their forces on that one point.
- The advantage of such flashy moves was that it'd make the imperial capital look thinly guarded. Someone was bound to try attacking it, and it'd undoubtedly be an elite force as well. They needed to be hit with maximum strength.
- The most important part: Chances are the monster nation is running short on firepower by now, so the Marshal, the greatest force in the Empire, would take them on. While Guy's eyes were pointed elsewhere, they would take the Storm Dragon, the strongest pawn of all, for themselves.

That was the long and short of it.

If they were gaining intelligence from the demon lord Clayman, it was safe to assume that he was under Kondo's control as well. I only had my suspicions before, but now it was crystal clear.

That wasn't even the important thing, though. I was shocked he revealed all that information, but let's not worry about that. There was a certain point he brought up, one that sent a shiver down my spine. *Whoa*, I thought, *wait a minute.* How many Marshals—or Velgrynds—would they need to carry out this plan?

That's right. I always did find it strange that Velgrynd was unleashed on the east city of the Dwarven Kingdom, where the current battle was raging. So who's this woman in front of me...?

...! Detected. Her ultimate skill grants her the ability to create multiple identical existences of herself. It is called...

"...Parallel Existence...?"

I spoke the words Raphael gave me, although I wished they were wrong. But reality was merciless as always.

"Oh, you're aware of it? How clever of you."

Velgrynd's smile was as beautiful as it was terrifying. The more you want to be wrong about something, the more correct you turn out to be, huh?

My unvarnished take on this was: *How the hell am I gonna beat that?!* No wonder Testarossa was sure she couldn't pull it off. I was so comfortable with this before because I figured I could call on Veldora here to even the odds. Now, though, I understand that I can't even count on that.

According to Raphael, Parallel Existence is an extremely dangerous power. To the uninformed, it may not seem much different from Soei's Replications. In his case, he can control several Replications at the same time. It's impossible to tell who's the "real" one, and no matter how many Replications you beat down, that'll never hurt Soei himself. He could also keep churning them out as long as he had enough magicules, which kind of seemed like cheating to me. That's because there's no difference in physical ability between Soei and his Replications, so it really is like having multiple Soeis on the field.

But let's take a peek behind the curtain.

Controlling multiple Replications at once is actually pretty tricky. The skill doesn't split his consciousness at all; instead, he uses

Thought Communication to operate the copies of himself without a time lag. He also uses Mind Accelerate to adjust his reaction times, so it only looks like they're all moving independently without any issues. I don't use Replications too often myself, because this is really an incredibly difficult trick to pull off. Soei, meanwhile, is a true master of his game and one of the most thoughtful people I know; an amateur like me could never handle it as well as him.

And one other thing; the Replications' physical abilities match the caster's body, but their magical abilities always lose out by comparison. The copied bodies don't have full access to the caster's skills. That's why Soei's Replications can only use skills that don't consume much magic power—and that's why, if you knew that little secret, it wasn't too hard to tell which Replication is actually the real thing. If you're defeated, of course, your Replications instantly disappear as well, so it's definitely not an invincibility code or anything.

Meanwhile, with the Parallel Existence skill Velgrynd had, she could divide bits of her consciousness into every copy. "Copy" wasn't even the right term any longer—it was simply like having multiple versions of your "real" self. It meant that even if you killed one of them, as long as there's at least one other "alternate" of hers left, that could serve as her main one. Plus, she didn't have to split up her magic force at all. Every "alternate" was connected with the main body, so she could replenish as much magic power as she wanted on any version of herself.

There's a limit, of course, to how much magic she has overall, so the more bodies she has out, the more that reduces the maximum magic each individual one can tap. Normally, you'd see that as a weakness to leverage, but this was a True Dragon, notorious for having scads of magicules. She could replenish her alternates faster than they could use up magic, so even a modicum of usage wouldn't mean much.

Frankly, I have no idea how to defeat her. I'm not Testarossa, but I can't blame her for publicly avowing that she couldn't win.

I returned Velgrynd's gaze, giving as arrogant a smile as I could.

"Well, thank you. I've got a really talented partner, you know, and when it comes to smarts, he's tough to beat. So I guess you think you've trapped us, but can you tell us what you want?"

In situations like these, bluffing is about all I got left. I had to make them think I knew exactly what they were up to; if it put them off guard enough to fear me, I had it made. But it was clearly not gonna work out that way.

"Aren't *you* rather confident? The way you refuse to admit defeat reminds me so much of my brother."

Meaning Veldora, I imagine. Having a sister like this must've been a real pain to him. *Do you see now, Rimuru?!* I thought I heard him say, but Ludora was talking, so I had to pay attention.

"What I want? Well, if you're *that* convinced of your intelligence, I don't think I need to tell you, do I?"

That's not really helpful, you know. If they wanted to rub us out, they'd be fighting by now. If they instead set up a roundtable of sorts, that meant there was room for negotiation. I think the answer here might just be that they're trying to win us over to their side?

Affirmative. This is believed to be correct. However, they may also be stalling for time. In that case, they may be attempting to defeat the subject Veldora Tempest and add him to their fold.

Hey, I did pretty good there, didn't I? I'm half right, at least.

Certainly, in Kondo's plans, "Marshal" Velgrynd would be taking control of Veldora. I didn't pay it much attention because I assumed it was impossible at this juncture—but if she had a Parallel Existence running around, was Velgrynd on her way to storm the labyrinth right this minute?

It was now an urgent question, so I contacted Veldora through our soul corridor.

(Hey, how's it going?)

(You fool! Now is not the time for casual greetings! Things are, um, rather hectic in here! My sister… My sister is pursuing me! She is outside the labyrinth right now, but at this rate, she is going to storm inside!!)

Yep. Sounds pretty busy.

(You gonna be okay?)

(I will have to come out for her. That would beat her laying waste to the labyrinth to reach me.)

Parallel Existence or not, I really didn't think Veldora would lose. So I decided to give him permission to exercise his full force.

(All right. I'll take full responsibility for the fallout, so just do something about Velgrynd for me. Can you do that?)

(Oh-ho? Well, in that case, allow me to handle everything for you! Kwah-ha-ha-ha!!)

(Great!)

I ended the call, now much relieved. Leave it to Veldora, and I've got nothing to be concerned about. That—and I now understood what Ludora's plan was. Time to return to the bargaining table.

"Your mission right now is to try winning us over. And also, you're trying to buy time with this meeting so we won't interfere with your fight against Veldora, right?"

I tried to look as smug as possible as I laid it on them. Ludora gave this an elated smile.

"Ahhh, you're *such* an entertaining person. It'd be fun to have you match wits with Tatsuya, but there's no time for more diversions right now. If you already know that much, then I don't need to explain matters further, do I? I want you to join us and serve under me. Do it, and I'll guarantee your sovereignty and grant you the title of archduke."

"Ludora! If you appoint a non–blood relative archduke, you know the nobles will wail over it."

"I'll live. That's how worth it he is to me, if he cooperates."

So not just a duke, but an archduke? I think you're supposed to be in the emperor's bloodline, and the title dies with you, and stuff like that? And Ludora's promised to let me have that. From the Empire's perspective, this must be an unprecedented offer. After all this talk about how they never offered surrender to their foes, too! And how they always subjugated and colonized the nations they conquered! This Empire that's expanded through countless wars of aggression was about to give me one of the best deals possible. Honestly, they were rating me a lot higher than I ever thought they would.

But sadly, I already had my answer.

"Well, I know that's an excellent offer you're giving me, but the answer is no. But here's a proposal for you: How about we just call it quits here? I don't need reparations or anything, but I'd like us to sign a nonaggression treaty with each other."

Judging how nobody here gave a second thought to the sacrifices they demanded from those who served them, it'd be nothing short of suicidal for me to give in. If I kidded myself into thinking I'd be the first exception in the Empire's long history, it'd be my one-way ticket to ruin.

So I firmly refused Ludora's offer. What's more, since I had the chance and all, I expressed my own request to him. Personally, we hadn't suffered any damage, so I wasn't gonna ask for an apology or anything. As long as they swear not to mess with us any longer, I'm willing to just sweep this invasion under the rug. I'm sure some people would complain about that, but if we can settle this without any more bloodshed, I think that's the best approach.

I know I was going too easy on them, and I know I couldn't rely much on promises. If we don't trust each other, they're bound to break the treaty at some point. But the most important thing right now is to buy time. By making peace here, we'd have more time to get to know each other. There was hope, I felt, that more time to deepen our mutual understanding could lead to a future where war could be avoided. If we kept fighting like this, we'd have no choice but to take it all the way to the end—and if that's how it was, I still wanted to take a chance on this possibility, however small.

But Ludora answered with a cold smile.

"Ah, I see you are not so fit to serve as a ruler, after all. You fail to see my mercy for what it is, and you spin a web of nonsense instead."

"*So* cocky. Ludora's made every possible concession for you, and you've thrown it all away."

They reacted like they had the absolute advantage here, despite having just lost an army of one million. They don't *really* feel, deep down, that they've lost at all. All the soldiers and officers who perished thanks to his orders were no great shakes. Something about that really frightened me.

"I believe that human beings are creatures who can learn to understand each other. That, over time, they will organize themselves into a single will and work together to create a better world. But to achieve that, it is first essential to unify the world through overwhelming military force."

Ludora's words might seem like the kind of ideals I go on about. But there was a major gap between us, one that would prove hard to fill. It was so frustrating. We both started at the same point, but he reached the exact opposite conclusion—I now had all the proof I needed of that. I wondered for a moment if he was even more of an idealist than I was. But he wasn't. He claims that only his own righteousness can bring about true justice; he's a dictatorial thinker who refuses to accept the ideas of anyone else.

Just as I thought, it's unlikely that we'd ever be compatible. And if we were this far apart in our arguments, it'd likely be impossible to find a compromise through discussion.

"Humans are creatures with free will, you know. There's no such thing as unchanging justice in this world—there are so many ways people can think about matters. And don't you think refusing to acknowledge this will only sow more seeds of conflict?"

"How foolish of you. My way of thinking *is* supreme—supremely just. If you keep catering to the selfish whims of the idiotic masses, you know you'll never reach that ideal world of yours."

"But people make mistakes, don't they?!"

"That I cannot deny. I do listen to the voices of my most trusted advisers. But I can't listen to all the voices from the people below me. If I did that, we'd be in constant turmoil."

Mmph. He might be right about that, yeah…

I feel like I'm gonna be losing the verbal argument soon, too. I hated to admit it, but Ludora had been pursuing his career as a ruler for far longer than I.

"Well, I don't see the point in further argument. What we want is your loyalty to us. Demon lord Rimuru, abandon your friendship with Guy and come to our side."

There's that offer again. No doubt trying to place the pressure on Guy. If I decided to give in to Ludora, I was sure that was gonna tip the scales. That, I suppose, is why we've been kept alive up to this point. Still, though, my answer was the same as before.

Now that negotiations have broken down, it seemed like a fight was inevitable. Perhaps reading my thoughts, Velgrynd smiled coldly and gracefully waved her index finger at me—two light wags. Then a video image appeared in empty space, the same kind of principle as my Eye of God. It showed the current state of battle.

What I saw there was shocking. Testarossa, Ultima, and Carrera had all fallen in front of Velgrynd. The three demonesses, the best fighting force our nation enjoyed, had just been defeated by one person.

"No way!" I muttered to myself.

In the video, I could see the three of them standing up again. They hadn't lost the will to fight yet, but they were struggling against an insurmountable difference in ability. They couldn't hold out much longer; that much was clear.

"Do you see how your faithful Primals perform before me? I'd suggest you think carefully. Someone as smart as you should understand that I'm still going easy on them."

She didn't need to go into detail. This was a threat. If Velgrynd wanted to, she could easily hurt more than just these three. I don't know what's motivating them, but Ludora's team has made every concession they could for my sake.

Now I could see that Gabil's forces didn't have any time to help the three demonesses. Airships littered the skies above the battle-field, imperial troops swarming down from them. Kondo's forces were on the ground as well. Yuuki's former comrades—with the exception of Kagali, who was continuing on with the ritual—were fighting with them against the Dwarven army.

"Teare?! And Footman, too!"

Laplace's shout made me notice those masked annoyances fight-ing for the enemy as well. It was a chaotic scene, and it didn't look very good for my side.

We had hit rock bottom. I could feel Benimaru's concern for me. But I just couldn't give in.

"I know what you're trying to do. If you could rope me in, that'd be a much easier way to recruit Veldora, after all. He's a real free spirit, as you know, so no way he'd take orders from higher-ups like you."

He tends to (mostly) listen to me these days, but still, he loses his temper a lot. Maybe he has trouble dealing with me or something; I dunno.

Anyway, that's probably why Ludora wants me so bad. After some consideration, I decided to throw the invitation back in his face. Then I tried to find another way out, but:

"I am not interested in negotiation. Give me a yes or a no."

Now I was confronted with a choice. If I refused, I'd be plunged into a battle I had little chance of winning. But if I accepted, it'd be throwing myself into a fight I didn't want. I'd be following the will of someone else instead of my own, and it could lead to all kinds of losses later.

"You know, you say that we can all unite into one and create a better world that way, but is that a world where everyone can be happy?"

"What?"

"Whether war and hunger are eradicated or not, if your free will's taken from you, then what's the point of living? What you're trying to do is take away the potential of all the world's people! Have you ever *thought* about that?!"

"Their potential? There's no need for that. Give people freedom, and it could lead them down the path to ruin. It's not what I want, and it's far from what Guy wants as well. So it's only natural that someone must manage them so they don't stray from the correct path, isn't it?"

"I understand that to a certain extent. I won't deny it at all. But are you going to find *happiness* there?!"

I suppose that, in the big picture, what I'm trying to do is essentially manage humanity. But I still think that, to some extent, you have to leave things to the will of the people. If you're too over-protective, you'll rob them of any opportunity to grow. People are stronger than we think, and I really don't feel we need to control them every step of the way.

"Happiness? What kind of naive nonsense is that? No matter

how much sacrifice it takes, it must be made for the sake of ever-lasting peace. You don't need the permission of people who fail to understand even that. A little patience is necessary, after all, for the great joy coming for all of us."

I could see his point, but I still couldn't agree with it. Ludora was trying to turn his eyes away from the individuals who make up a society. That just didn't seem right to me at all.

"Well, I can't abide by that. I feel like what you're aiming at will just create more misery for everyone, and I can't accept that."

"Then you are a fool not to take my hand."

"Fine with me. Look, what are you even sitting here being a king for? Is it because you want to act all fancy or have a bunch of toys to play with?"

"What are you talking about? It's for the people, of course."

"Yeah, right! I like to think I became a demon lord for the sake of all my people, too, but I still want more people than that to have a happy life. There's gonna be sacrifices, of course, but I'm working myself hard to keep them to as few as possible. I can't just make myself as cutthroat as *you* are about it!"

I'd love to make the world a better place without sacrifice, but that's not possible. Look at all the people who died to make me a demon lord, for one. It's not that I regret what I did—I still think they had it coming—but I'm not sure the victims' relatives would be too convinced by my argument. That's the cross I bear, and at the same time, Ludora has his own crimes he shouldn't take so lightly.

When he heard my words, he stared at me for a moment, eyes burning. But he immediately regained his composure.

"How young," he muttered, "and how naive."

"Ludora?"

"Don't worry, Velgrynd. It's just been so long since I've been so passionate about anything. I've failed to persuade you, perhaps, but you seem far too talented to be destroyed by us."

"That's a bad habit you're developing, Ludora. It was the same with Yuuki over there, wasn't it? Your odd hoarding habit as of late confuses me."

Quit treating us like toys, I wanted to shout, but I stopped myself.

Negotiation was a nonstarter now, so it was time to prepare for battle. I looked over at my friends; they all looked ready to go. They had been doing their jobs during our conversation, which I was glad to see.

We had to beat Ludora here. I made up my mind. So I opened my mouth. But:

"But it's too bad we failed to convince the demon lord Rimuru. His friend's getting stronger than I thought, you know. He just refuses to listen to me, though, so I thought I'd punish him a little. I won't strike enough of a presence if I leave Parallel Existence on, so how about I break out my full powers for the first time in a while?"

"Oh? He's not listening either?"

"He never *did* heed a word I said. That's exactly like him, but..."

I couldn't help but turn my attention back toward Velgrynd. Veldora was on my mind. I didn't think the invincible Storm Dragon could ever be defeated, but this was just an unimaginable monster here. There was no telling what would happen next, and out of nowhere, I was in a state of deep concern.

"Oh, are you worried about him? Then I'd suggest taking Ludora's hand while you can. Then I won't have to torment my little brother any further."

Velgrynd brought up another screen. This showed Veldora in dragon form, wounded and fighting frantically.

"I've been meaning to ask you, but how did you ever tame him in the first place?"

"What?"

"I said, how did you get Veldora to listen to you?"

I didn't, really.

"Veldora and I are friends. That's all there is to it."

"Oh? So you won't tell me, then? That's too bad." Velgrynd exhaled, visibly disappointed. "In that case, I'm afraid I can't go easy on him. In terms of magicules, at least, he's even above me."

Then Velgrynd disappeared.

This was surprising and upsetting in equal measures. We knew that Ludora's goal was to stall long enough to defeat and subdue

Veldora. I went along with that, because we were buying time for ourselves as well. Velgrynd's Parallel Existence might be nearly invincible, but it has one drawback—rapid energy depletion. If you eliminate each individual body, you can also deplete the magicules divided between them. Those can't be recovered immediately, so keep it up, and you can weaken her on an overall basis. The fewer magicules divvied up, the less often she can use her most powerful moves.

That was why I thought Veldora had an advantage... But looking at the screen, even one of Velgrynd's Parallel Existences was a bit too much for Veldora to fully defeat. In fact, I could tell through our soul corridor that Veldora was growing flustered.

On that screen floating in midair, I saw the Velgrynd that was engaged with Testarossa's group disappear. The three demonesses did their best to buy us time, but it was all for nothing. *Not good*, I thought. Velgrynd's power was even beyond my expectations. So they had seen through our intentions...and just used them to ridicule us instead?

"Curious, I imagine? Well, I'll give you one more chance after this battle is over. Perhaps you'll change your mind once you see the error of your ways."

Ludora's voice seemed far away to me. It was awful, but there was nothing I could do. Now that Velgrynd was gone, I really should've tried defeating Ludora there, but for some reason, I had a bad feeling it wouldn't work out. So I decided to watch Veldora fight.

In the second screen Velgrynd left for us, a crimson dragon roared. It was the clash of the century, a bout between two True Dragons—and it was about to get even more extreme.

EPILOGUE

RAGE

That Time I Got Reincarnated as a Slime

It was a scene that could only be described as a massive *kaiju* battle. No, really. That's the only way to put it.

There were two dragons fighting each other, and although their forms were different, they were both equally huge. Velgrynd the Flame Dragon was, in her original form, a very refined, beautiful figure. She was more flexible than Veldora, with a body that looked pretty well adapted for flight. What kind of battle approach would she take with that?

It was the middle of the night, but the sky was bright. The Forest of Jura was ablaze, turning the sky a bright red. The city of Rimuru was safe inside the labyrinth and undamaged, but if we left it outside, it would've burned to the ground, leaving nothing behind. That much was proven by the large gate that connected the labyrinth to the outside world. It was now thoroughly destroyed, and I was sure the upper floors of the labyrinth had sustained catastrophic damage, too.

The battle was now at a stalemate. That was why Velgrynd turned off her Parallel Existences. It was hard to imagine, given all the devastation to the forest, but they were both doing an admirable job controlling their power. We're talking huge amounts of energy clashing against each other, but the battle was actually being fought on a really sophisticated level.

They were also evenly matched in speed. Really, Veldora had

grown an incredible amount. He had expert control over his power, letting him fly at very high speeds, and he wasn't losing a single step against Velgrynd. He must have been training in secret, and the results of that were showing.

From what I could tell, Veldora had an ever-so-slight advantage. If you simply looked at their power—their magicule count—Veldora's was higher. It had gone up since back when he was sealed, and he had padded that with new skills and tricks of his own, leading to these results.

Still, I couldn't shake off my uneasiness. Velgrynd, after all, had a clear advantage in control over her magic—and now that she was focused entirely on Veldora, the battle was really just getting started.

And I have to say... Ludora's breeziness worried me. Velgrynd, his stoutest of shields, was no longer in the room, so how could he stay so calm like this? For me, the fact that I could call upon Veldora at any time was a sort of security blanket for me. No matter what kind of crisis I was in, I knew I could get through it with some of his assistance. I'm sure Ludora's a good fighter himself. Guy saw him as an equal, and the way he so easily took over Yuuki indicated how much of a threat he was.

But I've got an ultimate ability, too. And like I did with Benimaru, I have a little trick where I can grant people skills through my own discretion. If I'm being honest, I didn't see the top-ranking Imperial Guardians around us as much of a threat. Only the five Single Digits and Yuuki were a concern—in particular, that Damrada guy over there. I don't think he's undefeatable, though.

Even without counting Laplace, I figure we had the upper hand in a fight over here. That's how I felt about it, but it's also why I was so worried. Why isn't Ludora anxious at all? That was the question. Does he think he has an insurmountable power advantage, even without Velgrynd? Even so, it doesn't benefit him to take unnecessary risks. What makes him so confident? I had no idea, but I was also curious about Veldora's battle.

Velgrynd launched a flaming heat attack, which Veldora blocked with a barrier. Then he unleashed a howling wind attack in return, but that was dodged.

It was a tremendous battle, and I shuddered at how mythical it felt. This is the first time I've seen Veldora fight for real, and it's beyond anything I imagined. I never thought he'd be an equal match for Velgrynd, even after she dominated Testarossa and her friends. If you think about it, though, maybe it's only natural. Veldora had mastered Faust, Lord of Investigation, his personal ultimate skill, and that's why he was keeping it even with Velgrynd. His opponent had the edge in skill, but Faust made that seem moot.

As Raphael explained to me, his power involves manipulating probabilities. He also had Investigate Truth, a top-level analysis skill. With that, he can immediately gauge all his enemy's abilities and respond appropriately. It's so specialized for combat that I don't even get why it exists.

Honestly, I was wondering if there was anyone who could beat Veldora after mastering Faust. That's why I never doubted his victory.

Even now, he was unleashing an invisible attack on Velgrynd. I couldn't see it on the screen, so it looked like Velgrynd was suddenly hit by something out of nowhere. But I knew. This was one of the special moves he created, something he called Storm Blast. He'd been constantly bragging about it to me, but actually seeing it in action made me a believer. At first, it just looks like a bunch of meaningless energy waves that happen to intersect at a given point—but by the time the effect comes into play, it's already too late. You've already been hit by that point, so it's impossible to avoid or defend against.

It's just totally wacko, this thing he developed. The fact that each individual wave does nothing by itself makes it easily overlooked, so if you don't know what's coming, it's a deadly attack.

Storm Blast made a square hit on Velgrynd, too. I was glad to see Veldora perform as I hoped; it was a relief. But just when I was convinced that he had it in the bag, things started to happen quickly—and in the exact wrong direction.

Suddenly, an airship appeared in the battlefield. At its bow stood a man in a different uniform from the rest. It was Lieutenant Kondo.

I hurriedly turned my attention to the first screen. Kondo and his team, who should've been standing there, were gone. The ritual had ended the moment Velgrynd canceled out of Parallel Existence. I was apparently so engrossed in all this that I failed to notice.

Report. Forbidden Curse: Dead Birthday completed approximately one minute ago.

A single minute was all it took for Kondo to reach Veldora and Velgrynd's battle site.

The premonitions wouldn't stop in my mind. I had no idea what he was planning to do, which led to a surge of frustration in my heart that shouldn't have been there.

Then another person appeared on the bow of the airship—a man who looked exactly like the man sitting in front of me right now.

Masayuki...?

Wait, no!

"A Parallel Existence...?!"

By the time I realized, it was already too late. Everything after that happened in a split second.

Kondo shot at Veldora with the gun in his right hand. There was no way a handgun round would do much against a True Dragon... But the moment the thought crossed my mind, a bullet coursed into him at truly impossible speed. Well beyond the speed of sound; even approaching sub–light speed.

There was no exit wound, the bullet staying lodged in his body— and then its evil power was fully released. It made Veldora writhe in pain; he'd normally recover at once from something like this, but that extra moment proved fatal.

The Ludora on-screen reached a hand out to him.

"I'll let you in on a secret. That's known as Regalia Dominion. It's an absolute dominating force that rules over anything that has free will. Not even a True Dragon can escape its control."

The Ludora in front of me stood up. He was walking out of the room, as if his business was done with.

"Whoa, wait..."

"Heh... Ah yes, I did make a promise, didn't I? I'm afraid I've lost interest in you now, but if you serve me, I'll show you a whole new world."

Now Ludora couldn't care less about me. And I guess the Ludora here was an imposter all along, crafted by Velgrynd's Parallel Existence. It shared the same consciousness as the one on the airship, but even if I defeated him in this chamber, it wouldn't have counted for anything.

From start to finish, I was being rolled around the palm of Ludora's hand. It spelled total defeat for me.

"Don't you underestimate Veldora."

I know I was just being a sore loser now, but I muttered it anyway. But Ludora wasn't pulling punches any longer.

"He certainly *is* a True Dragon, is he not? It took a lot more trouble than I thought to get a handle on him, but now he's finally under my full control."

And he was right. I felt a pain in my chest right afterward, one so intense that not even Cancel Pain could alleviate it. It was like someone was trying to pull a soul out of me...

Report. The soul corridor between my master and the subject Veldora Tempest has been compromised. As a result, the skills Summon Storm Dragon and Restore Storm Dragon, derived from the ultimate skill Veldora, Lord of the Storm, are no longer available.

The reason for the pain shocked me.

What? You're saying they took Veldora from me? Veldora...from me...?

"God *dammit*, you asshole!!"

I tried taking a swing at Ludora, at the highest speed I could've hoped to achieve. He didn't attempt to dodge it. He didn't need to. My fist flew through the air in vain. He was erasing the Ludora over here, as he no longer needed it.

"And that's your answer? Very well. I would very much have liked to have you on my team, but it's a pity. I suppose my authority isn't quite as all-encompassing as I thought. It'll be difficult to apply any more control right now."

"What are you—?"

"But this has been quite productive, I think, so I'll give you a little more time to mull it over. I trust you'll have the time to do so, because you've been trapped inside this Dream Fortress since the moment I called you over to it. Let's hope that you'll decide to exit here…voluntarily."

And then Ludora disappeared. On his signal, the rest of the guards there teleported their own way out.

I couldn't bring myself to give chase, such was the intense feelings of loss and rage within me.

"You asshole…"

This was all a result of my carelessness. I had planned to take him by surprise, but I fell right into his trap. I thought I had a wary eye on Laplace, but they had anticipated that all along and devised an insidious ruse to take advantage of it.

I didn't need Ludora to go over it in fine detail; I knew the moment I was called over here. We were currently inside an isolated distortion in space, and getting out would be a formidable job. But I can do anything—and that confidence is probably what led me to be careless without realizing it. I thought I was being cautious, but my opponent was simply one step ahead of me. This is war, and wars aren't something you win every time. I *know* that. You don't have to tell me.

"*Dam*mit!" I shouted as I punched myself on the cheek. There was no pain, but it only accentuated the tearing ache I felt in my heart.

"Please, Sir Rimuru, stop!"

Shion's words didn't reach me. I did it again—and again. Then, on the fourth shot, Shion stopped me from behind. Not just her—Benimaru, Soei, and even Diablo rushed over to hold me down.

"…I'm sorry. I just lost sight of myself. I know I lose my temper too easily. So thanks, guys. I have my composure back."

That was a lie. Over and over, the anger poured into my brain.

Still, I stood up, trying to quiet my raging thoughts. I was punching myself with everything I had, but my face was undamaged. Before Shion, Benimaru, or anyone else could react, Raphael was defending me against myself. It made me realize all over again just how much everyone was protecting me. That's why, more than ever, I just didn't feel like I could forgive myself.

My anger kept brimming over the walls around my heart, as if to make up for the sense of loss. I wondered where I should even try to channel all this anger...

No. Now I knew. This was war. You don't want to let up right now. So why don't I take them on with all the power I have?

Was this just me venting my anger? Maybe. But so what? The Empire's pissed me off. If you want me, you can have me. I'll give you my destruction and call it a blessing. Those fools have offended me, and in my anger, I'm ready to unleash the power I've constantly been suppressing...

AFTERWORD

Good to see you once more. This is Fuse.

I caught the flu around New Year's 2019, which meant a lot of tough times for me. The deadline for this volume was at the end of the year, but I wound up overshooting it by, um, more than a few days. I really cannot thank I, my editor, enough for extending the deadline for me. I'll try to be just a little careful next time, so I'm not cutting it so close again!

"Just a *little* careful?" I can hear I saying, but let's ignore that for now.

The story covered in this volume develops in a different way from the original web novel version. How? I'll leave that as an exercise for the reader, but at long last, the full picture of the Eastern Empire has been revealed.

Who's the identity of that beautiful woman on the cover?! … Well, I'm sure most of you have already figured that out. Isn't that wacky dragon's sister real hot? I challenged Mitz Vah to try giving her a bewitching sort of sexiness, and they gave me the three main elements that form any man's eternal dreams—to quote the hero of a certain manga from long ago, "Breasts! Butt! Thighs!!!" I like how you only get a glimpse of each, without showing off too much. You can call it "flashiness," pardon the pun—but I digress. I must be getting all tensed up after my deadline, so please take what I write with a grain of salt.

So thanks to Mitz Vah for the excellent illustrations they provide every volume! And thanks also to the fans who support me. I've been receiving fan letters and stuff, and it's been a huge encouragement! I'd like to send replies to them, but frankly, I'm terrible at keeping up correspondence, and I have trouble finding the time to sit down and do it. But I do read them all, and I store them all for safekeeping as well!

Also, to everyone involved in the production of this work—thank you!

Thanks to all your support, we've announced a second season of the anime adaptation. As the creator, I know that people have high expectations for *That Time I Got Reincarnated as a Slime*. We all want to live up to your gratitude, and personally, I'll do my very best to make this an even better story for you all!

See you guys soon!

Premonition of Disaster

Art: Taiki Kawakami

SAVE THIS FOR AFTER YOU READ THE BOOK.

※ SPOILERS AHEAD!

YEAHHH, I KNOW I MADE THAT ONE RULE ABOUT POLYGAMY...

...BUT I DIDN'T CONSIDER **THAT** LITTLE HACK.

WHAT IF THIS HAPPENS AGAIN?

...BUT THE SAME CAN'T BE SAID OF HIS HEART.

HIS BODY MAY BE UNSCATHED...

CHARYS!

BUT I FEEL BAD FOR PHOBIO.

YEAH...

WHAT OF IT? IT SOLVED ALL THEIR PROBLEMS, DID IT NOT?

RIGHT, BUT SO WHAT?

I SHARE A PARTIAL MAGICAL CORE WITH HIM, AS YOU KNOW.

HE IS?

HE'S STILL IN A BIT OF A VOLATILE STATE.

OOOOO (ROAR)

OH, SEE?

ZAWA (SHUDDER)

I THINK PHOBIO'S EMOTIONS ARE PULLING AT MY CORE'S BODY A LITTLE...

CHARYBDIS IS ABOUT TO BE REBORN!!

t Time I Got Reincarnated as a Slime (manga) by Taiki Kawakami

The three demonesses are totally the best.

Sho Okagiri

HERE'S TO VOLUME 14!!

CONGRATS TO FUSE!

SHIBA 闇 2019.

I LIKE THE INSECT GANG.

Slime Diaries: That Time I Got Reincarnated as a Slime by Shiba

SHIZUKU AKECHI

VOLUME **14**!!
CONGRATULATIONS.

That Time I Got Reincarnated (Agai
as a Workaholic Slime by Shizuku Ake

FUSE, CONGRATS ON VOLUME 14!

I CAN'T WAIT TO SEE HOW THE STORY DIFFERS FROM THE WEB VERSION!

TAE TONO

I ALWAYS LOOK FORWARD TO MITZ VAH'S ILLUSTRATIONS!

※ALSO LOOK OUT FOR TRINITY IN TEMPEST, AVAILABLE IN MONTHLY SHONEN SIRIUS MAGAZINE!

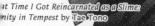